BD
AS
&2

A1 12/12.
D3 11/13
F4 4/15
F1 6/15

fc 18

OTHER PEOPLE'S SECRETS

OTHER PEOPLE'S SECRETS

Louise Candlish

WINDSOR
PARAGON

First published 2010
by Sphere
This Large Print edition published 2010
by AudioGO Ltd
by arrangement with
Little, Brown Book Group

Hardcover ISBN: 978 1 408 48768 6
Softcover   ISBN: 978 1 408 48769 3

British Library Cataloguing in Publication Data available

Printed and bound in Great Britain by
CPI Antony Rowe, Chippenham and Eastbourne

ACKNOWLEDGEMENTS

Thank you to Claire Paterson, Rebecca Folland, Tim Glister and Kirsty Gordon at Janklow & Nesbit. At Little, Brown, thank you to Ursula Mackenzie, David Shelley, Jo Dickinson (especially), Rebecca Saunders (you've been wonderful), Caroline Hogg (ditto), Alys Martin, Tamsin Kitson, Charlie King, Darren Turpin, Sam Combes, Madeline Meckiffe (for the lovely cover), and the sales team in its fabulous entirety.

Thank you to Nips and Greta, and to my long-suffering friends and drinking chums, including Mats 'n' Jo. I think you'll like this one.

PROLOGUE

Even though she'd rehearsed the line over and over, it didn't sound at all the way she wanted it to. The first word—her son's name—was lost completely in a nervous swallow and she had to repeat herself to be heard.

'I need to talk to you about something. Something important.'

'Oh yeah? So what have I done now?' He looked up from the little galley kitchen, where he stood at the counter splashing milk into their coffees, and for a second he was five years old again: expectant of a telling-off but trusting that she would keep it fair, as she always did. 'Don't tell me you and Dad want the deposit for this place back already?' And he grinned, back in the present again, droll and assured, confident she would never ask anything too painful of him.

'Let's sit down,' she said. 'It's a big thing I need to say and it's going to be a shock.'

He flicked a quick frown her way but remained silent as he brought the mugs to the coffee table— a battered old square of oak that had originally belonged to her sister, incongruously rustic in this city flat. As with many first homes, virtually everything in it had been donated by members of the family. When they'd delivered the table—along with an armchair and several other bits and pieces—her husband had joked, 'You can't expect them to buy their own furniture, can you? Not with booze and cigarettes being so criminally expensive . . .'

But that day, only weeks ago on the calendar, already seemed in reality like it belonged to a different age. The time before she told him.

I shouldn't have left it so long. I should have told him years ago.

He settled himself in the hand-me-down armchair, opposite her corner spot on the sofa; he was naturally graceful, had been since he was very young. She nodded her thanks for the coffee, but didn't dare touch it for fear of her hands shaking and spilling it.

'So, what's up?' he asked, innocent, beautiful.

Already she was anticipating the expression on his face of pure desolation, the plunge of his shoulders, the cries from his lips. She felt as if she carried his heart in her own ribcage: when his broke, hers broke.

How could she have expected anything less?

At last she drew a breath, her body reacting to the air as if for the first time, unfamiliar with it, hardly able to tolerate it.

'It's about Dad,' she said.

CHAPTER ONE

SATURDAY

Later Ginny would not believe that she had hardly noticed that first day how beautiful the lake was. And their position on it, right at the water's edge, with the island of San Giulio placed picturesquely to the left. The view was almost too immaculately composed to be real, more like something in a painting where the artist had rearranged the elements to satisfy his personal laws of perspective.

It was a little piece of paradise, Adam said, quoting from the guidebook he'd been studying on the plane. Possibly the most perfect view in all of Italy—and didn't that, by definition, also mean the most perfect view in the whole world? But Ginny didn't absorb the concept any better than she absorbed the view, and she didn't think fourteen days of it would make any difference, either.

Their rental had its own little garden on the lakefront, with a stone table and a set of four stools, each hewn roughly into the shape of a toadstool. There was also a pair of long, low curved wicker chairs, set at a delicate angle to one another as though intended expressly for convalescents. From her viewpoint at the window above, she judged that if you pulled one of those chairs to the edge of the grass, and leaned right over, you'd be close enough to the water to dip your fingers in. You could dip your whole self in, actually; there was nothing to stop you rolling right off the chair and into the cold. Alternatively, you

1

could do it properly: step up on to the stone ledge of the lake wall, stretch up your arms towards the skies and *dive* in. Swim right across the frame of that famous piece of paradise to the island itself.

She was fairly certain she wouldn't have the energy for that, though. And even if she did, she didn't think she would have the desire.

'What d'you think?' Adam asked, joining her at one of the two sets of French windows in the living room, which along with the oversized fireplace made the small room feel grander than it was. Ginny could tell that Adam was pleased, grateful even, for what they had found when they'd unlocked the door and climbed the steps. Holiday rentals were a leap of faith at the best of times and he'd been painstaking in his quest to find the right place for them. (Not trusting the Internet, he'd gone in person to a travel agency in West London that specialised in just this sort of thing: Hidden Italy, it was called.) Though she was sure she would have felt exactly the same wherever they'd gone, she didn't think he could have borne the disappointment of an obscured view or a decaying interior. He may have looked the stronger of the two of them—in truth, he *was* the stronger—but that didn't mean he wasn't still fragile too, in his own way.

'It's lovely,' she said, summoning a small show of interest. 'I've never stayed in a boathouse before. It feels . . . peaceful.'

'Yep, that's the idea. Italy without the crowds. No queues, no cruise ships, no tour groups . . .' He glanced about him for other notable absences. 'No computer, no TV . . .'

No children.

2

But neither of them said that.

He set about opening the windows—'Let's get some breeze into the place!'—and the air that entered was much warmer than that inside, its softness unreal after the cool London rain.

'I can't believe we got here so quickly,' Ginny said.

Adam looked as though he disagreed with that, but she was getting used to not trusting her own judgement and so didn't press the point. Car, plane, taxi; all the dragging of luggage and standing in queues in between . . . it was possible that it *had* been an arduous journey but she just hadn't noticed. These days, hours passed and she could not account for them. She wondered if it was because she didn't *want* time to pass; she wanted to hold it still before it took her too far from the day she counted as her happiest, the day before their lives capsized. April the fifth. And they'd been more than happy: they'd been euphoric.

Sometimes she thought it would have been better if the world had ended that day, or in the night, perhaps, as they slept, forever innocent.

'Right, shall we unpack?' he asked, briskly. Then, seeing her expression, 'I can do it if you want to rest?'

'No, I'll help.'

She followed him into the boathouse's only bedroom, which was even smaller than the living room, sharing as it did its half of the space with an access corridor to the external steps that led directly to the garden (the proper entrance was to the other side of the building, on the public lane). The room was lower-ceilinged, too, the walls wood-panelled, and all there was for lighting was a small, shaded lamp. Perhaps you were supposed to (*want* to) manage with candlelight alone, for the space had obviously been decorated with romance in mind. There were smooth white linens on the polished wooden bed, fresh flowers in a blue jug on the table, and at the window nothing but a length of that soft sheer muslin that seemed to move without any discernible draught, as if weightless. This was Italy, however, and the bathroom raised eyebrows, being as it was bath-free; little more than a showerhead, a basin and a loo. Not even one of those half-length sit-in baths you sometimes got in hotels. At home Ginny had got used to spending hours in the bath, often letting the water rise up to her chin, the trickling of the overflow at her feet enough to lull her to sleep. If she timed it well, she could get out, put on a towelling robe, and slip into bed without fully gaining consciousness. She was dismayed that that trick wasn't going to be possible here.

'Come on,' Adam said, from behind the lid of the suitcase. 'It won't take long and we'll be glad we did it properly.'

They began transferring their clothes to the wardrobe and drawers, and when it was done he found a cupboard by the front door big enough to store the empty luggage. He had become noticeably more thorough of late—some might say obsessively so—eking out practical tasks for as long as he could and often lining up the next in advance in order to avoid being faced with too long a break in concentration. Ginny was the opposite: formerly the organised one of the two, she no longer cared what went where or how anything looked. Live out of a suitcase for two weeks; wear

4

the same clothes every day; trip over a pile of shoes each time you came into the room: what did it matter? It didn't change a thing.

Though they'd finished their unpacking, Adam continued to take short, cautious paces around the room, a cat processing the dimensions of a new home. Watching from the bed, she wondered if he had also noticed that the cabin-like intimacy that made this place so romantic might in their case make it claustrophobic.

At last his gaze came to settle on her as if it could be avoided no longer. 'I might go into the village and explore. It's only a ten-minute walk along the lake path, I reckon. Do you want to come?'

With effort, Ginny rose to her feet, pulled back the wispy drape at the window and eyed once more the little garden, those invalids' wicker chairs. 'I think I'll stay here and read for a while. But we'll go out for dinner later, shall we?'

'Absolutely.' Adam nodded, pleased with this evidence of initiative on her part. 'I'll check out some places while I'm gone. Though I'm sure someone told me they eat donkey meat in the mountains . . . What's "donkey" in Italian?'

She had no idea and didn't answer—that was something else she'd lost, the ability to keep a conversation going beyond the required exchange of information—and, used to this, he abandoned talk and came to kiss her goodbye. As he did so, she stood quite motionless, hardly even blinking. It was only when she'd heard his steps on the wooden stairs and the lower door pulled shut behind him that she allowed her body to stir again, as if waiting for an intruder to leave the premises before daring

5

to emerge from her hiding place.

Crazy behaviour; incomprehensible.

She couldn't face the paperback Adam had chosen for her at the airport and instead picked up a folder marked 'Location Pack' that had been left on the breakfast bar in the kitchen. Settled in one of the garden seats, she squinted as the sun bounced off the white pages:

Dear Mr and Mrs Trustlove,
Welcome to the boathouse at Villa Isola, Orta's beloved Arabian-style folly—we know your stay here will be a happy one! Lago d'Orta is probably the least known of the Italian lakes, little sister of the more famous Garda, Maggiore and Como . . .

After managing only two sentences, Ginny closed the folder again. These days reading hurt her eyes, exactly as if she were still learning the technicalities of it and the effort overtaxed her brain. And the sunlight was so powerful here! It felt like they were on the equator. She supposed that explained the clusters of dark heads she could make out near the far shore, bobbing above the surface of the water alongside something bright and flashing. Adam had packed her a swimsuit, though she didn't intend to wear it. Seeing her body, all stretched and misshapen, was unendurable enough in private without having to display it to other people as well.

She never looked in a full-length mirror now; she rarely looked at her face, either, only in the mornings to check she hadn't smeared herself with toothpaste. She didn't need a mirror to tell her that her once artfully cropped and highlighted hair had been replaced months ago by a badly made nest—fitting, perhaps, given the crow's feet now established around her eyes. As for those eyes, they were strange, spiritless things, the blue re-blended to a drabber shade, the windows to this particular soul quite blacked out.

Remembering her earlier thought, she reached her arm towards the water. She'd been right: it was close enough to touch. She brought her face as near to the surface as possible without sending her chair toppling sideways, then, straightening again, felt herself consumed by a spinning sensation—she even lost her vision for a few seconds. But that was nothing to worry about: dizziness was a known symptom. She was familiar with the full list, as well as with the order in which they might be expected to come. What the experts didn't tell you, however, was that sometimes you got all the symptoms at once, in one huge chemical whoosh that knocked you off your feet. That was when you needed your bath and the warm water up to your neck and the merciful loss of pain that came with it. It was the closest you could get to not feeling.

Eyes half-closed, she watched a pair of white butterflies dance above the tall rushes on the far side of the boathouse. A fact popped into her head, where from she didn't know, though it was possibly from Adam himself: *the average lifespan of an adult butterfly is two weeks*. Was that true? And there was something with an even shorter natural span than that, though she couldn't remember its name. Something very simple that lived in the water. Maybe there was one in the lake out there, swimming about at this very moment, oblivious to

7

its own brevity.

That was the one saving grace in all that had happened, she thought: *you never knew*.

After that, she must have dozed. When Adam came back, the fresh infusion of enthusiasm the expedition had given him was clear in his whole demeanour. He bounced on the balls of his feet as he spoke, he used his hands to help describe the piazza and the steep cobbled streets and the little chapels on the hilltop; he even smiled. 'This place is incredible, Ginny! And you know what? I think we must be in the original boathouse of the funny villa we saw from the road. D'you remember: that pink and green thing with the watchtower? I didn't realise they were connected when we arrived because we've got separate entrances, but it's right there behind the trees. It makes sense now, what the agent said about sharing a jetty.'

Ginny gestured to the information pack. 'It tells you about the villa in here . . .' she began, but he was stepping past her, speaking over the top of her.

'That must be where this gate leads to. I wondered why it was there . . .' And he was already through it, closing it carefully behind him with that air he'd always had—and had not lost—of wishing to be above all else a good citizen, and now she could see only the upper part of him, his arms still gesturing eagerly as he reported to her what he was seeing.

He's behaving as if I'm blind, Ginny thought, *or disabled. He's my* carer. She pulled herself to a standing position and looked beyond him to a broad sweep of lawn, finished at the lake's edge with a row of horse chestnut trees whose overlapping branches created a long, inviting

8

canopy of shade. There was a private jetty, too, modest but well-kept. She couldn't see the villa itself, but whoever it belonged to had a park-sized piece of waterfront, the boathouse allotted only the tiniest corner of it.

Adam came to a halt with his back to the lake and his face upturned. 'Wow, come and look at this! It's not a house, it's a palace! Looks empty, though, which is just as well because we want to be alone, don't we? Shall we sneak up and have a nose around?'

It was only when he added, 'Oh, Ginny,' and came rushing back through the gate towards her that she understood that she had sunk back into her chair and begun crying. In a trice he was kneeling on the ground by her side, forcing her right arm against the hard edge of the wicker as he pressed her to him in an awkward hug.

'We will get through this,' he murmured, 'I promise we will. Coming here was definitely the right thing to do.'

He held her for a little longer, telling her he loved her. The way Ginny heard it, it was *I* love you, with that sorrowful emphasis on the 'I', as if he were only confirming what she already understood: that everyone else in the world had deserted her.

CHAPTER TWO

SUNDAY

'Right, crew, everyone strapped in? Then, let's go! *Andiamo!*'

Bea watched her husband grip the gear stick as if shaking the hand of an old friend. He was effervescent with bonhomie, jerking the huge rental vehicle towards the airport exit as if there was nothing in the world he'd rather do than drive on the wrong side of the road among the world's most dangerous lunatics. Had it been she at the wheel, she'd be turning it with her fingers crossed, genuflecting at every amber light, but not Marty. He was one of those people who treated driving as a sport, no lesser in the pleasures it gave than skiing or sailing or sex. The Italian roads held no horrors for him: the narrow lanes that needed cats' whiskers to judge, the sudden plunges into dark tunnel followed by re-entry into blinding sunshine, the *autostrada* system that required cars to line up like greyhounds at their gates—all of it he relished.

Naturally the children had been infected by his energy, just as they used to be on holidays when they were small. He'd been acting like a man possessed from the moment they'd assembled at Gatwick, slapping backs, squeezing shoulders, demanding high fives, even at one point lifting Pippi into the air in some sort of ice dance move (she was heavier than Esther but, still, Daddy's girl was Daddy's girl). His facial expressions were super-animated, too, exactly the way

10

photographers liked—'That was great, but this time can everyone look a *lot* more excited!'—as if the trip were being shot for their next catalogue. As they checked in, she saw people looking over from the adjoining desks, certain he must be someone.

And so he was.

Not entirely immune herself, even after twenty-plus years of him, Bea forced herself to turn from his determined profile and smile over her shoulder at her two daughters in the seats behind. You'd never have guessed at a glance that Esther was the elder by three years, partly because of the way she chose to dress but mostly because of the way her sister did. Esther's approach to clothing was that she might be asked at any time to tackle an assault course (though, to Bea's knowledge, she never had) and she'd opted therefore for running tights, T-shirt and a fleece that Bea happened to know was named 'Velocity'. Pippi, on the other hand, believed that few locations in life offered so extensive a captive audience as an international airport and had chosen for her public a sleek, elongating black dress, high-heeled roman sandals (if that wasn't a contradiction in terms) and enough silver jewellery to have stirred grumbles several men deep in the queue for the security scanners.

Dom sat alone at the back, alongside an arrangement of suitcases and garment hangers and—Marty's idea, not hers—a full-size Sale-branded parasol. She had only a partial view of her son's face and had not yet been able to catch his eye this journey, but she knew quite well that of the three siblings he had to be the least excited by

11

his father's performance today, the least inclined to play happy families. They were lucky he had come along at all and the possibility of him bolting back to London was even stronger than that of Marty's doing it (which was saying something: if you wanted to be statistically correct about it, four in the last five holidays had been interrupted in this way). But she wouldn't think about that, not now, not before they'd even reached the hotel. She would wait to see her room with a view before allowing her worries re-entry; she would wait to test the quality of the mattress before surrendering once more to the sleepless nights. And, who knew, maybe it would work out all right. Maybe she could find a way to talk to Dom again, to persuade him to let her soothe his fears.

'I think it's time for a clue,' Marty announced, and as he turned his face her way (*her* eyes would not have left the road so easily), there was an extra inch to that broad, devilish grin of his. It was a while since she'd seen him enjoy himself like this and, despite herself, she felt her heart respond. Habit, she told herself, that was all.

'Oh yes? Go on then, put us out of our misery.'

Chuckling at her choice of words, he glanced at the overhead mirror. 'You too, Esther.'

Esther leaned forward between the seats. 'Me too, what?'

'"Me too, what?"' Marty mimicked her suspicious tone as if there could be nothing more uproarious (he was not one of those men who treated his family less charmingly than he did strangers; they, too, could expect to receive the full force of his charisma). 'OK, so here's the clue: you two will be doing a lot of cooking where we're

12

going.'

'*Cooking?* Really? Oh.' Esther sat back, noncommittal, before at once moving forward again, now groaning deeply. 'God, Dad, don't tell me we're going to be filmed running a B&B or something horrendous like that?'

'No way am I making cappuccinos for a bunch of morons,' Pippi put in, in a voice that meant business. 'I can tell you right now I won't sign the release form.'

Marty guffawed. 'Who said anything about you, Pipkins? You lot are hilarious! Why would I take you to Italy to make you run a B&B? I did tell you this was supposed to be a *dream* holiday, didn't I? Anyway, you know we don't do that reality TV crap. Do you see Melissa in the car behind?'

Unable to help it, the three women looked, as if Melissa's black Mini might really be tucked behind them in the fast lane of the *autostrada*. Melissa was head of press and PR at Sale and Bea liked her as much for her honest lack of sexual attraction to the boss as for her excellent professional skills. But, sure enough, it was not she who tailed them but a young man with very high hair in a very low Alfa Romeo, clearly angling to undertake.

'Seriously, if your expectations are *this* low . . . !' Marty gave Bea another wicked smile. 'You know what? I might just let you all wallow a bit longer . . .'

'Oh, Marty, come on, this isn't fair. We're here now, so you might as well tell us.'

'No. You won't get another word out of me.'

'I can't bear this,' Pippi moaned. 'I need to get where we're going so I can charge my phone. Are we nearly there yet, Dad?'

Her father exploded with fresh laughter. 'She

said it! Did you hear that, Bea? The Pipster said it! *Now* I can relax. No family holiday can get underway without that time-honoured question!'

Which would almost certainly be featured in the next spring/summer marketing campaign. But Bea had to hand it to him. Not once had he given away his big surprise. It was only at check-in that she'd been told it was Italy at all, though the children seemed to know that much, at least. Until then he'd dismissed her requests for information with cries of, 'Don't worry, I'll do the packing!' or, 'Just trust me!' (a big ask if ever there was one, though she'd resisted pointing this out, given the circumstances). And whatever else was going on this summer, she could not deny him—or herself—the pleasure of a holiday with just the five of them, maybe, *certainly*, their final one as a family. They hadn't managed it for the last three years, after all, not since Dom left for university in the same year that Esther began her gap year, not since Marty's schedule had begun to resemble nothing so much as the foreign secretary's. No, the prospect of a full configuration of Sales in the same car with suitcases packed, schedules cleared, and friends and partners sidelined seemed to Bea little short of an act of God (or an act of Marty Sale—you'd be forgiven for thinking they were the same thing).

Having left the motorway and passed through a couple of country towns rapidly enough for her not to have caught their names, they came to a left turn signposted 'Lago d'Orta' and she willed Marty to flip down the indicator and take it. But instead he turned right, following a narrow road through woodland towards a place she'd never heard of. She sensed him glancing quickly across at her and

14

re-set her face in an expression of expectant pleasure. That was a shame, though; from the moment the destination airport had been revealed to be Milan, she'd hoped it might be Lake Orta they were heading for. They'd been to its neighbour Como a few years ago, to a stylish villa with its own speed boat and kayaks, and one of those small, slim pools that had a current you could activate with a switch. It hadn't been long before Marty had the kids—and a handful of locals he'd drawn into his games—taking part in some sort of competition involving split-second timings and medal tables.

They'd visited Orta only as an afterthought, a day trip towards the end of the break when water sports had ceased to thrill, and instantly Bea had wished they'd spent the whole two weeks there. It was small and green and tranquil, more like the English Lake District than glamorous, dramatic Como. It also had that sense of melancholy she hadn't realised until then she liked so much, that feeling you got when a place had been forgotten by all but the tourist minority. They'd parked in the main town, little more than a village really, and been taken across the water to a little island where they'd seen the convent where nuns still lived, and had a drink on a terrace overhanging the lake.

What she remembered most, however, was a building she'd spotted on the return crossing, visible only from the water and for a brief few moments. It was a bona fide folly, a miniature oriental palace decorated in green and pink. Among the classical, biscuit-coloured villas with their contrasting—but always tastefully just-so—coloured shutters it had stood out, a funny face

15

among the gracious ones, the only one with its tongue sticking out.

Perhaps they could manage another day trip to Orta, she thought, if they weren't heading too much farther. Being clueless was beginning to lose its charm.

'Apparently the weather is going to be amazing,' Marty said, narrowing his eyes at the particularly chaotic junction ahead. 'They've had heavy rains for the whole of the last week and now it's all green and not nearly so humid. Hopefully that means the mozzies won't be out in such force.'

It was as though he controlled the elements from on high. Zeus Sale. Bea imagined them arriving at the hotel in the same blistering heat that was making the road blur and shimmer through the windscreen before them, only for a perfect breeze to start up from thin air, pools of heavenly shade materialising everywhere they stepped.

Once, in an interview, her husband had been asked to say in one word what he considered to be the secret of his success, the secret of any business success as phenomenal as his. Without needing to think about it, he'd chosen 'timing'. She should not have been surprised, then, when he'd announced this holiday. As timing went it was immaculate, nothing short of brilliant, for it was the only thing he could have done—bar, perhaps, a revelation of terminal illness—to keep her in the marriage. She had made her decision as long ago as March and had mentally prepared herself for an announcement in July, just as soon as Pippi's exams were safely over—about now, in fact. (Of course, the irony was that Marty knew nothing of

16

these private machinations; he thought they were doing just fine. *That* was the true genius of timing—it was nothing to do with experience or strategy, it was a sixth sense, a gift.)

How often they'd talked about it in the past, how it would feel when little Pippi took her A-levels, the last hurdle in the sprint to independence for the youngest of their family. The last eighteenth: everyone knew that was when parenthood moved into its next phase (and its next phrase, one which Bea hated with a passion: empty nest). But as the landmark approached, she had been reluctant to resurrect the talks, fearful they might run her own decisions off course, and she'd been grateful when Marty appeared simply to have forgotten. After all, with Pippi set on a career in fashion, she'd be working in the same industry as him, perhaps even, eventually, for the Sale brand itself; it wasn't the same as losing her completely.

But he *had* remembered, he *had* known, and he'd come up with this magical mystery tour.

'I know I've neglected you lately,' he'd said. Marty did that naturally, without guile, spoke of Bea and the children as a single organism (a habit that had not helped when it came to discussing their marriage). 'With everything taking off in the States, it's been impossible to think about anything else this year. Well, I've just told Ed I'm taking you away. I've cleared the diary. Two weeks, a proper holiday.'

'When?' Bea asked.

'The weekend after next.'

'*What?*' They were supposed to be visiting friends in Ireland then; the flights had been booked months ago, with Bea scheduled to go for a

17

week and Marty, if he could manage it, two nights. None of the children were to be involved, though Pippi had said she might tag along with her father if she had nothing better to do. 'What about Tom and Julia?' she asked. She felt cross at being ambushed like this at exactly the time she intended to start freeing herself. Though she didn't say so, she had fully expected him to pull out of the Ireland weekend owing to work pressures.

'Cancelled.' He made a chopping gesture with his right hand, a magician who could make things appear—and vanish—with a single flourish.

Bea began to protest. 'But we can't do that to them, it's much too late to—'

'Don't worry,' he said, shrugging (it was a myth that powerful men expressed their authority in brawn and bluster; in her experience, they were more likely to command with a twitch of the shoulders). 'They were cool about it when I explained.'

'Explained what, Marty?'

His eyes bulged with mischief. 'Where I'm taking you, of course. Believe me, you're going to be seriously chuffed.'

She was certainly seriously amazed, for he had not arranged a holiday for the family in its whole history. The occasional weekend, yes, back in the early days, when you had to have a break from small children if you were to be stopped from throwing yourself out of a window and yet couldn't hope to organise it yourself because you spent eighteen hours a day wading through laundry and bottles and nappies and the remaining six in the sweaty purgatory that passed for sleep. He'd taken her to the Cotswolds, to the Kent coast, even to

Paris once. She remembered each weekend as a peculiar combination of blissful release and aching loss, and sex, too, the kind that combined catching-up with storing-up; the kind that, by the time Pippi came along, was more often than not the victim of cancellation (as were, eventually, the weekends themselves).

'Look, we can't just take off for two weeks and ignore everything in the diary,' she said, fearful of his fun and games for all sorts of reasons. 'This isn't enough notice.'

That was when he produced his masterstroke. 'It'll be just us and the kids. No partners or friends, either. Just you, me, Dom, Esther and Pips. We won't even give the office the address or phone number.'

'No partners?' she said, doubtfully.

'No partners.' His conviction faltered then, just a fraction. 'The girls are on board already.'

'The girls, yes.' Esther's partner Vicky was working in Guatemala for the summer break, so that wouldn't be an issue; Esther was joining her for part of August and was at a bit of a loose end until then, anyway. As for Pippi, she had the whole summer free before starting work for one of Sale's suppliers for six months, followed by the half of her gap year that *really* mattered: the search for the world's best beach. She had no boyfriend at the moment, had declared herself a bachelorette after a succession of local romances had fizzled out ('local' was her own adjective, as if it were only a matter of time before her love life went international). But Bea knew not to be worried by this. Pippi was like her father: a part of her would be a bachelor even when she was deeply in love

19

with someone.

No, it was Dom who was the tricky one, the cause of that rare hiccup in Marty's self-belief. There was no way he would be willing to be parted from his girlfriend Chloë, who, it was taken as read these days, joined them for all family events, including holidays. What was more, the two had recently moved into a flat-share with university friends; whisking Dom off for a fortnight when they'd just started living together was unthinkable.

And so it proved—at first. Unlike his sisters, Dom was *not* on board, and his father was staring a stranger in the face: failure. Then, just days before their departure, Bea had had that distressing conversation with her son, the one that had left them in a state of utter stalemate. She had never imagined he would change his mind and come to Italy, not until Chloë stepped in and urged him to do just that, to get away from London and take some time with his family, think things through. And Marty, without knowing why, had his last acceptance.

'Almost there,' Marty said, sing-song cheerful, and she began to pay attention to the route again. The signs were saying 'Orta San Giulio', which was confusing since they'd surely missed the turn a while back and headed in the opposite direction. Her own internal navigation system had placed them somewhere in the countryside above Turin but, no, here was a sign with three curved white lines on blue—the lake—and now they were turning towards it.

'Didn't you just take the road *away* from Orta?' she asked her husband, mystified. 'How did we get back again?'

20

'Insider tip,' he said, smugly. 'The sign we passed is just for freight. Locals take the road through the woods.' As he spoke he braked smoothly on the left-hand side of the road, where a pair of grand iron gates stood at the foot of a pale cobbled driveway. The words 'Villa Isola' were visible on the wall in raised script, and, smaller and more official-looking, *Proprieta privato*.

There was a sudden exclamation from behind— 'Is this it?'—and Pippi was craning over her sister for a better view. 'Dad, this place is completely crazy!'

'Hmm, as hideaways go it's not very discreet,' Esther added in obvious delight.

Puzzled, Bea reached across Marty's body and rolled down his window. In a glorious instant she felt heat begin to melt her make-up and curl her hair. 'Oh my God,' she said, softly. Beneath her, his body remained still and cool in anticipation.

It was the villa, the one she had been so fascinated by all those years ago. She'd thought she'd never see it again but here it was in all its fairytale flamboyance: three storeys of mullioned windows, horseshoe arches, lacy fretwork and pink and green paintwork, the whole confection topped, as if by a celebratory birthday candle, by a minaret. The gates pulled back—how? None of them had pressed anything—and as the car curved towards its parking spot, you could get a better sense of the size of the grounds, which were home to what must have been hundreds of trees, among them larch, palm, fir and lemon. A series of terraces led to a wide green lawn, with a row of trees shading the water's edge, and beyond was the view from a Canaletto: the island, a little piece of Venice

21

floating in the middle of the lake.

'So is this a cookery school or something?' Esther asked. She'd clearly been working on her father's 'clue' these last few miles.

Marty shook his head. 'No, you're going up the road for that, to the famous Casa Mista. This is where we're staying. We've got it completely to ourselves for two weeks.'

'It's enormous,' Pippi said, laughing. 'How many bedrooms are there?'

'Seven. And eight bathrooms. And three sun terraces. Oh, and its own private beach on the lake. There's no boat, but we can sort that out easily enough.'

Squealing like infants, Esther and Pippi began unclasping their belts and pulling open the car doors. There were even signs of life from Dom in the back, a widening of the eyes as he too absorbed the magnificence of the edifice in front of them.

Still seated, Marty turned to Bea, his face aglow with the excitement of the reveal. 'You don't want to know what I had to do to get this place.'

He was right: she didn't want to know.

CHAPTER THREE

SUNDAY

The first day they took the ferry to the island. Adam said you should never leave the main sight till last; it had to be explored at the outset or its mystery would only grow and lead to tourist anticlimax. (He warned of this as one might tennis elbow, a muscular affliction with lasting effects.)

There was no mystery as far as Ginny was concerned, but it didn't matter because she had already decided to go along with his schedule of sightseeing, at least at first. That was the whole point of this trip, after all: long enough after the event for the raw pain to have begun to fade (supposedly; but could three months really be considered long enough? Could three *years*?), it was time for the beauty of the mountains and lakes to work its magic and restore their faith in life. Lessons in loss number one: find a slice of paradise and explore it to the point of exhaustion, the point at which weariness generates an energy all of its own and, if you're lucky, recharges your heart.

Yes, if she let Adam think she was submitting to the programme in the early part of each day then he might be more willing to leave her to her lakeside trance later on. He might choose to enter it with her, of course, reading or snoozing in the adjacent chair, but she doubted that enough to already be thinking of the late afternoon as time to herself. And she also knew precisely how she would spend it, the same way she did her private time at home: she would pick herself a particular hour from that world-altering week in April and she'd replay it in her head minutely—literally, minute by minute. Whenever she did this she would, without exception, remember moments she'd forgotten until then, precious, hidden details. It was like re-watching an episode of a very complicated drama series and spotting peripheral elements you'd missed the first time. She knew what they called this in therapy: 'revisiting'—a term the special counsellor at the hospital had

23

introduced them to. But for Ginny the word was all wrong, with its connotations of pleasurable expectation. You could revisit a favourite place—the Italian Lakes, for example—but you could not revisit what she had lived through.

'It's so beautiful, isn't it?' Adam said, as the ferry—hardly bigger than a private launch—skimmed the short stretch from Piazza Motta to Isola San Giulio, making a perfect V on the surface of the lake behind them. 'So *ancient*. I mean, how long has this body of water been here? It really puts things into perspective, doesn't it?'

'Hmm.'

He'd already said something similar when they walked down Via Olina, the narrow cobbled lane that counted as one of Orta's main thoroughfares and where the buildings had every appearance of being untouched by the renovating zeal that had transformed their own neighbourhood in London (did *any* of the hotels here have bath tubs, she wondered?). She wished he wouldn't feel the need to spell out the message quite so frequently. Not only did she not agree with it—*nothing* put things into perspective; being on the moon wouldn't put things into perspective—but it also made her feel guilty, because he was concentrating so devotedly on her when she could spare so very little for him.

'Please don't worry so much about me,' she'd said, weeks ago, when the rhythms of grief were still new to them. 'You'll forget about yourself.'

'It's harder for you,' he said. 'I realise that.'

'It's not harder,' she said, 'but it's different, I suppose.'

Different because it was harder, but you couldn't say that to your fellow unconsoled. In any

24

case, he was right about something: it *did* help to be somewhere else, anywhere else, because nothing could be worse than being at home in their flat, where a stranger could step through the door and know at once that something terrible had taken place. It was as if the walls themselves ached. The confusing thing was that she missed it at the same time, not the way it was when they'd left it yesterday morning, but before that, before everything happened. She missed the smell of expectation, the clean corners of a newly prepared nest. Most of all she missed the little ritual she'd established there and which could not be reconstructed here. Every morning as soon as she was up she'd go into the room next to theirs and open the blind, sometimes the window, too, to let in the morning air, to start the day. Then, at night, she'd go back in and wind the blind down again, ready for bedtime.

Sleep well, darling.

*   *   *

The island looked better from the mainland than it did when you were actually on it. The famous convent Adam had told her about was strictly off-limits, its buildings and lush tropical gardens protected by high walls and railings with heads shaped like sharpened spears. (She wasn't sure what she had expected: to be able to join the nuns in prayer?) There was just a single loop of narrow path for the tourists to follow, and this brought you back to where you started long before you expected to get there—another disappointment. The way was broken only by the occasional track

25

down to the water where you might see a boatman smoking a cigarette in the sunshine or talking on his phone. Other than the sisters, no one seemed to *live* here. Notices declared the route a Way of Silence and called at frequent intervals for reflection and contemplation, but as if in rebellion the other tourists kept up a ceaseless stream of chatter.

'Nuns make people feel uncomfortable,' Adam told Ginny.

'But we haven't even seen one.'

'It doesn't matter, it's the whole idea of them. It's like people think something awful must have happened for them to have chosen a life of seclusion.'

Ginny considered this. 'Well, hasn't it?'

'Maybe, yes.' His expression was earnest, as it often was these days when he answered her questions. It was as if he'd been told (and perhaps he *had*) that he must never dismiss her views out of hand, however bitterly they were expressed and regardless of his own feelings. 'But not necessarily. I don't see why someone can't just really love God. There doesn't have to have been a terrible tragedy.'

She couldn't bring herself to answer that. She stared instead at the message in front of her: *Nel silenzio accetti e comprendi*. The English was given below: *In the silence you accept and understand*. She thought of all the ways in which people might apply this to their own situations—it was a catch-all, like a horoscope—and then she thought of its total inadequacy in respect of her own.

The old basilica, open to the public, housed the remains of St Julius and, fittingly, smelled of death.

26

Ginny refused to climb down the stone steps into the crypt and so Adam went to look on his own. All she could see from her pew at the top was wooden surfaces crowded with lit votive candles; it was so still down there the flames weren't moving at all.

'He's got very small feet,' Adam reported on his return, drawing a guffaw from a nearby American in yellow trousers and a tight-fitting polo shirt.

'They built them different in those days.' He grinned.

'Didn't they just,' Adam said, and both the phrasing and the tone—jocular and matey—made Ginny feel irritated with him, then at once guilty for having begrudged him his moment of 'normal' interaction. His attempts to take part in the everyday, her resentment of those attempts and the guilt that followed: it was becoming a pattern.

'Can we go now?' she asked him, her voice weak and dry. It was so airless, she felt as if she were breathing cobwebs, and yet no one else seemed to be having this reaction. In all directions, tourists went about inhaling and exhaling as easily as if they were standing in an open meadow.

'I just want to look in the souvenir shop,' Adam told her, 'I'll meet you by the jetty.'

'OK.' She shuffled back to the landing-stage alone, hunted for a patch of shade. The sun was high, utterly unforgiving in its withering heat. All in all, she wasn't sure she liked being on the island; it made her feel captive. Even at the point of departure, where you could clearly see the village on the lake's eastern shore no more than a few hundred metres away, she felt overwhelmed by the idea that there might never be another ferry, she might never get back, stuck here for ever with the high walls and the spearheads and the candlelight that never flickered, the sun that never dimmed.

That was when she had her shaky moment, the shakiest to date, the one when she thought she might really be going mad. For as she looked back at the steps to the basilica, she saw a man approaching and found that though she knew that his name was Adam she did not know *who he was*. She had to remind herself that he was her husband by scanning each individual feature of his face— the strong nose and serious mouth, the light-coloured eyebrows that had thickened with middle age just as the hair above had thinned—and it was almost like working through a police photofit to build the face that sparked a memory. Then the words came into her mind, fully formed and with a frightening foreboding: *I share something huge with this man, something permanent, something terrible. Will it make us stronger or will it break us apart?*

Because it was already beyond question that the third option—the easy, natural, optimistic kind of love they had shared until three months ago—was no longer open to them.

On the boat on the way back, Adam said, 'There was a prayer in the crypt, pinned up by the casket. I picked up a copy from the shop.' He held out a pamphlet, a single sheet of paper folded into three.

Ginny read the first few lines:

La mia fede è debole,
La mia preghiera è povera:
Sono preso da tanti affani,
Ho bisogno di luce,
Di aiuto e di conforto.

28

'What does it mean?' she asked him.

Adam didn't know. 'There wasn't a translation.'

She looked again. 'I like it. I like not knowing what it means.'

'That's what I thought. It's just the way Italian sounds, isn't it? It sounds right.'

For the rest of the crossing she clung on to the rail as if she expected to be tipped overboard at any moment, even though the water was still and smooth, the only waves the ones made by them.

*　　*　　*

Arriving back at the boathouse it was immediately obvious that there was something different about the place. Perhaps it was nothing more than a picking up of the breeze or a degree's rise in air temperature, but it felt as if their little square of land had sprung shoots for the first time.

When she came outside after her shower, Ginny found that Adam had been spying on the main house from the dock.

'Gin, come and look, someone's moved in. They're setting up dinner on the terrace at the top. *Very* civilised.'

She went to join him. The villa was further away than she'd realised and further uphill, too, separated from the water by both the sloping lawn and a steep rise of terracing, but you could clearly make out the figure of a woman at the top, arranging place settings on a large circular table. The wide curved balustrade of the terrace and the woman's precise, systematic movements gave her the air of a dresser preparing her stage for the evening's performance.

'Looks like she's wearing some sort of overall,' Adam said. 'Must be a maid or a housekeeper. I suppose it makes sense that a house that size would be staffed.'

'Yes.' Ginny couldn't think of anything worse— to have people fussing around, not allowing you to be yourself and scream and cry and beat your fists and . . . well, she supposed whoever it was who'd just arrived at the villa would be unlikely to be doing any of those things during their stay.

Please let them not have a baby, she pleaded, silently. *That's all I ask.* And before she could stop she was busy torturing herself with a vision of the worst possible scenario: the newcomers were English, they were people she and Adam knew— no, worse, they were one of the couples from the same maternity ward as theirs, or the same antenatal group. Their baby was getting bigger every day, feeding well and holding his head up. Yes, they were finding it challenging, yes, it was mind-blowingly tiring, but already they couldn't imagine life without him . . .

That would be the worst. And it would be almost as awful for the other couple as it would be for Ginny and Adam. One or the other of them would have to leave. By this time tomorrow, they'd be back in their flat in London.

But of course this sort of thinking was what they called catastrophising, another term she'd heard for the first time at the hospital (as if there could be any more catastrophic situation than the one they were already in!). Besides, anyone wealthy enough to own or rent this huge place would not have been taking classes in an NHS teaching hospital as she and Adam had; they'd have been in one of those private maternity hospitals where they had movies on demand and wine lists, where catastrophe never occurred.

Later, coming back from dinner in the village by the upper road, they could hear voices as they followed the passageway down to their entrance, and she allowed herself to loosen her grip on her fears a little. All the voices—too many to pick out individually, but it was a group of six or so—were adult. It wasn't concrete proof, but it would have to be enough for now.

They sat in the garden and sipped the brimming measures of the liqueur Adam had bought from the *enoteca* recommended by his guidebook. When he handed hers to her he lingered by her side as might a nurse who'd delivered a dose of medicine and wanted to be sure it got properly taken. *Come on now, every drop* . . . It was already clear to Ginny that part of her husband's strategy for her, for both of them, was to deaden the pain with alcohol. She didn't think it would work any more than the keeping busy with tourist activities did, but as a short-term measure it at least meant they could fall asleep more easily. (One thing everyone agreed on was that the nights were the worst, just before you fell asleep; those and the very first seconds of full consciousness in the morning, when you remembered again.)

As the light began to fade, her eyes were drawn naturally to the glowing windows and loggias of the island in the distance, as if something might suddenly happen there—fireworks or orchestral music, perhaps. But the only signs of revelry were coming from the other direction, from the villa on the hill; high spirits released into the night air like

31

party balloons, bobbing higher and higher. After listening for a while Ginny thought she could catch a rhythm to it—statement, protest, laughter—and wondered if it might be teasing, the good-natured teasing of a large family or group of friends. Whatever it was it was exactly as if someone had switched on 'happy holiday' sound effects to remind them of the true purpose of a trip to Italy in July.

Adam, meanwhile, was producing his own 'normal' sound effects, thinking aloud about tomorrow's schedule: 'I thought maybe a big walk south . . . If we follow the lake around we'll come to a village that's supposed to have a good place for lunch. *And* wine tasting. Oh, unless it's one of those places that closes on Mondays . . .'

Suddenly his murmurs were interrupted: 'Hello, I've been sent to see if you'd like to come up to the house for a drink!'

It was a girl's voice, loud and bright and at close range—close enough to startle Ginny, who had been completely unaware of anyone approaching. She and Adam gazed towards the gate, towards the source of this abrupt invitation, their eyes searching the darkness for a clearer focus on the speaker's face.

'We've got plenty of good, honest local wine if you're interested?' The absurd over-familiarity of the girl's manner was only emphasized by a sound of laughter from the upper terrace, as if in direct response to her comment, though her words couldn't possibly have been audible from such a distance. They must have followed her movements, Ginny thought, seen from her body language that she'd made contact. Had she been sent, then, or was this her own idea? She thought it very likely that whatever the reason for her arrival the joke was on *them*.

'Er, thank you,' Adam said, politely, 'but we were just about to turn in for the night, actually.'

The girl reacted as if he'd made a hilarious quip, shouting out in delight: ' "Turn in"? You make it sound like you're confessing to a crime or something!'

'That's turning *yourself* in,' Adam said, pedantically.

'That's the one!'

Sitting closer than Adam to the fence and her vision by now fully adjusted, Ginny had an excellent view of the girl. She was blonde, her hair worn long in the snaking ropes favoured by the younger women in Ginny's office (her colleague Tracey called it 'bed head' but it was a style that made Ginny think less of Sleeping Beauty than Medusa), and neat-featured rather than pretty. Though her demeanour was assured and worldly, the smoothness of her skin and the natural suppleness of her frame told Ginny she was probably still a teenager.

'But it's very nice of you to ask,' Adam added, correctly.

Something occurred to the girl and she brought the fingers of one hand to her mouth. They, too, were smooth and slim and there was a large ring on her middle finger, made of components that moved and sparkled. 'Oh God, I haven't . . .? Oh, *how* embarrassing!'

'What?'

'You're not on your honeymoon, are you?'

'No,' Adam said, 'no, we're not.'

33

With an air of theatrical relief she let her fingers fall to her collarbone, delicately tracing its outline as if she'd never noticed her own clavicle before. As well as the ring, there were several silver bangles, falling together to form one solid gleaming cuff. 'It's just that the last people were. That's what made me think . . .'

'The last people? We thought you'd just arrived today?' There was a slight sharpness to Adam's tone; it had meant something to him that they had got here first. A stake claimed—for that famous view, perhaps.

'Oh, we have, yes,' the girl agreed, 'we came this afternoon. What I mean is when we came to the lakes a few years ago there was a cottage in the grounds a bit like this and the couple who stayed there were on their honeymoon. They were Americans. We got to know them quite well, actually.'

She was either naturally very open or temporarily drunk on her 'honest' wine, for she continued to chatter without further prompt or encouragement. 'Mum *totally* fell in love with this place, but when she looked into it for the next summer she was told it's never available. It's rented by the same people every year, literally from June to September. We never found out who it was, but it was obviously someone pretty important. I thought maybe Berlusconi? Or Brad Pitt? I hope not, because I would have hated to have missed *him*. But Esther saw George Clooney in Bellagio. He's a bit old, though, and anyway Esther's the *last* person who'd go for him . . .' She spoke as if Ginny and Adam knew who this Esther was and why George Clooney might not be to her

34

taste. Her head tilted thoughtfully as she added, 'Yeah, I expect they booked your place as well for security reasons. You probably only got it because we got ours.'

Adam frowned. Vaguely Ginny recalled him saying the boathouse had come up at the eleventh hour, the travel agent having offered him first refusal just as he'd despaired of ever finding the perfect hideaway for them. 'So you obviously *did* manage to get the villa then?' he asked.

The girl nodded vigorously. 'Yeah, that's because *Dad* sorted it. He knew Mum was still dreaming about it and he decided it was time to act.' Again there was that sense of assumption that the two of them should understand at once why 'Dad' should succeed where others had failed. 'Well, if you're sure you won't come up? Maybe another night?'

'Sure. How long are you here for?' Adam spoke in the kind of neutral tone that Ginny knew masked keen interest.

'Two weeks, supposedly.'

' "Supposedly"?'

'Well, the rest of us, but I don't reckon Dad will last that long. Not all in one go, anyway. He's *way* too obsessed with work. Esther predicts he'll be gone by Friday.'

'I see,' said Adam.

No doubt in debt to the deep measure of liqueur she'd just drained, Ginny couldn't help being rather charmed by the girl and her stream of consciousness. Despite herself, she found elements of it intriguing. All right, her casual sense of entitlement—her family took the main estate while lesser mortals were consigned to cottages and boathouses—was not so attractive, but the fact that her father had 'sorted' the villa for her mother, well, it was romantic. Ginny glanced at Adam to gauge his expression. It was either fascinated or irritated, she couldn't tell which.

'Well, I shall leave you to it,' the girl said, cheerfully. '*Salute!*'

They watched her withdraw, not back to the terrace but a little way along the waterfront to the far side of the pier, where the click of a lighter and a bright dot of orange indicated the event of a cigarette break. A faint plop made Ginny picture feet being lowered into the lake, though it was too dark now to be sure that they had. Then, all at once, the voice returned to them, fainter, of course, but feverish with excitement: 'Milla! Hi, babes! Yeah, I know, I'm here. It's gorgeous, we're in this completely amazing villa, it's like *Arabian Nights* or something! I know, *I* wish you could too, there's *so* much space and we're going to get *so* bored with just each other.' There was a brief pause. 'Not even Chloë, I know, incredible, but I reckon they're having some kind of *issue*, y'know? He hasn't even mentioned her name, it's *so* weird. So, listen, did you get those silver flip-flops in the end?'

A sloshing sound and a general fading of excitement told them she was on the move again and out of earshot. Adam grimaced. 'Great. They're British, over-privileged, and within adequate range of a mobile phone mast. My favourite combination.'

Ginny smiled. Her throat felt sticky and constricted from the liqueur, and when she spoke her voice seemed to have altered; it sounded

36

thicker, more nocturnal. 'She was sweet, I thought. And who were you expecting, anyway? It was obviously going to be someone super-rich—that place must cost a bomb to rent. Ten thousand pounds a week, I bet. Maybe even more. You'd have to be a Berlusconi or a Brad Pitt.' She was unexpectedly cheered by her little allusion, and by the sheer length of her speech, but Adam didn't appear to have noticed either miracle.

'I guess I was hoping it wouldn't be anyone at all,' he said, quietly, as much to himself as to her. 'I'm not sure we can handle neighbours.'

And, as quickly as it had risen, Ginny's new-found spirit subsided. For, once again, Adam's was the 'we' of the doctor speaking on behalf of the patient.

CHAPTER FOUR

MONDAY

When Ginny married Adam there was undisguised relief among his family that he, the eldest sibling of four and by common consent the most hopeless, was finally ready to do what his two sisters and one brother had already done (and, indeed, were now in the process of raising to an art form): be a parent.

'He'll be a brilliant father,' Karen, the bossiest, told her. 'Kids *love* him.'

Ginny had of course seen this first-hand. It was true that children of all ages were fascinated by Adam, which you might not have expected of someone so bookish and, in his own sweet way, physically awkward. It was his dispensing of strange animal facts and his weakness for revolting jokes that did it, she supposed, though she was not so sure that these skills automatically translated to outstanding fatherhood—or, indeed, to the desire to become a father in the first place. She knew there was a part of her new husband that was tempted to break the Trustlove mould, and not only for the hell of it, either. Though he loved his nieces and nephews, of course he did, he also associated them with noise and exhaustion, with checklists and schedules and the loading of heavy musical instruments into car boots; with *fuss*.

'It's never straightforward,' he'd complain to Ginny, whenever arrangements were made for a family lunch. 'It's never, "Let's meet here at one o'clock and we'll all be on our way by three." Oh no, it's always, "We might be a bit late because Izzy's got cello," or "We'll have to leave half an hour early because Jack's got two parties to go to." They behave as if their children are going to have them shot if they make them miss anything.'

Ginny, who had no siblings of her own and to whom the child-centric world was quite new, saw it differently: it wasn't the children who were driving all the activities, it was the mothers. To varying degrees, Adam's sisters and sister-in-law were stage mothers, damned if they weren't going to uncover the one thing at which each of their children shone and which might thus propel him or her to global (or at least school-wide) stardom. And it was all the more frightening because they each professed themselves guilty of not doing *enough* for their kids. The one with the cello-

38

playing daughter, Samantha, was even learning it with her, for goodness' sake, sitting alongside her in twice-weekly lessons as if she'd completely forgotten that she was the parent and not the pupil. As for Karen, she was known to keep French flashcards in the glove compartment of her car (Ginny imagined her holding one up every time they hit a red light, refusing to pull away again until the correct answer—sorry, *la réponse juste*— was presented). Whatever happened to a bag of Fox's Glacier Mints?

Adam agreed that it was sheer madness. He could produce no insider evidence to disprove the suspicion that these women had no interests, no identity, beyond their family. 'It's the Trustlove way,' he said, dryly. 'A good name for a cult, eh?'

'But what would happen if something went wrong?' Ginny asked, in all seriousness. If a spouse left or a child rebelled or one of their own began to act outside her assigned role? Adam didn't know, but she could form her own picture well enough: the women would simply *shrink*. They'd fold in on themselves, their life force removed, like something out of a sci-fi movie.

Still, she and Adam were different, she thought. They would find their own way, if and when they decided to do it themselves. *If and when*—a figure of speech, nothing more, for she meant *when*, of course. She never imagined *if*.

*   *   *

By the second morning Adam's plans were becoming more elaborate. They were at the garden table drinking coffee (made by Adam) and eating

39

croissants from the bakery on the hill (fetched by Adam), when he declared with sudden energy, 'It's a shame this place doesn't come with its own boat. After all, it *is* a boathouse.'

Ginny thought of the musty bowels below their rooms, the discoloured stone and industrial-strength cobwebbing she'd glimpsed from the main stairwell, the ribs of wood that once cradled the boats and were now eroded by a decade's worth of bird droppings. 'But it's disused, isn't it?'

'I don't mean we'd keep it down there. We could probably use the jetty next door. I think we should rent something for a few days, don't you? Really see this place the way it's meant to be seen.'

Ginny looked at him from beneath the brim of her hat. Already sweat was making her cotton shirt stick to the skin between her shoulder blades. 'Wouldn't it be expensive? And, anyway, do you even know how to sail?'

'You don't need to know how to sail to point the thing away from one edge and towards another. I just mean a little rowing boat or a dinghy or something.' He paused. 'I just think we should try new things.'

Whenever he made a call to action like this, Ginny knew he must have read it in a book or been fed it by one of the hospital counsellors. She also knew that, just as he humoured her apathy, her disinterest, her occasional truculence, she needed to support these whims of his, this evidence of his survival instinct, even if—or especially since—hers had yet to show any signs of resurrection. And if they did hire a little boat, well, it would pass the time as well as anything else.

'It's an idea,' she said.

'Karen's kids sail,' he added. 'She and Richard took them on that course on the Isle of Wight, do you remember?'

She nodded, understanding. He'd been thinking of his nieces and nephews. Despite his best intentions, he'd been doing exactly the same as she was: imagining this place with children. Children wouldn't recoil from the derelict innards of an old boathouse, they'd clamour to explore them, make a climbing frame of those crumbling beams, they'd use their imaginations to bring it back to life.

Adam left the table and hopped on to the ledge of the lake wall, the better to consider the rental question. He'd be up on the jetty practising his knots if it weren't for the fact that the new neighbours were out in their garden playing a rather excitable game of cricket and he was nervous of accusations of trespassing. 'Have you seen them on the lawn? Like the Kennedys,' he'd said to her, when she'd first emerged. This, she knew, was as much a criticism of his own family as it was their new neighbours. All those gatherings with the Trustloves, their undisguised delight in the size and complicatedness of their group, they didn't just exasperate Adam, they embarrassed him.

'Mr President's batting,' he added.

Ginny had caught only quick glimpses of 'Mr President', the man of the house, the one with the power and money, but even at some distance he had already given her an unwelcome feeling of intimidation, one that she recognised from her first few terms at university over fifteen years ago. Then, she'd been unable to think of anything to say to the almost insolently self-assured public school

41

boys she'd met there, and they, in turn, had made no bones about their lack of interest in her.

He was one of those, but grown up—in his mid-forties, she judged, not far off Adam's age. If she was right about that then he'd been quick off the mark in starting a family, for there were two more grown-up kids besides the teenager they'd met last night. That was assuming the others she could see—a young man and a young woman, identifiable as siblings even from a distance by their dark curly hair and long pale legs—were brother and sister to the drunken blonde one. The girl, presumably, was Esther, though Ginny couldn't remember any mention of a boy. Both looked of student age, mid-twenties at most.

She raised her head slightly for a better view. The way the cricket game was set up said it all: as Adam had noted, the man of the house batted from a makeshift wicket set plum in the centre of the lawn, while the others took turns in taking him on (there was a fifth figure, an Italian boy wearing dust-smeared trousers—a gardener, perhaps? Some kind of servant, anyway, Adam said). But there was no mistaking who was in charge, who was the fixed centre, the one to which all things moved or were drawn.

As if to prove the point, Ginny surprised herself by getting to her feet and, without saying another word to Adam, bypassing him to step on to the stone ledge herself and walk beyond the boundary of their premises into the main estate. Reaching a set of steps that gave access to the lake for swimming, she detoured briefly across the grass before hopping up on to the pier and walking right to its end, turning only at the very last moment to face the lawn.

She had not moved with such momentum in months.

Even allowing for her hat, she knew she could be seen to be openly studying her neighbours. Indeed, from here she had a perfect view of the alpha male, of his athletic height and broad shoulders, his thick head of dark hair, gleaming in the sun like the rump of a chocolate Lab. He wore long shorts the pale blue-grey colour of the Atlantic, and some kind of designer sports shirt in white. His feet were bare and his calves taut and muscular. The tan of his skin looked like that of someone who was ending his holiday, not beginning it.

Physical details examined, Ginny's thoughts moved automatically to their natural focus: family. Three children this man had, at least three, which meant three sets of grandchildren to come; days and nights filled with children's voices for as long as he lived. They'd be encouraged to start young, she decided, her imagination carrying her away. She pictured him turning to his wife (absent in this vignette but in every way adored, she was certain— the heart and soul of the clan) and declaring, 'It didn't do us any harm, did it? We'll all muck in!' She was sure of what his voice would be, too, deep and patrician and commanding. Her next thought was inevitable: how quiet and lonely she and Adam must seem in comparison to all this, how bereft. Yes, that would be the word you'd choose, even without knowing: *bereft*.

'Ginny? *Ginny?* What are you doing?' Speaking with a hiss of alarm, Adam came hurrying to join her. She turned on him with an exasperation she knew was unfair.

'It's all right, Adam, I wasn't going to fill my pockets with stones and jump in!'

The hurt showed in his face, his fair complexion flushed. 'That's not what I thought at all, don't be silly. I'm just not sure yet we're allowed on this side, not officially . . . Oh God, look, it's too late, they've seen us . . .'

Just as Ginny had hoped and feared, the tanned patriarch had indeed turned at the sound of their voices. Without a moment's hesitation he dropped his bat and came striding towards them, arm raised in a cheerful salute. The blonde girl followed, waving at them as if greeting lifelong friends and leaving the older girl and two boys to the remains of the game.

The next moment the man was springing on to the pier, moving with such thrust that Ginny thought he might stride right past her and off its end, striking out across the lake in championship freestyle—she even found herself stepping aside to allow him room for the required dive. He did not, of course, but came to a halt at a respectful distance and held out his hand, first to Adam and then to her. 'Martin Sale. I think you know Philippa already.' His voice was smoother than she'd expected, and subtler, more king-maker than king.

'Pippi,' the girl told him, with a playful prod of his arm. '*No one* calls me Philippa.'

'Sorry, Pipsqueak. And those two down there are Esther and Dominic.'

'Dom,' Pippi corrected, with the air of a set piece. '*No one* calls him Dominic. And you forgot Emilio, our boy Friday.'

'Oh yes. Our very own *ragazzo venerdì*. Is there such a thing in this part of the world? Is that even the right translation?'

Pippi pulled a face of exaggerated dumbness. 'I don't know, Dad. My Italian is rubbish.'

To Ginny's faint disappointment, Adam was instantly deferential to the other man. If he'd been wearing a flat cap he would have doffed it there and then. 'Adam Trustlove, very nice to meet you. I hope you don't mind . . .' He motioned guiltily to the deck beneath their feet and his laugh was meek and unnatural. 'We didn't mean to encroach . . .'

Encroach. It sounded such a wheedling, small-minded word.

'Of course not,' Martin said, easily, 'you do know it's a shared mooring, don't you? There may not be boats in your boathouse any more but you've as much right as we have to this. Besides, we've got nothing to hide, have we, Pips? Or at least nothing that we can't be asked to take indoors.'

Pippi giggled and gazed admiringly at her father. Ginny saw at once that no man had yet eclipsed him in her life view. Demonstrations of the hero worship of a parent were impossibly painful on so many counts that she was forced to avert her eyes from Pippi altogether and take refuge in her impressions of Martin Sale at close quarters.

His face was fascinating, large and strong-boned and with enough flaws—including a slightly crooked nose and the most slender of gaps between the two front teeth—to make the effect far more powerful than conventional good looks might have. And though he had natural authority he was also quite boyish, almost giggly, which seemed to come partly from a sense of restlessness in him—not the kind that couldn't wait to lose you for something more interesting, however, but the kind that made you hope you'd be taken along too. It was charisma, pure and simple and as strong as scent. You could have seen from orbit that he was the one who held the attention of this little group; even those still playing cricket were looking across at regular intervals in the hope of regaining his focus.

'Gaio in the piazza is your man,' he was telling Adam, 'on the other side of the main jetty. He'll sort you out.' He was going to organise a boat for himself later that morning, he added, and at once Ginny imagined a glamorous cruiser of some sort, Adam's rowing boat, were it ever to materialise, bobbing humbly in its shadow.

'You'll meet my wife Bea at some point soon, I'm sure. She's just gone off with the housekeeper, on the hunt for some special goat's yoghurt or something. Nothing else will do, apparently.'

The fond indulgence in his face when he mentioned his wife was striking, and it produced in Ginny a sensation too close to envy to deny.

'Susanna's an *amazing* chef,' Pippi put in. 'I am *so* going to put on weight while we're here.'

Martin mimicked her speech. 'You *so* don't want to. Look at the size of you already.'

'Hippo size,' she returned, and the look they exchanged made Ginny see the remark had some sort of private significance. She'd already lost count of the number of times Pippi had done that in their two short encounters—not felt the need to explain an in-joke—and Ginny was certain this was not a mistake the father would make; he was far

46

too attuned to other people's feelings. She'd been wrong to link him to those entitled boys of university days, for he entirely lacked their brand of arrogance. His was the confidence of proper achievement. She wondered if he were a cabinet minister or a retired sports star or a famous character actor, someone she ought to recognise but who, in the shock of the last few months, had been deleted from her memory.

He smiled again at Adam and her. 'Listen, I'm sure we can spare her if you want her to come and cook for you one night?'

There was a slight delay as Adam and Ginny worked out who he was talking about and Martin guffawed at the confusion, squeezing his daughter around the waist. 'Susanna, I mean, not this one. You'd be lucky to get a Cup-a-Soup out of her. But seriously, we'll be eating out a lot; she's at your disposal.'

His offer was both extremely generous and exactly the sort of thing that made Adam uncomfortable. He never accepted an invitation he couldn't return.

'We were planning to work our way around the restaurants in the village,' Ginny said, feeling the unfamiliar strain in her cheeks of a smile. 'But thank you, anyway, that's really kind.'

Martin looked at her properly then, not saying anything himself and yet somehow suspending speech in everyone else, as well. He didn't seem to blink as frequently as a normal person, which gave him an expression of fascinated attention. Ginny had no idea if this was supported by real interest or whether he was simply one of those (invariably very successful) people she'd read about who

47

understood that the key to world domination was in making everyone feel they had something extraordinary to contribute. Her instinct said it *was* real, that he was seeing her as she was, maybe even guessing right now at the source of her unhappiness. The smile shrank on her lips as his expression altered to one of compassion, and she wished at once that she had not started this, had not put herself on this platform and demanded he notice her.

'Well, look, we'll leave you to your lake,' he said, finally, and began to usher Pippi away. 'And don't even think about holding back if we get too loud and obnoxious, will you? We won't take offence, I promise.'

She knew he was talking to her, showing her he had understood her vulnerability, but at the same time and with equal accuracy he had picked up on something in Adam, that territorial bent of his— *we'll leave you to* your *lake*. It was as if he'd got the measure of each of them in only a few minutes. But how could he have done that? He knew *nothing* about them.

She raised her head, blinked as the surface of the water reflected sunlight into her face. 'Bye.'

'Good to meet you!' Adam called.

Together they watched father and daughter stroll away and then, after a wordless interval, they too began to walk towards land, Adam subconsciously aping Martin's body language towards Pippi, his hand on Ginny's back, protective, paternal.

*   *   *

48

'They did say their name was Sale, didn't they?' Adam asked, later.

'Yes, that's right.'

'Hmm, that's interesting.'

'Why?' she asked, dutifully.

It was her husband's habit to preface any revelation with a drawing-in comment of this sort. 'Hmm, that's interesting' was a favourite, as was, 'I thought so', or the more direct, 'D'you know what I think?' Only when you had made your obligatory prompt would he share with you the original opinion or piece of information. She had experimented in their early relationship and discovered that to not give the required prod was to elicit a rather infantile sigh, followed by silence, as if he'd been told his idea needed further refinement before he might try again. (And if she was cross with him, then to *deliberately* not play along was a sure way to torment him.)

'I think I know who they must be. Who *he* must be.'

'Who?' Ginny's curiosity was genuine now. 'I thought there was something familiar about him. Is he on TV?'

'No, no. Well, he might be, I suppose. He's that clothing guy. You know, the Sale catalogue? Linen shirts and all that. Haven't we bought some stuff from it?'

'Oh yes, *that* Sale.' In fact, Ginny knew more about Sale than its reputation for linen shirts. It was a household-name brand for all kinds of good-quality clothing, both for adults and children, and one of her treats over the last year had been to pore over the newborn section of the catalogue, occasionally checking the stock online and making

49

a modest order (the label was not cheap). Then, after everything happened, she threw the catalogue away and stopped looking at the website. That left only the items she had already bought—four rompers—and these remained in the top drawer of the changing unit at home, along with the other unworn clothes. Sale sold rompers in pairs and both sets were soft white cotton, two printed with bumblebees and the other two with penguins. Imagining them now, pristine and perfect in a silent room, in a silent flat, caused such a gush of anguish it jerked her upright in her seat.

'All right?' Adam asked at once.

'Yes, fine. Tell me more about the Sales.'

He looked pleased. 'Well, there was that article in the *Sunday Times* magazine a few months ago, do you remember? "The Sales of the Century" or something—him and his brother. They started the business together in the eighties, straight out of university. Didn't one of them sell his car because they couldn't get a bank loan? Or was it his guitar? Anyway, now they're big in the States and worth millions.' He let out a puff of disapproval, quite at odds with his approbation on meeting Sale in person. 'Well, they'd better not be doing any photo shoots here, I'll tell you that for nothing. That thing he said about complaining if they make a noise—it makes it impossible for us *to* complain now and he knows it. A classic passive-aggressive manoeuvre.'

Ginny looked at him. 'Don't get obsessed, Adam. Even if they are the Sale Sales then they're just as entitled to a holiday as anyone else.'

He glanced up in surprise. 'I'm not obsessed, I'm just, you know . . . making conversation, that's all. I'm sure we'll hardly see them while we're here.' And she watched as he replayed what had been said, noting for the first time, perhaps, this role reversal that was taking place between them and of which Ginny had been aware for weeks. Was this how it was always going to be now? she wondered. And was it going to grow, finally reaching its logical conclusion in his becoming the fully-fledged busybody she'd once been and she letting the world wash over her as once he had? Was there a way of stopping the process, or putting it into reverse?

She doubted it. If she knew anything for sure it was that she could never go back to being her old self. She could survive this, the fact that she could open her mouth and have this conversation proved that, the fact that she could feel curiosity about the Sales in the first place proved that, but she could not be the same. And the horrifying part of it was that she was probably more interesting this way to someone new, someone like Martin Sale. When he looked into her face that morning on the pier, she had had a feeling she'd awakened a curiosity in him, possibly even unusually so. Tragedy had distinguished her. If he'd met her before, he would have found nothing remarkable about her at all.

CHAPTER FIVE

TUESDAY

Before Ginny got pregnant she had no reason to expect that anything would go wrong. Negligent as

51

it now seemed—criminal, actually—she knew nothing about her family medical history, had hardly given it a second thought. As she told the midwife at their first meeting, she could quote her blood group but that was about it.

'You'll have to treat me as a one-of-a-kind,' she said, happily, when a succession of routine antenatal questions had drawn blank after blank.

'She *is* a one-of-a-kind,' Adam agreed, sitting next to her, 'I can vouch for that.'

And the midwife smiled at them, a proper smile with real human warmth, as if she could still sincerely share in the joy of a couple's first pregnancy, the special togetherness that brought, even though she must have seen it a thousand times before.

'So no Down's in the family? Or cystic fibrosis?'

'Not that I know of.'

'Anything else?' Other conditions were listed on the off-chance that one should ring a bell: muscular dystrophy, sickle cell anaemia, and ones Ginny had never heard of.

'Your parents died in their late thirties, you say. Any heart or neurological issues there?'

'No. It was a car accident, nothing medical.'

Nothing medical. She couldn't repeat that throwaway phrase now without shuddering.

The fact was she *hadn't* known anything medical, she hadn't known there was anything medical to know.

Of course, growing up after her parents' accident, she'd been aware of the occasional remark on her father's side about her mother's— the Sharp curse, they called it—especially around the time that her maternal grandparents died, in oddly close succession. No one said it explicitly, she was still a child, after all, but it was generally thought that their grief at losing their daughter had had a hand in their early deaths. 'You know their first child died in infancy,' Ginny's grandmother said. 'He'd be your uncle if he'd lived. So all they had was your mum, and when she died they lost their will to go on. Without a will we just wither away.' (It did not occur to Ginny that her mother's parents might have found in her some of what they'd lost with their daughter.)

The Sharps were like a family from centuries ago, her grandmother said on another occasion, by which time Ginny was a teenager with a passing interest in genealogy. They could have been from the time of the Black Death or some other epidemic, back when whole households would be wiped out by a single unlucky hand. And with Ginny's mother having taken her husband's name in marriage, the name itself had died out, too. 'She was the last of the Sharps,' her grandmother sighed.

'Surely *I'm* the last of the Sharps?' Ginny said.

'Well, not in name, but of course you have half the blood.'

It was funny to think of it like that—as two separate sets of blood mixed together, fizzing slightly, like one of her grandmother's gin and tonics.

'And who's to say you're the last, anyway?' her grandfather said. 'I for one would be interested to meet my great-grandchildren.'

Sadly, that proved optimistic, for he passed away years before Ginny met Adam and began to plan a family. Her grandmother was still alive, but by the time Ginny had gone to her for information she was no longer able to give it, having succumbed to dementia.

Not once in her childhood was Ginny made to feel grateful that her grandparents had taken her in—and for that she *did* feel grateful. Growing up, she had everything her friends had, including family fellowship. She was secure and happy, well prepared for adulthood, filled with expectation.

Her grandmother was right about the Sharps, though. When you itemised it, laid it out on paper, it was impossible not to see the repetition of stunted lives. Ginny's was a family tree with one half in the sun and one in the shade.

*   *   *

She was surprised to find how keen she was to see the woman who had married Martin Sale, who had given him his handsome brood and shared his *Sunday Times*-worthy success. Adam, encouraged by her interest, wracked his memory for further facts from the article he'd read. He was sure there was nothing complicated or dysfunctional about the Sales' set-up: there was one marriage, one mother, one nuclear family. Their togetherness was of the wholesome, old-fashioned (and of course supremely well-dressed) variety. If it hadn't been for the 'amazing' housekeeper dragging her off to look for dairy products, Mrs Sale would have been there in the thick of the cricket game, keeping wicket, perhaps. Bea, Martin had said she was called. Busy as a Bea. Ginny imagined someone tall and cool and blonde, someone who believed there was no such thing as good luck, only

54

good genes.

Not like hers.

Of course they met in exactly the opposite way that she would have liked or expected. The whole episode was beyond unexpected, in fact: it was distressing. Had she told Adam about it, he would have had no compunction about labelling it a setback. It was late afternoon the following day, Tuesday, and Adam was out shopping for provisions (it had been established without discussion that he should take care of meal planning and preparation, just as he did these days in London), and for the first time Ginny had had the impulse to bypass her lakeside chair and walk along the path towards the village.

The way was narrow in parts, narrow enough for her to be cautious of those coming the other way, in particular the arm-in-arm couples you saw everywhere in Orta (sometimes their reluctance to break apart made Ginny think they'd rather see the other person fall in the lake than risk a split-second of not touching). But the path was quiet, weaving in and out of the sunlight as shore and tree dictated, and she was not even a half-mile from the boathouse when she stopped to rest. It amazed her sometimes how physically weak she'd become; the air here had the same effect on her as high altitude might on a normal person.

It was a still, melancholy spot. She settled on the second of a pair of stone benches, set at right angles to one another and divided by the low-hanging foliage of an old oak. The water, shaded by the overhanging branches, was liquorice black-green, the light touching its surface in distinct drops, and watching it had a hypnotic effect on her.

She wasn't sure how much time passed—perhaps only a few minutes—but when she came to she was reaching instinctively for her handbag, for the zipped compartment meant for keys and other valuables. From this she withdrew half a dozen photographs. There was one in particular that she kept coming back to, her favourite, if such a term could be used for it. At home, when she was sure visitors weren't coming, she had kept it out, not on display exactly, but within reach. She wasn't sure if Adam would like it on view in the boathouse; it went against the spirit of the trip. The funny—or sad—thing was that if a stranger were to look at that picture he'd see nothing unusual in it, nothing wrong, just a peaceful, sleeping infant.

She tucked the other photos back inside their pocket, keeping this one on her lap, and sat for some time without being aware of anyone passing. Then she heard the rush of approaching footsteps—two sets—and a woman's voice raised in unmistakable agitation:

'Dom! Don't run off like that! You must have heard me calling!'

And then again, making Ginny start: *'Dom! Wait!'*

There were further sounds of feet, heavy on the broken twigs and dried leaves, and then a second voice came into earshot, young, male and English, as exasperated as the first: 'For God's sake, you don't have to stalk me halfway round the lake!'

'I wasn't stalking you, don't be ridiculous. Look, I'm out of breath, let's sit here a minute. I want to talk to you.'

'There's nothing to say, Mum, I told you.'

'Well, sit anyway. Keep me company for five

minutes.'

'Fine. Five minutes.'

From this short exchange Ginny gathered that she now found herself just metres away from Bea Sale and her son Dominic and, judging by the way the shuffling stopped and the voices lowered, they'd done as Bea suggested and settled on the stone seat. Already Ginny knew she was not going to be able to close her ears to any further conversation she might overhear. The Sales were too close and she was too curious.

'Have you thought any more about what you're going to say?' Bea asked. Her voice now was soft-edged and tentative, which gave it a girlish quality. It didn't match at all Ginny's pre-conceived idea of how the woman might look; with the thick partition of green between them, she could still only guess at that.

'No, and I don't *want* to think about it, all right?' Dom's voice, in contrast, was bitter and sullen.

'But it won't go away, Dom, however much we want it to.'

There was a scoffing sound. 'A bit of an unfortunate choice of words, don't you think?'

'Oh, darling, don't be like this.'

'Like what?'

'Shutting yourself off from me. I feel awful.'

There was no reply, which was a reply in itself, Ginny thought.

'You haven't said anything to Esther or Pippi, have you?' Bea asked.

'Of course I haven't. They'd go crazy.'

'Or Dad?' She was audibly more nervous when she said this.

'Oh, come on, Mum!' In contrast, the son's tone

was impatient, disrespectful. 'Like you wouldn't know if I had! We'd all be back home now sorting it out.'

'Is that what you'd like, to get it sorted out? Out in the open?' There was no challenge to the woman's question, Ginny observed, simply an eagerness to understand the other's desires.

Again frustration sharpened the boy's tone, and to a degree that made his eavesdropper wince: 'I thought you said *you* wanted to talk to Dad first?'

Ginny found herself holding her breath, as if Bea Sale's reply would have some impact on *her*, too. She was shocked by how quickly she'd been gripped by this private conversation, and mortified that she was so readily allowing herself to listen. She considered putting her fingers in her ears, but somehow that seemed more shameful, an admission of guilt for what she'd already heard. It made not the slightest difference to her that she didn't understand a word of what they were saying.

'I did. I do,' Bea said, at last, 'at least I thought that was what *you* wanted.' She sighed. 'And with this holiday happening . . . it makes it difficult, you know that. He wants us to all be so happy. If we could just go along with it, just while we're here . . .' Now it was the sentiment rather than the tone that held a naive quality, but there was no trace of manipulation in it. This was not a woman who played games, Ginny thought.

'Nothing will happen while we're here, will it?' Bea added. 'That's agreed, isn't it?'

'Supposedly,' Dom muttered.

Bea sighed again, more heavily this time, her dislike of her own impotence palpable. 'Even so, maybe you should have stayed in London, after all.

58

Maybe this isn't going to work. I should have realised how hard it would be for you. Two weeks—that probably feels like a long time at the moment, doesn't it?'

'I *want* it to be an eternity,' Dom burst out, startling Ginny. 'The longer I leave it, the more chance there—'

Thanks to the approach of a speedboat from the north, she couldn't make out the rest of this, or whether there was any rest of it at all, for when she next tuned in she got the impression the boy had broken down in some way. Bea was distressed, too, speaking to him with a cooing sound, 'Oh, darling, this isn't the end of the world, I promise you, however it may feel now!' And Ginny pictured him stooped, crushed, unable to lift his own head. 'Do you know what? I think maybe we should just tell Dad now, after all—'

'No. No. I don't want to ruin it for everyone . . .' And there was a gulp in Dom's answer that twisted Ginny's heart. As she often did now, even with strangers, she found herself connecting to this person's pain as directly as pins being slotted into a socket.

'Then why don't you just try to rest and relax,' Bea said, gently. 'Make the most of being here.'

'It's a bit late for that.'

There seemed to be a moment of agreement before Bea said, 'Will you at least tell me if you've spoken to Chloë since we've been here?'

Pippi had mentioned someone of the same name, Ginny remembered, when she was on the phone to her friend. She supposed Chloë must be Dom's girlfriend.

'No, I haven't.'

'Well, maybe you should. You need—'

'Need what, Mum? To hear her say for the hundredth time that she totally disagrees with me?' His cry was angry and raw, distressing Ginny afresh.

'I just thought you might need an outlet, that's all, if you don't want to talk to me . . .' Bea trailed off, as though already regretting her comment, a possibility borne out by the boy's explosive reaction.

'An *outlet*? Are you kidding me? A time machine, that's what I need.' Then, the next thing, his voice had lapsed again into pleading and desperation: 'Why won't you just leave me alone about it, why won't you just let me—God!— *pretend*?'

'Because you're obviously suffering, darling. I can't watch you crucifying yourself like this.'

'Stop trying to talk to me and I'll be fine.'

He sounded anything but fine, even to a stranger—especially to a stranger—and Ginny had to resist the urge to rush forward and comfort him, to cry out, *Of course we can pretend!* The contrast between this anguished exchange and the frivolous banter of Martin and Pippi was utterly bewildering. It was hard to believe that the four of them belonged to the same family.

Now it was Bea who was doing the groaning. 'OK, OK. But when we get back to London, the first thing we'll do is all sit down together and try to—' Abruptly she broke off, and her voice, when it came again, vibrated with alarm. 'Oh, Dom, quick! I think there's someone sitting there!'

'Sitting where?'

'*There*. On the next seat along. I heard

something.'

There was a horrible moment of paralysis for Ginny as the foliage began to rustle, presumably being prodded aside by the Sales in an attempt to assess just how close to them the witness was (and, given their conversation, perhaps to establish that she was not a member of their own household). Then, not knowing why she was reacting in such a preposterous way, she sprang to her feet, lunged unsteadily back on to the pathway and began dashing in the direction of home. Passing her neighbours, she kept her head low, imagining rather than seeing their open mouths at the sight of her flight, for both were on their feet and turned her way. All she was aware of was a triangle of crisp white skirt and a fork of denimed legs; she dared not raise her eyes to their faces. Then Dom was calling out 'Hey!' and Bea was crying after her—'*Please, wait!*'—and tears were blurring Ginny's vision. She was feeling a second, stronger rush of panic, as if by leaving the scene like this she was doubling the crime. Irrationally, as her feet pounded on the flagstones, she felt a sudden hatred for Adam, for his not being here to tell her how she *should* be behaving.

The panic faded as quickly as it had arrived, however, and, even before she'd pushed through the door to the boathouse, she was already wishing she'd simply stepped forwards and introduced herself. She could have pleaded ignorance of listening—or, better still, made no reference to it at all—and retreated with dignity, whether they believed her or not. After all, Dom was sure to have recognised her from yesterday's cricket game—though they hadn't been formally

61

introduced, he must have been aware of Adam and her as they chatted with his father and sister on the pier. And even if he didn't make the connection, she could hardly keep herself from sight for the rest of the trip.

She didn't know herself, acting so hysterically; she must surely have lost her mind. How she had managed that show of normality yesterday, she honestly didn't know.

Upstairs, she poured a glass of water and drank it in a few gulps, but instead of calming her, as she had hoped, it acted as a fresh shot of adrenalin and her pulse began to throb harder than ever, her eyes darting wildly to the door as if she awaited the arrival of arresting officers. Sure enough, when she opened up the French windows and edged to the corner of the balcony, she could see a woman in a white sundress standing at the garden gate. She'd come to confront her, ask her why she'd been spying, demand to know what she'd heard.

Reluctantly, Ginny opened up the garden door and took the steps down, clutching at the rail in case she tripped.

Her visitor held out a small rectangle of paper—it took a few moments for Ginny to realise what it was: her photograph, the picture-side discreetly averted. 'You left this on the seat.' Bea remained as softly spoken as she'd been in her exchange with her son, and if anything less breathless, despite the fact that she must surely have hurried back herself to have got here so quickly.

Though she continued to hold out the photograph, Ginny didn't move beyond the shield of her wicker chair. 'May I come into the garden?'

'Yes, of course.'

Her visitor let herself in and laid the photo on the table, face up now, perhaps to avoid scratching the image on the stone. Without thinking, Ginny placed her sunhat over the top of it, hiding it from view. If this hadn't felt so necessary she would have seen how absurd it must look, like an amateur magician setting up a trick. As if to heighten the sense of ceremony, for a few moments the two of them stood on either side of the hat, neither speaking.

She was the one with the curls, then, Ginny thought. They were silky and sculpted and, combined with the clinched waist of the sun dress, gave her the look of the 1940s or 50s. Her hair colour was a warm mid-brown, and natural, too, if Ginny judged correctly; there was even a thread or two of grey at the parting. She *was* beautiful, very beautiful, but in a natural, rose-skinned, shiny-eyed way, not in the superior, untouchable way Ginny had imagined. She looked as if she'd be the first to admit to the lucky hand she'd been dealt.

'It's Ginny, isn't it? Marty said he met you yesterday. I'm Bea. I meant to come and introduce myself earlier, but the days have just disappeared.' When Ginny didn't reply but continued to stand staring dumbly at her, she added, 'My daughter Esther and I are doing a cooking course every morning at a restaurant up in the hills, and then we come back and there's lunch . . .' All of this was said in a tone of apology, even regret, making Ginny feel even worse for her rudeness.

She blurted out: 'I didn't mean to hear you . . . I was walking along the lake and I saw the seat and I sort of got caught up in my thoughts.' As her eyes drifted to the hat, Bea's followed. 'I should have said something, but once I'd waited a minute or two it seemed—oh, this is stupid! I'm just really sorry, OK?'

For the first time Bea looked vexed by her behaviour. 'It's fine, please don't worry. You were sitting there first—we disturbed *your* peace. Anyway, we're strangers, aren't we? You couldn't possibly have known what we were talking about.'

This last statement demoralised Ginny. Unlike Martin, who had naturally drawn Adam and her into his realm, first with his sheer presence and then with his offers and his advice and his conspiratorial remarks, his wife seemed more inclined to establish the line between them. Given the choice, Ginny thought she would rather have dealt with the anguished son; at least his was a key she could think in.

'I don't know if we should stay here,' she said, voicing an instinct she did not fully understand but that she knew had been sliding its way to the surface from the moment she'd met Martin yesterday.

Bea was taken aback. 'Why not? Listen, you really mustn't worry about what just happened. Let's just forget it.'

'No, it's not that. It's everything. I was mad to go along with this.'

'With what?'

'This holiday, being away from home. It was never going to work.'

Too late Ginny saw that she was echoing the phrasing Bea herself had used less than half an hour ago in comforting her son.

'What do you mean? I don't understand.' With a delicate inclination of her head, Bea did what

Ginny knew she should have done, suggested the two of them sit down.

'Please . . .' Ginny gestured to the chair—Adam's one of the pair. Palms smoothing the back of her skirt, Bea slid into its low seat with the grace of a debutante negotiating an E-type.

'Tell me what it is,' she said. 'What's happened?' Again, her eyes found the hat, returning to Ginny's face with faint apprehension. Though Ginny did not reply, her guest seemed prepared to wait in absolute silence for as long as it took, and after a minute or so Ginny found herself drawing breath and answering the question.

'We're not here on a normal holiday like you. We came here because our baby died.' It sounded bald, horrifying in this civilised place, with this calm, groomed woman, as if she'd thrown a bucket of blood over that crisp white dress. 'We're supposed to be recovering,' she added.

'The baby in the photo?' Bea asked.

'Yes.'

'When did it happen?'

'April the twelfth. Three months ago.' She had absolutely no idea why she was telling the other woman this, or at least no clear single idea. She needed to explain her peculiar reaction earlier, perhaps, or she wanted to erase that subtle line Bea had drawn between them by being so protective of her own secret. Maybe she had been subconsciously longing for a confidante who was unconnected to her tragedy, who was not Adam. Or, most confusingly, most dangerously, it was possible she wanted Bea to go straight home afterwards and tell Martin her story—as simple as that.

Bea reached forwards to pat Ginny's hand, just once and very gently. As she withdrew her arm, her wrist caught the brim of the sunhat on the edge of the table, dislodging it, and she pushed it precisely back into position. 'So recent,' she said, her voice low and steady. 'You must still feel it very deeply. I'm sorry, I really am.' Then, 'I have a friend who this happened to. It took her a long time to get back to normal.'

Knowing she should be satisfied with the general sympathies of this response, Ginny instead felt the urgent need to spell out her position more brutally. 'I'm not talking about a miscarriage. He was eight days old. We thought everything was OK, we thought he was a normal baby, but then they found heart defects . . .' She swallowed the last two words, forced herself to repeat them. 'Three heart defects. He had to have surgery straight away and, well, he didn't stand a chance.'

Bea nodded again, biting her lower lip before repeating her condolences. 'I'm sorry. That's devastating. You must give yourself plenty of time, Ginny.' She paused, looking to her right, to the dazzling expanse of lake. 'And being here, where it's so beautiful, that must help a little?' Asking the question apparently reminded her of Ginny's rather wild claim that she couldn't stay, for she added, 'I still don't see why you feel you should go.'

It was too late now to try to disguise the truth. 'It's just, seeing you all, seeing you and your children, everything we're never going to have. You're such a perfect family.'

'Well, hardly.' Bea gave a reluctant smile. 'Have you already forgotten you've just heard me arguing with my son?'

But Ginny remembered only, *This isn't the end of the world, I promise* . . . 'You weren't arguing. You were offering your love.'

Bea blinked at this appraisal, apparently more surprised by it than by Ginny's original confession. Ginny saw that while she was practised, almost professional, in giving comfort, she was perhaps not so ready to receive it.

'And besides, with three children, you're always going to have one who's in trouble or has fallen out with you, aren't you?' Ginny was aware that she sounded like a child herself, earnestly describing how she thought it was that the grown-up world worked. 'And you're on your holiday, you probably don't get much time together like this, and here I am . . .' She felt the sting behind her nose that signified the beginnings of tears, and sniffed firmly. 'I shouldn't have told you. It's an awful by-product—I can't help making everyone else miserable, whether I tell them or not. Even someone happy like you.'

'Oh, Ginny, that's not how it is.' Bea hesitated again, evidently searching for precisely the right thing to say. Ginny was used to this—making people feel fearful of their own words—and she tried to look responsive. 'I think in going through what you're going through you might be imagining the rest of us are a lot happier than we are. When you get back on more of an even keel, you'll see none of us is living a dream life.'

Ginny couldn't help herself reacting resentfully to that remark. 'Well, you are, aren't you? My husband says you run that clothing company. I've seen the catalogues.'

'Well, if you have, then you'll know *that* is the dream life, the one with the models and the beach houses, not this one.'

'It looks pretty perfect to me.' Ginny gestured in the general direction of the villa, though from her seat all that could be seen was the slender spire of the minaret.

Bea nodded, as if Ginny had just proved her point for her. 'You obviously have a wonderful husband and that's the most important thing right now.'

Though she was indisputably right in this observation, Bea had not yet met Adam and therefore couldn't possibly know if he was wonderful or not, and it caused in Ginny the same crushing sensation she'd felt earlier to realise that the other woman was resorting to platitudes. Or perhaps this was simply her way of turning the conversation from herself, from Ginny's ill-disguised envy and uninformed assertions about perfect lives. She felt a sudden need for something more from this woman, something deeper; she felt a cold fear that she might never get the chance again.

'You do, as well,' she said in a bold tone. 'Pippi told us that Martin arranged the villa for you as a surprise.' She knew that in using the names of Bea's husband and daughter so familiarly she forced a closeness between them that the other woman might not care for—but she couldn't stop herself. 'He must be very . . .' She struggled to find the appropriate word; after all, she had barely met him. 'Devoted,' she said, at last.

Bea made no sign of agreement. She narrowed her eyes—the irises were bright hazel—and drew in her breath, as if it was no use, she could hold her tongue no longer. 'Ginny, if I tell you something, will you promise never to repeat it—I mean to anyone in my family?'

'Of course.' Both thrilled and frightened by the promise of a confidence she had as good as extorted, Ginny wondered what on earth her visitor might be prepared to share. She thought it unlikely to be the dilemma involving Dom, which she'd just been at such pains to conceal and which had brought her to the boathouse in the first place. ('You couldn't possibly have known what we were talking about,' she'd said, the statement of someone who had undoubtedly retraced every last word of it.)

Bea said: 'The day Marty sprang this surprise trip on me I was about to spring something on him.'

Ginny said nothing, only watched and waited, her nervous system alive. She had what she wanted: there was no danger of platitudes now.

'I had made up my mind I was going to leave.'

'Leave? Leave where?'

'Not where, *whom*. I was going to leave him.'

Ginny stared in disbelief. 'But why?'

Bea was unruffled by her amazement. Clearly she was experienced in the nature of the world's first impressions of her husband. 'Because . . .' And the way she widened her eyes and angled her head reflectively gave the impression that this was the first time she had been asked to state her reasons, which couldn't be true, surely? Or perhaps it was, Ginny thought; after all, she hadn't left him, she was here with him now. It had been nothing more than an impulse, the kind had by husbands and

69

wives everywhere. '. . . Because he has not been faithful to me since the day Dom was born.'

'Oh.' Not an impulse then; something huge and unpleasant. Ginny hated herself both for her mean-spirited assumptions about the other woman and her manipulations to discover if they were true. Her provocative stance of a moment ago had vanished and now she only saw her own appalling neediness. And she didn't like to ask how old Dom was.

'Twenty-two years,' Bea said, supplying the answer. 'And that's a long time to be married to a cheat.'

There was an uncertain silence. Ginny's first thought was, If this is what she chooses to trade, then what on earth is the deeper secret, the one she shares with Dom? Then she thought, I must be misunderstanding, she wouldn't tell me. No, this must be an arrangement between the Sales, something rich people did. An open secret, which meant it wasn't a secret at all. 'You mean . . . have you always known, then?'

Bea shook her head. 'I didn't for quite a while. Years, actually. And then, for a long time, I just couldn't act. I thought I was being punished. I don't mean by Marty, or at least not for any specific reason as far as he was concerned, I mean by some higher power.' She seemed satisfied with this definition, repeating it to herself with greater firmness. 'Yes, I thought I was being punished.'

'But what for?' Ginny asked, still not understanding.

'For thinking I'd got away with it.' Bea said this sorrowfully, almost dreamily, and Ginny did not feel she could ask what 'it' was. Life, she supposed,

70

the illusionary perfect life they had just been discussing. Then Bea was closing her eyes and sighing, and when her eyes reopened her manner changed completely, as if in that moment of shadow she had reconsidered this whole conversation. 'Oh, don't take any notice of me,' she said, cheerful, charming. 'I'm sure that must all sound absolutely crazy.'

Ginny didn't know what to say. She couldn't say yes, because actually it didn't sound crazy, not especially. She felt overwhelmed by this scene and not least because every instinct in her told her this was not normal behaviour for this woman. Her conversation with her son, Ginny's outpouring of her own problems and her pushing for something in return, they had created a freak climate in which Bea had had no choice but to be honest—with herself as much as for any desire to swap confidences. 'You are a stranger,' she'd said at the outset, and yet now they knew the single most important thing about one another: in Ginny's case the tragedy that defined who she now was, who she would always be, and in Bea's the secret she had chosen to keep from everyone in her family, and perhaps from everyone in the rest of her circle, too.

Bea said, with a little laugh, 'Oh dear, now that's two conversations I've asked you to forget, and we've only just met.'

Ginny tried to laugh too, though she didn't make a very good job of it. In the end, she was saved by the return of Adam, who seemed quite willing to take charge of proceedings, offering Bea the cold drink Ginny should have, asking after Martin and his progress with boat hire, even

71

remembering the housekeeper's name. He was far more relaxed with Bea than he had been with her husband, Ginny noticed, and she was struck by the understanding that Martin would not have come down and done this, Martin would not have chased after her and sat here at their little table trying to convince her his life was as troubled as hers.

He doesn't know how she feels, she thought. He believes she is living the life of her dreams, just like everyone else thinks she is.

When it was time for Bea to leave, Ginny walked a little way into the main grounds with her.

'What did you call him?' Bea asked. 'Your little baby?'

'Isaac,' Ginny said.

'That's a very beautiful name.'

'Thank you.'

'Yes, it is, it's lovely.' And Bea made the sound Ginny was familiar with now, the slow, guilty sound that said, 'There but for the grace of God go I . . .' The one she didn't think she'd ever grow used to hearing.

CHAPTER SIX

WEDNESDAY

'So what d'you think, Bea? Conch Silver or Loveheart Lavender?' Marty spoke only half-jokingly as he held up the two shirts for his wife's inspection. More than two decades after the company had been founded he still liked to say that he needed her to tell him what to wear, even though he knew as well as she did that he was going to choose the Loveheart Lavender.

It was Wednesday. You could take Marty Sale out of the office, you could even confiscate his BlackBerry and throw it in the lake, but you could not hope to take from him the office traditions he was famous for and, 600 miles away in their South London HQ, Wednesday was Sale Day. Whatever they chose to wear for the rest of the week, all staff dressed in the brand on Wednesdays, and that included the executive chairman himself. Yesterday, he'd worn Ralph Lauren or Gap, Bea couldn't remember which exactly and was enjoying not thinking about labels at all, but today he was in Sale Nantucket deck shorts and Sale Montauk shirt (for the US line, the names were changed: Penzance shorts and Cowes shirt).

'Lavender,' she said, and he gave a deferential nod.

Once, long before this show of uxoriousness had developed into a sub-brand of its own (for the last four seasons, selected items had a sun-shaped stamp by them to announce 'Bea's Bestest!'), he *had* valued her opinion. Many times in those first creative discussions he'd insisted to Ed that she have the casting vote. (Not that she could fit into any of the first clothes—except perhaps for the largest-size man's shirt. Though they'd hidden it from their parents, she was already pregnant with Dom when she and Marty got married.) She was still asked about it sometimes, how her power of veto had been established, for those early years of Sale had become retail mythology. Every time there was a new Top 100 Entrepreneurs, or a Retail Rich List, the country would be reminded of

73

it, as it would the story of how Ed Sale had been persuaded by his older brother Marty to sell the car he'd been given for his twenty-first birthday and spend the money on a run of linen shirts (the colours then were plain old Cream and Mint). Bea herself had designed the launch catalogue (launch? They hadn't known whether they'd be able to afford to produce a second) and worked the streets with the finished product, baby bump and all, posting copies through letter boxes, a process that yielded success in more ways than the obvious for in peering through windows and listening to kerbside conversations she had also found their first flat. This, on top of her full-time day job as an art teacher.

Now, when Marty talked about it in interviews, she wondered how much of it was false memory, or at least memory reconceived by art directors and copywriters. How close to the breadline had they really been? (How many new graduates *did* have money to spare, after all?) No, their rags to riches story had caught on partly because the rags in question were Made in England of finest cotton and softest wool at about the time the market was beginning to move east and scrimp on quality, and partly because Marty and Ed and their wives were more photogenic than the average retailer.

Some bits of the story were true, of course; for instance, there was documentary evidence of the afternoon they and their less knobbly-featured friends from college had modelled, all fees waived, their jumbo cords and fisherman's sweaters. When you saw the pictures now—proudly hung in the boardroom—they were laughable, the self-consciousness in their faces plain to see.

As for baby Dom, far from being an impediment, he was an inspiration. It was Marty's idea to have Esther so quickly afterwards. He called them his little variables. The variables doubled as models when the junior line was launched, though as time went on it became clear that their third child, Pippi, was the only one to take any pleasure in the role. Luckily, Dom and Esther had only begun refusing point blank at about the time turnover was healthy enough for budgets to accommodate professional models. After that it wasn't long before a director of photography had been poached from a fashion magazine and an agency hired to come up with the line names and catalogue copy. Soon they were less a company than a brand, a much celebrated one at that, as an invitation to Number 10 to celebrate Best British Design had last year confirmed.

And they were rich, having long ago upgraded from that first flat in Wandsworth to a large detached house in Kew, its footage increased by a third when they'd opened up the attic to make a suite of rooms for the kids.

Ironically, it was just as life appeared to be reaching something close to perfection, allowing Bea to sit back and count her many blessings, that she at last had her eyes opened to her husband's infidelities. 'At last' because she quickly came to see that it had probably been going on long before that first moment of revelation; she'd been too busy and he too protected for her to see it before. His first assistant Colette had been something of a sphinx, the type who preferred one master to two and treated Bea as no different from any of the other daily claimants for the top man's time. She was long-serving, too, putting in almost a decade before her boyfriend got a job in the northwest and brought her devotion to an end. (To think, Bea had been as sorry as Marty to see her go!)

The next girl, Sandy, however, was less adept at covering up her boss's sins—or, more to the point, at mastering the office switchboard system. She had gone now, as well, but Bea still remembered her with a mixture of gratitude and revulsion. She had called Bea at home one morning and without waiting to hear her voice in greeting had announced, 'I've got Marty for you, can you hold?' (Communications had become rather more presidential by this stage.) Next thing, her husband was murmuring in her ear, 'I can't make it this lunchtime, sweetheart, I've got to get to New York.'

Putting aside the peculiarity of his voice—low in his throat and oddly mid-Atlantic—Bea already knew about her husband's trip to New York because she'd only the previous evening packed his suitcase and located his passport for it. But, obviously anticipating trouble of some other kind, Marty steamed on before she could point this out: 'I'll make it up to you, Kitten, I promise. Friday night, how about that? A whole night together? It's been a while since we've done that, huh?'

A whole night together? Simple confusion gave way to something deeper and darker, causing her to reach in her dizziness for the nearest seat. The information on the desk pad in front of her, supplied earlier in the week by Sandy herself, gave a return flight arrival time on Saturday morning. There it was in front of her in black and white:

Arrive LHR Saturday 0845. Marty had promised to take a taxi straight to the house, easily in time for brunch with her and the kids before he zipped quickly into the office for a debrief with Ed.

'Are you there, Kitten?'

Kitten?

Shocked, she'd hung up without saying a word. Only when she'd fully calmed down did she ring the office and say to Sandy, 'Did you just try to put Marty through? All I got was your voice and then the line went dead.'

Sandy had agreed at once, the relief evident in her voice. 'Yes, I thought we must have been cut off. He's on another call now, but I'll get him to try you again later.'

'Fine.'

She hadn't known what to do. It had taken another ten years before she'd made up her mind. Now, Bea thought, she must not let it take another ten for her to put her decision into action.

Standing at the window of the watchtower suite, she said to her husband, 'Did I tell you I met our neighbours in the boathouse yesterday?'

She knew full well she had not told him. Having returned to the house after talking to Ginny, she'd been grateful to leave soon after for a restaurant in town and, once there, scrupulous to avoid referring to either of the afternoon's conversations. The one with Dom or the one with Ginny: she wasn't sure which she cared to recount the least.

'Oh yes?' Marty strapped on his watch—also a Sale. A limited line of jewellery had been introduced last season and was doing very well. 'What did you think?'

'It's very sad, actually. She told me they lost

77

their baby a few months ago.'

'What, a miscarriage? You know, I thought she looked a bit low.'

'No, worse than that,' Bea said. 'He was born, but he died when he was eight days old. A congenital heart thing. She said they didn't even know anything was wrong at first.'

Marty grimaced. 'Jesus, poor sods.'

'Imagine burying a baby. The tiny coffin . . .' She shuddered, the faces of her own babies passing before her in vivid succession.

'Dreadful. How on earth did you discover all this so quickly?' He gave her an indulgent look, a look almost of admiration, and she realised he was feeling proud of her! He was thinking, Only my wife can draw this sort of private information out of people; she's got the touch.

She felt faintly sickened by him. 'The husband seems very devoted to her, though, and that's what counts.'

Of course Marty took this, along with the cool look that accompanied it, as a comment on *their* marriage. The same boyish insecurities that led him to seduce other women also prompted him to seek reassurance from her. He wanted it both ways, *all* ways. 'Are you happy we came here?' he asked, other people's tragedies swept aside as easily as the Conch Silver shirt. 'This room is fantastic, isn't it?'

'Yes, it is.' She looked around her. He was right, the suite was fantastic, but not for all this luxury, for the magnificent assembly of antique furniture and sumptuous fabrics, nor even for the intricate tiling on the walls and superbly restored parquet floors. It was for the view. Their suite was in the

78

lower part of the minaret, making the view from the windows the most breathtaking Bea had ever seen. See Naples and die, it was said, but on the only occasion of her arrival in that city she had not agreed (though, to be fair, it *had* been raining). Now, in Orta, she understood the emotion. For a moment, more than a moment, a full minute, when she'd first stood there she'd forgotten everything at the sight of such natural beauty, the rugged curves of the mountains, the swoop of the sky, that motionless skin of water. What her eyes saw was so pure she felt it could be breathed into her lungs like air, used to sustain life itself. It was profound. And yet it made her feel sad, in a way, for how were you supposed to hold on to these moments when there were a million everyday ones for each of the special ones? You were lucky if you even recognised it as it was happening.

'Anyway,' she said to Marty, 'I've invited them for drinks this evening.'

'Who?'

'Ginny and Adam. From the boathouse. The couple I was just talking about.'

'Oh. OK. Sure. If you think it'll be fun.' He didn't remind her of the family-only rule; their expectations of that, they both knew, had after three private dinners in a row already been exceeded. It had been only a matter of time before others were invited into their circle. Last time they'd come to Italy, to that villa in Como, there'd been a lot of fun with the neighbours. The woman had got Marty straight away, tuning into his frequency and beginning a banter that had soon reached the standard of a professional double act, rather as it had these last days with Pippi. Of

79

course, being on her honeymoon, she had not had the slightest interest in taking the connection beyond the verbal and Bea liked to think Marty would draw the line there himself, whether the woman did or not.

She raised her eyebrows. 'Maybe not fun, exactly, given their circumstances.'

'Do we need to brief the kids not to put their foot in it?' he asked. 'Not to talk about babies? Not that I can see any reason why they would.'

Bea waited for the shiver to pass over her arms. 'No, don't say anything. I imagine the only reason they said they'd come was because it's a chance to take their mind off it all. The last thing they'll want is for everyone to be walking around on eggshells.'

Gazing out the window once more, she caught sight of Adam down by the water. From this distance you'd never guess he was anything but an ordinary holidaymaker, a man of average looks and standing, dressed in typically anonymous English style in jeans and a shirt. What would he call its colour if you asked him? Blue. He'd say he was wearing a blue shirt—and he'd be right.

She felt a sigh build in her chest and slowly fill her throat. All that midnight oil she and Marty and Ed had burned, all that chasing of their own tails, but they weren't so unusual in having worked hard, were they? Adam and Ginny had probably slaved in exactly the same way in their fields, whatever they were. Adam didn't look much younger than Marty and she were, and Ginny was in her mid-thirties. They'd married late, she guessed; either that or they'd put off having children until they'd judged themselves able to afford them. To give them the sort of childhood the Sale children had

had.

Sometimes she wondered if her family success owed less to Sale genes—Sale genius—than to the simple roll of the dice.

*   *   *

Despite what she'd said to Marty, she did decide to have a word with Esther before their guests arrived. She couldn't help it: already she was feeling a special responsibility for Ginny. No doubt it was partly a form of survival instinct; it took her mind off Dom to anticipate the other woman's pleasure—however small, however involuntary—as she climbed the steps to the villa and saw the terrace at the top, with its old stone urns and its potted trees, the wall lamps that made the green and pink patternwork glow like stained glass.

But it was more complicated than that, of course. If she was honest, she hoped to please Ginny because she wanted to be sure the other woman had fully understood the restricted nature of the information she had shared. Had that unexpected trading of confidences *really* taken place? How, when Bea had disclosed her intentions to only two of her closest intimates at home, had a stranger drawn it from her so easily? And since she had gone on to share Ginny's story with Marty, did that mean Ginny had shared *hers* with Adam? She had a sense that she had not. The baby's death was a tragedy, a truly terrible one, but it did not constitute dangerous or secret information. If anything, it was of the kind that needed to be brought into the open, shared with a wider world, in order to be fully accepted.

Her own revelation, on the other hand, had been made much too recklessly. Talk about too close to home! She should have been much more careful, that was obvious now, but there'd been something about the other woman's rawness that had made an expression of honesty irresistible. And more than that, it had confirmed to her—if she *still* needed confirmation—that hers, unlike poor Ginny's, was a situation that could be reversed. The only life that had been lost was her own; she *could* get it back.

She found her elder daughter leaving her bedroom and heading for the staircase. There were no outward signs that she had dressed for the evening, but you were never quite sure with Esther. In this family, she wore her casualness as a badge of honour and there were times when Bea longed to dare to do the same.

'Esther, come upstairs a minute, I just want to brief you on this couple coming for drinks . . .'

'What couple?'

'That's what I need to tell you . . .'

There was no greater pleasure than time alone with Esther and Bea had been of this opinion from the day the girl was born. What they had was exactly the bond she had seen her own older sister share with their mother: they were natural teammates, captain and deputy (third in command had never had quite the same ring). Now, when people remarked on how alike they looked (all those cheesy questions about their being sisters), she truthfully couldn't see it, not even in photographs, for to her Esther looked only like Esther: beautiful, peaceful, happy in her skin. Bea would never admit to favourites, of course not, but if you injected her with a truth drug you'd learn that Dom was her eldest, Pippi her youngest and Esther her dearest. Bea's Bestest. Even the discovery that the love of Esther's college years was a woman and not a man had not changed a thing between them. Bea blamed her own naivety for her having not suspected sooner, certainly not any deception on Esther's part. And her lack of self-consciousness in a family that often blurred the line between teasing and mockery made her even more special.

'Mum, this room is unbelievable . . .' Esther rolled back on the huge four poster bed, with its swags of silk damask and fat embroidered cushions. 'Don't you just feel like, I don't know, Aladdin or something? What was the princess called again?'

'Yasmin. She used to be your favourite, if I remember . . .' Bea joined her on the bed, allowing herself a moment of laughter, before returning to her subject. 'Like I say, I've invited Ginny and Adam from the boathouse for drinks.'

'That didn't last long,' Esther grinned.

'What?' Bea was startled, but quickly covered it with another smile.

'The family-only rule. I must admit I thought it would be Dad who cracked first, but he must have been really trying hard. Bless.'

Sometimes, when Bea heard her children praise their father for something that to her should be a given (his insistence on family-only time was a perfect example), she had to consciously stop herself from criticising him to them.

'Yes. Well, the thing is, they've had a horrible experience lately and could probably do with a

83

distraction.' In a few words, she told Esther Ginny's story. 'They wouldn't want us to talk about it, I'm sure, but I just wanted you to know they might need more delicate handling than your usual guests.'

Esther raised her head from the pillows, her expression quite changed. 'How awful,' she said. 'I can't bear it.'

Bea was moved to see the tears that wobbled in her daughter's eyes. She wanted to cry out, 'You are a wonderful girl, a wonderful woman! I'm so proud of who you've become!' But that would be no different from Marty's admiration of her earlier, using someone else's misfortune as an opportunity to congratulate themselves. 'I know,' she said, nodding, 'I think it's one of the worst things that could happen to anyone. I'm not going to tell the others, but if you, at least, could just be aware.'

'Of course. Of course I will.' All excitement gone, Esther shuffled from the bed and to her feet, settling by one of the trio of windows with a view of the lake. 'Why have they come here?' she asked, at last, over her shoulder.

From the edge of the bed, Bea said, 'To try to recover, I would imagine. A change of scene.'

'But why here?'

Bea didn't understand. 'What do you mean, darling?'

Esther motioned to the natural portrait of blue and green in front of her. 'Why here, to one of the most beautiful places on the planet?'

'Well, because beauty is supposed to heal, I suppose.'

'Do you think so?' Esther demanded. 'Do you

really think so?'

Bea considered it. First, she remembered that it was she who had suggested this very notion to Ginny and not the other way around. Ginny in fact seemed, at best, entirely unmoved by her surroundings. Then she recalled that extraordinary feeling she'd had when she first breathed in the view, how she had believed, just for a moment, that it had the power to consign all that had gone before to history, to wipe the slate clean. It hadn't lasted, no, but it had existed, of that she was certain. And it might come to exist for Ginny, too. 'Yes, I do,' she said, at last. 'In some situations, anyway.'

Esther shook her head. 'Well, I think the exact opposite. I think you'd need to go somewhere horrible to make you see that home is the right place to be. I think being somewhere like this must just seem like a cruel trick.'

Bea didn't know what to say to that. But since Esther didn't seem to expect an answer, she decided it was best simply to give her a few moments' quiet reflection. Making as little noise as possible, she began searching her vast carved hardwood wardrobe for the scarf she wanted to wear that evening.

*　　　*　　　*

As it went, she needn't have worried about a suitable welcome for their fragile guests, because Marty handled everything.

Just as Esther had pointed out, it was he, not Bea, who usually invited others into the fold—the Sale Open House of their parallel catalogue life—

85

and over the years of holidays, summer, winter, Easter, autumn, hundreds of people had been welcomed by him to share drinks, play a game of cricket or take a swim, taste the best risotto/curry/tagine they were ever going to taste in their lives courtesy of his wife/daughter/chef/housekeeper/new favourite restaurant. Business contacts, friends of friends from London (not to mention real friends, too), strangers he'd fallen in with on a square or in a shop: it was hospitality gone mad. At first Bea had worried that he didn't want to be alone with her and the children, but she soon gathered that he simply didn't know *how* to. From school to university to the happy little fraternity at Sale that grew steadily bigger with every new collection, he had operated in larger social groups than their nuclear family.

And so, as he had countless times before, he identified at a glance the person among them who would benefit most from his attentions and he concentrated on her (for it was, invariably, a female target). That satisfied Bea that Ginny, at least, would be taken care of. The problem was that Pippi, becoming every year a little more like her father, seemed to be doing the same with Adam, only without knowing *why* he might need her special attention, and that could mean only one thing: she felt like flirting with someone. But at least Esther hovered discreetly in support, chatting to Dom (a task in itself at the moment) while keeping half an ear on her sister.

Satisfied that everyone had a fresh drink and was standing within stretching distance of an olive, Bea felt it safe to go and help Susanna with the canapés. When she came back, bearing a plate of local goat's cheese sprinkled with crumbs of Casa Mista white truffle, she heard Pippi telling Adam:

'I just *love* thc name Adam! If I had a boyfriend called Adam I'd change my name to Eve and I'd dress us in fig leaves for fancy dress parties. We'd *always* be going to fancy dress parties.'

'I don't see why you literally need the name to appropriate the costume,' Adam replied. 'Anyone can dress as Adam and Eve if they wish.' He was rather pedantic, Bea observed, though that didn't necessarily preclude a sense of fun. To her relief, he looked considerably more amused by Pippi than he might reasonably have been expected to.

Long experience told her that he was going to be among those who knew they ought to find Pippi irritating but, when it came down to it, couldn't help but get a little carricd away by her. It was her daughter's saving grace, that flair for instant connection. On the plane coming here, they'd boarded late and had to be broken up into smaller groups, Pippi ending up on her own in the row behind Bea and Esther. She'd immediately cngaged the woman to her left, evidently over the fastening of seatbelts. 'I always likc to scc if I'm fatter than the person before. Do you do that? Oh look, hurrah! I'm thinner!' The woman had roared, happening to have a kind of bark to hcr laugh that had at first silenced their section of the plane and then caused an outbreak of giggles. After that Pippi was off, chattering away for the whole flight, saying fond farewells to people as they disembarked.

'I know you want to design hats,' Marty said to her as they queued at passport control, 'but you really should consider PR. You're a natural,

Pipster.' (This was the first Bea had heard of any millinery ambitions.)

It was a performance, she told herself whenever she needed the reassurance; a comedy persona that Pippi had constructed expressly to make people feel good about themselves. It was virtually a charitable venture. She wasn't *really* so blithe, so self-absorbed, so unconcerned for the feelings of others.

Even so, there were good reasons why it was Esther Bea had chosen to confide in that evening.

She held the plate of cheese in the vicinity of Dom, hoping he might eat more this evening than he had at lunchtime. He was doing a decent job of appearing carefree, or at least aware of his immediate environment. Smoking Pippi's cigarettes seemed to be helping—not a habit Bea approved of in either of them, but she had long developed a policy of not protesting publicly. How terrible it had made her feel to hear his anguish yesterday, his begging her to allow him to treat this holiday as a way of prolonging hope, when he obviously knew it was really just denial, a stay of execution. And equally terrible was the fact that his instinct had echoed her own: for a stay of execution was precisely what this holiday was. And yet there was no solidarity in the knowledge that they felt the same, no comfort to be had. No wonder he was avoiding her; he had hardly looked at her in the twenty-four hours that had passed since.

'Are you all right?' she asked him, in a discreet voice, and she caught the inquisitive look Esther sent their way. They were so close, the two of them, was it really possible that he had managed to keep his secret from his sister?

He shrugged, dismissive of both her and her canapés. 'Yeah, fine.'

Noticing his son at a loose end, Marty began to guide Ginny his way, saying in his best gung-ho tones, 'Come and meet Dommo. Did you know, he just got a first from Bristol? We're all very proud. He starts law school in September.'

'Congratulations,' Ginny said to Dom. She seemed much more cheerful than yesterday, Bea thought, pleased, but then she saw the particular intensity with which her new friend was looking at Dom and she felt another stirring of unease. A state of mind like Ginny's couldn't possibly have recovered overnight. 'Do you have a special area of interest?'

Dom nodded, eyes fixed on Ginny, as if his father were not in the conversation at all and it was just the two of them. 'Since you ask, yeah. I've been doing a lot of reading about fathers' rights.'

Bea's skin chilled exactly as if the air temperature had dropped by ten degrees. Why would he say that? It was for her benefit, surely? Certainly not for Ginny's for he appeared quite heedless of the soft collapse of her face. Bea wished now that she had followed Marty's advice and let all of the kids in on their guests' sad situation.

Whether Marty made the connection or not, she couldn't be sure, for his first recourse, as was usual in his relationship with Dom, was to tease: 'You mean those activist groups? The guys who climbed on to the roof of Buckingham Palace? Or was it Nelson's Column? Wish I'd thought of that when we were starting out. A pair of Sale boxers flying from the Queen's flagpole, how about that?'

Ginny smiled at the idea but Dom did not. 'It's a lot more than publicity stunts, Dad. It's a civil rights issue. These people are our Martin Luther Kings.'

Marty gave him a look of exaggerated surprise. 'They are? I didn't know *that*.'

'Well, it's true. Did you know that if the woman decides not to put the father's name on the birth certificate, he has no legal rights whatsoever?'

'Or if he's not around to register,' Esther suggested in her measured way. Bea joined her in moving closer towards the central trio, the better to rescue the situation.

'The law about that has changed, though, hasn't it?' Ginny asked. Her tone, artificially breezy, showed the effort she was making to take part in this debate. 'I thought it only affected fathers of older children.'

'And there's always DNA testing,' Esther added, pleasantly.

But Dom dismissed these comments with an angry shrug. His body language had transformed completely over the last week or so; he was once again the dark, disaffected teenager he'd been years ago. 'You shouldn't need last resorts like that, and even then it doesn't help you in practical terms, like visitation. I think it's scandalous that the father should need the woman's permission to see the person who has fifty per cent of his genetic make-up. They should be considered exact equals.'

He kept saying 'woman' for the mother and yet 'father' for the man, Bea noticed. It was a very long time since she'd felt so fretful in a conversation— too fretful to trust herself to contribute—for this

90

was already putting yesterday's awkwardnesses in the shade; at least she'd felt partially in control of those. There were too many people involved in this one, which gave the atmosphere a dangerous, swirling undertow, and she, who had drawn the groups together, could only guess at the individual agendas being concealed. Secrets were rarely the problem per se, it was the sharing of them that made things go wrong, and—mostly thanks to her, let's face it!—there was not a person present who wasn't party to some form of forbidden information. All except . . . as Pippi opened her mouth to make another of her flirtatious pronouncements to Adam, Bea finally appreciated who the real loose cannon was here. The one she had left in the cold. All it needed was for Pippi to ask Ginny if she wanted children, or to demand to know why Dom was so interested in fathers' rights all of a sudden and they'd have uproar on their hands.

She tried to catch Dom's eye, but he was much too busy ranting to notice her. He was frighteningly wild-eyed. 'And if they're living apart it's often because *she* decides to bugger off, not him. The myth of the absent father—it's just that, a fucking myth! *She* holds all the cards, he's just the joker!'

His voice had become so domineering that Adam and Pippi turned to listen to him, too, which meant he now commanded the attention of everyone present.

'Come on, Dom, I think most people would want to put the best interests of the child first,' Esther said, politely waiting for her brother to draw breath. 'Every situation has its own separate

91

complications. Every family is unique. You can't possibly say what works and what doesn't.'

Bea couldn't have put it better herself, and she was relieved to see Ginny nodding quite calmly. But Dom merely scoffed. 'Bollocks,' he said, disagreeably, and Bea felt sure he would have been even ruder had the offending comment been made by anyone but Esther.

Marty put a hand out to his son and spoke gently, somehow making it sound as if they were alone. He reminded Bea of a vet. 'Hey, what's eating Gilbert Grape? You're going to need to work on that air of impartiality, mate, if you're ever going to appear in court.'

'And who cares, anyway?' Pippi burst out, with the attitude of having been unwillingly distracted from far more amusing matters. 'Why is everyone being so unbelievably *earnest*?'

'Spoken like a true fashion student,' Marty said, easy again. 'Even fashionistas get into family difficulties, Pipkins. *Especially* fashionistas.' He winked at his youngest child. 'Hang on, though, apart from me and Ed, *are* there any straight men in fashion retail? You'll have to let us know when you start at St Martins next year.'

Pippi pulled a long-suffering face. 'Yeah, like I'm going to tell *you* who I'm sleeping with!'

Marty pulled a face back at her and Pippi groaned theatrically. Then, just as the others were making their first efforts to use this comic interlude to change the subject, her voice came again, carrying high above the others: 'Oh, I do love Lago d'Orta, but it's all just a bit *too* quiet and civilised here. There's no *fun*!'

There was a moment of general uncertainty

before Marty arched an eyebrow and said to their guests, 'Don't take it personally, will you? She's always like this.' And as he led the laughter, as deftly as any conductor, Bea couldn't help noticing that some of those present took their cues more gratefully than others.

CHAPTER SEVEN

THURSDAY

For as long as Pippi Sale could remember it had been her lot within the family to move around the house from room to room looking for someone to play with. No one ever seemed to come to *her* room looking for a game. And ever since she could remember it was worse when her father was away or, more accurately, when he was about to go away. Every time, the atmosphere changed; her mother changed.

And here they were, Thursday of the first week of their holiday, and he was already disappearing!

He had made the announcement at breakfast. 'Sorry, guys, but I'm going to have to head back to London today. Work stuff.' He made it sound as if he were simply nipping into Milan for a quick meeting.

'Oh, Dad!' Pippi groaned. 'Can't you just do, like, a web link or something?'

'No can do, Pipster. One of our investors is making noises about pulling out and I need to meet with them face to face. Shouldn't be anything too painful, I hope, but it's either that or invite them out here, and we don't want *that*.' He was getting the one o'clock flight from Malpensa, he said, and wasn't sure when he'd be able to get back, but if it were not tomorrow then it would be at some point over the weekend. Definitely.

At first Pippi didn't dare look at her mother's face—she *hated* it when her father was in trouble—but sneaking a glance she saw that her mother was merely nodding, and not in that blank way that she often did, to save face, but properly, as if everything Dad said was perfectly acceptable. Pippi supposed she must have had pre-warning.

'Why can't Uncle Ed handle it?' She continued to ask the questions, since no one else was, and she looked to her siblings for support. But Esther was pulling her 'Leave me out of this' face and Dom, well, it was odd, but he was looking kind of *pleased*.

'I'm sorry, guys,' her father said again, mock-sorrowfully. 'What can I say, it's *my* ugly mug they seem to want to see. I always did want to be irreplaceable.' And he began discussing with their mother what time he should get the taxi to come and pick him up for the airport.

So much for the family being together, Pippi thought, thoroughly disgruntled. She *knew* she should have stood her ground when she signed up and insisted on being allowed to invite Milla along. Maybe a couple of the other girls, too. It was ridiculous: there were three bedrooms upstairs standing empty! *Now* who was she going to hang out with? She and her father had been natural allies this week, what with her mother and Esther being so preoccupied with their cookery course (who wanted to go on holiday to cook? And to *pay* for the privilege!) and Dom being so busy being a

94

wet blanket. They'd had some good chats about her career, she and her father, as well as a very successful trip to the designer factory outlets outside Milan (the statute of limitations on eighteenth birthday presents could run and run as far as she was concerned).

After breakfast, discovering Dom's room empty—of course, it was ten in the morning, he'd already be out mooching—she sought out Esther in hers. Her sister was in the middle of changing from her Sale pyjamas into her Sale shorts and Sale T-shirt, both fresh from their packaging. Once she'd tried and failed to remove the corresponding creases in the garments, she stooped to tie the laces of her Sale velvet-toed plimsolls. Pippi herself, understanding that one should *never* wear a single label from head to toe, had on only denim flip-flops from the Sale summer collection—she would never hurt her father's feelings by deserting the brand entirely and, besides, they had some quite cool stuff this season—but otherwise wore an artful mix of TopShop and vintage. Her sunglasses, a gift from her father at the aforementioned factory outlets, were by Prada, and still newly-loved enough for her to keep them on indoors.

'So what's up with Dom?' she said, spritzing herself with scent from the lone bottle Esther had placed on her mantelpiece, alongside less decorative items such as deodorant that by Pippi's reckoning ought to have been stored out of sight in the bathroom. (Esther may have struck lucky in inheriting their mother's looks, but Pippi was the one who'd got Bea's famous eye for detail.)

'How d'you mean?' Esther asked. 'Er, can you leave some of that perfume for me, please?'

'Fragrance,' Pippi corrected her, replacing the lid. 'I mean, he's acting all weird, don't you think?'

'That's because he *is* weird. You must have got that by now.'

Behind her dark glasses, Pippi rolled her eyes. They were protective of each other, Dom and Esther. Just sixteen months apart, they had a kind of twin thing going on. Over the years this had proved infuriating and useful to her in equal measure.

'What was all that about last night? He was *so* obnoxious. It was embarrassing.'

Esther just pulled a face (a non-committal one).

'And he never wants to do anything. He's always just skulking about by the lake. Not that he ever goes in for a swim, even though it's boiling.'

'The water's not, though,' Esther said, reasonably. 'It's bloody cold.'

'He seems very off with Dad, as well, don't you think?'

'We're *all* off with Dad.' *That* got her going, at least. Now she adopted the same critical tone she'd used fifteen years ago when they'd played schools and she'd cast herself as headmistress opposite Pippi's dunce. 'I can't believe he's going back to London already. After everything he said about us having proper time together and he's managed, what? Four days! And Mum let him off lightly, didn't she? If I were her, I'd . . . hmmph!'

They both let that one hang. Though it was obvious to Pippi that their father was no saint, she was too wary of Esther's closeness with their mother to get into anything too speculative about their parents' marriage. And, in any case, their father was only doing what he always did, which

96

was to put the business first; it was Dom who was acting out of character here, Dom who she was most curious about.

'He's been weird ever since we got here—before, actually. When he came home for Sunday lunch the weekend before last he was like a zombie. And he left without saying goodbye, which I thought was *very* rude.' She mused. 'It's obviously something to do with Chloë.'

'Maybe it's because Dad said he couldn't bring her?' Esther suggested, evidently intent on their father remaining the villain of the piece. 'She came on holiday with us last time, didn't she?'

'Nah, that's not it. If anything, he's pleased she's not here. I haven't seen him phone her once and when Mum mentioned her name yesterday at lunch he looked seriously pissed off.'

Esther snorted. 'What is this, have you got him under surveillance or something? Pip, can you take those sunglasses off, please? I can't see your eyes.'

Reluctantly Pippi propped them on the top of her head, checking the angle in the mirror. The effect was good: her face was too round for her liking and this made the shape appear more oval. A low beehive did the same. There was no flaw that could not be corrected with styling and accessories, in her view. 'Seriously,' she said, 'd'you think they've split?'

Esther looked at her in such a way that Pippi wished she'd kept the shades on. 'Don't stir, Pip.'

'I'm *not* stirring!'

Her sister held up a hand like a lollipop lady, the kind with the power to bring an overeager van driver to his knees. 'OK, I'm just saying. Leave it. Things are on a knife's edge as it is.'

Pippi frowned. 'What's on a knife's edge? Oh, you mean Mum and Dad?'

'I mean everything. Let's just all enjoy the holiday, OK? It's costing enough.'

Honestly, if you closed your eyes it could be Mum speaking. Middle-aged at heart, that was Esther; *born* sensible. Why couldn't she be more like Milla's sister Jess, who even when they were practically still kids had let them hang out with her university mates and smoke her cigarettes? Now she was working for a record label, far more glamorous than the career in charity fundraising that Esther hoped for. Yes, Pippi had learned a lot from Jess. There'd been no closed ranks with her.

'Fancy going to the piazza for a coffee?' This was as close to people-watching as Orta San Giulio got, and Pippi thought the guys who ran the boats to the island were cute, if a bit elderly.

'I can't. Mum and I are heading off for our cooking class in half an hour.'

'Oh yeah, I forgot you had that. Don't you usually go earlier?'

'Yes, but we're seeing the working kitchen today. Observing the lunch service.' Esther looked kindly at her younger sister. 'I'm sure you could come for a one-off session if you wanted to?'

'No, thanks.' Casa Mista, where the classes were being held, was the Michelin-starred restaurant in the hills where they'd had dinner the other night. It was so expensive that even their father, who *never* questioned the price of a treat, had commented on the unlucky exchange rate as he paid the bill. No, having a bunch of bad-tempered fusspots instruct her on how to pipe mushed-up artichoke into a perfect spiral was not Pippi's idea of fun. She'd

98

have plenty of time for that kind of thing when she worked in fashion.

'Don't worry about me,' she told Esther, airily. 'I'll amuse myself.'

*   *   *

She headed alone to the piazza. The café terraces hadn't been open long and so she had her pick of the tables, selecting one right on the water, next to the shaded walkway where the boatmen prowled in their long navy shorts and captain's hats. She lit a cigarette, holding it limply in her left hand while she wound her hair around the index finger of her right. She thought about her new linen hat, ordered from the website of a designer in New York, and wondered if she should have gone for Seaweed with a horn buckle rather than Sand with a leather one. When the waitress came she ordered an espresso and looked at the boats lined up in front of her. They were halfway between rowing boats and gondolas, old and with the paint stripped away, the kind of distressed look her mother liked. Hopefully the one her father had requested would be a bit more glam than that. Answering the captains' admiring cries of '*Signorina*' filled the rest of the time before the coffee came. She put out the first cigarette, then lit a second to have with the coffee. When she'd finished those she ate the half-melted square of chocolate that came on the saucer. Now what?

That was the problem with this place: the quality of the *passeggiata*. It was all very well *Glamour* magazine naming the lakes as *the* place for celebrity-spotting, but that was all happening in

99

Como, not here. Here there were only retired people and families with young children, the kind that screeched unbearably if they didn't get what they wanted right away, the kind that Pippi didn't recognise at all from the pages of her father's catalogues. As for the men, the only ones she'd seen in their twenties were the bridegrooms and the honeymooners; both groups, by definition, unlikely to want to indulge in any casual flirting with someone who wasn't their wife. If only she hadn't failed her driving test that time—OK, both times—she could have rented herself a little Fiat and driven over to Como. Or to Milan, in a convertible! Picturing herself at the wheel—left-hand drive, so glamorous—she felt a gush of pure delight in being alive, being here, being Pippi Sale. Even if there was no one to share herself with.

She reached for a third cigarette.

'You haven't got a spare one of those, have you?'

The voice at her shoulder was English and of a similar accent to her own, though, crucially, male, and Pippi fluttered to its call like a turtle dove to its mate. She liked what she saw, too, to the extent that she made herself blink a couple of times in case it was part of her Como fantasy and not an earthly creature of flesh and blood. And *what* flesh and blood! He was about six feet tall and rakishly lean, his hair dark, thick and either completely unkempt or growing naturally outwards rather than flopping down into his eyes in the usual British boy style, which, either way, looked fantastically rock 'n' roll. She couldn't see his eyes for his aviators—were they vintage Ray-Bans? Yes, she thought they were—but she could tell that he was older than she was, mid-twenties she guessed, which happened to be her ideal. She felt like swooning: at last, a beautiful person to look at!

'I certainly have,' she said, extending first the pack and then her lighter. Kill her slowly and painfully though cigarettes most likely would, she still knew of no better way to break the ice with a man (provided he was a smoker, of course). She gestured for him to take the seat next to her and was delighted when he did so, stretching his legs out and signalling to the waitress for a coffee. She looked at her watch—barely eleven—and then at the empty tables around them. *The early bird catches the worm*, she thought, happily.

Despite the heat—and his luggage, which included a much-stickered guitar case—he wore a leather jacket, ancient and scuffed, and made no move to take it off. He wasn't perceptibly sweaty, however; the opposite, he was very, very cool. She tried to imagine his smell close up.

'How did you know I was English?' she asked.

He shrugged. 'Not enough bling for Italian?'

That made Pippi smirk. They smoked for a while in silence, then she thought of something amusing and said, 'What are the worst two words in Italian?'

'I don't know, what?'

'*Vietato fumare.*'

'No smoking. Very good.' He grinned at her. His jawbone was clean-cut, kind of heroic, but his lips were curved and pink, a beguiling combination of soft and strong.

'So you just came in from Milan?'

'Yep. Just walked down from the station.' He motioned inland, to the hill above the main village where Pippi had yet to venture but where she understood there to be located such public necessities as a multi-storey car park and a train station. She eyed his guitar case again. Could it be . . .? No, it was too much to ask. Could it be that there was some kind of venue in Orta—or better still a festival—and he was here to play?

'Do I know you? Are you, like, in a band?' Far from sounding gauche, she used a casual, equal sort of tone that showed that if he *did* happen to be famous then he certainly needn't worry about her not being able to hold her own.

'I'm not, no,' he drew on the cigarette, 'but, hey, you never know, I might do a bit of busking while I'm here. Italy's not cheap.'

She smiled, uncertain whether he was joking, though you would not have guessed it from the knowing quality of her smile. 'What do you do then?'

He groaned, a sound that made her want to arch her back and groan right back at him. 'As from two days ago, nothing.'

'Nothing?'

'*Niente*. I *was* working in a bar near my flat in Bristol, but I walked out the day before yesterday.'

'You walked out? Just like that?'

'Just like that.'

'Wow,' Pippi breathed. 'Why? Did you feel you had to, y'know, get away from everything? Escape?'

'Sort of. It's complicated.' He frowned, shifted a little in his seat. 'They don't even know I'm not going in tonight for my shift. I should call, I suppose.'

Pippi stared at him, scandalised. Of all the Sale

102

children (including her cousins, Ed's daughters), she was the most goal-orientated and had had her career mapped out from the moment she'd found an old copy of *Vogue* under a pile of her parents' catalogues (they only had it because they'd somehow got one of their shirts photographed in it). The thought of free-spiritedness such as this man evoked was alien and exhilarating.

'How about you? You're here on holiday?' he asked her.

'Yeah, with my family, you know.' In world-weary tones she described the villa, the luxurious terraces, the many en suite bedrooms and louche little lounging areas. 'It'd be a great club space. The only thing is there isn't a pool, but you can swim from the beach at the end of the garden. And we're getting a boat tomorrow, which'll be cool.'

'Sounds fucking amazing,' he said.

'It is. The fabulous Villa Isola.' Remembering a comment Esther had made last night to Ginny, she added, 'But I warn you, this whole place is like something out of Edith Wharton. I mean, it's great, but it's *so* quiet. Apart from the couple in the boathouse we haven't met *anyone*. I can't think of anywhere else I've been where I've felt so *isolated*.' She considered. 'Or maybe it's just after the whole party scene back home when school ended. It feels so *dead* in comparison.' At once she regretted mentioning school, which told him her age so precisely—it would be tragic if so promising a connection as theirs were to be broken by something as prosaic as an age gap—but it was OK, because he didn't seem to have picked up on it.

'The couple in the boathouse? What, are they

103

Brits, as well?'

'Yeah, they're really nice.' She liked the way he watched her so intently when she spoke, really looking. Gisele could have strolled by and he wouldn't have noticed. 'He's quite sexy, actually, the guy.' She said this as though it had just occurred to her, though she'd fantasised about seducing Adam for a full ten minutes after he and Ginny had left last night. 'But they're a bit weird, as well. They have this, like, air of doom about them, you know, like they've just had a huge row the minute before.'

Her new friend tipped up his chin and exhaled smoke in a thick upward stream. He looked thoughtful, even a little troubled. 'That doesn't sound so good.'

'I know. And the hilarious thing is their name,' Pippi said.

'Their name? Why, what is it?'

'Trustlove.'

Two small parallel dents appeared between his eyebrows. 'That's unusual.'

'Yeah, but what I mean is they don't seem like they *do*, you know . . . ?'

'What, trust love?' He said this with the faintest crack in his voice, like he was really getting into the scenario. Cool *and* sensitive: every girl's dream! So much so that Pippi began to revive her suspicion that she'd invented him, that the Italian cigarettes she'd just bought from the *tabacchi* across the piazza might have a little something extra in them.

She threw out a challenge. 'Why do couples stay together when they obviously hate each other? I've never got that.' Not only was this extremely unfair to their neighbours, who she had met only a couple

104

of times, but it was also far too large a question to expect anyone to answer, particularly someone she very much hoped didn't *have* a partner. But to her surprise he did answer, and quite seriously, too.

'It's because humans aren't supposed to mate for life. Hardly any animals do. There's all this changing opinion about it, actually. So, even if they don't hate each other to begin with, something will happen out of the blue that *makes* them hate each other. And then it's time to do what they were designed to do all along: move on. It's not sad, it's natural.' He seemed to realise he was getting a bit intense and smirked at her. 'But what do I know?'

'More than I do,' Pippi giggled. She was getting very pleasant flutterings at the thought of the two of them as animals.

'So,' he said, 'you and your Trustloves, you're which way?'

She motioned north. 'Along the lake path, about fifteen minutes. But you can only see the villa properly from the water. Hey, you should come and see it if you're around for a few days, it's like a tourist attraction. Yesterday a whole boatload of people pulled up when I was sunbathing on the pier and started taking photos. I felt like Britney Spears or something.'

Wishing she hadn't chosen someone with quite such well-publicised weight issues, she instinctively lengthened her leg stretch and straightened her posture. Now that this *god* had turned up, she'd need to put a stop to the piggery. Damn Susanna and her amazing cooking, not to mention Mum and Esther and the treats they kept bringing home from the restaurant; they'd turned this holiday into a weight-gain programme.

'So you're not here with anyone, then?' She wanted to get it straight—was there someone or not? (Know your competition: a key component of any marketing strategy.) Or had it been a girl who had caused his sudden upping and leaving? (Rebound, that worked!) She regarded him with such perfect insouciance she almost convinced herself that it was real.

'No. I'm on my own. Just me and my guitar.' This he pronounced 'gee-tar', in a southern drawl, like Elvis. 'And phone and iPod and laptop, obviously.'

'Where are you crashing?'

'Where am I crashing?' Already she was thrilling to his habit of repeating her question after her (mirroring: a sure sign of sexual attraction). 'I'm crashing . . .' He consulted a piece of paper fished from his jacket pocket. 'Hotel Motta. It should be just off here. I got the last room, apparently. It's bound to be a pit.' As if reminded of a purpose he might otherwise have totally overlooked, he got to his feet, stamped out the fag end, slung his bag over his shoulder and went to hook the guitar strap over his other arm. 'So I should probably go and make sure they don't give it away to anyone else.'

'I'll help you with your stuff if you like?' Pippi offered. 'How did you manage to walk even one street with all this?'

He shrugged and let her take the guitar, but not before he'd thrown down enough euros for their coffees.

The instrument was a lot heavier than she'd expected, but luckily his hotel was close by, in a building in one of the narrow lanes off the eastern edge of the piazza. Clearly no pool; maybe not even a bar, though of course he had only a matter of metres to walk to the square for one of those. Would he even get breakfast? she wondered. But that was an Esther sort of question and she was glad she hadn't uttered it out loud. Someone like this wouldn't be up in time for breakfast; he probably wouldn't have gone to bed till then.

As she watched him approach the reception desk, she imagined she was checking in with him, handing over her passport, the two documents pressed together as if they belonged in a pair. The moment the door closed behind them they would fall on the bed and have sex. The whole of the rest of her holiday would be spent having sex with this man. He would overpower her, devour her, *own* her—while at the same time worshipping her every move and fitting in with all her family commitments.

Or perhaps they should start by getting a drink somewhere?

There was a moment of hope when it turned out you couldn't check in before one o'clock, but that didn't last long as it was announced that the room had already been vacated and cleaned. He could take it now if he wanted. He did, and the manager plucked the key from its hook.

'What's your name?' Pippi asked, suddenly.

He turned to her with a start, almost as if he'd forgotten she was there. 'Zach.'

'I'm Pippi.'

'Well . . .' He had the key in his hand, was being ushered towards the stairwell. 'Great to meet you, Pippi. Thanks for the porterage. And the cigarette.'

'Thanks for the coffee.' She didn't move. If you

107

don't ask, you don't get, that was what her father always said (as a child, it had jarred slightly with her mother's 'I want never gets' teaching, but never mind, she'd dealt with it). 'Maybe you'd like to come for a drink this evening?' She gave a little exhalation of mirth as if she knew it was crazy talk but she just couldn't help herself. 'Up at the house? We need a bit of male company. Dad's buggered off and Dom's no fun.'

He looked a little wary of the offer.

'Dom's my brother,' she clarified, not remembering if she'd already made her availability fully explicit to him.

'Right.' But he still hadn't agreed to come.

'I know,' she said, decisively, 'I'll swing by the same café at sixish and if you've got nothing else to do . . . ?'

He looked amused. 'All right. And if I'm not there . . .'

'Then I'll know you've been waylaid,' she finished for him, raising her eyebrows suggestively. It was her most fervent hope that if there was any waylaying to be done with him then she would be the one to do it.

Not looking back (*never* look back, especially when walking in heels on cobbles), she hugged her arms around herself and strolled back into the sunshine. *Good job*, she thought, beaming at a pair of children with a skipping rope. Why did girls always moan about not meeting decent blokes? The truth was they were everywhere, there for the taking!

Sometimes she was conscious of her own charm even as she was speaking, the way her voice beguiled its prey (a little charm goes a long way,

Dad said, and she didn't think it was *that* deluded to think that people might say she took after him in that respect).

Other times . . . well, other times she just opened her mouth and waited to hear what came out.

CHAPTER EIGHT

THURSDAY

Maybe it was the Sales' success in rousing in the Trustloves something roughly approximating a show of normality the evening before, Ginny wasn't sure, but in bed the next morning she felt Adam touch her in a way that was more hopeful than comforting.

'No,' she said, her face colouring hotly. 'Please don't.'

His mouth was suddenly too close to hers on the pillow. 'Why? Are you still very sore?'

'*Sore?*' What kind of an inadequate word was that? Even though she knew he was talking about physical damage, she was quick to misunderstand. 'What do you think, Adam? Our baby died three months ago!'

Her voice was much harsher than she'd intended, explosive in the tiny cabin room and Adam recoiled from her as if she had kicked him. 'I think I'm aware of that,' he said in a mutter.

Ginny felt frightened by the force building inside her chest. 'For your information, I'm *always* going to be sore. And what's the point, anyway?

109

We can't try again, can we?'

Eyes averted as if from the scene of excruciating carnage, Adam said, cautiously, 'People do have sex for other reasons.'

'There *are* no other reasons!' Ginny exclaimed. There was a silence, and then she added, 'Not yet,' because she knew this was wrong. *She* was wrong. Every day she was allowing herself to be a little sharper with him, every day she was pushing him a little further from her. She knew it was not right to go limp when he tried to hold her, like some technique designed for self-defence, or, just as bad, to tense, as she had just now, the moment he attempted a caress. She knew she should listen to the voice—the special midwife's, her friends', her own—when it told her, 'You mustn't let what's happened drive a wedge between you. You need each other. You love each other.'

Not for the first time she wished the grandmother living in that nursing home near Reading was the one of her childhood and not the lost, drifting old woman she had become. *She* would know which voice could make Ginny listen.

They were sitting up in bed now, both jolted upright with their backs against the headboard, keeping themselves a safe distance apart. Trying her best to calm herself and start this conversation again, Ginny was the first to turn inwards. 'The thing is, I can't handle it yet . . . you know, working out contraception and all that. Just doing that, it would remind me of everything.'

Adam nodded. 'I've been thinking about that. I thought I could maybe do what Richard did.'

After the birth of his fourth child, their brother-in-law Richard had had a vasectomy. He called it

110

The Big V and was boastfully free with his descriptions of post-operative bruising. It was his version of a labour tale, Karen said, his badge of honour.

'You can't do that,' Ginny said in a small, dry voice that didn't begin to betray her horror at his suggestion.

Adam looked back at her with nothing but simple sincerity. 'If it means we don't have the reminder every time, like you say, then why not?'

'Because you could . . .' But she couldn't finish, hoping they might just leave it at that, but knowing it was already too late: they were in this conversation now.

'I could what?' It was the tone you might use with a child you knew had something painful to confess, full of love and encouragement, knowing the answer before it was given. She couldn't have said what tone she would have preferred, but she knew she hated this one.

'You could have a baby with someone else.'

There, it was said, and now that it was she found she had the same instinct she'd had with Bea Sale in the garden, the need to make it brutally clear, for herself as much as for the other person. To show herself no mercy. 'It's me who's caused this,' she added, grimly, 'it's my genes, not yours. You could go out there today and father a perfectly healthy baby with someone else.' She had no idea why but the youthful, and doubtlessly perfectly fertile, figure of Pippi Sale rose before her eyes. Only then did it register that the girl had been flirting with Adam yesterday evening, she had completely monopolised him for the two hours they were with the Sales, and Ginny had cared so little she hadn't even *noticed*, not at the time. Over dinner afterwards, they had hardly mentioned her, concentrating instead on Martin and Bea and the scale of their business empire. Adam, in particular, had been full of conversation, sparkling by their recent dismal standards. No, she thought, she shouldn't have been as startled as she was by his tentative attempt at intimacy just now.

'It's me who's caused this,' she repeated. And she wanted to see the words in writing, printed on a medical document, etched into the wood panelling on the wall in front of them, scrawled across the sky outside: *Ginny's fault*.

'Ginny . . .' Adam's expression was horrible to see, part beseeching her to take her words back and part resigned to the truth of them. And not only resigned but also grateful that it had not been left to him to say it. She reminded herself that this was exactly how she would look if their situation were reversed, if it were she who still had that whisper of a choice. 'We don't know that's true,' he said.

'We *do* know. Deanna's email confirmed it.'

'She's not a cardiologist, Ginny. She doesn't know anything about it. She hadn't seen your father for years before he died.' The disapproval in his voice was, Ginny knew, for her aunt having allowed herself to fall out of touch with her dead brother's only child, his *orphaned* only child, an issue of rare dispute between them. Ginny was weary of pointing out that Deanna had already been living in New Zealand for five years before Ginny's father was killed, and that she'd been reassured by her mother that Ginny was in safe hands. In any case, there'd been birthday and

112

Christmas presents, letters from her faraway cousins, and even two visits. As far as she was concerned, there was nothing to forgive.

'And that's certainly not what the fertility guy said, anyway,' Adam added. But the shake of his head was too defiant; it felt false.

She gave an impatient sigh. 'He said the same as all the others, that if it was *his* wife he wouldn't want to risk it.'

'Oh, but that was off the record.'

'Off the record is what counts, Adam. We were lucky he was so honest with us.'

Lucky: the word hung between them like a taunt. As long as they both lived, neither would consider themselves lucky.

'Besides, he probably didn't want to suggest that you dump me and find a new wife, someone in full working order. Not very tactful, given the circumstances. But, then again, he'll probably spell it out when you go in for your vasectomy, eh?'

How spiteful she sounded, how self-pitying; even cold fury would have been preferable. She wouldn't have blamed him if he'd flounced off, or slapped her even, but by contrast his reaction was one of unbearable tenderness, made all the worse by his gentle grasping of her hand in his. 'Ginny, I don't want to have a baby with anyone else, you know that. I never wanted one *before* you and me. I think I can be happy again with it being just us.'

'Just us,' she repeated after him. It couldn't have sounded more wretched if he'd said, 'Alone for ever'. Still the wrong words continued to spill from her mouth, or at least the right words wrongly delivered: 'Well, I wish I could say the same, but I don't think I can. I can't live every day of my life being "Just us". It's not right. It's not fair. It's second best.'

During this little speech Adam had looked completely at a loss, but with her last words there seemed to be a sudden shift in his understanding and he nodded. 'Ah. I wondered if last night would lead to something like this.' He shook his head. 'Maybe we shouldn't have gone for drinks with them after all.'

Suddenly Ginny didn't want her hand in his any longer. It felt bound. 'What are you talking about? This has got nothing to do with the Sales.'

'Are you sure? I wouldn't blame you. What that woman's got, anyone would be envious. *I'm* envious.' Again he spoke with that special delicacy of an adult leading a child towards the higher ground of truthfulness.

Cross and confused, Ginny snatched her hand away. 'I'm not envious of Bea Sale, I barely know her. And nor do you.'

'Come on, there's no point pretending we haven't noticed. We spent a couple of hours last night discussing it. The woman's got everything.' He paused, before beginning his list: 'The looks, the amazing lifestyle, the husband making zillions . . .'

The kids, he meant, but he bottled out of that.

'Nothing's as wonderful as it seems,' Ginny said, remembering the tension in Bea's body, the livid twist in her eyes as she'd confessed her husband's betrayals. 'She's got her problems, just like everyone else.'

She thought she saw disbelief in Adam's face, then, even a trace of disdain for her pig-headedness, and she felt more defensive than ever:

114

'Don't look at me like that. You started this conversation!'

He didn't refute this, though he might have, since all he'd done was run his hands over her hips, not invite an argument. Had she responded more dutifully in the first place, then they'd be locked together now—be it in pain or pleasure—and not having this terrible discussion. Maybe the landmark of it would have helped, too, another demarcation line between then and now, like coming here, putting half a continent between Isaac's still body and their moving ones.

Adam allowed the vehemence of her last exclamations to fade before he spoke again. This time he made no move to touch her, but kept his distance as though from an animal that had already taken a chunk out of his fingers. 'You say it's not right or fair, and that's true, it isn't. But it is what it is and we have to face it. And we haven't even talked about other possibilities yet.'

Ginny's head whipped round. 'What other possibilities?'

'Well, adoption for one.'

She gaped. A new dawn, indeed! Sex, vasectomy, her own genetic horror show, adoption: all the taboos of the last months were tumbling from Adam's mouth, one on top of the next, on top of her. She couldn't breathe with the weight of them.

'But you just said you'd be happy without a child?' she said, at last.

'I said I *could* be happy. If that was what we decided.'

'And I thought you always said you would never consider adoption?'

There'd been a conversation about it, she remembered, a general one when she was pregnant, with Karen and Richard, and with Samantha, the younger of the sisters and mother of two (and counting, for she and her husband Tom were trying so publicly for a third they might as well have been blogging their efforts to the whole world). It's not the same, was the consensus among those who had no need to doubt their own fertility. There would be too much extra effort needed to make up for the lack of a natural connection. Ginny alone had said she didn't see the difference. 'That's because you lost your parents young and you have no brothers and sisters,' Karen pointed out in her bald way. 'You're virtually adopted yourself.'

Ginny had stood her ground. 'Which is why I know it makes no difference. I'm the only one here who's qualified to say.' But glancing in turn at those around the table, she knew that each one of them—as well as anyone else who cared to analyse her—was thinking the same thing: that the reason she'd been attracted to Adam in the first place was the security and comfort of a big family, a *real* family, with mothers and fathers and brothers and sisters; with aunts and uncles and cousins who lived half an hour away, not on the other side of the world. Because she craved what she hadn't had.

Even now, she didn't know if this was a fair judgement or not.

Adam turned earnestly to her. 'Look, if I said that then it was when I thought I would never *need* to consider it. But now . . . well, we have to accept that we are like the other thousands of couples who, for whatever reason, cannot have children of their own. There are options for them and there will be for us, too.'

Ginny was silent. Like Adam, she'd never believed they'd be in this position. When they'd had that conversation with Karen and the others it had amounted to little more than idle chat while they were waiting for desserts to arrive, not mentioned a second time; after all, she'd been pregnant, blissfully confident she'd never be faced with such a dilemma. But since Isaac's death she'd come to understand better the fear behind the opinion voiced that day: no matter what she'd said then, the fact was she *couldn't* imagine taking someone else's child, feeling the same about him or her as she had Isaac. And that was assuming a small child could be found in the first place; the stories she heard suggested otherwise—these thousands of other couples Adam conjured, millions maybe, they'd all be in line ahead of them, hungry for the call, ready to drop everything and mobilise.

By her side, Adam sighed heavily, evidently wishing as dearly as she did that they'd never started this. 'I'm not saying we're ready to think about any of that yet, just that, when we are, then all the options will still be there, they'll still be open to us. Actually, I think we should give it at least a year before we even think about making any plans. That's what the counsellor said, as well, and she's right.'

'A year?' Ginny felt as if he were handing a sentence to her, one she had no hope of overturning. 'But what do we do with ourselves for a year? How do we live? In some kind of limbo?'

'Not in limbo, no. We live like we used to. We do our jobs, have our holidays, see our family and friends . . .'

Nausea engulfed her. She'd thought Italy was doing nothing for her—other than tormenting her with the beautiful Sales—but now the thought of returning from this tranquil hideout to England was intolerable. Adam had gone back over two months ago to the large accountancy firm for which they both worked, but she remained on leave, signed off indefinitely by her GP. Going to the office—where she had not set foot since her leaving party—sitting in meetings, bumping into people in the lift, in the sandwich shop or the queue for coffee. Some of them wouldn't have a clue what had happened. They'd say, 'You're the one who went off and had a baby, aren't you? How old is it now?' And she'd be forced to watch their expressions collapse as they realised their polite enquiry was in fact a hideous faux pas. Faux pas— that was what this would be to them, nothing more, a slip-up that would make them go back to their desk and say to their neighbour, 'Oh, God, I just put my foot in it with that woman from HR . . .'

She turned to Adam, shaking slightly. 'That's just it, I can't go back. I couldn't survive it.' Again her words felt unstoppable as she blurted, almost against her will, 'I need to feel that something is different. *Fundamentally* different.'

'What do you mean, "fundamentally"?' He spoke slowly, as though reading between her lines and supplying the answer for himself simultaneously.

But she didn't know what she meant, and the fact that it could be interpreted so dangerously only added to her despair. She thought of Bea and her plan to leave Martin—was that what she saw for herself? To leave her marriage, to escape Adam's grief and thus free him of hers? Wouldn't there be a kind of mercy in that? No, it was insanity, not mercy. She remembered the feeling she'd had on the little island a few days ago, her sense of the enormity of what they shared, the immovability of it. They would always have this, whether they lived in the same house or on opposite sides of the world. And she loved him, she needed to remember that; she had loved him best of all—until a more powerful love had come along.

What then? A change of job, of home, of neighbourhood? Live closer to the other Trustloves and the many nieces and nephews they provided, or farther from them? *Something.*

'I'm getting up,' Adam said, miserably.

'OK.'

Nothing was resolved. He went into the bathroom and Ginny stayed under the covers, edging into the centre of the bed to escape the sunlight now coming through the window. But the moment she heard the water splashing in the shower she shuffled back to her side and reached for her handbag. Without hesitating, she drew out her mobile phone and switched it on. She knew very well that it had come to represent a low moment when she did this—and so early in the day, too!—and a particularly weak-willed one, but she couldn't stop herself.

Fingers moving quickly, she found the text message she wanted. It was the one Adam had sent an hour or two after Isaac's birth; he'd sent it to her too, so she could see what he had written to their family and friends, though of course she hadn't looked at her phone until afterwards.

> Dear all, finally some news,
> a baby boy! Isaac Joe
> Trustlove, born April 4th
> at 13:33, 7lbs 3oz. Mother
> and baby tired but very
> happy! Love Adam x

Once, she'd been groggy with sleeping pills when she'd read it and had had a full sensory memory of the moment he'd sent it, the joy speeding through her body like an aftershock. She had Isaac in her arms and Adam was sitting on the edge of the bed, his back to the door (you weren't supposed to use mobile phones in the rooms), tapping away with his thumbs.

'There,' he'd said, turning to his wife and son. 'It's official. Now everyone knows.'

He'd released the news into the world like a gift, a cageful of doves on a wedding day. And together they'd looked forward to getting the replies.

*   *   *

Isaac arrived five days late. Until then, everything had gone along just as the book (and Adam's family) said it would. Even the little celebration they arranged for her at work was familiar, the same one she'd seen a dozen times before, only this time it was she who opened the bottle of massage oil to sniff its scent and joke about its uses, she who read aloud the label on the packet of raspberry tea that was supposed to bring on labour.

120

('Maybe in a lab mouse,' Adam said, when she took it home. 'A human being would need a kilo of this stuff.')

When the contractions did start, they made the same first-time parents' mad dash to the hospital as millions had before them, saying to the receptionist in the same panicked cries, 'It's happening! It's happening!', only to be told, 'No, it's not,' and to go home again and sit it out for another six hours. It was during this stretch, she remembered, that she had said to Adam, 'I've almost forgotten what this is all for!' And it was true; it was as if the labour had taken on a life of its own, a test of endurance like a triathlon or one of those half-marathons where you get everyone in the office to sponsor you.

But that feeling only lasted a short time. Of course she hadn't forgotten! As she looked around the living room, she held her stomach and whispered, 'The next time I'm here I'll have you with me. You'll be in your Moses basket over there by the sofa, or maybe in the funny little rubber seat we just bought for you yesterday. Or in my arms.'

Mostly she pictured the baby in her arms. Or in Adam's, of course, but she would always be close by, always within touching distance.

*   *   *

Later that morning, when they were up and dressed, they did just what Ginny had hoped they would do (and Adam too, evidently): pretend the horrible conversation had never taken place. This was achieved initially by setting out for the latest of Adam's adventures, on foot up to Sacro Monte, the hilltop collection of chapels where the story of St Francis was told in sculptures and frescoes. The idea was to take the sequential route around the chapels and appreciate the changing architecture as you followed the story. She wasn't sure if it was deliberate on Adam's part or simply owing to the fact of Italy itself but there was a definite religious bias to these excursions of his. Neither of them had been churchgoers in London, though Trustlove pressure had secured their agreement that Isaac would be christened as each of his cousins had, but she supposed it counted as well as any other as a 'new thing' for them to try. And it was true that she had liked the prayer he'd found in the basilica on the island.

They'd hardly begun up the steep path alongside Villa Isola when she slackened her pace and allowed him to walk ahead. He didn't object, if anything picking up his own speed a little in response. It seemed that neither wished to risk another exchange of opinion—on any subject.

It felt strangely smothering to move away from the lake's edge; until now Ginny hadn't realised how she'd got used to the space and light of open water, its sounds of glugging and smacking. She was grateful, therefore, when she emerged at the top of the alley, where the path crossed the traffic lane and where she could get respite from the claustrophobia. She stepped into the road, eyes scanning the signpost on the opposite pavement, which, confusingly, showed two separate directions for Sacro Monte. That was when she saw the Merc braking, or, more correctly, heard it, and not so much the screech of rubber on road, though there was that, as the odd, mechanical swallowing sound

122

that accompanied it.

The vehicle was less than a foot from her, close enough for her to see the glossy walnut fittings inside—and the figure in the back seat: Martin Sale. All at once Ginny saw exactly where she was, realised that the car must have come from the villa's driveway and braked expressly in order to avoid hitting her. It had been an emergency stop. She looked down at herself. No contact had been made, but only through a miracle of reflex on the part of the driver.

The rear door opened and Martin jumped out. 'Ginny, I *thought* it was you! Are you all right?'

'Yes, I'm fine.' Her voice sounded ridiculously carefree, as if she had simply not noticed she'd been the cause of a near accident.

'Did we hit you?' He thought, perhaps, that shock was the reason for her failure to take this seriously.

'No. Sorry, I shouldn't have stepped out like that. I wasn't looking.'

'My God, we could have broken your legs!' He sounded as if he hadn't yet decided whether to be angry or sorry. He made a relieved gesture through the windscreen to the driver—a taxi driver, Ginny gathered—and swiftly took command of the situation. Since she was still standing motionless in the middle of the road and showing no signs of removing herself from the taxi's path, he reached out to put an arm around her shoulders and lead her to the pavement. She didn't resist; his chest and arm felt solid against her—in a way that the threat of two tons of steel and rubber had not— and she let herself sink against him as if she had decided she was injured after all and in need of propping up. He smelled of unfamiliar smells, exotically so, in the way it struck you when you flew to another continent and stepped outside of the airport for the first time. Just inches from her face, his skin was warm and glossy and tanned.

They'd stood in close proximity last night, of course, but being at the villa at dusk, with all that extraordinary light and colour, the blur of drinks and food and conversation, not to mention Dom's disconcerting outburst, there had been such sensory overload that Martin himself had seemed unreal to her, an actor playing a part. Now, though, he was real.

'Where's Adam?' he asked, discreetly disentangling himself. He kept one palm on the back of her shoulder and she shifted the weight of herself upwards slightly to increase the pressure of it.

'Just ahead . . . up this path here if it's the one towards Sacro Monte?'

His eyes narrowed as he examined the various signs and then the steep lane ahead. 'Yes, I think it is. Just carry on up the hill. Do you want me to walk up with you and find him?'

Yes, she thought.

'It's no trouble,' he added.

But she saw his quick glance at his watch and remembered the waiting taxi. The engine was still running. 'No, it's OK, you're going somewhere.' She paused, hoping he might tell her where, for she suddenly felt she *needed* to know. 'Thank you, though. I don't know how I didn't see you coming.'

'Easily done, don't worry.'

Her nostrils still full of his smell, she strove to prolong this closeness, even if only by a few seconds. 'And thank you for drinks last night. I had a good time.'

He smiled, open and easy. 'My pleasure. Very glad you could come.'

They looked at each other. Why had she said *I*, she wondered, and not *we*? Especially when it had been Adam who had had the good time. It seemed suddenly significant that she had done this— crucial.

'You go,' she said, finally.

He must have decided it was easiest to take her at her word, and after offering her grateful shoulder a last squeeze and baring his not-quite-perfect teeth in farewell, he was in the back seat again, closing the door between them. The driver pulled away with exaggerated care, accelerating properly only when the car had cleared Ginny by ten metres or so, which meant she could clearly see Martin turning to check on her through the rear windscreen. She stood watching until it disappeared completely from view, overpowered by the desire to be in the car with him, crushed against him as they rode away, being taken far from this place.

Continuing her life under his command.

CHAPTER NINE

THURSDAY

Marty had hardly been gone five minutes when the message came. Susanna's son Emilio brought it to Bea when she and Esther got back from Casa

125

Mista in the middle of the afternoon:

Signor, phone Cally Hastings.

The accompanying phone number was for a UK mobile line.

'You mean this person called the number here?' she asked Emilio, puzzled. To her knowledge, not one of the family had yet to take a call on the villa's permanent line. The few calls that had come had been for Susanna and to do with the business of the house.

Emilio shrugged. '*Si, Signora.*'

'When?'

'*Oggi.*' Today.

'Are you sure?' She didn't mean to suggest he was lying, it was just that Susanna had spent quite some time this week complaining to her of the long Italian school holidays and of the tendency of teenage boys here to unlearn everything they'd been taught in the previous eight months. ('Every day, he forget something new!') It was a concept that, for someone whose children had friends who'd been brutally tutored in school holidays, had given her a vicarious thrill.

'*Si, Signora,*' Emilio said, once more.

'OK. Thank you.' She peered again at the name: Cally Hastings. Though she didn't recognise it—perhaps *because* she didn't—it wasn't hard to deduce who this woman might be. Marty had promised that no one from the office had been given the number of the private line here, no one from the office would *need* it; they'd simply leave a message with his assistant Angela or try him on his mobile. No, Ms Hastings could only be a personal

126

friend—which in Marty's world meant a lover. Quite why he would have given her this number was beyond Bea, frankly, but if it was a question of conjuring up worst-case scenarios, well, she'd had plenty of practice. She experienced a brief flash of her greatest, longest-lived fear: that her husband had a parallel family, other children who were half-siblings to her own, just like the patriarchs of old. He had them based in Paris or Marrakech or somewhere such arrangements were considered stylish and necessary.

There were more outlandish theories in the world; after all, he *had* just flown home in a hurry. For all she knew, the message she held in her hands could be her husband's summons to the maternity ward.

Though she fought it, she couldn't quite stop the image of Dom's face appearing in her mind's eye then.

Seconds later—she could still hear Emilio's footsteps on the tiled floor as he returned from the hallway where he'd found her to his jobs in the kitchen—she had already updated her deduction: this Cally could not be the only one Marty had on the go at the moment. If she was calling him here today, then she obviously *didn't* know he was on his way to London. Alone in the Kew house, with no one else about to burst through the door, it was a free pass, and if Cally didn't know about it, then someone else did. Then again, the message might have taken its time in reaching the family—this was Italy, after all, and *oggi* didn't always mean *oggi*. Marty could be planning to sleep with this Cally woman that very evening—assuming she wasn't in the labour room giving birth to his child.

She could go around in circles with this, round and round indefinitely, or at least for as long as she was prepared to remain married to her husband.

Still holding the note, she lowered herself on to one of the recessed stone seats in the hallway that had become her favourite place in the villa to sit with a book. On this occasion, however, she struggled to get comfortable on the flattened antique cushions, for old feelings of wretchedness were washing over her and making her body heavy on the stone. It was no more that a conditioned reflex, of course, and the sensation subsided just as soon as she reminded herself that women like Cally no longer mattered. Really, they didn't. She'd made her decision before this holiday and the fact that she was here, determined to enjoy herself for its duration, did not change a thing.

She couldn't remember the exact moment when she'd come to accept the truth (only that it was several years after she had become aware of it): no matter how hard she tried, however many times she agreed to trust Marty, she would never be allowed to have her marriage to herself. And it wasn't only the other women, it was also Sale itself, the company and all its successes, the public persona of her husband's that had long since ousted the private one. Only someone who was thoroughly deluded could imagine it would be any different for the next twenty years than it had been for the past twenty. And the saddest thing was that, beneath it all, beneath the layers of her years of forgiveness and fresh starts, there stirred the suspicion that if theirs were not a business that traded on idyllic family living, if she were not integral to that image, then might *he* not already have left *her*? She imagined Ed or Melissa counselling against a divorce: 'The damage would be pretty bad, Marty. Stick it out for another five years, eh? The brand should be untouchable then.'

Well, they would soon see how resilient the brand was, wouldn't they?

Phone Cally. No, she'd been here a million times before and she could quote the order of play in her sleep: discovery, confrontation, appeasement. The only thing unusual about this—apart from the fact that it would be the last—was that it was the only time there would be a confrontation *during* an appeasement, for she was in no doubt that this holiday was appeasement of the highest order, the most extravagant there had been. Though neither of them had said it explicitly, both she and Marty knew it represented an attempt on his part to make amends for all that had gone before. It was his best offer. The problem was that he could have given her the moon at this stage and it wouldn't have been enough.

She wondered if there hadn't been a kind of comfort in the way she had first reacted to Emilio's message, even nostalgia. Jealousy for old times' sake: who would have thought it?

*　　　*　　　*

As with all crimes, the first had been the hardest to suffer. The girl he'd been phoning before that trip to New York: Kitten. (Even now Bea thought of her simply by her pet name.)

It had taken her some time to track down her rival. It was before mobile phones were commonplace, before itemised utility bills came as standard, and even before the family had email at home. She was reluctant to follow him—he'd recognise her car in an instant and in any case she couldn't get very far before she had to come back and pick up the children from school—and she didn't want to use a private investigator to tail him, either, in case she'd somehow misunderstood the whole thing and there was nothing to uncover. Then she'd just feel bad, as if she were the guilty party, not him.

She should have just gone to the professionals in the first place.

Four months of watching and listening, that was what it had taken. She paid special attention to overnight trips, cross-referencing the itineraries Sandy forwarded to her at Marty's request with any documents she found in his possession, both before and after the event, and scrutinising hotel bills and credit card statements. Finally, she noticed a small discrepancy, so small she was sure she wouldn't have thought anything of it before. It was a printout of his itinerary for a buying trip to Hong Kong, prepared in the usual way by the travel agency Sale used to book international flights and hotels. One line had been crossed out, but not so fully that you couldn't still read the typed words beneath: *Passengers in party: 2.* Why had someone done that? Bea wondered. If it had been a mistake, and should have read '1' (Marty had told her he was travelling alone), then you'd just correct the '2', not cross out the whole line. Then again, there might originally have been two travellers, someone else from Sale, someone quite innocent who had had to cancel for reasons not worth relaying to wives or partners.

But by now she'd come to see that she had nothing to guide her but her gut instinct, and what that was telling her was that she should follow her husband to Heathrow Airport for this flight to Hong Kong, or, more accurately, to beat him there. At a safe distance from the check-in desk, she watched him approach, suitcase wheeled to a halt behind him like a pet brought to heel several steps from the business class kiosk. He made no move to engage any of the staff, even though there was no queue. He waited like that for several minutes, after the first few pulling a copy of *Private Eye* from his carry-on and chuckling as he read. Then, after no more than ten minutes, a tall blonde girl walked up, pushing a trolley laden with designer luggage. One hand still on the trolley, she slipped her other through Marty's arm. At once he dropped the magazine to his feet and pressed her to him, kissing her hard on the lips. Then they checked in together, Marty handling the girl's bags as well as his own. While the airline worker checked their documents and taped the luggage, Marty ran a hand over the girl's bottom, tightly encased in non-Sale denim, then up under her T-shirt, idly tracing the outline of her spine with his thumb.

The feeling inside Bea was one of nausea, a primal, world-ending feeling, something like she imagined you'd feel if someone tore your child from your grip and sped off with him in a waiting car. Her breath shortened and her vision swam; her legs and arms trembled of their own accord. But she didn't have much time here, and even while these symptoms held her in a physical seizure her brain was busy with some simple calculations.

131

The girl's height and wholesome beauty, her youth, the way she dressed, and even the way she wore her hair, pulled back in a glossy ponytail, made it more than likely she was a model. Bea was sure she was not one Sale had ever booked, however; she was still involved enough with the business to know the last few seasons' campaigns inside out. But that didn't mean the girl hadn't been called in for a casting at some point in the past, or wasn't being considered for future work.

She could have sprung them then and there, of course, but after having been held for four months in that grim, wordless purgatory (like awaiting the results of a secret biopsy), she found she wanted to keep to herself for the time being the small power of knowing about them before they knew she knew. It felt like the only thing she *did* have. And so she allowed the lovers their path through to Departures unaccosted, watching them vanish through the automatic doors before she fled from the terminal building and drove directly to Sale's HQ near Tooting. Luckily the alarm code had not changed since she'd last needed to use it, and she was able to walk through the darkened rooms towards the bank of filing cabinets kept between the twin desks belonging to Sandy and Ed's assistant Frances. She quickly located the drawer that held the hundreds of models' cards, along with the staff notes made during castings and go-sees. And there she was, among the 'No's. Her name was Lara Morton. No age was listed (Bea guessed mid-twenties) but the rest was all there: *height 5ft 9ins, bust 34C, waist 24ins, hips 35ins, hair blonde, eyes blue, shoe size 6 1/2.* She'd done catalogue work for Next and Harrods and for several

American clients.

Bea looked at the notes scribbled in the white space at the bottom of the card: 'Too sexy. Not believable as a mother.' It wasn't Marty's writing, it was the art director Claire's, but even so. Too sexy. Not believable as a mother. In the days that followed, the lowest of her life to date, Bea thought of herself in a way she never had before, despite the nature of their business. She thought of herself as not believable as a model.

The agency was only too happy to pass on a message for one of their girls to call Beatrice Sale in person to talk about a forthcoming special project. Lara was on holiday right now, they said, but just as soon as she came back, they would be sure to have her phone her.

'There's no hurry,' Bea said, leaving her number.

She never did phone, of course, this Lara girl, at least not on the number Bea had left for her.

Two days after he got back from Hong Kong, Marty came home from the office earlier than expected and said, 'I think we need to talk.'

'Yes,' she said. 'But only if you're going to tell me the truth. I'm not interested, otherwise.'

He nodded.

'So? Talk.'

'You obviously know about Lara,' he began.

It wasn't a question and she didn't reply.

'I want you to know this hasn't happened before,' he added.

Bea gave him a long look of disdain. 'That's crap and you know it. You don't take someone to Hong Kong on a first date.'

He frowned slightly. 'No, I mean, she's the only

one.'

But the fact that he was answering a question she hadn't thought to ask told her only that the opposite must be true. Now she knew he wasn't telling the truth, not the whole of it, and when he said he'd been seeing Lara for six months she automatically doubled that. When he said he did not love her, she modified that, too: *not yet*.

'Does everyone know?' she demanded. 'Am I a laughing stock at Sale?'

'No, of course not. No one knows.'

'Well, Sandy does, doesn't she? She's the one who puts your calls through to her.' She told him about the call that had started it all, what she had heard him say. Remembering the desire in his voice, the casual intimacy, it was just as heartbreaking then as it had been at the time.

'I wondered about that,' he said. He was watching her face, processing hard, problem solving.

'Look,' she said, sharply. She couldn't bear to be embroiled any deeper in his vain little cover-up. 'What's your bottom line here, Marty? Do you want to stay or do you want to go?'

That shook him. He'd been leaning towards her across the kitchen worktop, his demeanour soft and pleading, but now he straightened, a squaddie caught slumping on morning parade. 'Stay,' he said, and then, with more feeling, 'Stay, of course! It's over with her,' he insisted.

Bea took a step closer to him, hating the feeling of instant relief his words had given her. Was she not going to make this harder for him? She felt as disgusted with herself as she did him. 'Why? Why is it over? Because I found out?'

There was no point his denying this, though she did believe that he had ended it—or was about to.

Absurdly, he went on defending himself (or convincing himself, it wasn't clear which). 'Why would I want to risk all this?' he asked her. Though he gestured generally to the space around them, the interior-designed, light-filled, perfect-for-entertaining kitchen extension they'd had built, his eyes rested on a large framed photograph on the wall of her and the children before returning imploringly to her face. 'Why?'

'You tell me,' she said, coldly. 'Because evidently you *have* risked it, haven't you?' She'd hated him in that moment, but hating him was new territory and traditionally new territory had been negotiated together, as a team. And so he helped her find a way to forgive him. As time went on she found things improved between them, most notably in bed, where the scare had made her want to give rather more than she had before. Her divorced friend Patricia told her that this was one of the typical outcomes of a husband's infidelity. 'Either way, he ends up getting more sex. It hardly matters to him who it's with.'

Bea tried not to think of it like that, especially as Patricia's children were not coping as well with their parents' divorce as had been hoped.

Why would I want to risk all this? he'd asked, his eyes little-boy innocent. Had it happened any later, of course, she'd have understood better that 'all this' meant the business, the brand, his status as someone who not only upheld family values but also cherished them, someone who needed to be seen to be practising what he preached. But back then it was still just about credible that he should be talking about her, about her and their three young children. Family and family alone.

*　　　*　　　*

Slipping the phone message into a nearby drawer—she was damned if she was going to aid and abet his adultery, even at this stage in the game—she looked through the high horseshoe arch of the rear doorway and out to the pale lake beyond. She needed to get out of here, to clear her head. Funny how quickly that happened. You left your home for a dream holiday, but it was never very long before you were looking for a change of scene from that, too. She knew why it was, she'd read an article about it recently, it was the great holiday fallacy: you went away to escape your troubles, but no matter how far you travelled you could not escape your own mind and that was what gave you the biggest trouble of all. Ultimately, human beings were no different from dogs chasing their own tails.

Nonetheless, she thought a walk into the village, a nice coffee somewhere on the water, might put a little wag back into hers.

Though she went through the motions of asking the others if they wanted to come, it was with the certain knowledge that she'd be given the solitude she needed. Esther was expecting a phone call from Vicky in Guatemala; Pippi, she knew, had been into the village before lunch and was now sunbathing down on the jetty (a coincidence, perhaps, but she was in full view of anyone who happened to be out on the boathouse balcony); as for Dom, Bea felt confident, if a little sad, that he would reject any proposal that involved being on his own with her for fear she'd start again on the troubles *he* was trying to escape.

And so she made her expedition alone. Reaching the piazza, she hardly paused at the sight of a young bride and groom having their photographs taken, for wedding parties were common here, if not two-a-penny then at least three-a-day. The first couple of times she'd stopped to watch, memories surfacing of her own special day, but already she'd stopped noticing them; it was like working in the theatre and getting used to everyone walking around in costume.

She lingered to gaze at the derelict building on the south side, at the scars all over its facade, the permanently shuttered eyes. It was clearly centuries old, once a grand hotel and the venue, no doubt, of a thousand fascinating liaisons. She imagined herself buying it, restoring it, re-opening it as a chic guesthouse—single-handed, of course. With or without Marty in residence at Villa Isola, she was starting to realise that she'd been visualising life alone from the moment she'd got here, her mind gently sifting ideas of what she might do next. Anything might inspire one: the sight of an Italian woman of about her age, without a wedding ring and with an intriguingly brisk purpose to her step; a boutique full of the luxurious scents and lotions she'd always enjoyed buying and now wondered if she might sell instead; or a beautiful building, like this one, ripe for renovation.

Could she take on a project like this? For a lovely sun-filled minute it seemed perfectly within her grasp, the obvious solution to everything, a sign meant especially for her, but then she remembered the work that went into a single dinner at the villa and wondered if she was really willing, at the age of forty-four, to begin again, to sustain the kind of energy and drive she and Marty had taken for granted when they'd started Sale. He had it still, that was plain to see, and at least one of their children had inherited it, but somewhere down the line she herself had let it slip away. Well, that was fine, she decided, absolutely fine. She no longer wanted to live life at breakneck speed. At her age she should simply be grateful that no one's neck had been broken thus far . . .

There was a sudden shout in English—'Hey, watch out there!'—just in time she stepped from the path of a car gliding silently at speed towards her. All but those with permission from the municipal authorities were banned from driving in the centre of the village, and she, like everyone else, had quickly taken the car-free streets for granted, attributing any approaching engine sounds to the little tourist train that shuttled, at five miles an hour, between the car park and the piazza.

Seeing the car pull up safely at the waterfront (and disgorge wedding guests—of course!), she turned in the direction of the shout and saw a dark, languid figure leaning against one of the pillars of the colonnade. He was a young man of about Dom's age, his black clothes and mirrored aviator glasses giving him the look of a rather glamorous ant.

'Thanks for the warning,' she called, raising her hand. 'I was miles away.'

'That's OK. I don't think you were in mortal

danger, but you never know.'

She smiled to herself, remembering how she'd just been thinking of broken necks. 'No, you don't, that's true.'

He stepped out into the sunshine and came to stand a couple of paces from her. She half-expected a girlfriend or a wife to come out from behind the pillar and claim ownership, but it presently became clear that he was on his own, just as she was.

'Bit of a waste of prime real estate, eh?' he said, gesturing to the building. 'You look as if you might have plans for it?'

She wondered how long he had been standing there before the speeding car had drawn him from the shadows. 'In my dreams, yes,' she said, dryly, 'but I think it would be a bit of a tall order for real life.'

'What would you do with it?'

'I think I'd re-open it as a hotel.'

'Would you?' he said, playfully disappointed. 'Aren't there enough honeymooners in this place already?'

She pulled a face, made a show of reconsidering. 'OK, maybe I'd put up a sign saying "No Romance". Yes, that would be my USP.'

'*Amore vietato?* I have a feeling you'd end up with a lot of empty rooms.'

She liked his voice, which was low and grainy and had a confidential tone to it that made you instantly attentive, as if something special might be shared if you only came a little closer. Without being able to see his eyes behind the reflective lenses, the voice was all she had for a clue as to this approach of his, that and the wry set of his mouth

139

(his lips were dark pink, stained, as if he'd been biting down on them with his teeth). It was impossible not to speculate on eye colour: a classic deep brown, she decided, to go with that dark and somewhat wild hair.

'What would *you* do with it?' she asked, feeling bold.

'Oh, easy. I'd tear it down and build a mooring.'

'A mooring?'

The lips curled. 'Yeah, for something totally inappropriate, something that would cause national controversy.'

'Like what?'

'I don't know, HMS *Warrior* or something. Whatever the Italian equivalent is. They could do the wedding photos by the guns.'

Bea gasped with laughter. 'And how would you get it here? You know the only outflow to this lake is up in Omegna, and that's just a glorified stream?'

'Oh, is it? I didn't know.' He pretended to be crushed. 'You've scuppered my plan, then. Literally.'

'I'm sorry. I don't like to scupper plans if I can help it.'

There was something very disarming about the way he stood looking at her then, at least she assumed it was her he was looking at and not the waterfront over her shoulder. He was assessing her, taking an educated guess at her age, perhaps—he'd have to be half-blinded by the sun not to arrive at somewhere close to forty. For her part, she felt sure he was no older than twenty-five, perhaps not even that. He was more self-assured than Dom, had a worldlier air, but there wasn't much to choose between them in terms of physical condition. They had the same quick, lean frame, the same carelessly lush hair, the same laughter lines that vanished into perfect smoothness the moment the face was straightened. Youth, beauty, charm: it was impossible not to stare right back at him.

'Well,' she said, when the length of time that neither of them had broken gaze felt indecent, 'thank you again for the warning.'

'Any time.'

But he didn't move, he simply continued to hold her in the grip of his scrutiny, which left her with no choice but to turn around and walk away herself. She strolled down to the water, giving a wide berth to the group of elderly tourists boarding a ferry for the island. She could still see the dazzle of those silver sunglasses in the centre of her vision, almost as if she'd looked directly at the sun—twin suns—and glanced away again just in time. It was weird, but she couldn't quite shake off the sense that he'd been watching her long before she became aware of him, that he'd been lying in wait for her.

Crossing the square towards a café in the shade, she issued herself with the humorous but necessary rebuke: *Come on, Bea, you should be so lucky.*

CHAPTER TEN

THURSDAY

It seemed to Ginny that, since Isaac, time no longer had anything to do with the way the earth turned on its axis or circled the sun, but was something fragmentary, inconstant, past episodes breaking into her mind and obliterating the present with neither warning nor recourse. Even so, she was keenly aware of the hours passing at Sacro Monte, of the light actually changing while she and Adam were up there.

It was inevitable from the moment of arrival that she was not going to be able to stand the full course of twenty-one chapels, and, sure enough, she began to make her excuses after only four or five. Who were these people determined to follow the route around, she wondered, diligently turning the pages of their travel guides, ticking each one off? And where *did* they get their energy?

Adam was one of them, of course, and though she was married to him she still didn't know the answer to either of those questions.

Simple exhaustion was only part of the reason she dropped out so quickly, as was her continuing reluctance to be alone with Adam so soon after the ghastly scene in bed that morning (who knew what part of St Francis' life might bear comparison with their own? If there was any link, she knew Adam would find it). For there was a third, more complicated reason, one she was reluctant to give voice to: her fear of the fresh dissatisfaction she felt in her husband after having encountered Martin Sale, having been *touched* by Martin Sale.

This had begun the moment Adam came into view at the top of the path, hovering a little cautiously for she was a good ten minutes behind him, telling her how he'd been about to come back down to look for her. And she just gazed up at him, not replying, which unsettled both of them. The way she felt, well, it was almost as if he'd failed her by not being the man she'd just left at the bottom of the path. How tentative he was in contrast, how colourless! *Martin* wouldn't have been bothered by a ten-minute absence. She'd had to look away from him, as if dullness was as painful to the eyes as brightness.

Which made her feel guilty and ashamed and afraid of what she might say when she finally *did* open her mouth.

In gestures as much as words, she excused her strangeness by being out of breath from the climb and to her relief Adam swallowed it. She didn't mention the incident on the road below. He had his own fascination with Martin Sale and she didn't want him making something of it that it was not— bad enough that she should be in danger of doing that herself.

And so she dropped out of the trail. With the sun burning feverishly above, she waited on a seat shaded so heavily by pines the sky was all but screened from sight. For a while she just sat in her usual way, coming to from her self-hypnosis every so often to note the variety of tree life—as well as the pines there were oaks, beeches and hollies—or to wonder if she was going to be able to resist looking at the photos again. And then she did something new: she took from her bag a small hard-backed notebook, the spine of which was still stiff, the pages unmarked. Not troubling to fish for a pen, she opened the book and stared down at the white pages. Though she was off the beaten track in a relatively unpopulated park, she looked from side to side, for it was on her mind that she would want to hide the notebook if Adam were to approach unexpectedly. She wanted this to be just for herself, even while it remained nothing more than an idea, even while there were still no words.

*   *   *

There was one day, one whole day, of normal, innocent joy. And they got to experience it in comfort, too, because they were given a hospital room of their own—a rare treat in an NHS maternity unit. Ironically, the special treatment was for Ginny's benefit, not the baby's. She had suffered traumatic tearing during the birth and had lost enough blood to require a transfusion; the staff wanted to keep her on an IV and away from any colds or bugs going around, monitor her while she built up her strength. She wondered sometimes if they would have noticed what was wrong with Isaac earlier, early enough, if it hadn't been for her getting all the attention. They said not; they said that what happened was inevitable from the moment he was conceived. And had it been spotted earlier, even as early as in one of the routine ultrasound scans, there would have been no happy ending, only a decision to be made about termination.

But that one day . . . if she was sure of anything

144

in her constantly shifting state of mind, it was that there would be no day more precious as long as she lived. She hadn't slept much in the night and had fed Isaac just before dawn, but she still woke up at about the usual time, seven or so, and there he was. There he was! Lying in the little plastic crib to the left of her bedside, all wrapped up, his sleep deep and sweet. When he woke to feed again he made eye contact with her straight away and it felt like something so pure and essential, like a cub memorising the markings of its mother's coat. Already, they could have picked each other out by cry alone. As he fed, she kept saying, 'I love you, I love you,' over and over again so it would be the first message to be imprinted on his brain, all the while supporting his tiny skull in her palm. She remembered thinking, all that religious nonsense from Adam's mother about a baby being a blessing, a gift from on high, and it turns out they were right! Her conversion was instant, if not to God Himself then to Isaac, to the faith between mother and child.

Then the hospital came fully to life around them and Adam arrived. He gave Isaac a cuddle and took some more photos of him. He stretched out beside them on the narrow bed. Then he took Isaac to the window, began pointing out the London streets below.

'This is the greatest place in the world to grow up,' he said. He was thinking of his family, too (what influence they had had on them, that she should have a presence in both their thoughts on a day like that). Karen and Samantha said you should move out of big cities when you had children, but all their advice about school

145

catchments and proper swimming lessons still seemed too far in the future for them.

It was hot in the hospital and they weren't allowed to open the windows. The food was unpleasant. Ginny began to think about getting herself discharged. In spite of being physically depleted, she wasn't scared to look after Isaac without the help of the midwife and nurses; on the contrary, she longed for it to be just the three of them. The nurse said she would see what they could do in a day or two. They had more tests to run on her; she was not to forget that she was still being cared for in her own right. 'You need to be strong and healthy to keep *him* strong and healthy.'

That was what they said, that was really what they said.

They had no visitors that day. Adam was holding everyone off on the grounds that she wasn't up to seeing people yet. She'd heard the chatter and smelled the excitement from the main ward and she had to admit he was right. She heard him tell his mother that she was weaker than she realised, that adrenalin was still running the show single-handed. He told his mother she could come the next day, she and Karen and the others.

But by then the nightmare had begun.

She still wished she'd been able to take Isaac away from there, even if it had been for just a little while. She wished she'd been able to show him his home.

*   *   *

'Have I been ages?' Adam asked. He held his

guidebook to his chest, still open on the relevant page and with his thumb stuck inside it for a bookmark.

'I don't know. My watch is . . . I don't know where. Maybe ages, yes.'

He sat beside her. 'It's *really* interesting. Absolutely incredible how much money they used to spend on this Madame Tussauds stuff! And you can really tell the periods when they had their budgets cut, as well.'

'Hmm.'

'It's worth remembering that the vast majority of the pilgrims would have been completely illiterate, of course.'

'Oh.'

There was a silence, one of the easier ones of the day so far.

'Have you been OK?' he asked, solicitously.

'Yes,' Ginny said, truthfully. 'I've been . . . thinking. I was just—'

Eagerness caused him to interrupt for he'd seen the notebook. 'What's that?'

'It's a journal.' She might have said it was a cure for cancer the way his face changed. 'I haven't written anything yet, but I will, I think.'

'You mean . . . a journal about Isaac?'

She nodded.

'But that's fantastic!'

The word was so wrong she couldn't keep her eyes from wincing at it and, seeing this, Adam corrected himself. 'Well, that's a really positive step, Gin. Healthy.'

Her second wince was fainter, faint enough, perhaps, for him not to have noticed. It concerned her that her physical rejection of him was extending beyond his touch and to his speech. 'It's nothing yet. But I want to do it on this trip. It makes sense to use the time.'

She knew he would think that it was their discussion that morning that had inspired this development, and he'd feel better knowing some good had come of the row. She also knew he wanted to ask her if he might be allowed to read the journal when it was done and was grateful when he didn't. She was relieved he didn't bring up the letter again, either, the one he'd written to Isaac before he was taken away from them and which she'd been adamant she didn't want to see, much less sign.

'I'm sorry about earlier,' Adam said. 'This morning. I should have been more sensitive.'

'I'm sorry as well.'

'We mustn't fall out.'

'No.' Still, she couldn't bring herself to tell him about running into Martin Sale, even though she knew that to conceal it was pointless since the story was sure to come out one way or another, but at that moment, when she'd been feeling quite peaceful, enjoying the cool woodland around her and being visited by memories that fell on the 'before' side of her tragedy, she couldn't bear to create a new reason for him to fuss over her.

'Shall we get a coffee before we go down?' Adam said. 'I noticed a place just back by the entrance that looked quite nice.'

'OK.'

They walked together quite contentedly. Passers-by might have taken their subdued expressions as the natural result of their pilgrimage. On their way they passed an

148

observation point where Adam stopped to take photographs of the view. Putting his camera down, he lingered for a moment, his elbows resting on the wall. He looked quite transformed, Ginny thought, his face livid with the beauty of what he saw, as if the lake had settled there at the foot of the hill just for him, strong and whole and alive.

*   *   *

Later in the afternoon, when Adam was inside resting (he said they'd been over three hours up on the hill, though Ginny would have guessed at twice that) and she'd been left alone in the garden once more, she saw Dom Sale approaching from somewhere beyond the horse chestnut trees. She had yet to discover what lay in that direction, the grounds of another elite hilltop villa presumably; the two properties were divided by a lush stretch of larch.

He came to a halt on the other side of their fence, farther down from the gate than was natural, deliberately bypassing it, she assumed, in order to avoid being invited in too readily. She didn't say anything at first, eyes half-closed, waiting to see if he'd just planned a glance into their garden without expecting anyone to be there, but after he had hovered in nervous contemplation for at least half a minute, she decided that one of them had to break the silence.

She opened her eyes. 'Hi, Dom.'

'Ginny.'

'Is everything all right?'

It was a ridiculous question when everything so plainly wasn't. He was even more tortured-looking than she'd remembered from the previous evening, and paler, too, in the sunlight, as though anguish were keeping his skin from tanning. Not that she needed visual clues to begin experiencing those instant feelings of kindred spirit for him—she needed only hear his voice. She couldn't help it, right from the first encounter, before she'd even seen his face, her instinct had been to go to him and comfort him. What had Bea said to him? 'This isn't the end of the world, I promise you, however it feels now.' Ginny wanted to repeat that phrase to him now, the same phrase mothers murmured to their children the world over, until she felt him relax in her arms. And she wasn't a hundred per cent confident she could stop herself from doing so. (Maybe he sensed this, maybe that was why he kept the fence between them, to protect himself from her hunger.)

But it was he, she soon learned, who sought to make amends. 'I came to say sorry,' he said in a mumble. The awkwardness of his gaze, the rigidity of his stance—he didn't even touch the fence, as if he thought it might electrocute him—everything about his body language spelled the message that he wanted to keep this exchange brief.

'Sorry?'

'Yes.'

'Why?' Her head was still so full of Martin and the incident that morning with the taxi that she thought Dom must have been sent to apologise on his father's behalf. 'You weren't to blame,' she added. In the back of her mind, right in the most shameful recesses, she had the idea that if she rejected this apology by proxy, then Martin would have to come to her himself . . .

150

Dom was frowning. 'For ruining everyone's evening with my drunken ranting? I don't see who else's fault it could have been.'

'Ah.' So he was talking about the previous evening, the drinks party, already relegated to a single faded still in the unholy mess of her mind's archive.

At least she could *remember* it, she thought, which was something.

'You didn't rant,' she said, 'you just spoke your mind. I think it's good that you feel passionate about things.' *That was what the young were for*, she thought, already consigning herself, in her mid-thirties, to the side of the old. *I'll never feel passionate about anything again*, she decided, and, though the resolution was grim by anyone's standards, there was a certain comfort in having made any kind of resolution at all.

Over the fence, Dom was regarding her with a quizzical expression. How like Bea he was in feature and colouring—there was nothing of his father in his facial bone structure—but he was obviously much less adept at hiding his feelings than his mother was (he'd had no cause to until now, perhaps), and Ginny could read clearly the doubt in his eyes: he was thinking that she must have misunderstood him and this was frustrating him all over again. As the silence lengthened, she tried to work out what it was about last night he was really apologising for if not for the forcefulness of his opinions. It was obviously something unspeakable, which meant . . . which meant it must be the subject matter.

'You know about the baby,' she said, quietly.

He closed his eyes, slightly longer than a natural

151

blink, and though his hands didn't move, that small motion of the eyelids reminded her of someone entering a church and crossing themselves before God. 'Yes,' he said. 'But I didn't know last night, I swear to you. Esther told me just now. Otherwise, I wouldn't have said all that stuff. I was totally out of order.'

So Bea had told her elder daughter, Ginny thought, before Dom, perhaps even before she'd told her husband. What a gift to have that closeness with your grown-up child, especially a daughter. All at once the feeling descended on her like a foul, wet cloud, the knowledge of all she would miss in her future life, on top of all she had missed already, and without knowing why she reached for her memory of Martin that morning, of leaning into his strong body as he guided her to safety. He'd felt invincible, her bodyguard, her protector. It mattered not that he had also been the one to put her in danger in the first place.

'Well, I hope you *would* have said it,' she said to Dom, with as much brightness as she could muster. 'You mustn't think I can't sympathise with other parents, especially the ones you were talking about, the ones who aren't allowed to see their children as much as they'd like to.' This, in theory, was true; the problem was that in practice her sympathy was far too intense to be anything but damaging to its subject, and much too complicated by the anger she felt with those she perceived to not appreciate what they had, the parents she read about in the newspapers who used access to their children as part of a war against one another. But she did not want Dom to know this, any more than she wanted to damage him with the empathy she

152

felt for him. No, much as she sought to reassure him that he had not caused offence, she had no desire to re-open last night's debate.

In any case, he seemed content with her answer. Changing the subject and disproving her earlier point in one fell swoop, he said, with utter dispassion, 'Our boat arrives on Saturday morning.'

'Oh?' She realised he must mean their rental and they both looked automatically in the direction of the pier, only visible by the tip of its posts from Ginny's ground-level vantage point.

'Yeah.' Dom looked back, his stance marginally more relaxed. 'We wanted to get it earlier, but Dad insisted on this particular one and they've had to bring it over from Como.'

'That should be fun.' Before she could prevent it she had an image of Martin again, this time of him sitting opposite her in one of those long wooden gondolas she'd seen by the piazza, gazing at her as though bewitched. It was such a pure, romantic image she was confused as to how it could have emerged from her.

'It's a Riva,' Dom added.

'I don't know what that means,' Ginny said, apologetically. She expected to hear an explanation of how this type was the *ne plus ultra* of boat craft, but again he failed to enthuse.

'It doesn't mean anything, I suppose.' He said this with great world-weariness, as though it might *once* have meant something, but not any more. With his bruised eyes and his arms hanging long and heavy by his sides he was the picture of disaffection.

'I'm sure it's a beauty,' Ginny said,

153

encouragingly. She was starting to feel thrown off course by this meeting; it was a while since she'd been the optimist in a conversation. Amid her confusion she had a sudden insight that it *was* within her grasp to overcome her losses and become someone else, someone like Bea; the wise one, the protector, if not of her own children then of society's in general. She *could* fit into the natural order of things, even without Isaac. But the feeling passed rapidly, adding to her sense of disorientation. In an attempt to remind herself of her physical environment, she plucked at the pages of her notebook, laid once more in her lap, the lines still blank.

'I'd better go . . .' Dom murmured. But he'd noticed her fingers fidgeting and as he turned to leave he asked what the book was.

She decided there was no harm in telling him the truth. 'I'm supposed to be writing down my feelings about what happened, with the baby.'

His eyes widened fractionally. 'Wow.'

'I know.'

Remembering, perhaps, why he had come to find her in the first place, he roused himself enough to add, 'Sounds like a really good thing to do.'

She had no idea if he meant it or not, but at least he hadn't used Adam's word: healthy.

'Do *you* ever do that?' she asked. 'Keep a diary, if things are troubling you?'

The question didn't surprise him as much as she'd thought it might. 'Not a diary, exactly. More like when you make a list, you know, to weigh up the good stuff and the bad stuff. Sort your head out.'

'The problem is there *is* no good stuff in mine,' Ginny said.

They looked at each other. 'There's not that much in mine, either,' he said, morosely.

'That can't be true.'

He shrugged, and for the first time she had an instinct of what his secret might be, the news too awful to be broken to his father: he must be ill—properly ill, something life-threatening. Then she thought, No, Bea wouldn't keep that from Martin. I wouldn't keep that from Adam. It would be too much for a parent to bear alone.

Another silence yawned between them. Ginny waited for him to remember he was about to leave.

'Don't you want to do it then?' Dom asked, at last. 'Your journal?'

'I do, in a way. The problem is I don't know where to start.'

'Why don't you write that?' he said. '*I don't know where to start*. Then you've started.'

He said this with such simple resolution Ginny felt she had been given a glimpse of what he must have been like as a little boy, back when everything was logical and there were no irregularities, back when his parents really could protect him from the world.

She nodded. 'That's a good idea.'

'Cool.' He chewed at the skin around his thumb. 'I'd really better go,' he said, a second time.

And she didn't argue, though she felt sure he had no particular engagement to meet, just as she did not.

CHAPTER ELEVEN

THURSDAY

Self-confidence though she had in spades, Pippi was uncertain enough of her target on this occasion to feel a quick rush of triumph when she saw Zach waiting by the café at six o'clock. She had already decided she would not seek him out at his hotel—that looked far too desperate—but as it turned out she needn't have worried because there he was, one hand in his pocket, the other smoking a cigarette, just like the song her mother used to listen to. And people were looking at him: passers-by, customers at tables, some openly, some more discreetly. That was the mark of true beauty, she knew. People dropped their masks around it, they couldn't help themselves.

He wanted to set off straight away for the villa. 'Come on, then, show me this folly of yours . . .' He made it sound excitingly risqué.

She beamed at him. 'OK. *Prego, signor* . . . Have you had a good first day?' she asked as they set off across the cobbles.

'Yep, I think I've got the lay of the land.' That sounded pretty risqué, too.

'And you said you're travelling alone, not meeting friends while you're here, then?' She'd prepared this question—one of many—during an afternoon of excited anticipation.

'Not anyone I already know,' he said, which made her think. What the hell, she decided, that's good enough for me.

156

Oh, it was so romantic strolling down via Olina at that time, and against the tide, too, so you could see the faces of all the couples coming out of their hotels and heading for the piazza, hand in hand, as if their lives had only at that very moment begun. Not normally given to such yearnings and certainly not having felt any in Orta until now, Pippi wondered if this was female intuition at work—or, better still, Cupid!—and if Zach might turn out to be more than a holiday fling.

Ever the pragmatist, she reminded herself that she hadn't got the fling in the bag yet.

'This town is a honeymoon favourite,' she told him. 'Did you know that?'

'I'm starting to appreciate the fact, yes.'

'And for the weddings themselves. I've seen four completely different brides so far today.'

'Pleased to hear it's not just the same one, then. Wouldn't that be polygamy?'

She picked up his humour at once, catching his slow smile out of the corner of her eye. 'I think it would, yes. Oh, and old people, too. Have you seen them all?'

'Why, are they lined up somewhere for our inspection?'

'I hope not!' She giggled, enjoying herself, ready for something bolder. 'That's why it's so cool to have come across *you*. You're not the usual type.'

'I'm glad to have such rarity value.'

'Oh, you do, believe me.'

He laughed, casting an appraising look her way. This was going so well already, she thought; what on earth had she done to deserve luck like this? Talk about inspection lines—if every man in the region were paraded before her, he was the one

157

she would choose.

'The house is a bit out of town,' she said. 'I'm taking you the lake way. Have you done the waterside walk yet?'

'No, I haven't come this far before.'

But it turned out he was one of those people who had a compass in his head because he anticipated each turn, however sudden, as though he'd walked the route dozens of times before. Or perhaps he was just responding to *her*, shadowing her every move like a dancer. When they reached the water, she noticed he walked very close to the edge, giving her the less hazardous wall side. 'Hey,' she said, 'this is like in the Middle Ages, when a gentleman walked on the kerb side in case the woman got her skirts dirty.'

'Oh, right,' he said, grinning. 'I'm not sure they had kerbs then, but I get what you mean.'

Of course her comment had partly been a ruse to get him to notice her clothes. Though she said so herself, she was looking pretty hot this evening, having chosen one of her favourite ensembles—an asymmetric blouson top in pale yellow chiffon and a fringed skirt in petrol blue. She'd kept off the sunglasses, thinking it might be time for him to see her eyes, which were her best feature, a bright black-brown and long-lashed, if a tiny bit too close set for her liking. He still wore his, though, which made her think she might have been premature. It felt a bit like having all your clothes off when the other person was still dressed (now she came to think of it that was quite sexy too).

It also made it harder to check him out without him seeing. Sneaking a couple of sidelong glances, she admired for a second time his attitude of

158

elegant dishevelment. She knew from her own efforts that this was a hard look to achieve artificially (it was one thing to look as though you'd slept in your clothes when you really had, and had the odour to prove it, but quite another to pull it off having just showered), maybe even impossible, despite the attempts of Sale and its competitors. She knew without asking that Zach would never, ever wear anything by Sale, and just imagining him in her father's embarrassingly faux-distressed Hendrix jeans made her blush under her tinted moisturiser.

Just as well Dad wouldn't be around this evening, then.

As they walked, she kept the pace as slow as comfort allowed, not wanting to share him yet, and he seemed happy enough to drag his feet. Orta was *so* beautiful all of a sudden, the mountains smoulderingly close, the evening sun making everything silver and gold. The light would have been perfect for one of those fashion stories you saw, the retro ones where they backcombed the models' hair and put all the eyeliner on to make them look like Sophia Loren and Brigitte Bardot, and all the men were like Jude Law in *The Talented Mr Ripley*. That had been a defining moment in Pippi's life, seeing that movie when she was nine years old (her mum had needed a bit of persuading on the matter of its 12 certificate). It was when she'd seen how she wanted her life to look when she grew up—and a beautiful boyfriend was a key part of the package.

She asked Zach if he'd seen the film.

'No,' he said, 'but the book is cool. She's an amazing writer.'

'Really? I'll have to get hold of it.' This was getting better and better—they were practically in a book club already. Next stop: soulmates.

'It's pretty unsettling,' he added.

'Oh, but so glamorous!' Pippi exclaimed, and he laughed at that. He began to tell her of an earlier French film adaptation of the same novel, his voice getting all hoarse and intense. Whenever he paused, his lips came together in a pretty bow shape, its softness at odds with the rough bristle above the top lip and on his chin. She very much hoped that by the end of their time together this evening she might know how the combination *felt*, as well as looked.

'So did you study English at university?'

'English and History. You?'

'Fashion.' She took a breath. 'I will after my gap, that is.'

And there was no reaction, no broken step, no sudden excuses; he just murmured, 'College seems a long time ago now,' and Pippi thought, once more, *Just as well Dad won't be around.*

Far sooner than she would have liked, the boathouse came into view, marking the end of the lakeside trail. 'When you get to this point you either have to turn back to the village or go up this footpath here. The traffic road at the top takes you to the car park.'

'I'll remember that,' Zach said.

'Not you, silly. You're with me!'

She hadn't meant it to sound quite so presumptuous but he just shrugged and said, 'Lead the way.'

They turned into the passageway behind the boathouse, walking in single file, right up close to

160

the bones of the old building, and he asked, conversationally, 'So this is where that other couple's staying? The one you told me about?'

'Adam and Ginny, that's right.'

'Adam and Ginny,' he repeated after her.

'The Trustloves,' Pippi agreed.

'Are they in now, d'you think?'

Pippi glanced up at the only window to the rear, whose blind featured a shell motif; the bathroom, presumably. 'Maybe. Hang on, no, they said they were going out for an early dinner. I saw them a bit ago, on my way out to meet you. I'm surprised we didn't pass them.' But catching the look on his face she saw she must really have captured his imagination with her opinions about the Trustloves and at once felt eager to offer something more substantial than this. 'Come and hang out tomorrow if you like and I'll introduce you. They're always out in their garden first thing.'

There was a faint furrowing of his brow, which she interpreted as acceptance (result!).

By now they'd emerged from the shaded passageway into the main garden and Pippi moved deftly aside to let him by, crying, '*Voila!* Or whatever that is in Italian!'

He stopped just ahead of her, gazing up at the main house. 'Wow, you weren't exaggerating, were you?'

'There wouldn't have been any point,' Pippi said, simply. As they began climbing towards the pink and green castle, she launched into the story of her mother having fallen in love with the property from a boat, of the prior claim of Berlusconi (or another) and her father's having moved mountains to wrestle the place from him for this special holiday. 'Everyone has their price,' she added, knowingly.

For every couple of steps climbed, Zach would turn and glance back at the lake and the boathouse; she wasn't sure if it was her story or just the beauty of the view but he seemed to have entered some temporary state of hypnosis.

'Pretty romantic, huh?' she remarked.

'Yes,' he said. 'Yes, it is. It doesn't seem real.'

The way he continued to turn back and forth, she couldn't tell if he meant the house itself or just everything about this situation, including her, in her yellow chiffon top and swishy fringed skirt.

'It *is* real,' she said, kindly, and then, a little embarrassed by the tenderness he'd inspired in her, added, laughing, 'and there's alcohol at the top of the steps to prove it, hopefully in the form of one of Mum's cocktails. Come on!'

It would have been amazing if they could have walked up the last steps hand in hand, especially when she saw her mother and Esther sitting at the table on the terrace, their heads raised at the sound of footsteps approaching. She'd said nothing to them of meeting a friend when she'd waved goodbye forty minutes ago and now, as they looked on curiously, she felt a certain pride in bringing the first offering (well, not including Adam and Ginny, but somehow they didn't count).

'Hi guys, I've brought a friend for drinks. What are we having?' This proved to be a rhetorical question because the other two were far too busy gawping at Zach to answer her.

He hesitated before stepping forwards for introductions, smoothly slipping off his sunglasses just as a gentleman in the olden days might have his hat. Seeing his face properly for the first time, Pippi felt her chest clench. He was way, way more attractive than he was with his shades on (a first in her experience: it was usually the other way around, well-chosen eyewear conferring mystique and inscrutability on the dullest of boys. One of life's greatest lessons, in her view). His eyes were grey, cast a sort of pale silver by the light, the same as the lake, and they were wide set, with long soft-brown lashes. What stopped him from being too pretty—for there was a limit, even for Pippi—was that bold jaw and cheekbones that were clean and sharp, like a Northern Italian aristocrat, or the sexy Fiat heir she'd seen photographed in *Vanity Fair*.

The hilarious thing was, as he reached for the hands offered by her mother and Esther, it was *he* who was reacting as if in the presence of intimidating beauty, not them. Pippi rolled her eyes to the sky, quickly getting it: Esther. Because her sister was not a direct rival, she tended to forget how pretty she was in that natural, almost moral way some men liked. And she did look good this evening, Pippi had to admit, in a little pink vest and denim shorts, arms tanned, face freckled. No, this wasn't the first time a boy had reacted in this way and she decided to put him out of his misery before he fell too hard.

'Esther's gay,' she said, with just the right dash of theatricality to her regret, like she *hated* to be the one to have to break it to him.

'Esther?' Zach looked confused as he withdrew his hand from her mother's.

'I'm Bea,' her mother explained with a slow smile, 'Pippi's mum.'

'She means me.' Esther pulled a face at Zach.

'I'm afraid my sister finds it necessary to announce a person's sexuality at the first opportunity. I assume she hasn't known you long enough to discover your own predilections but, rest assured, when she does she'll be spreading the word.'

'Fuck off, Esther,' Pippi said, sweetly.

'Fuck off, you. Did she tell you what an erudite family we are, Zach? Back home our exquisite manners are known in three counties.'

'Girls,' Bea murmured, but Zach was laughing and Pippi could see that she wanted to, too. It was a Sale fact of life that their mother *never* told Esther off. Smiling at Zach again, Bea said, more to him than to the others, 'And anyway, we've already met, haven't we?'

He nodded. 'We have.'

'When?' Pippi cried, dismayed by this news—she had so wanted Zach to be *her* discovery. She turned to him, hiding her accusation with a particularly toothy smile: 'But you only arrived this morning!'

'We met a couple of hours ago,' he said, 'down in the piazza. I saved her from being run over.'

'You did?' Now Pippi batted her eyelashes at him, instantly re-conquered. So he was Lancelot in a biker jacket, cool. And *she*'d met him in the late morning, which meant she *had* been first, after all.

'Well, what a coincidence,' Esther said, her eyes bright with attention, 'because I was just telling Mum that Dad rang earlier from the airport and apparently *he* almost ran over Ginny today.'

'No!'

'It's true. Poor Ginny,' Bea said, in a voice that suggested this wasn't the first time she'd uttered the phrase that evening.

Esther turned to their mother, frowning her detective's frown. 'I'm surprised you didn't mention your accident when we were talking about Ginny's.'

'I was exaggerating,' Zach intervened, quickly. 'It wasn't an accident, exactly. Your mother's number was never really up.'

'I was just being a bit absent-minded,' Bea agreed. 'I forgot about the local cars being allowed into the square.'

'Oh, you said "run over",' Esther said, 'so I thought—'

'You're always so literal, Esther,' Pippi cut in, mocking. 'Can't you allow us a bit of poetic licence? Where's Dom, anyway?' She'd only just noticed her brother was missing. That was another good thing about having Zach about: he'd make up for Dom's poor form this holiday.

'Upstairs having a bath,' Esther said. 'He'll be down in a minute.'

'Is he still being Mr Killjoy?'

'Pip,' her mother said, in the same voice she'd used ten years ago when she'd warned her not to show off in front of guests. 'I don't think that's very fair.'

'Why? He *is* a killjoy.'

'He's just preoccupied, that's all.'

'Well I don't see what about!'

During this small family squabble (the Sales rarely modified their banter in front of guests; if anything, especially if Pippi's father was around, they exaggerated it), Zach had retreated a few steps across the terrace to take in the full height of the house, minaret and all. 'This place is incredible,' he said, dividing his focus politely between their three faces. He settled on Bea. 'I've never seen anything like it. Well, maybe in Istanbul or somewhere.'

'But not in Italy,' she agreed. 'It's a genuine one-off. The owner was a cotton trader who made his fortune in the east. It really is like something from a fairytale. Would you like a quick tour inside? I need to go in anyway.'

'Sure. Yes. That would be great.'

'Take this with you,' Esther said, handing him a glass of some kind of *granita*, which Pippi hoped had plenty of vodka in it. 'Whatever she says, you'll be hours.'

Zach took the drink and placed his sunglasses on the table. His wrist was smooth and his fingers slender and pale, making Pippi wonder for a moment about body hair (her preference was for it, but not to the extent of fur). 'OK. I'm all yours . . .'

And Bea responded with a look that said she was personally touched that he should indulge her like this. Seeing her mother's instant kindness to their guest, Pippi felt suffused with love for her, love and pride. For her age, she looked amazing, almost young. Pippi remembered a photo shoot there'd been when she was little, something for a newspaper supplement about glamorous mothers. The pictures were fantastic, Dad loved them, got the photographer to sort him out some extra prints, but Mum hated the whole thing. Pippi hadn't understood that, just as she hadn't understood her mother's gradual withdrawal from the Sale business, or her belief that she was needed at the school gate, at their desks as they did their homework, in the kitchen making their tea every

166

day. Of course Pippi liked having her there, but the point was what had she been left with, now they were all gone? Nothing but cookery courses and love affairs with weird houses.

Not that she was complaining about being brought to this one, not when she could see how impressed Zach was with it. She thought of her bedroom upstairs, the only one besides the master suite to have a four-poster bed. A shame that her mother's tour would probably only cover the ground floor—a glimpse of Pippi's chamber might have whetted his appetite.

'Pipster? You want one of these as well?' Esther held up the jug, slippery with condensation, and poured her sister a glass. She moved the plate of olives closer to her, too (her way of apologising for her earlier meanness). Acknowledging this with a gracious nod, Pippi took an olive and busied herself trying on Zach's sunglasses. She enjoyed the warm smear of them against her nose, knowing they'd been on his face all day long. Ignoring Esther, she looked out to the lake below, already a shade paler than ten minutes ago. When I fall in love with a villa in Italy, she thought, I won't wait for my husband to rent it for me for two weeks one summer. I shall buy it.

And with this happy thought she settled into her seat to wait for Zach to come back.

CHAPTER TWELVE

FRIDAY

Friday morning brought fresh blue skies, fresh lapping waters and fresh Pippi Longstocking. Now the seal had broken, there was no avoiding her, it seemed to Ginny. She'd stopped by for a chat yesterday afternoon en route to the village and here she was again, standing at the gate, full of energy and promise, like a cheerleader with a new routine to perform—or at least with a new costume to parade. Even in London Ginny had never seen anyone dress for the evening when it was eleven o'clock in the morning—not unless they were returning home *from* the night before. Yesterday, it had been a floor-length skirt that swept silkily across the grass as she'd proceeded towards them; today it was a short slate-coloured dress that wrapped around her like a long bandage, with a constellation of silver stars embroidered across the bust. And always there were accessories: a beaded hat, a sequinned bag, chains laden with charms, and lipstick, too, applied properly with a brush, the way women did when they wanted to remodel their mouths completely. Goodness knew what time she got up to get all of this done.

Today the girl carried her high-heeled sandals in one hand and had some sort of ball under the other arm. And she was not on her own, not this time, for shuffling to a halt alongside her was Dom—by yesterday's standards, he looked almost cheerful—and a second man Ginny had not seen

168

before. Judging by the broad beam on Pippi's face, it was plain she was feeling in her element to have this handsome pair in tow, and for a lovely brief sunburst Ginny remembered how it felt to be young and popular, not knowing what life held in store but feeling fairly certain it was going to be good. Seeing the three youngsters made her think about the gap in years—almost ten—between Adam and her, something she hadn't considered in a long time.

She realised she must have been staring, quite frozen in her thoughts, because Pippi was calling out to her as though to a small child: 'Ginny? *Ginny?*'

'Oh, hi, Pippi.'

'You had me worried for a minute—it was like you were in a trance! I was going to ask Adam for the magic word!'

'Sorry, I was miles away.' The warmth she had felt drained in an instant. Whereas Dom invoked (what was left of) the better part of Ginny, for some reason his younger sister had begun to stir only the worst. She wished Pippi were not here quite so often. She wished she would wear normal clothes, she wished she would just *go away*.

Straining forward in her wicker chair, she called out: 'Adam! We've got guests!'

Only at the sight of Adam at the top of the steps did Pippi actually release the latch and lead the others into the garden. Ginny saw that it was not in fact a ball that she held but a large roundel of bread. Sensibly the girl offered this directly to Adam, fearing perhaps that Ginny might become deranged and throw it into the lake.

'Mum and Susanna sent you this. Have you ever

tried *dolce pane*? It's got figs and walnuts and raisins, oh, and the secret Casa Mista ingredient: chocolate! It's amazing with coffee. I could eat the whole lot all by myself!'

'Then you must stay and have some,' Adam said, smiling. For a moment Ginny thought he was going to lean forward and kiss the girl on the cheek, but then she saw he was merely reaching to push the gate shut, an act that made the little garden feel very crowded, even with the open stretch of water beside them. 'Come and sit down. I was just making some coffee anyway.'

'Fab,' Pippi said. 'I was going to say, you have to eat it while it's still warm or the chocolate will harden and it will be a totally different experience.'

Only Dom looked unconcerned about saving the baked item from so careless an act of God. The other boy had yet to say a word, having come into the little garden after the two Sales and followed Pippi's exchange with Adam with an expression of slight caution. Well, Ginny used the term 'boy', naturally thinking of him as such, but of course he was a man, being at least Dom's contemporary and probably older—it was hard to tell without seeing his eyes, hidden as they were behind a pair of triangular reflective lenses. He was skinny and restless, dressed in narrow black jeans and a long-sleeved shirt, oddly wintry in the building heat.

Though introductions had not yet been made, Adam hurried back up the steps to tend to refreshments, leaving Ginny to watch helplessly as the others dragged stools to her immovable spot, exactly as if they were visiting a patient in hospital.

'This is Zach,' Pippi told her, indicating the newcomer. 'Zach, this is Ginny. And that was

170

Adam. Can we smoke?' she asked her hostess.

Ginny nodded, half-thinking she might ask Pippi for a cigarette for herself—anything to get her through this impromptu little tea party—but Adam's reaction would be sure to be so humiliating it wasn't worth bothering.

Pippi lit herself one, offering the pack to Zach, who shook his head. 'God, you're good,' she drawled. 'I can't speak in the morning without nicotine.'

'We'll have to block your supply, then,' Dom said. 'Finally, the solution to a lifelong problem presents itself. And so simple!'

'Ha ha,' Pippi said. Despite her sunny mood, there was an edge to her voice when she spoke to her brother. He hadn't been invited, Ginny intuited, he'd tagged along for reasons of his own. And her first impression had been right: he *was* in considerably better spirits today—perhaps something to do with the arrival of this Zach character? But it was hard to believe that an injection of new blood was enough to rescue him from so profound a gloom. It occurred to her that it was possible he found being here with her, at the very epicentre of misery, helped put his own troubles into perspective. Where could *she* go, she wondered, for the same comparative effect?

'So . . .' Adam had returned with a tray of coffee things. 'Who takes what?' He began serving coffee into the little cups. There was no plate for the bread, so he placed it on the stone table to slice it.

'Like a sacrifice,' Zach said, giving a chuckle low in his throat.

Adam looked at him as if noticing him for the first time, which it occurred to Ginny might actually be the case, so focused on Pippi had he been when the group had arrived. 'I don't think I've met your new friend?'

'This is Zach,' Pippi said. 'Sorry, you missed introductions. Zach, this is Adam.'

There was a pause as the two men eyed one another. Zach's fingers rose to his sunglasses, he looked as if he might be about to take them off, but then he decided against it and lowered his hand once more. Ginny found this curiously provocative. *It's like he's masked*, she thought.

'Where are you from, Zach?' Adam asked.

Zach cleared his throat. 'Er, I live in Bristol.'

'A friend of Dom's from university?'

'No, no, though we were both there, it turns out. But at different times.'

'I see. Mates from somewhere else, then?'

Adam was like an old family friend, Ginny thought, making all the polite prompts, all the right links. She knew she should help pour the coffee and offer the sugar and ask the polite questions but she had not got the energy. It was all she could do to reach out for her own cup and hold it steady in her lap.

'We just met,' Dom told Adam, bringing an end to the rather dry Q&A. 'Yesterday.'

'*I* found him,' Pippi said, proudly. 'He's our new friend and he's amazing. He knows *everything*.'

Zach shrugged in amusement, apparently already adept at taking Pippi in his stride. 'I wouldn't say that.'

'No, it's true,' she protested, taking the coffee cup that Adam offered and passing it along the line to Dom. She naturally filled the role that Ginny ought to have taken, reaching out for the next cup

172

and making sure that this one went to Zach. Only when the men were supplied did she accept a coffee of her own, at once detaching the saucer to use it for an ashtray. That's going to stain, Ginny thought. She couldn't help being fascinated by the girl's combination of excellent manners and utter self-absorption. She couldn't imagine any situation that Pippi would not be able to make her own. 'He just told me all about the dragons and the saints and Mozart's broken heart. It's amazing stuff.'

'Nietzsche's,' Zach corrected her. He rubbed the back of his neck with his left hand. 'I don't know if Mozart ever came to Orta.'

'What dragons?' Ginny asked, a little out of sync.

'I told you about the dragons the other day,' Adam said, in mild reproach, but nonetheless he didn't protest when the others brought a halt to their chatter to address her query with a conspicuous gravity. They were treating her quite differently from Adam, whether by following his lead or by acting on her own clues, she didn't know, but pretty soon Pippi was petitioning Zach to tell his story again just for her. Make sure it's good, Ginny thought, darkly, since the lunatic has made a special request for it.

Zach was smiling at her, and casting a modest look of acknowledgement Adam's way (was it Ginny's imagination or was her husband looking ever so slightly miffed by the arrival of this outsider? It was that territorial strain of his again, she supposed). 'Well, I'm sure it's in all the guidebooks, but they say the island was infested with dragons until Julius turned up and asked the locals to row him across. Naturally they refused and so he got across using his coat for a sail . . .'

As he continued to speak, Ginny began to see what it was that he had that was evidently pleasing Pippi so greatly, besides the obvious outward glamour. Though he was quietly spoken, he had that same natural magnetism that Martin did, a way of absorbing others' attention and feeding it back to them. And he was clever, clearly, had a good memory for details. This was someone's son, she thought, suddenly, just as Dom was Bea's. How often she had wondered during her pregnancy how it was going to feel to see her son grow to be an adult, and at just the time that she began to age and weaken, making a natural protector of him.

But she would never know how that felt now. She would never have the experience of watching Isaac hold the attention of a group like this, orchestrate its intensity. For he *was* intense, this Zach, in his own way. Even with his wry comments and chuckles, he still had an underpinning of something very deep, even melancholy. Or perhaps that was an attribute she projected on to other people, perhaps in reality he was behaving— feeling—entirely typically.

'. . . He got wolves to help him build the basilica, so I guess the whole thing wasn't completely single-handed. And he had a brother, too, Julian, though some people think Julius and Julian were the same person.'

'Not that he went around pretending to be two different people or anything,' Pippi clarified, 'just that they spelled his name differently in some of the sources.'

'They are very similar,' Adam agreed, 'so that would be my conclusion.'

Zach said to him, politely deferring, 'Though it's always possible there could have been a brother anyway, who didn't make it into the picture?'

Adam didn't reply, but after a second or two Dom said, as though in agreement, 'I wish *I'd* had a brother.' And Pippi made a huffing sound, perhaps interpreting his comment to mean he wished he'd had one instead of a second sister. There was a peculiar silence then, with everyone looking at the next person in the ring, as though it had been choreographed in advance. Ginny looked at Pippi, who looked at Dom, who looked at Zach, who looked at Adam. Adam broke the chain, biting into his piece of chocolate bread for the first time. 'Oh, this is good,' he exclaimed, mouth full. 'You didn't say your mother made this herself, did you, Pippi?'

Pippi dragged on her cigarette. 'Her or Susanna. I'm not sure whose loaf you got.'

'Well, it's spectacular.' Adam turned to Ginny. 'We must make sure we thank Bea when we see her.'

'Yes.' Two days ago Ginny would have put good money on him dubbing Bea Lady Bountiful for sending down bread like this. Or Marie Antoinette—let them eat *dolce pane*, or whatever it was. But, no, he had been won over, just as Zach clearly had. The two of them were as charmed by the Sales as they were apparently expected to be. She wondered if the family had ever had a failure.

As they drank their coffees, she became aware of a prickling sensation in her stomach and chest, a kind of hunger, and it took her a few moments to identify what it was she craved: news of Martin. That overwhelming sense of need she'd felt when

175

they'd almost collided in the road, and her inability afterwards to resist comparing him with Adam, had turned out to be just the beginning of an unstoppable fixation on the man. Even though she had still kept the incident from her husband, it tortured her that neither Pippi nor Dom had made any reference to it, or to their father at all, for that matter. It suggested he had not even thought it newsworthy enough to report to them, it had meant nothing to him; a minor inconvenience in a day crammed with adventure. Then again, she supposed the fact that she had been found wandering across the road without looking where she was going was not such a scoop to anyone who'd spent longer than five minutes in her company.

Where had he been going, she wondered for the hundredth time, and why in a taxi and not the family's hire car? Off hunting for ideas, perhaps. Pippi had told Adam that her father collected ideas like the Apache collected scalps. He was always on duty, she said, especially in a country like Italy where design innovation was part of the fabric of the place. Adam had also mentioned a local town he'd read about that was said to produce the world's finest cashmere and Ginny had put the two together, picturing Martin touring the workshops, buying a whole pile of stock on the spot. He'd come back with gifts for them all, sending Pippi down with a blanket for her. She even imagined a little note: *G, I'm so sorry about earlier, please accept this gift, love M* . . .

But that was ridiculous. There'd been no cashmere shopping spree and no reason for him to offer her anything. And, besides, Bea was the one

176

who took care of those sorts of errands (hence the gift of the freshly baked bread?), not Martin. How Ginny feared the notion that was beginning to creep up on her, the notion that she wanted to be pitied, that she took a perverse pleasure in being the victim of the piece. That she wanted, in particular, Martin Sale's heart to bleed for her. Of all the comforts offered to her here—by Adam, by Bea, even by Pippi—it was Martin's arm around her shoulders that she craved.

The little party didn't linger long. There was a plan to show Zach the hidden beach Dom had found on a hike he'd taken the day before, which would pass the time until Bea and Esther returned from Casa Mista (and presumably made their lunch for them). As their guests left, Zach was the last to say goodbye and there was something about the way he hovered over the gate, not ready yet to close it behind him, that convinced Ginny that her instinct about him had been correct—there *was* something troubling him.

But whatever it was, he had no wish to share it with *them*, nodding to her as the latch clicked into place and turning to follow the others back up the path to the villa.

*   *   *

Ginny was right: Bea did take care of Martin's errands. She, if not the children, *had* heard from him about yesterday's near miss and she made sure she came in person to check that Ginny was suffering no unpleasant after-effects. In an echo of their first meeting, she apologised for not having found the time sooner; she'd been out with Esther

177

for her cooking course, then organising lunch for everyone and, well, it was like that here, wasn't it? The days were just slipping by. They'd all be back home before they knew it.

In contrast to her apathy of the morning, Ginny roused herself sufficiently to make tea and put some *biscotti* on a plate. They sat on the balcony of the living room, a concerted effort on Ginny's part to show she could move her limbs from the wicker chair below. In the hours since Pippi's visit, she'd become increasingly embarrassed about the girl's comment that she'd been lost in a trance. She thought she'd try doing what Adam did: pass herself off as normal in the hope that she might trick herself into *being* normal.

'You seem to have adopted another one,' she remarked to Bea. A little distance to their right, Dom and Zach were diving from the pier into the water. Judging by the heckling coming from stage right, Pippi was nearby, sitting in the shade of the trees perhaps.

'Yes, you could say that.' Bea watched the young men with obvious pleasure. Ginny supposed she was relieved Dom was finally having some fun. His body moved differently in sport, it had energy and grace; the heaviness she'd had no choice but to associate with him had vanished completely. He must forget, she thought, when he's concentrating on something physical, he must forget what it is that's been dragging him under.

That reminded her of another of Adam's and the grief counsellor's commandments: exercise. It *will* help, they said. It wakes the endorphins up again, reminds you you're alive. Right.

'He's nice, isn't he?' Bea said, of Zach. 'I can't

believe he's persuaded Dom to swim. I thought he'd never go in.' She turned to smile at Ginny. 'Pippi said you met this morning? She found him in the village yesterday.'

She made him sound like a stray animal, not a grown man. (Well, if he was, then there were worse families to rescue you, that was for sure.)

'Where's he staying?' Ginny asked.

'Oh, in some dive near the piazza, apparently. You don't always get the best deal in Italy when you're travelling alone. We asked him if he wanted to move into the villa for a few nights, we've got plenty of room, but he said no.'

Ginny checked her guest's face to see if she had heard correctly. Charming though Zach clearly was, and galvanising company for Dom as well as Pippi, she couldn't understand why the Sales should invite a near-stranger to move into their holiday villa, even for just one night. Was he sleeping with Pippi? If so, that was liberal-minded of Bea to the point of recklessness. Quite apart from the clear age gap, he could have any disease or hidden psychological condition. He might be a criminal, a fugitive of some sort. She wanted to ask what Martin thought of this invitation of theirs, but decided that would be out of line. (Where had all this self-righteousness come from, anyhow? Imagine if she'd said any of that aloud!) And, besides, what did *she* know? She didn't know the first thing about motherhood, did she? Or, perhaps it was more accurate to say that she knew the first thing, but nothing else.

'Just as well he refused,' she said, lightly. 'You said it was supposed to be family only this holiday, didn't you?'

Bea raised her eyebrows. 'Yes, well, it *was*. But that's fallen by the wayside now Marty's gone back.'

'Gone back?' It took immense will power for Ginny to stop herself from physically doubling over with the emotion this news caused in her: intense, disembowelling dismay. It was all she could do to keep the grief from her voice as she repeated, 'Martin's gone home? You mean back to England?'

Bea looked at her, surprised. 'Yes, didn't the kids tell you this morning? That's where he was going yesterday when he almost ran into you: to the airport for a meeting in London. He won't be back here for a few days, probably not till Sunday.'

'Sunday!' Still struggling to manage her reaction, Ginny hoped she didn't sound a tenth as devastated as she felt. She could sense her temperature rising as her body was revisited by that feeling she'd had in the road of wanting to go with Martin in his taxi, recognising it now as less a wish to be spirited away than an impulse to be absorbed into his greater strength. And now she knew where he'd been headed she was able to add the next frame to the fantasy: the two of them sitting together on the plane to London, she snuggled against him, that solid, muscular wall of his chest. In tune with her need, he would gather her closer to him, kissing her face through her hair, knowing he should not let go again until she was ready. The plane would be in the air until *he* said she was ready to land.

'What a shame for you,' she added with a little more self-control.

'Oh, I'm used to it,' Bea said, without a trace of

self-pity, and to Ginny's disappointment her tone also had the air of a final word about it. She was obviously not inclined to discuss her husband's shortcomings today and it was impossible to tell if she was concealing deeper feelings on the matter of his departure or if she simply had none. For her part, it seemed incredible to Ginny that Bea should not be able to read her thoughts, see her husband's name in Ginny's eyes, his face in her fantasies. Every new minute that the other woman did not leap up in anger and splash her drink in her face, Ginny felt gratitude.

The subject returned to Zach and his accommodation. 'The Italians are very odd about people travelling alone,' Bea said. 'They find it unnatural. I went for a weekend to the Amalfi coast once. They kept saying to me, '*Sola? Sola?*', as if it was the most bizarre thing they'd ever seen. Everyone I met had a theory about me. I was a bride looking for a venue for the wedding; I was just divorced after my husband had run off with someone else; I was a travel writer pretending to be a widow. I realised they'd been speculating from the moment I got in the taxi.'

She didn't say why it was she *had* been travelling alone. Having guessed she must have been extremely young when she'd married Martin and started her family, Ginny surmised the solo trip had taken place at some point during their marriage. Then again, given how unmoved she was by Martin's having cut short the family holiday for a business meeting, perhaps it was routine for them to operate quite separately. How different from Adam and her; the only nights they'd spent apart since marrying were the first two after Isaac

181

was born, when hospital policy had forbidden him from staying.

'My children have wills of their own,' Bea added, as if realising a fuller explanation of Zach's sudden attachment was necessary. 'Very strong wills. Even when they were younger I found it was better to respect their actions and decisions rather than fight them. That way I got to see more of them. I'm sure you could pick holes in the approach, but it's the one that works for me. Believe it or not, Marty is the one who comes down hard on them, when it's needed. I suppose in a way I've used him to do that.' She chuckled. 'The Italians would like the traditional arrangement of *that*, at least.'

Ginny felt a flare inside her as Martin's name was brought up again. All at once she could not bear to talk of Zach or Pippi or anyone else. She could hardly believe what she was doing, but she was suddenly changing gear quite fearlessly, fixing Bea with intense attention and speaking a set of urgent, probing words: 'Why didn't you leave him? I mean, that time you said you were going to.'

Bea looked taken aback, but only momentarily (how had the Sales come about this eerie self-possession of theirs? Ginny wondered. Had they learned it from shamans or had they been born with it?). Her mouth twisted prettily to one side as she considered her answer, while Ginny used the time to convince herself she wasn't prying, that this was partly why Bea had come down to see her, even if she didn't realise it herself. She *wanted* to talk about her marriage.

'Well, partly this holiday. Marty went to such lengths to organise it all for me. It would have

182

been cruel to make him cancel it, not only to him but to the children, too. They were sort of in on it.' Bea sighed. 'But not just that, there was another family thing that needed to be resolved. I realise now it's going to have to be dealt with properly before I do anything for myself.'

'The thing with Dom?' Ginny ventured.

Their eyes met. Bea's were very soft again. 'Yes, the thing with Dom.'

'He does seem quite up and down.'

'He is. He's always been quite, I don't know, introverted, hard to read, especially compared to the girls. Maybe even a bit dark sometimes. But nothing like this.'

'Have you . . . have you not been able to deal with it yet, then?'

Slowly Bea shook her head. 'Not yet. It's out of my hands for the moment.'

'Can I help?' The words came quite instinctively, from the person she used to be, and she wouldn't have blamed Bea if she'd thrown back her head and laughed. How could she, *this* Ginny, this useless blob, help someone so manifestly better equipped than she was for emotional dilemma? She could barely get herself through the day. No, she had nothing to offer a woman in Bea's position.

But Bea did not laugh. She gave another, deeper sigh and said, 'No. Thank you, though. I'm sorry to be so mysterious about it, Ginny, but it's not my secret to tell.'

Once again Ginny was both disappointed and relieved by the distinction. Even without knowing the facts, her empathy for Dom was abnormally acute; who knew how piercingly she'd feel his pain

183

if she was actually invited to examine its cause? 'And Martin still doesn't know the reason?'

Bea shook her head. 'As I say, it's hard to explain.'

'No, I understand,' Ginny said. And she sat on her hands, telling herself that she must not mention Martin again in this conversation, under any circumstances. If *she* couldn't understand this new obsession with him, then the man's wife most certainly would not.

Or, more painful still, Bea might be the one person who did.

CHAPTER THIRTEEN

SATURDAY

'Bea? There you are. Adam says we're ready to go when you are . . . ?'

It was Pippi's idea that Adam should be captain for the boat's inaugural crossing to Isola San Giulio, and it was Zach who was sent up to the house to tell Bea that the ship was ready to sail.

She was in the kitchen with Susanna, finalising plans for dinner. It was the third time Zach had appeared in front of her unexpectedly and the third time this had caused her to pause and take note of him. (If she was honest, she'd taken note a few times in between, too.) He was truly good looking, that was the first thing to say—to be got out of the way, really. And he was good looking in a way that she could only describe as *non-Sale* (not wholesome enough, that's what the casting notes

184

would say. Not believable as a husband). His appearance, his whole demeanour, was frustratingly indefinable, elusive. On the piazza, when she'd first seen him, he'd struck her as urbane and glamorous, conscious of his own power (the way he gripped her with his gaze, as if by invisible ropes!). But presented to her only hours later he'd been something else altogether, more like a mythical creature, half man, half fawn, rare and delicate.

And yet, despite the changeability of this, there was something quite familiar about him, too, which made absolutely no sense at all.

The second thing she'd noticed was the old-fashioned attentiveness of his manner; he exuded an air of chivalry that made her feel as though she were the object of a courtly seduction. Delusions of grandeur, she told herself. Living here, however briefly, had filled her head with strange ideas. Marty had given her her very own knights' palace and she was queen of it. Or, put another way, she was making the most of her last hurrah as the great Mrs Martin Sale.

But there was something more to Zach than both of these factors, something special about the atmosphere he had been able to create among the group so quickly. His arrival, on the very day that Marty had left, had a strange symmetry to it; it felt exactly right, almost as if they *needed* him. He fitted in with them and yet he improved them, too. In an effort to deconstruct this effect (goodness, she *had* spent time thinking about him, hadn't she?) she noted that in the few conversations they'd had he had said strikingly little about his own family or his life back in England. She wondered if this hadn't conferred on him a rootlessness, a perpetual present, as if nothing mattered to him except the place he stood and the people in his sight. Maybe he made everything more pleasurable because he took such easy pleasure in it himself.

Yes, however casually she'd spoken of him to Ginny, he had not passed her by, this new friend of her daughter's.

She picked up her hat and handbag from the kitchen table and turned to leave.

'*Ciao*, Susanna!' Zach waved goodbye to Susanna.

'*Ciao, Signor* Zach.' To Bea's amusement Susanna adopted a somewhat star-struck attitude when she was around Zach. She wondered if the Italian woman thought he really *was* famous in the UK.

He was smiling broadly as they hurried down the steps in the sunlight, keeping exact pace with her as if he'd had the benefit of a rehearsal. 'The boat's amazing, isn't it? Like something out of James Bond. I think Adam's fallen in love.'

'I'm glad everyone's enjoying it,' Bea said. 'Let's just hope we haven't run it aground before Marty gets to have a go.'

She wasn't sure, but she thought he raised an eyebrow at that, just a whisker, as if he thought she had meant something more significant, something that he alone could decode. Or, more likely, their nautical conversations were becoming a sort of running gag between them.

'Not quite HMS *Warrior*,' she added, playfully. 'But this is more practical, I think.'

'We wouldn't want to frighten the nuns by

186

turning up in a warship.'

'Absolutely not. God would never forgive us.' They'd reached the lawn and she could see the others at the jetty, clustered in and around the boat. 'What *has* Adam got on his head?'

'Er, it's a captain's hat. Pippi got it for him.'

And not just any old captain's hat, Bea saw, but one of the official ones, the same model the ferry operators wore. She hoped it wasn't a federal crime to wear one without the relevant permissions. 'Just tell me she didn't steal it,' she said.

'Just don't ask,' he smirked.

Inevitably, the way they bantered so easily, it reminded her of nothing so much as Marty and her—except in this case Marty would be the one wearing the captain's hat.

At the jetty there was a brief delay as they tried to convince Ginny to join them on the outing. Though with them on the pier she stood slightly apart from the melée, insisting she would not be coming. Much as she felt for Ginny, Bea couldn't help being relieved when it became clear the other woman meant what she said and wasn't simply looking for attention. Yesterday, when they'd had that cup of tea together, Bea had become painfully conscious of the strain of having to find exactly the right words, for Ginny was a person who *needed* you to say the right words. She listened minutely, she searched your phrasing for new levels of meaning, maybe even for some kind of epiphany. It made having a conversation with her feel like a serious responsibility.

Adam was different: it wasn't epiphanies he was looking for, or homespun wisdom, it was newness, something different for his brain to lock on to, if only for an hour or two, and that Bea could relate to—and supply—a whole lot better.

'No, really,' Ginny pleaded with Pippi, who was being rather shrill in her persuasions. 'And I don't see how we could all fit in there even if I did want to come.'

'But that's part of the fun,' Pippi exclaimed, 'the close quarters!'

'For you, maybe,' Esther groaned.

'One of us might have to sit on the sun deck,' Dom agreed, beginning a headcount. 'Who's least likely to fall in? Maybe you, Esther.' Absorbed in the business of the boat, he seemed closer again to his normal self, something for which Bea felt quite certain they had Zach's presence to thank, at least in part. And, in spite of Adam's appropriation of the captaincy, her son was demonstrably the one in charge, causing in her a quick charge of maternal pride.

'Well, if you're sure you won't miss Adam too much,' Bea said to Ginny, the first to capitulate, and the other woman looked gratefully at her. Bea could see that she longed for them to go, to leave her to her silence.

'Will you be OK on your own?' Adam asked his wife from under the beak of his hat. There was something longsuffering about the set of his jaw.

'Of course I will.'

'Do you want to use my laptop while we're gone?' Zach offered. 'You haven't got Internet or TV down here, have you?'

Bea noticed that Adam looked less than delighted by this idea, to the extent that she might have been moved to intervene had not Ginny been

188

so very pleased. 'Actually, that would be great, thank you, Zach. Will I be able to get a connection from here?'

'If you go up to the main house, you'll pick up the Wi-Fi,' Bea said. 'Susanna's there and the doors are all open.'

'The laptop's on a coffee table in the Room of a Hundred Ottomans,' Zach deadpanned, making Bea laugh, 'just across the way from the Master Opium Den.'

'Sit out on the terrace,' Bea told her, 'the shade is so lovely and cool there. Ask Susanna to bring you something to drink. Make yourself at home.'

'Thank you,' Ginny said, looking a little overwhelmed, 'that's really kind of you.'

And so at last they were all aboard, Adam at the controls and Pippi and Dom in close attendance (well, as Ginny had pointed out, they were *all* in close attendance), and the boat began to reverse from the pier in a dramatic curve that caused a sharp slap of water against the lake wall. Adam didn't know what he was doing, of course, but it was just a little caper on a short stretch of empty water, nothing could really go wrong and he certainly seemed to enjoy his stint in the captain's seat, which was the main thing.

To Bea's left, Zach was drawn into a conversation with Esther and so she tuned out, looking back dreamily to where they'd come from, watching the dimensions of Villa Isola shrink, its lines recede, its colours soften. Only from the water could the true apportionment of land in Orta be properly seen, for when you were on it, inside the little lanes and alleys, even down by the water's edge, the vast majority of it was completely hidden

189

from view. But from the lake you could see every one of those grand old villas, their hilltop perches and vast grounds, the snaking pebbled drives that connected them to the public roads.

Once more she remembered seeing their villa for the first time (she couldn't recall exactly the state of play that day, but she felt sure she must have been going through a better time with Marty for there was no bitterness associated with the memory); the dreams she'd had of pulling up at the little private jetty and running up the steps to the door, exploring every nook and stroking every surface, climbing up to the tower and feeling the height of it as something meant only for her, reaching out and touching freedom with her fingers.

The reality of it, when they'd arrived last weekend and turned the key in the lock, was so close to the original dream that she wondered if premonition might not be the better word for what she'd felt back then. Could it be possible that, in the intervening years of procrastination, she had known all along that this was where events would finally happen, the events that would change the course of their lives?

Yes, she thought, it *was* possible.

*　　　*　　　*

When they reached the island's landing-stage, Dom took the controls from Adam and eased the boat expertly into the mooring. A few berths along from them the public ferry was rocking itself into position, heavy with tourists, and as ropes were secured and gangways lowered Bea could feel the many eyes on them, on the elegant little speedboat and its luxurious fittings. A different time, a different life, she would have felt like something from James Bond herself.

Once disembarked, the six split naturally into pairs: Dom and Esther strolled off together without thought or consultation, while Zach made as if to fall into step with Adam, sensing perhaps that of all of them Adam was the least taken with him. Pippi got there before him, however, ushering Adam off with that air of VIP solicitude she'd learned from her father, hardly giving Zach a backward glance. Though she tried very hard not to worry about such things, Bea felt sure her daughter was deliberately favouring Adam in an attempt to keep Zach on his toes, a trick that might not have concerned her had Adam not been well over twice Pippi's age. The occasional snatch of phone conversation she'd caught between Pippi and her best friend Milla had told Bea that Pippi's feelings for Zach were not being reciprocated, though it was of course only a few days since they'd met.

She wondered if she'd played such games at this age; she supposed she must have done. These days, she didn't think much of her life before Marty, the boys she'd been with in her first two years of college. It might benefit her, she thought, to remember a little more how ably she'd filled her days, how determined she'd been to make a success of life in her own right, before she decided to join hers with his. Not that she'd had much choice in the matter, for his pursuit of her had been irresistible; having fallen for her almost on sight, he'd made it clear he would not rest until she agreed to be with him. (And so she had. And still he had not rested.) You were subsumed at a young age, her friend Patricia said, but it was a word Bea disliked—it had the same feeling as *drowned*.

The little basilica of San Giulio was right by the jetty and the natural route took tourists straight to its heavy wooden doors. 'Shall we go and look inside?' she said to Zach. 'It's only tiny, if I remember.'

Ahead of them, she heard Pippi say to Adam, 'Best to get the culture out the way first, don't you think, before you start drinking? Then you can't beat yourself up for not having done it.' Her laughter was light and sunny, the sound of summer itself.

By contrast, Zach was earnest. 'There's supposed to be fantastic frescoes in here.' He took off his sunglasses and lifted his face to look—Bea had had a bit of a shock when she'd first seen those eyes, for they were an arresting feature by anyone's standards, large and pale and a little mournful—and in that one gesture of removal, he was transformed from invulnerable to vulnerable. This confused her. She was used to men being one or the other (Marty invulnerable, Dom vulnerable); it fascinated her that someone could be both.

Together they picked a path through the thronged interior, agreeing without consulting one another that they would not bother to queue for the crypt (virtually every last body from that overloaded public ferry now stood between them and the bones of St Julius), and by the time they emerged on to the empty lane they'd lost the other four either behind or ahead of them.

'Let's take our time,' she said. Adam had

192

reminded her that the stroll around the island was disappointingly short. 'They're not going to leave without us.'

As they walked, she felt she ought to say something to Zach about Pippi having abandoned him. 'Don't mind Pippi,' she said, lightly. 'For some reason she's decided Adam needs taking under her wing.'

Zach looked as if minding Pippi had been the last thing he'd been thinking of doing, which made Bea worry that she might have badly misread her daughter's desires (surely Adam wasn't the one who really *had* attracted her?). She watched as he studied one of the convent signs overhead. The English translation read: *If you can be yourself, you are everything.*

'Do you think that ever happens?' he asked her. 'Someone arrives on the island a fraud, but leaves his own true self?'

Bea couldn't tell if his question was serious or not. 'Well, the average length of a visit is probably about thirty minutes, so perhaps not. It takes longer than that to find yourself, surely?' Twenty-four years, she thought, her smile fading on her lips; that was how long she'd been with Marty, almost a quarter of a century. But put like that it became surreal, neat and rounded off, as meaningless as the words on the sign in front of them. 'It's a nice thought, though, isn't it? Instant enlightenment. People would pay good money for that.' Personally, she found the aphorisms both twee and intrusive. She preferred to look about at the lovely old flint roofs, the hidden causeways and ancient pebbled paths. 'Look how flattened the stones are. Just think how many people must have come this way before us. Imagine all the conversations, all the little human dramas.'

Zach looked down at the path and then back at her. When he spoke again it was with a choked abruptness that took her by surprise: 'Why didn't Adam's wife want to come with us today?'

Bea hesitated. As if in recognition of the seriousness of the subject, they had come to a halt, facing each other square-on. In the narrow silence of the lane, their stillness felt tense, intimate. She realised there was no way she was going to be able to evade his question and her first attempt sounded inadequate even as she offered it: 'Well, they've already been over here once, they came earlier in the week, so perhaps she didn't want to come a second time.'

But that was not going to cut it. Zach frowned. 'Is she ill or something? She just sits all day in that chair.'

'Not ill, exactly, no, but she's very low.'

'Why? Please tell me.'

Bea explained the Trustloves' situation as briefly as she could, finishing with a sigh. 'Oh, I feel as if I'm doing nothing but going around gossiping about them, which is awful. But somehow you need to know.'

Zach nodded. 'I'm glad you told me. I knew there was something very wrong.' He was quiet for a while and then he said, 'You sound as if you're the one who's taken them under your wing.'

She folded her arms, gripping her elbows with her hands, not sure why she was adopting so defensive a pose. 'Not really. I just think . . . well, I can't help thinking there's more to it than this one loss. I wonder if it's happened to them before.

194

Even Adam . . . I know he looks as if he's full of the holiday spirit, but he's just as broken as she is.'

'I thought that, as well,' Zach said.

'Did you?' And when Bea met his eye, he was looking at her with such great tenderness she felt as if it were *her* loss they were discussing, *her* brokenness. She hugged herself more tightly still, had to stop herself from stepping away from him, from all his intensity.

'Yes. I thought that the second I met them. They seemed as if . . .' He spoke with the same choked gruffness, struggling to find the words. '. . . They seemed as if they couldn't take much more. And yet they're in this amazing place. It wasn't . . . it wasn't what I was expecting.'

'Expecting?' Bea was puzzled.

'Yes, when Pippi first described them to me.'

He seemed so troubled by all of this that he reminded her for a moment of Dom, which instinctively made her want—need—to make things better for him, cheer the moment up as best she could. 'So you see, it's great that Pippi's stepped in. She doesn't know anything about the baby, she's just being herself and that's what people need in these situations. That's why she didn't warn you.'

Thinking she'd said too much (truly, it was becoming a habit), she began along the path again, and they walked the next part without speaking. Soon, the way narrowed and a feeling of confinement came over her, as if she was trapped permanently between these high walls, and the next time they came to one of the dank little passageways that cut between the buildings she slipped into it, desperate for the water's edge and a

195

fuller swallow of air. After a moment's wrong-footing, Zach followed and their feet were almost in the water as they stood side by side, blinking in the sunlight, straining forward to get a closer look at the loggias and balconies that flanked them.

Bea, instantly soothed by the open space of the lake and feeling a little silly for having rushed her companion off course without warning, gave him a sidelong smile and said, 'Who knows what illicit activities have taken place in these alleyways over the centuries.' She turned her face full to his, hoping he'd tell her one of his stories about smugglers or serpents, or at the very least make a comment about the gloriously crumbling architecture, but to her great surprise he didn't speak at all but moved towards her and kissed her. It was no split-second contact, either (though that would have been startling enough), but a kiss on the lips that kept on, and that she seemed to be taking part in. As her mouth moved against his it was like being transported backwards and forwards and sideways at the same time—she was herself twenty years ago, she was who she would be in ten years' time, she was someone from a different life doing things a different way; she was not Bea Sale at all but a stranger to whose responses she had no access. Inevitably, the result was a sensation of extreme giddiness.

When, at last, they broke apart, it was a relief to see that Zach looked as unnerved by what had taken place as she felt. His expression—flushed and glittering—even made her wonder if she had been the one to initiate this extraordinary leap, but when he said, 'I shouldn't have done that,' she knew it had been as she'd thought. *He* had kissed

196

her. But why?

'No, you shouldn't,' she said, quietly, the gentlest of admonitions in her voice, and she took a step backwards, feeling cold water creep through the sides of her sandals.

'I couldn't help it,' he said, and, to be fair, he did look utterly helpless. It was the news about Adam and Ginny, she thought. Tragedy made you reach out, especially to those who offered comfort, and if anyone offered comfort it was she—she exuded the stuff. Giving comfort, making people feel secure, even in the face of their failings and hers: it had been her life's work. That explained her part in the kiss, too, then. She'd just been thinking how easy he was to be with, well, perhaps her mind had simply got its wires crossed and confused it with 'easy to kiss'. But even as she thought all of this she knew it was just a convenient denial, a reflex; she didn't really believe it. Something else was going on here, something much simpler.

Then Zach said, in a terrific rush, 'I want to be alone with you, Bea, but it's impossible in that bloody place.' The way he gesticulated, vaguely, wildly, made her think he meant the world at large, though he of course meant the villa. 'There's always someone lingering about in an alcove or coming in with a tray of drinks. It's like a stage set, it's not real. I want you on your own, like this, where I know it's you.'

'What . . . what do you mean?' She could hardly keep pace with what he was saying, or understand him at all, for he spoke as though they'd known each other for weeks—months. But they'd only met two days ago and the attraction was supposed to be for her daughter, not for her. And yet, far from seeking to confuse her, he appeared to be deadly serious.

'I want you,' he repeated, and there was no emphasis on the 'you', no hint of correction. His voice, his expression, his stance: all emitted frankness, pure desire.

And there *was* desire, she could see that now. She'd been too overloaded with other concerns to register the symptoms. She'd mistaken it for fondness; she'd mistaken the enigmatic fascination of him for her interest in human behaviour generally. She'd studied him from the point of view of someone who no longer had proper feelings of her own (and particularly not any that might mirror her daughter's . . .) and yet she did have them, of course she did.

He was speaking again, in the same low, thickened voice. 'Come to my hotel later. It's pretty awful, but at least we won't run into anyone else there.' He added the name, its position by the piazza, as though this were a confirmed assignation.

At last, she found her voice. 'Oh, Zach, you know I can't do that. Let's just forget this, OK?'

He stood observing her with some of the same tenderness of ten minutes ago, when they'd been talking about Ginny. 'Is that what you do? Whenever anything interesting happens? You make yourself forget it?'

She didn't know what to say. Quite apart from anything else, she was rather guilty as charged. The kiss certainly fell into the interesting category and there was no question that she had an established history of sweeping trouble under the carpet. She looked imploringly at him, noting that he was only a little taller than she was in her heels, their faces needing to tilt only very, very slightly to fit together. To her astonishment, she found she was hoping for another kiss. *Exactly like the first*, she thought.

'Well, I refuse to,' he said, vehemently, and she felt his breath on her skin, wondered which of them had inched forward again. 'This is the last thing I expected when I came here and I'm not going to ignore it. Come after dinner. You *have* to.'

Even as her brain struggled to make sense of his words—this was the second time in the last half hour that he'd talked of his 'expectations'—her mouth raced ahead, betraying her. 'But how can I? What would I—'

He interrupted. 'Tell them you're going out for a walk, something like that.'

'But what if someone wants to come with me?'

'I don't know, put them off. I need to be with you.'

'No, Zach—'

But there was no sense in continuing because he had taken his mesmerising grey gaze and his hot, unfamiliar breath and moved from her reach, out of earshot, climbing back up the walkway to the main path, while she could do nothing but watch, her feet lapped almost to the ankles by water. At the top of the steps he was silhouetted against the sunlit wall of the lane and even just the shape of him, the solid figure with none of the details visible, felt powerful to her, the new centre of her present. She was amazed that she was able to find the memory in her muscles to remove herself from the water and climb the steps after him.

Neither of them spoke again as they completed

their circuit of the tiny island. At the jetty, the other four were waiting, relaxed and easy, unsuspicious. Esther and Pippi held bags containing purchases from the souvenir shop; Dom drank from a can of Coke; Adam was sliding a dog-eared guidebook into his pack.

'*Andiamo!*' Pippi announced, seeing them, just as her father would have if he were here, raring to go, ready for the next part of the adventure. Her eyes settled on Zach as if she had him exactly where she wanted him—one step behind, in her wake—which made Bea feel even more confounded by what had just happened. No one would ever guess, she thought, and she felt no relish in the deception that phrase implied, only the conviction of a true statement of the facts.

On the ride back, she felt his eyes on her again. Now he'd declared himself he seemed to be making no attempt to contain the force of his interest. Thank God, then, that the others were either busy with the controls of the boat or were gazing off across the water, their heads full of dreams of their own.

CHAPTER FOURTEEN

SATURDAY

Ginny ran a hand over the cool stone wall of Villa Isola, her fingers exploring the raised joins between the greens and terracottas of the painted pattern before finding the delicate fretwork below the window—so minutely done you'd think it had been carved from softest wood. Then she turned from the building and crossed the sunlit terrace to the balustrade. In front, rolled out at her feet just for her, was The View, and a plum version of it, too, probably one of the best to be had in the village. Four levels of manicured terracing shimmered slightly as they settled into place, leading the eye naturally to the thick fringe of horse chestnuts between lawn and water and to the quicksilver of the lake itself. From up here, only the inner right-hand corner of the boathouse was visible, the relative insignificance of the structure all too clear. It was amazing that the Sales had even noticed it on their first night, when Pippi had stumbled down to say hello (she'd made more of a journey than Ginny had appreciated at the time). You couldn't imagine grown men fitting inside a place so small, let alone believe that life-changing conversations might be contained within it.

She felt glad to be up here instead.

Having been out for an early walk that day, she and Adam had quickly gathered on their return that Martin's boat had at last been delivered. After racing around the lake all morning, the younger Sales and their inseparable new friend Zach were planning an excursion to the island. As sure as night followed day, Pippi had appeared at the gate with her customary show of bonhomie, dressed this time in the pale linens and wide-brimmed hat of Happy Valley.

'Please come!' she begged Adam. '*Please*. We *need* you. You're the only one who knows about the island . . .'

Ginny didn't point out that last time they'd talked about the island it had been Zach who'd been crowned the group's principal historian.

'. . . and you did say the other day how much you're *dying* to get out on the ocean wave . . .'

'I don't actually know how to sail,' Adam admitted, but Ginny could tell he was excited by the invitation. Their own investigations into taking a boat for any length of time had ended with the first glance at a price list.

'You don't need to know,' Pippi said, 'and you don't need a licence or anything. It's only a diddy little speedboat, look!'

Despite the girl's careless shrug (and Ginny's memory of Dom's lacklustre comments on the subject), even a fool like Ginny could tell the boat was some sort of design classic, with its sleek fibreglass body, aquamarine leather seats and metres of warm polished wood. Adam had admired it from the garden when it had arrived, evidently greatly impressed.

'And don't worry,' Pippi added. 'Dom will park it for you. I wouldn't have a clue either!'

Ginny wondered why she liked to make herself sound so stupid when she was obviously so extremely clever. The day before Bea had told her, without any semblance of bragging, that her youngest daughter was expected to receive the highest grades in each of her four A-levels, an achievement that, if realised, would easily eclipse the corresponding results of her siblings. Her choice of college, Central St Martins, though it delighted her father, had come at the expense of almost certain acceptance to Oxbridge.

'You go, I'll stay,' Ginny told Adam, though she wasn't entirely sure if she'd been invited in the first place. Just the thought of being crushed into those 'diddy' seats alongside Pippi and the others made her body clench with anxiety.

Now, on her own at Villa Isola, she was experiencing as opposite a sensation as the human body could expect: she was free-falling in the space and the light and the solitude. She was wondering if Martin would arrive back while the rest of the family was out. Far from putting a stop to her wild imaginings, as she'd told herself sternly that she must, she'd begun to expand them to include his perspective: Bea had finally done as she'd threatened and told him she was leaving him ('Why didn't you?' Ginny had asked her outright yesterday. How impertinent that sounded now—what had she been thinking?) and he had fled to London to consider his position.

He would already have been deep into the process of soul-searching when Ginny had walked out in front of his car, and the incident had set something in motion within him, the memory of it over these last days guiding him towards the realisation that he was as ready to let go of Bea as she was him. Almost knocking Ginny over was a sign, a message from on high, and when he came back to Orta it would not be to save his marriage but to rescue her, Ginny, to *cure* her. Being in love, they would want to live together, of course, and all the distractions of his wealth and status would work where Adam's more ordinary brand of care had only stifled. This was the change she yearned for: a completely new life!

Of course, all of this was pure, shameful fantasy, not worthy of a twelve-year-old, not to mention a grievous insult to both Adam and Bea. She put it down to the madness of grief; just another form of respite her mind had decided to try for size, along with anger and resentment and all that desperate, bottomless sobbing. Acting on such insane urges was the last thing she would do, not least because of the extreme kindness and consideration Bea continued to show her.

Lovely Bea. Had it been her imagination (everything else seemed to be, after all) or had the other woman seemed especially carefree today when she'd left for the boat trip, radiant in her Wedgwood-blue sundress and floppy white hat, laughing delightedly as she took her place on the wobbling vessel?

That kind of grace and spirit was so far out of reach for Ginny she might as well have been sitting in the gods at the Royal Ballet and admiring the prima ballerina on the stage below, the superiority of the spotlit star so manifest it rendered utterly worthless any feelings of envy the spectator might have.

*　　　*　　　*

Without being asked, Susanna brought a pot of coffee to the terrace table, as well as a plate of macaroons. In the Villa Isola kitchen, the baking continued apace, apparently.

'How are you, *cara*?' she asked Ginny, her expression full of kind significance.

'Fine, thank you.' They all knew, then. And yet they still went about their boat trips, their gourmet dining, their incorrigible storytelling. If life went on for everyone else in the world, then how could two people expect to resist its force? One person, she corrected herself. The other had already hitched his star to the Sale Holiday Express.

But she wasn't about to begrudge Adam his day in the sun. She knew that under his skin, behind his smile, he was still as desolate as she was. And any bitter thoughts she might have had about the others, they were wrong, plain wrong.

After sitting dreamlessly for a stretch of time that was, as usual, neither as long nor as short in her own estimation as it was by the hands of her watch, she opened Zach's laptop and turned on the power. Now that she had it in front of her, she didn't know what to use it for and, inevitably, the first site she thought to bring up was the Sale one. The connection was fast and at once the slogan announced itself: *Welcome to our Open House Summer!* The letters were loose and curvy, like the handwriting of a woman in a state of great excitement, and the words had been run across a family beach scene of dazzling happiness. She couldn't tell if the man in the old Mini convertible holding up the Union Jack was a younger Martin Sale or someone who looked a lot like him. Certainly, the woman by his side could have been Bea twenty years ago (or even a present-day Esther); she had exactly the same brown curls and heart-meltingly wide smile.

She clicked on 'Bea's Bestest', a selection of sundresses and pool accessories, none of which she'd seen Bea in, though she thought Pippi might have been wearing that woven silver belt yesterday. Nowhere she looked, not even in the company history section, did she find what she was looking for: a photograph of Martin.

Working her way through the various sections, she soon tired of the shots of Cornish rock pools and Suffolk beach huts, the model who looked like Martin sitting cross-legged on the roof of a pistachio-green camper van or stepping from a pod of the London Eye, the Esther girl gripping the hand of a gap-toothed infant or stooping to take a lick of its ice cream. It was relentlessly idyllic, so far out of reach as to be extraterrestrial.

Clumsy with so small a keyboard, Ginny must have hit a combination of keys she didn't intend to because a page sprang open on top of the Sale one, something previously saved from Explorer. It was a local map and directions to the villa from Milan Malpensa. This made her wonder briefly why Zach should have needed it: hadn't Bea said yesterday that Pippi had picked him up in the square? Then again, any one of the others might have needed the page for one of their excursions (considering the trouble—and, presumably, expense—Martin had gone to in order to rent the place, none of them seemed to spend much time inside it). Or maybe Zach was now inviting more friends to the Sales' open house?

Well, whatever Bea said, you couldn't accuse the family of not living the brand.

She closed the Sale site, then, after a quick scan of the British news, keyed in the password for her email. At once she was faced with the familiar column of unopened mails, messages of sympathy from friends and colleagues that she could bring herself neither to read nor acknowledge, and scrolled down to find the only name she wanted— Deanna Magnuson—the only message she knew she *would* open. Again. She clicked on the subject, 'Your family questions . . .', and began to read, not from start to finish, as she had the first time, but back and forth, picking out words and phrases and letting her mind supply the rest: . . . *feel so devastated . . . hadn't made the link . . . several miscarriages . . . eight months pregnant . . . doctors called it a miracle . . . you would be their only child . . . loved you dearly . . .*

Looking at the words again it was like taking a hammer to your own limb long after the first blow had shattered it irreparably, continuing to hit and hit and hit and see if there was any pain left to be wrought.

It was the email from her aunt in New Zealand that had filled the gaps her grandmother could not, not all of the gaps—she could never have that— but enough for her to know that she was *not* the blank canvas she'd presented herself as to the midwife, and that what had happened to Isaac, while it could never have been prevented, might at least have been predicted.

*   *   *

On the second morning he was not feeding well. He had also begun making little grunting noises she hadn't heard before and that didn't sound right. The duty nurse said she was sure it was nothing to worry about, but Ginny should mention it to the doctor just the same. Routine tests were planned for the morning rounds and there'd be an opportunity to talk to him then.

Mr Roberts arrived from his previous patient with the kind of harried briskness that made her wonder about hospital workloads and blunders made out of simple exhaustion, but almost as soon as he began touching Isaac his movements slowed

207

visibly. It was as if he was reminding his hands to take their time and do this properly. He used his stethoscope to check the baby's chest, then he repeated his actions as if he'd missed something vital the first time, all the while frowning quietly to himself.

'He's not feeding very well today,' Ginny said.

He glanced at her. 'What do you mean, not feeding?'

'Well, I don't think he's taken more than a few drops. He doesn't seem interested. But it's hard to tell, I don't know what normal is . . .'

She was about to take it back, worried she was making an unnecessary fuss owing to basic ignorance of breastfeeding, but Mr Roberts said at once, 'That is worrying. Especially with this breathlessness I'm detecting.'

'Breathlessness?' The sound of those three syllables caused an instantaneous mimicry in her own chest, a fast and shallow rhythm that, along with a pounding pulse in her head, made it impossible for her to hear her own thoughts. She wanted Adam at once, willed him to arrive earlier than the time they'd arranged. Already the consultant had called for the nurse and was asking her if she'd noticed any blueness or any limpness in the baby. The woman's attitude was different now, tense and alert, her watchful eyes not straying from Isaac's tiny form as the doctor continued to handle him.

'Yes,' he said, finally, 'I'm afraid he seems to be struggling a bit.'

From that moment onwards the only feeling Ginny had that was plainly identifiable was terror—first the terror of not understanding, then the terror of understanding. It was a pattern that would continue without relief, even during the short lapses of sleep her body insisted she took.

Adam arrived in time to hear the worst: theirs was not a healthy baby and a series of tests would need to be performed without delay. It was to do with his heart. Phrases like 'pulse oximetry' and 'echocardiogram' and countless others were being used, and there was a suggestion that they were lucky (*lucky?*) because this was one of only a handful of hospitals in the UK with the equipment to make the diagnosis.

That was when Ginny's relationship with time began to change: having for the last few days been governed by the regular beat of contractions and the steady pulsing of the monitor hooked up to both the baby's and her own heart rates, it now seemed to move irregularly, faster and then slower—sometimes it even disappeared from her awareness altogether.

Tests showed that Isaac had congenital heart disease: three separate, critical defects. He was transferred to the intensive care unit and prepared for surgery. The chronology became even more blurred after that: there were whole nights when Ginny didn't sleep, whole days when Isaac wasn't conscious. There were bewildering briefings on the two six-hour surgeries required, surgeries that looked like criminal acts when you saw the smallness of him next to all that towering, monstrous apparatus. Her perception of the hospital staff fluctuated wildly: one minute the gowned and masked figures looked to her like witches convened for a ritual sacrifice, the next they were angels of mercy radiating nothing but love and duty. They were her only chance, *his* only chance.

And all the time they kept saying they were worried about her. They kept saying to her, 'You're exhausted, you mustn't forget you're recovering from a trauma. Try to rest.'

She couldn't answer. There was not a drop of spirit left in her for herself. If she could have given Isaac her own heart she would have.

The defects had not been detectable in the ultrasound scans she'd had in the first and second trimesters of her pregnancy. The difference between not detectable and not detected had since been debated long and hard by Adam, looking at first for someone to blame. But his anger blew itself out; he didn't want to make a battle of it. Pretty soon he saw that refusing to accept was not the same as bringing back.

*   *   *

Aware of signs of life at the waterfront, Ginny shut down the laptop and returned it to the room where she'd found it. Zach had been right, it was quite a salon, filled with the most beautiful jewel-coloured sofas and floor cushions, rich red carpets on the chequered marble flooring and on the walls delicate oriental paintings that looked like they'd come from the British Museum. No wonder he was camping out here every hour of the day. This was a hundred times more fabulous than any hotel she'd ever stayed in. Standing in this room she even thought she could understand why Bea had fallen in love with the building on sight. It was entirely different from that simple, transparent, open-armed world of the Sale catalogue; it was exotic and idiosyncratic; with its hidden corners and secret alcoves, it was as if it had been designed specifically for whispered confessions of love and forbidden clinches.

How exciting that must feel for someone whose heart had not caved in on itself.

Slowly she walked back down the steps, reluctant despite herself to bring her time as lady of the manor to an end. To her surprise she saw that the party was out of the boat and in the water. You could see the smudges of their dark heads and the gleam of white skin moving in the sun. At first she couldn't tell who was who, but then, as she got closer, she made out Bea, her shoulders shapely and fit, a stronger version of the very slender Esther, who was a little way off, swimming with Pippi. Esther must have been tugging at her sister under the water, or splashing her perhaps, because Pippi was shrieking, the sound of her exhilaration slicing across the surface of the water.

Moving closer, Ginny saw Zach, treading water alongside Bea and Dom. He had the most extraordinary bone structure, like something from forties Hollywood; more than any of the others, it was he who looked as if he belonged in this playground for the privileged, he who did justice to the famous beauty spot. She felt ashamed of having thought of him yesterday as a freeloader, someone diseased or capable of criminal acts. What on earth was wrong with her? Quite apart from anything else, she should be grateful he'd fallen so easily into line with his hosts in accepting her misery for what it was, not allowing her to ruin their holiday as she was her own.

211

And then she saw him, striking out with joyful abandon, just as she'd pictured Martin doing that first time—was it really less than a week ago?—when he'd come striding along the pier with all that energy and purpose: Adam. He was perhaps fifty metres out before he turned back for the shore. Strings stretched within her, as if with every stroke he was separating himself from her, and yet she could see quite clearly that he was moving *towards* her. She felt suddenly rocked with grief, a new complicated kind, a kind she knew she couldn't begin to understand but must simply allow to pass.

Zach was the first to spot her and he raised an arm to wave. Bea did the same; even from this distance Ginny could see the friendliness in her face. Then they all saw her.

'Ginny, come in!' Pippi cried. 'It's bliss!'

'Yes, yes!' someone else called out. 'It'll only take you a second to get changed!'

'There's a spare bikini on the boat if you need it!'

As if she was going to step out of her clothes and stand naked in front of them! She noticed now their clothes, some strewn on the pontoon, others in a heap under the trees, including a bright splash of blue that must be Bea's dress—all, evidently, torn off in a great hurry. Adam, she knew, had not had his swimming things with him when he'd left; he must have been up to the bedroom to change.

She regretted coming down to the water. After an afternoon in perfect shade, the sun felt brutally hot on her head and the clamour of the Sales' voices deafening, suffocating. Other people's excitement worked differently on her now; in the

212

old days, it had been a virus passed happily from person to person, but now the sound of it, the smell of it, closed her airways, shut her down.

'Ginny, hello!' At last Adam swam up, his chest heaving as it emerged from the water, and joined the row of dark, glossy heads, father to Bea's mother in a family of beautiful aquatic creatures. 'Are you coming in?'

But Ginny just stood there, her discomfort impossible to conceal, until one by one they gave up on her and turned back to their swim.

CHAPTER FIFTEEN

SATURDAY

With Marty still in London, Adam returning to the boathouse to be with Ginny, and Zach deciding to go back to his hotel, dinner at the villa was a relatively flat affair. Then again, thought Bea, the Cirque du Soleil might have felt flat after the day she'd had.

'Have you spoken to Dad?' Esther asked her, as they began on Susanna's spectacular antipasti. There was easily enough for eight and yet she found she could eat almost none of it. 'When's he coming back?'

'I'm not sure. I left him a message on his mobile earlier and he hasn't rung back.' She hadn't liked to phone the office yesterday; though she didn't doubt that Marty would have made contact with Ed, if not have spent the whole day with him, there was still the outside chance that this crucial face-to-face with 'investors' was in fact something quite different, in which case his assistant Angela would express only astonishment at her calling. *But Bea, isn't he with you, in Italy?*

No, he was not in Italy, and now all sorts of unscheduled events were taking place in his absence. Unscheduled *feelings*. Just being out on the terrace for their evening meal brought it home to her how much things had changed, even in a single week. When the five of them had sat down for their first dinner last Sunday, it had seemed that no more magical backdrop could exist for the beauty and energy of her family; whatever her plans to end her marriage, whatever her anxieties for Dom, Marty's force of personality had made it as high-spirited an occasion as any they'd had together before. She had felt absolutely capable of treating this holiday as a self-contained experience, a treat she thoroughly deserved. It had all seemed easily within her control. And yet now—though the architecture was just as unique, the evening light as dreamlike, the food, if anything, better—her experience of it was completely different. Maybe it was that strange remark Zach had made, but all at once it *did* feel like a sound stage, a place where events were not under her direction at all. She had not even been given a copy of the script—and nor had anyone else, it seemed. Except, perhaps, for Zach himself.

Through plain old-fashioned will power, she had managed to banish all thoughts of him, his kiss, and the proposal that they meet alone later, of the extraordinary urgency of it all, but not a moment had passed without her being conscious of her body's open betrayal of her. The alert sensitivity of

214

her skin beneath her clothes, the new way she was conscious of the nerve endings between her toes, the hairs on her neck, the heat behind her knees, all of it told her she had not forgotten a second of the encounter. Her mind may have trapped it efficiently enough, like a wasp in a glass, but her body was giving it free flight.

When they'd been about to part, soon after the swim, she had found herself both relieved and disappointed that there was not a moment or two alone to allow her to repeat her opinion that they should treat what had happened on the island as an aberration—if not deny it wholesale. Zach's custom (*custom*? Now she was at it too, speaking as if they'd known each other long enough to have customs!) on saying goodbye after spending time with them was to seek her out and thank her particularly, and she now realised that Pippi's shadowing of him as he'd carried out this little courtesy had not suited him at all. In retrospect, and through no fault of Pippi's own, her presence had taken on the air of man-to-man marking—a crude act of rivalry.

Then technology had intervened: Pippi's phone rang just as she and Zach began to head towards the gate. 'Oh, it's Milla, let me just . . .' And with a little waggle of her fingers in their direction, she had moved out of range, leaving the two of them alone after all.

'See what I mean,' Zach said in a tortured undertone. 'You're always surrounded.'

Bea smiled. 'Maybe it's *you* who's always surrounded.' Half of her was hoping Pippi would come back before any more could be said, while the other half willed her daughter to stay away

215

indefinitely—she was so utterly torn she might have been stretched by either wrist into the shape of a cross.

Zach stepped a little closer to her. 'Will you come later? You remember where I said, don't you?'

She swallowed. 'You know I'm not going to, I told you.'

But he just looked at her with all that youth and intensity, reminding her of how difficult it had been not to stare when they were in the lake, and worse, far worse, not to fall against him and allow him to fold his arms around her, feel their chests against one another's, sliding with the wet, or sticking perhaps in the way skin did as it dried, to forget completely that all three of her children were with them in the water. The fact that they were standing here now with damp hair and glowing faces made the idea of denial even more absurd than it was. In the space of three hours something enormous had surfaced, something as perspective-altering as the news of a birth or a death. She told herself it was the years of being kept on her toes by Marty that had made her overbalance so precariously at this first approach from someone else. But there was a big hole in this theory, for Zach's was not the first; she'd attracted plenty of interest before. She had simply felt nothing in return.

'You'll come,' Zach said in a murmur so faint she only just caught the words.

Then, before she could reply, Pippi was by his side once more—'I said I'd ring her back later'—and Bea was able to turn from his sight and restart the necessary process of suppression.

'I don't know why Zach didn't want to stay for dinner,' Pippi grumbled now. She finished crunching a breadstick and loaded her fork with food. 'Mmm, this stuffed pepper thing's gorgeous. What is it, Mum? Anchovy or something?'

'Anchovies, tuna, peperoncino and a little salt.' Bea was grateful for the orderliness of a recipe, but at the same time she realised she had subconsciously omitted an ingredient—olive oil— in the hope that Esther might jump in and correct her, keep the conversation on the safe subject of food. But Esther was too busy looking at her sister with a dangerous smirk.

'Er, maybe lover-boy didn't stay because he's got a life of his own? He isn't prepared to be kidnapped by you for his *entire* trip.'

'Face it, Pip, you've got no chance there,' Dom put in, mouth full.

Pippi ignored Esther and glared at her brother. Bea hoped she wouldn't dignify his remark with a reply, but of course she was as provoked as Dom had hoped she'd be. 'He told you that?' she demanded, hotly. 'When, exactly?'

Dom rolled his eyes. 'No, 'course he didn't, but it's obvious. He's not here to have a holiday romance with a kid. He's a seriously cool dude.'

'Cooler than someone who uses the word "dude",' Pippi sneered. 'Listen to yourself, Beatnik boy.'

Bea tried to hide her anxiety as she watched for Dom's reaction. There was an unusual tension between Dom and Pippi this evening (was it new, or had she, as with everything else, apparently, simply missed it until now?).

'Why *is* he here, I wonder?' Esther said, as usual

cutting through the fog of high feeling to identify the real point of interest. As she paused to fold a piece of prosciutto into her mouth, Bea felt herself hold her breath.

'What d'you mean?' Pippi said, exasperated. 'He's on holiday, of course.'

Esther chewed, making her sister wait. (Unlike the other two, she always remembered not to speak with her mouth full.) 'Don't you think it's an odd choice of destination for someone travelling alone, someone who's just left his job? The expensive Italian lakes in the middle of the tourist season, when everything costs so much more if you're on your own? If you wanted to take off backpacking, wouldn't you go to India or Thailand or Mexico, somewhere like that?'

'You'd go wherever you wanted.' Pippi shrugged.

'He might have a sentimental attachment to Italy,' Bea said, sounding rather more reasonable than she felt. She was beginning to see that this was not one of those subjects on which she could count on Esther to fall into line, especially as Esther was right: if Zach wasn't interested in Pippi, then there had to be another reason for his having chosen to stick around. And now Bea knew just what that reason was.

'And it's not like he's some kind of pauper,' Pippi said, crossly. 'You're so condescending, Esther. OK, so he's just been doing bar work, but when he gets back he wants to get into the music industry, or journalism, maybe.'

'He'll need to be in London for that,' Dom put in.

'Well, good,' Pippi said, as though that settled

218

the matter. 'I have no problem with that.'

Bea realised she'd been holding her breath since her own last comment, and now her lungs were reaching the point of optimum expansion; if she didn't breathe soon she'd pop. She had a sudden vision of Zach appearing on her doorstep in Kew, forcing her to admit her feelings, taking command of them whether she liked it or not . . .

'Maybe we can rent him your old bedroom,' Pippi added to Dom. 'What d'you think, Mum?'

Exhaling and wincing at the same time was a new experience for Bea. Oh God, she thought, he'd be waylaying her on the landing, smouldering at her across the breakfast table . . .

But Dom wasn't finished yet. 'I don't see why you're so desperate for an older man,' he told Pippi. 'You always do this. And anyway, if you ask me, you've got more chance with your original choice.'

Pippi turned on him with fresh fury. 'My original choice? Who's that, then?'

'Adam, of course.' He seemed determined to tease his sister until she submitted to one of her rare but legendary flouncing fits. 'Get him while he's feeling vulnerable, why don't you?'

'Cool it, Dom,' Bea warned.

But Pippi evidently found his last remark hilarious. 'Can you imagine?' she squealed. 'Seducing a man in the honeymoon boathouse!'

Bea began to feel a little blurry; she wasn't sure if she was still seeing in colour. But there was worse to come than this low-level goading, for Esther was putting down her fork and frowning across the table at her. 'Don't tell me she still doesn't know? Oh, Mum, now we're seeing so much of them you *have* to tell her.'

'Tell me what?' Pippi snapped, her forehead puckering as she looked from one to the next. 'What are you on about?'

How Bea wished she had simply gathered everyone together in the beginning and told them about the Trustloves all at once. One by one she had drawn the others into it, as if into a plot with some darker purpose. There'd been no sense in keeping it from Pippi. Yes, it was possible that her ignorance had made her less cautious with Adam and Ginny, but it might just as easily have made her insensitive. She saw now that she needed to start treating her like the other two, like an adult. After all, hadn't her youngest's eighteenth birthday always been her landmark, the point at which she could stop fighting someone else's battles and start to think about rearming herself for her own? 'Pip, Adam and Ginny lost their baby not so long ago. They're here to take their minds off it. That's what Dom means when he says Adam's feeling vulnerable.'

'So he's not looking to be seduced by anyone,' Esther said, reproachfully, 'even a Lolita like *you*.'

'Pippi hasn't been seducing him,' Bea said, sharply. Esther had always had a tendency to over-press her point, especially when it involved her sister. 'No one's saying that.'

But Pippi was looking puzzled. 'Lost it, lost it where? You mean it was, like, snatched?'

'It's a euphemism, moron,' Dom said. 'The baby's dead.'

The others may not have noticed the edge of bitterness to his voice, but Bea certainly did. She hoped fervently he wouldn't begin again on

220

fathers' rights; that really would be more than she could cope with.

Pippi's frown faded as her eyes widened, her natural soft-heartedness quick to surface. She was too far down the table for Bea to be able to reach for her hand. 'Oh. Oh. That's awful. I didn't know. How do *you* know?' she asked Dom.

Dom nodded in Esther's direction.

'Mum told me,' Esther added.

Though Esther and Dom were hardly disguising that they were ganging up on her, it was, of course, inevitable that it should be Bea who Pippi chose to turn on. 'So it's just me then! Why did you leave me out, Mum? So I could look a complete fool? A complete, horrible, heartless fat fool!'

'You're not fat,' Dom said, infuriatingly flip. 'Though if you go on pigging out like this, you might be by the end of the holiday—'

'Dom, I want you to stop this now! What is *wrong* with you?' Bea was as alarmed by the genuine spite Dom was displaying as she was the fury it was provoking in Pippi. When things flared up like this it was the collective energy of it that defeated her; only individually did she have the strength to talk them down. 'I didn't leave you out deliberately, Pip, I just didn't know if we'd be seeing them again after they came for drinks that time. And don't think you've offended Adam in any way, darling, because you haven't. He enjoyed today's trip, we all saw that. And to be honest, I wonder if it might be better if none of us knew. I'm sure they'd prefer people to act naturally than to be making sympathetic noises all the time. They'd probably hate to think we were sitting here discussing them now. It's a totally private matter.'

But somehow all of this emerged off-key, like a telling-off of Pippi, though the truth was it was herself she was angry with for having let it all develop in this way. Sure enough, Pippi ate the final few mouthfuls of her starter in icy silence and when Susanna came to clear the plates she told her she didn't want anything else. Susanna's look of surprise only incensed the girl further.

'Is it so incredible that I don't want to stuff my face all night? I'm going to my room!' She got to her feet, her glare sweeping from Bea to Esther and growing more thunderous still as it rested on Dom. 'Then you'll be free to discuss all your other secrets.'

'Oh, Pippi, don't be silly . . .' Bea began, but she was speaking to her daughter's back. As Susanna retreated, no doubt quite baffled by this unpleasant scene, she let out the long groan she'd been holding in her chest since the meal began.

'Well, that was a quiet tantrum,' Dom said, looking pleased with himself.

'She's growing up,' Esther said. 'She doesn't throw cutlery any more. One of these days we'll have a conversation and she'll finish the meal.'

'I don't think either of you helped,' Bea said, her tone short. 'You know you didn't.' She put her napkin on the table, letting her gaze settle on Dom. Whatever his private agonies, he had deliberately stirred up unnecessary drama. But, as ever, he refused to meet her eye. 'I'll go and see how she is.'

But the worst thing was, she thought, as she climbed the stairs with wobbly legs, the terrible, shameful thing was that she was feeling secretly relieved that Pippi had chosen her room to storm

222

off to, and not the town, not the hotel of the only other friend she had in this place.

*   *   *

Yellow light glowed at the open windows of the boathouse as she hurried past; you could see the drapes moving in the breeze, but there was no sound of voices. She supposed Adam and Ginny were still out at dinner; she'd need to be on her guard in case she should bump into them. Not that there should be anything suspicious about her taking a stroll alone, for she'd done it many times before on this holiday—the distance between Villa Isola and the centre of the village was the perfect leg-stretching mile—but the way she was feeling this evening she worried she might *make* it awkward. She might draw attention to herself because of this mania she was experiencing—for surely other people could see it as plainly as she felt it? (Not her children, however, thank goodness. After dinner, Esther and Dom had followed Pippi to their rooms, as if an early night was the only fitting conclusion to their unlucky dinner.)

Though the lake path was safe and well lit, her blood dashed about her body as if she were being stalked, and she was conscious of every chemical component of it: alcohol, of course (when she'd returned to the table from placating Pippi she had drunk far more wine than she'd intended), and a cocktail of hormones, the lion's share claimed by adrenalin. Guilt, fear, exhilaration—all three raided her nervous system with such force she could not tell the invaders apart. Countless times

223

she had wondered how Marty found his energy, countless more why he continued to be unfaithful to her when he'd had it spelled out to him repeatedly what it was that he risked losing. Well, now she had her answer to both: the high. It was very, very high, both vertiginous and irresistible. She had not felt like this for twenty years. Anger!

As she reached Via Olina the way thickened with tourists strolling after dinner, crowding the entrances of the wine bars and *gelateria*, taking photographs, stopping to read posters and look in shop windows, absorbing the special atmosphere of the place. At the entrance to the piazza, a crowd had gathered in the loggia under the town hall, a tiny, elevated building that made Bea think momentarily of the boathouse. She hoped she'd been wrong about Adam and Ginny and they were indoors after all, cuddled up together, finding comfort in one another.

On the piazza yet more people congregated— locals and tourists alike—sitting at the café terraces drinking wine, eating spaghetti, licking ice creams, or just standing in easy clusters in no hurry to get home. A family of geese had strayed on to the marble and a line of small children trailed after them, crying out with excitement at each new turn of the chase. The older kids played with a football. They'd be up till late, all of them, even the very youngest, for that was the way here, with everyone out together, everything out in the open, nothing concealed. Bea imagined her own illicit thoughts played aloud, amplified for all to hear, and reaching the centre of the square she stopped and drew a long, warm breath deep into her lungs. She was no more than ten feet from where he had

224

called out to her that time. I could just turn around and go back, she thought, there's nothing to stop me. No one would ever know I'd come this close. He wouldn't know.

But she wasn't going to do that.

She found the *albergo* easily. It couldn't have had many rooms because she had only to say '*Signor* Zach' (she realised only then that she didn't even know his surname; did Pippi?) to be at once directed to the first floor and a room at the front. The receptionist, an older man who looked her over with unconcealed interest, made no move to phone up to warn Zach that a visitor was on her way, giving her a last opportunity to turn around and abort her crime. But she wasn't going to do that, either.

The bulb on the stairwell ceiling was operated by a timer and despite making a noise like an aggravated insect it cast very little light on her path, causing her to trip slightly as she came to the first turn. She steadied herself against the wall, enjoying the coolness of it on her palm, before at last straightening and knocking at the door.

It was pulled open at once and he stood there in front of her. Neither of them said a word, but only stared. Once again, she was struck before all else by his eyes; incredible things the way they seemed to issue light rather than reflect it. He'd obviously showered and his wet hair was combed flat and gleaming on his head—he'd caught the sun today out on the water and his face had turned flushed and golden. He was barefoot, wearing jeans and an unbuttoned white shirt, rumpled and smelling of freshly washed old cotton—one of her favourite smells.

225

'Hey,' he said finally, in a gentle voice, the sort you'd use if you were consoling someone rather than seducing her, which made her wonder what kind of look she wore on her face—as wild and frightened as she felt, probably.

'Don't say it,' she told him. 'Please don't say it.'

'Say what?'

'If I tell you, then I'll just be saying it for you.'

He looked at her differently then. The way his eyes searched her face, curious and hungry, it was as if he hadn't seen her for months. 'Say what?' he repeated.

'That you knew I'd come.'

'Ah.' He smiled, amused. 'OK, I won't then.' Only then did he reach out and take her hand, reeling her over the threshold. 'Come in. Come and sit by the window with me.'

There were two windows in the room: a narrow rectangle to the side street, where the entrance to the hotel was situated, and a wider one that overlooked the square itself. This one had a broad marble sill, an improvised seat judging by the flattened cushions, paperback book and wine glass set on it, and its shutters were open to the world. Beyond, easily within touching distance, were the curved iron rails of a tiny balcony and the effect of these, along with the lowness of the ledge, gave her the sensation of being caged. Slowly, her other senses adjusted. There was the smell of cigarettes, either from within the room or drifting from the café terrace below, and of frying from the restaurant kitchens. Conversation—mostly in Italian—was as audible as if it were taking place in the same room. She was reminded that Susanna and Emilio called the square *il salotto*—the

226

drawing room—and now here she was, sitting with Zach in a hidden corner of it.

He handed her a glass of red wine and sat down next to her on the ledge. A half-drunk bottle stood on the dressing table, an incongruously grand piece of mahogany wedged between the window and bathroom door.

'You saw me.' Bea nodded towards the square, to the spot where she'd been standing just five minutes earlier. It hadn't occurred to her then that he might have been able to see her from his room. She had pictured him somewhere set far back from the piazza, with a view of the rooftops, perhaps. She swallowed some wine fast, hoping he would say he had not.

'Yes, I did,' he said. 'I wanted to see your face, to see if there'd be any indecision.'

She squirmed as she imagined it as it might have looked, transfigured by lust and deceit and the sheer foreignness of what she was about to do. Embarrassment made her prickly. 'So you've been stationed here all evening, have you?'

He grinned at her, drew up his fingers to rub the side of his nose. 'I wouldn't say that. But I've looked up once or twice this evening, sure, and I happened to catch you arriving. This is the big view, you know, you can't *not* look.'

There was a pause. The way they were sitting, sideways to the window and facing one another, meant that her left knee and his right one almost touched, and their hands were no more than a gesture apart. This wasn't Villa Isola, or the middle of the lake: here the scale was small and there was nowhere to camouflage a movement or an emotion. She raised her eyes to his face; in the

227

evening shadows, his bone structure looked particularly finely wrought, lit exactly as one of the Italian masters would have had it. She replayed his words, *I happened to catch you*, and felt a lurching feeling, an unmistakable descent, the free fall of sexual desire.

'So, was there any?' she asked, finally.

He lowered his wine glass. 'Any what?'

'Indecision. In my face.'

'Oh. I don't know. You had your back to me, I couldn't see you properly.' And he chuckled at her indignant expression, his left forearm crossing his chest as he reached to scratch his opposite earlobe. She couldn't believe how relaxed his body language was; this was insultingly easy for him, it wasn't fair.

For she, still horribly self-conscious, couldn't shake her defensiveness. 'Well, I only came because things got a bit . . . a bit heated at home.'

'Did they?' But he didn't seem at all keen to hear about it, perhaps because he didn't believe for a second that this was her motive for coming to him, or perhaps because it really was she and she alone in whom his interest lay (poor, poor Pippi!). She abandoned the story of the argument after a couple of lines and decided to say instead what was really on her mind:

'I'm twenty years older than you, Zach.'

He shrugged. 'So what? No one would bat an eyelid if it were the other way round.'

'That's not true. If it were Pippi or Esther with someone that much older than her, *I'd* bat an eyelid.' And to think that it had crossed her mind when he had first arrived at the villa that Marty (if and when he reappeared) would be bound to

228

object to his being older than Pippi—and yet the difference between them was only a few years. Nothing compared to *this*. 'I'd do whatever I could to stop it,' she added.

'Well, you wouldn't succeed,' Zach said, simply. 'You'd only alienate them. An adult is an adult, and we're adults.'

There was a pause then, a length of time that fitted precisely the protest one of them *should* have made and yet declined to, not about age but about marital status—for surely that was the main impediment here? But the silence only grew and the words went unspoken and it seemed to Bea that that was that, all of her objections had been made and dismissed in the first two minutes. And it would have been the biggest lie of her life to say she hadn't wanted it this way. Now, already, Zach was putting down his glass and taking hers from her, placing it next to his on the sill, turning to draw her by her elbows to her feet. It was as if by holding her peace she was giving him permission to go ahead with the ceremony—in this case, the ceremony of doing with her exactly as he pleased.

They continued to stare at each other. In spite of the command in his eyes, that unstoppable urgency, she was sure she could also sense a current of something more complicated, something that reflected her own animal shock at being in this situation.

'Shall we go to bed?' he said. 'Come with me.' And led the half-dozen steps to the one item of furniture she had, until then, avoided looking at.

After that, neither of them said a word. He began kissing her. He removed his clothes, and then, more slowly, hers. The air in the room was

229

twisted with heat and her skin felt scarcely cooler without the clothes than with. When he pressed the full length of his body against hers she could feel the stickiness between them and taste the salt and sweat on his skin. She could feel the muscles and tendons in his legs, the hooking together of their ankles and shins, their wrists cuffed together, and she could hear the silence being broken by the gathering strain of their breathing, their murmurs mixed together, impossible to separate. There was no part of her he didn't touch with his hands or his lips. Then her legs were apart and he was pushing inside her and the murmurs were turning to groans, and it was all building far, far faster than she had imagined (for she *had* imagined it, whatever she chose to tell herself), and the rush of what was happening was propelling her body far beyond the range of her brain's surveillance.

But that didn't make sense because she remembered from helping Pippi with her biology revision that it was transmitters in the brain that let the body know what it was feeling. It wasn't the other way around.

She put Pippi from her mind and crushed her face against his, biting at his neck and ear. *And we're adults*, she thought, reaching and reaching with her body, growing frantic with pleasure until, unconscious of the cries they were both making, she had emptied everything from inside her and could feel only a great light-headedness.

For a whole minute—maybe longer, two or three—they lay there, still fitted together like the solution to a puzzle, not uttering a word, just sucking the air, refilling their chests.

'That was easy,' Zach said, at last, and she

230

smiled, for it really was the only word he could have chosen. He shifted on to his side and gestured to the open window. 'And I guess not *too* noisy, or we'd have heard applause by now.'

Bea agreed. It was far too late in the day to start being coy now. 'We wouldn't want you to be chucked out of your hotel.'

'Doubt they'd do that.'

'No, you're right. This is Italy. What are hotel rooms for if not for secret assignations? We're a good advertisement.' And it felt as illicit to use that casual post-coital plural as it had to have sex with him.

It occurred to her as they lay on that narrow double bed that they were not completely hidden from view. From the island (just 400 metres from the eastern shore, Adam had informed her today), with a powerful pair of binoculars, someone might just be able to get the angle right and see into their room—one of the nuns, perhaps—and the thought made her laugh, loudly and freely, an unfamiliar kind of laugh that surprised her and made her want to prolong its sound, just for herself.

'What?' Zach said.

She told him. 'I like seeing you laugh,' he said. 'That was one of the first things I noticed about you.'

That was a sweet thing to say, she thought. 'My laugh?'

'No, the fact that you don't very much.'

'Oh.' Not so sweet, then; sad. 'Don't I?'

'Not really, no.' As he spoke his hands began to roam her body in the most proprietorial way, as if he were committing to memory every crevice and bump and curve. It was completely different from

231

the way Marty touched her; it was as if it were an absolute necessity to Zach that she know that she belonged to him. Had Marty ever needed her to know that? Or had he taken her as given, right from the start?

'Yes,' he said, 'I was looking at you with Ginny earlier, after we were swimming and you went up to speak to her, and you know what I thought?'

'What?' She forced herself to remember. It had been a strange moment: Ginny just sitting there watching them all with an expression on her face of pure horror, as if the lake had turned blood-red or something. After a few minutes of it, Bea had climbed out and gone over to say hello properly; in truth, she'd half-wondered if the other woman might have been sleepwalking.

Zach said, 'Even with everything that's happened to her, what you told me about her on the island, I think you're by far the sadder.'

'Well, I doubt very much she'd agree with that,' Bea said, trying not to show how taken aback she was. But her heartbeat had picked up. She waited for him to notice that, too.

'No, it's true,' he said, and sure enough his fingers were above her left breast, exploring the grooves between the bones that protected her heart. 'Every day she moves away from the terrible thing in her life, but every day you move deeper into yours.'

'What do you mean?' But to her shame his words had had a second effect, giving her goosebumps, and he saw it straight away, smoothing his fingers over her arms to flatten the little hairs.

'See, you know it's true, you've got the shivers.'

232

'But . . . what's my terrible thing?' Her question caught in her throat. She didn't think she'd ever listened with such apprehension for an answer.

He was frowning, his front teeth cutting into his lower lip, turning the skin of it a deeper pink. 'I don't know what it is. Your marriage, I suppose it must be, unless there's something else going on that I don't know about. In which case tell me, because I need to know.'

At this, Bea laughed again, a different sound from the one that had started this conversation, shorter and grudging. Even in the circumstances she was determined to regain *some* of her self-possession. 'Oh, Zach, there's a lot going on that you don't know about. My whole life! And you certainly don't know anything about my marriage.'

Indifferent to the rebuke, his fingers moved deftly from her arms to the soft skin of her stomach, continuing their original mapping; it was unsettlingly sexy to be explored in this way. 'I'm not saying your husband is a monster—' he began, and she interrupted, 'Good, because I can assure you he isn't,' and she slithered a little under the preciseness of his touch. But, undeterred once more, his hands simply followed the movement of her body, as easily as a swimmer riding the swell of the water. I'm trapped, she thought.

'I just mean he's obviously not right for you,' he said, matter-of-factly, 'not any more.'

'I see.' She knew he couldn't be basing this purely on the fact of her presence here, in his bed. She wondered if he'd picked something up from Pippi, or even from Dom or Esther. It was likely that remarks had been made by at least one of them, if not all, especially with their father having

233

disappeared so soon after making his solemn vow to devote himself exclusively to them. Another in a long line of broken vows. She also knew the three of them were aware, if not of each individual betrayal then certainly of the general existence of betrayal in their parents' marriage, just as she knew that the natural, if heartbreaking, result of this knowledge was not a loss of respect for *him*, as one might have expected, but for her—for not having done enough to stop it.

Yes, there was a lot Zach didn't know, and couldn't begin to guess at, however confidently those hands of his roamed.

'You haven't even met Marty,' she said to him, with a final effort at defiance.

'I don't know if I want to.' He looked at her with a bemused expression.

'Well, he'll be back soon, tomorrow probably, so you'll have to give me your opinion . . .' This was bravado, of course, for she was already quite sure she wouldn't be able to handle seeing the two men together in the same room, much less in conversation. Wouldn't they be able to smell her on one another? For didn't everybody possess the almost forensic detective skills she herself had honed over the years? Then a new thought struck her, one that both overwhelmed the pride of her last statement and obliterated the unease that it had set in motion. 'You're not leaving, are you? I mean, before he comes back? After tonight, after this? Because of me?'

He heard out her rush of questions and then said, very certainly, 'No.'

'You still have stuff to do here?'

'Yes,' he agreed. 'I still have stuff to do.' He

234

kissed her very hard on the lips. Then he said, 'You're incredible, Bea. I love saying your name. Is it Beatrice?'

'Yes.'

'Stay the night, Beatrice.'

She gasped in thrilled disbelief. 'You know I can't do that.'

'I don't see why not. You just said he's not back till tomorrow.'

'The others, though.' She couldn't bring herself to say 'children', because after the point she'd made about his age it would surely imply that she thought of him that way, too, as a child. 'They'll be getting worried already.'

His expression made quite plain his dismissal of this idea. 'No, they won't. Why would they? Do you check each other's rooms at night just to see if everyone's there, tucked up in bed, all present and correct?'

'No, of course not, but someone might need me.'

'They can look after themselves, Bea.'

'But if they saw my empty room . . . in the morning . . .'

'Wouldn't they just think you were already up? In the garden or down at the boathouse with Ginny? Or out getting things for breakfast?'

'Maybe.' She got the impression he could go on conjuring up alibis for her ad infinitum. She couldn't believe how powerful her desire was to stay.

'Text them, if you're bothered. Text Esther and say you'll be back late. Then you can at least stay another couple of hours. I'll walk you back later, when there's no one about.'

Fumbling, she did as he said. She thought he could have persuaded her to swim naked in the lake in front of the whole village if that was what he wanted from her. As she pressed 'send' and dropped the phone, she felt the muscles in her arms loosen, the feeling spreading quickly like anaesthetic in her veins, and she knew he had felt it in her too.

'Good,' he said, pleased, 'now stop worrying and let's start all over again. I've waited a long time for this.'

'Zach, stop saying that. It's creepy. You've waited two days.'

'Two days, then. But time feels different here, much, much slower, like a day is a month.'

There was a new darkness in his face as he said this, and even without knowing its source she felt she understood and shared it.

'It's because so much is happening,' she said, her throat constricting as he kissed it, turning the words into a groan.

'Not enough, if you ask me . . .' He kissed her neck again, at various points and very, very lightly, only a degree of torment away from tickling her. The pressure of his tongue was almost unbearable. *Almost.* 'So, you find me creepy, do you? That has interesting possibilities.'

Entirely drained of argument, Bea just stretched her arms high above her head and closed her eyes.

CHAPTER SIXTEEN

SUNDAY

Ever since Adam had returned from his jaunt to the island with the Sales, Ginny had been aware of the presence of a new—and quite unjustified—anger existing inside her. It was a bodily thing, knotting itself tighter and tighter, ulcerating like a tumour, scaring her with its hard, consuming presence.

But why? Why was she angry?

The obvious cause was that she resented the change in him, for this holiday seemed to be performing on him the very cure he'd hoped for in her: every new day they spent in Orta, his spirits lifted a little more. And it was not so much the location that was proving the tonic as the presence of their glamorous, moneyed neighbours and their endless ideas for pleasure seeking. Even the brooding Dom was willing to throw on a pair of Ray-Bans, jump in his vintage speedboat and *pretend* he was living the dream.

The boat was a part of it, she realised. Adam had been visibly on a high after his trip in the Riva, overflowing with descriptions of how it felt to steer it, to handle the controls, to follow in the footsteps of all those who'd graced its decks in the past (one of the Sales had suggested theirs was the very boat Brigitte Bardot had once owned—imagine that!). She'd hidden her irritation well enough in the evening, listening with a semblance of interest to the ever-smaller details, even letting go a rather questionable comment about Zach being a hanger-on (what did Adam think *he* was, then? A second cousin?), but by the following morning she had become conscious of a frightening new development. The ball inside her was unravelling, the threads ready to reveal themselves like snakes' tongues. If anger was what she had felt before, then the only word to describe this was *poison*.

He was out on the sitting room balcony in the morning sun, craning over the rails to take elevated photographs of the boat, and the moment he heard Ginny's footsteps behind him he began to gush once more his admiration for the perfection of its design. It was when he complimented Martin's taste—'He knows the best, I'll give him that,' as if he had documentary evidence that the man's life was in other ways not quite up to scratch—that she knew she could control herself no longer.

'Adam, for God's sake, stop acting like such a groupie! It's embarrassing!' Her voice, like the crack of a whip, actually made him jump. Filled with self-loathing, she tried to cover up with a laugh, as if she'd been berating him only in mock irritation and not the real thing, though it was stupid to imagine that he wouldn't be able to tell the difference. Not trusting herself, she turned away, but it was too late: she'd crushed his enthusiasm for his task and he was now trailing her through the sitting area and into the bedroom.

'What's the matter, Ginny? Has something happened?'

Has something happened? Did he really, in all seriousness, think that a suitable question? She closed her eyes, not wanting to look at him, and

238

muttered, 'Nothing's the matter.' But the flatness in her voice did little to contain the emotions swarming to the surface, the press of the vipers' heads.

'Well, it's obviously not nothing, is it?'

'I'm just saying, it's only a bloody boat! You're behaving like it's the Apollo Missions.' Still she couldn't bring herself to look at his face, but it hardly mattered for she could have pictured his expression blindfolded; it had become a default setting these last weeks: puzzlement layered with hurt, softened with tenderness. It was as if he was as much at a loss with *her* as he was with what had befallen them both. *She* had become a part of the tragedy in a way that he had not, and yet she couldn't begin to express that to him.

He drew breath and even the small sound of it, the peripheral sense of his chest rising, seemed to transmit how disappointed he was in her. 'Well, I'm sorry if you feel I've been off having fun this holiday. I know it's probably not appropriate.'

'Oh, don't say that,' she cried, furiously. '*Appropriate*—I hate that word!' Her voice was loud and, with all their windows and doors standing open, she knew it must be audible to anyone down by the water, but she didn't care. Finally she met his eye, looking, just as she'd expected, into that horrible depthless concern. 'And stop staring at me like that! Go and take some more photos of the famous Riva, be as inappropriate as you want, I'm not stopping you!'

There was a silence as he processed this petulance. Knowing he was analysing her tantrum with a therapist's ear only renewed her resentment of him. 'What? *What?*'

239

'I know what this is,' he said, quietly.

She said nothing, though the wording was familiar enough—one of those opening gambits of his that in the past would have prompted a dutiful query from her, her part in the conversational double act of marriage. But she knew that on this occasion her lack of participation would not force him to retreat; he would tell her what he 'knew', whether she liked it or not.

'You're trying to make me hate you,' he said, simply.

'No, I'm not. I don't care if you hate me or not.' Still, her voice was vicious, a weapon that raised itself the second it was provoked. She could do nothing to control it.

'You are,' he insisted. 'Listen to yourself.'

'I don't want to "listen to myself",' she spat. 'And can you please stop telling me what to do all the time? Why can't you just, oh, *go*! Get away from me and don't come back!' She'd never said anything like this to him before, it was new ground and sufficiently terrifying for her to feel a pinch of relief when he stared back at her with an unchanged expression. He had been expecting this and he was going to be able to absorb it. He wouldn't *really* go and not come back.

He took a cautious step towards her, a trained negotiator in a volatile hostage situation. 'Well, listen to me, instead, OK?'

She scrawled. 'If I must.'

'What I think is that you've lost so much already that you want to lose everything.' He corrected himself. 'You *think* you want to lose everything. And hurting me is the only way left you can think of to hurt yourself.'

Though doubtlessly true, all of this was straight from the textbook and Ginny felt her customary exasperation at being so easily reduced to a case study. 'I already *have* lost everything,' she said, tonelessly.

Adam shook his head. 'No, you haven't. You haven't lost me. And I don't care what you say or what you do, or how annoyed with me you get: you won't get rid of me.'

There was a sad little break in his voice when he reached the last portion of this, and at the sound of it Ginny felt tears rise. (If she could have had one wish granted at that moment it would be that she could just stop crying! Crying didn't wash feelings away the way everyone said it did, no, it only made them soggy and heavy; and then afterwards you had to wait hours for it all to dry out again before you could return to where you were in the first place.)

'I mean it,' he went on. 'Nothing you say will make me go.' Though his voice had recaptured its original conviction, the effort seemed to drain him of his physical strength and she watched as he lowered himself forlornly on to the edge of the bed, shoulders slumped forward. Only now did her pitilessness vanish and allow her to see him the way she knew she should have all along, the way she would have in any other life but this, as a suffering man who needed her love. And more than that, far more: someone who had every right to think he deserved it. He was her husband! How could she have pushed him to say such sad things to her, to feel the need to make such pledges of loyalty? Was it really only two years since they'd exchanged wedding vows?

241

But remembering that occasion—the joy she had felt, the sense of completeness that you couldn't put into words without invoking every cliché in the book, that had to be felt to be truly understood—well, it was just another form of masochism, another self-inflicted beating to an already broken body.

It was too exhausting.

She closed her eyes, leaned back against the wall, her head hard and heavy against the wood pannelling. 'I'm sorry.'

The words acted magically on him, for he straightened at once, obviously much heartened. He had been expecting her to go on raging, she realised. Was he . . . was he *scared* of her, then?

'I'm so sorry,' she repeated, firmly. 'I shouldn't have said what I said. I don't want to be like this.'

'You mustn't be sorry,' he said, shaking his head. 'It's completely natural. It's a process.'

But it was the worst thing he could have said and fury flamed again in her chest, licking upwards through her throat to her mouth. 'Don't you see that saying things like that makes it worse? It's like saying what we're feeling isn't real, it isn't worth anything because it's just a mechanical thing, like something you could programme a robot to feel.'

Adam looked astonished. 'That's not what I mean at all.'

'I know you don't, but that's how it sounds to me. And I don't like it. I *hate* it.'

They stared at each other, reflecting one another's anguish as clearly as in a looking glass. His face told her exactly what he was thinking: that that apology of hers had been a false dawn, that there *was* more darkness to come, just as he'd

242

feared. When she spoke again, she made an effort to make her voice more reasonable. 'Maybe I don't need to know my feelings are predictable and *appropriate*, the same ones felt by people who've lost a child for however many thousands of years. Maybe I just want them to be mine.'

'Ours,' Adam said, softly. '*Our* feelings.'

She nodded. 'Yes, ours. But please just let it happen. Don't tell me what I *should* be doing. You have your way, I have mine. I'm sure we'll get to the same place in the end.'

If she was honest, she wasn't sure at all, not then, but at least she'd said it. She'd given her inch and that was as much as she could manage right now.

'OK. I'll try,' Adam said in a sad voice, and if she'd had any heart left to break, it would have fractured then and there to hear him speak as if he were the one at fault, not her. He stood up and moved towards her. 'Let's not argue any more, Ginny. Please can we not argue any more.' It wasn't a question, it was a plea to which there could only be one answer.

'All right.'

He held her against him for a long time, not saying anything more, but stroking her back with his hands to ease the emotion away. She tried to take stock of the embrace: it felt . . . OK, not contact she especially wanted but not like leeches either. When he didn't let go, but steadily increased the pressure of his body against hers, she could no longer ignore the message that he wanted to have sex, and remembering the awful discussion that had ensued the last time she'd rejected him she tried to relax, to show more willing. The encouragement—or lack of protest—made him handle her more insistently.

At the bedroom window, the little porthole that overlooked the garden, he spun her slowly from him and stood protectively behind, undoing the buttons of her shirt until it gaped open. Then he began running his hands over her breasts and kissing her neck and shoulders.

'Adam . . .'

'Don't tell me to stop,' he murmured, cutting her off, 'because I don't think I can . . .'

Now it was she who gazed down at the Sales' speedboat, at its gleaming red mahogany and its soft blue-green leather, the spangles of sunlight on the chrome trim, the easy way the vessel rode the wobbling, current-less water. She studied these details intensely so as not to let revulsion take a grip as Adam slid the sleeves of her shirt down her arms, groaning as he did, and unhooked her bra, letting both items fall to the floor and leaving her upper body naked; she hoped that if she kept the distaste at bay for long enough her body would triumph over her mind, remember how it was supposed to respond to the touch of its mate.

Out of the corner of her eye she caught sight of a figure at their garden gate, and stiffened despite herself, for she knew she couldn't be seen properly from below.

'What?' Adam didn't look up, but continued kissing and nuzzling her. His chin and throat were scratchy against the bare skin of her shoulder; she could feel its surface reddening.

It was Zach. He'd come from the main house, presumably, but for once he was alone. Holding her breath, Ginny watched as he put his hand to

244

the latch and then hesitated, uncertainty on his face as he reminded himself, perhaps, that this was not the proper entrance to the boathouse and to come in this way was to take too much of a liberty. Did he know that their front door was in the lane on the other side? A second later he had removed his hand and ducked from view and she had no way of telling if he'd chosen to wander back up to the villa or to turn right after just a few steps, to come through the passageway to the public path, look for their door, raise his fingers to lift the knocker . . .

'I've missed this,' Adam was saying, his lips in her hair, his voice a soft purr, 'I've missed you.' There was no escape from his hands, the left one still drawing her body possessively against his, the other on her right breast, thumb playing with her nipple.

She blinked, removed her focus from the spot where Zach had stood and concentrated instead on Adam's head next to hers. She saw the silver in his hair, smelled the gel he'd used in the shower earlier, and experienced that same sensation she'd had on the island of him being a total stranger to her. Who is this middle-aged man kissing my neck? What does he want? *What is he trying to take from me?*

Then, just as she expected, there was the rap of the knocker at the front door downstairs.

'Adam, that's the door.' Though she was genuinely distracted, she knew she was also hopeful that the interruption might release her from the relentless pressure of his hands, the clean-smelling insistence of his head.

'Ignore it.'

'Who d'you think it is? Pippi?' This, she was

245

under no illusions, was pure manipulation on her part. Adam was very taken with the younger Sale daughter and if anyone could interrupt him in his task of making love to his wife, it was she.

The caller knocked again, harder, and then a third time, but more tentatively now, as if he'd already admitted defeat. As Adam's fingers drifted to the button on Ginny's jeans, she felt herself give up too.

'They've gone. Come and lie down . . .' The raw desire in his voice was making her remember how it used to be between them and she was sliced through with sadness for what she felt sure they could never recover.

'OK.' The best she could hope for now was that he would not taste the deadness on her skin, or feel its shameful absence of arousal.

As with all other activities these days, he practically did everything for her. He undressed her, positioned her legs and hips beneath him, showed her hands where to go, led her lips with his own. All she had to do was follow his cues and then, when he was inside her, move her hips gently in the rhythm he set for her.

'Does it hurt?' he asked, whispering.

'No,' she said. 'A bit, maybe. But it's all right.' And it was, it was perfectly bearable. In a way it was nice because the feeling of being crushed so tightly together made her forget that this collection of arms and legs and breasts and hips belonged to her. Just as Adam felt like a stranger to her, so, for those few minutes, did her own body parts. Hardly the point of the exercise, but at least *he* seemed to get pleasure from it, and quickly, too, because his cries of climax had come and gone sooner than she'd expected.

He didn't say so afterwards, but she knew he was thinking it was an important milestone they'd got out of the way.

She let him continue kissing her, telling her how he needed her, all the while wondering what it was that Zach had wanted. She wondered why he should come to see them on his own; she wondered whether they would ever find out what it was he wanted to say.

CHAPTER SEVENTEEN

SUNDAY

It was time to show Zach that she was no airhead, Pippi thought. It was starting to occur to her that she might be coming across a little bit *too* fashion.

The two of them were alone on the south side of the upper-most terrace of the gardens, a sheltered suntrap with easy access to the kitchen and, should any public be wandering along the woodland path at the side of the estate, just a chink of a view through the railings and past the firs and cypresses that screened them. She imagined tourists whispering to each other, 'Who's that glamorous couple? Is one of them someone?' and she had chosen her plunging red polka-dot bikini as much for them as for Zach. (It wasn't a Sale, no, but she had pointed out to her father that his swimwear designer needed to go a lot more 1950s next summer.)

Among the pots and urns on the terrace there

was a little stone statue of a girl with a watering can, which Pippi thought was cute. She'd moved their sun loungers right by it so the girl was almost standing between them, and she joked, 'Look, we're a little family! A lot easier than a real kid, eh?'

But Zach didn't seem very talkative today. Had it not been for the fact that he'd arrived this morning at exactly the time Esther and their mother usually left for their cooking class—giving the clear impression he wanted to get Pippi on her own—she might have wondered if he cared about seeing her at all, especially after yesterday's early exit. And, soon enough, she *did* start to wonder. Having accepted with good cheer the news that there was no class on a Sunday and that Bea and Esther had instead joined Dom for the latest of his interminable lake walks, Zach promptly suggested that he and Pippi try to catch them up. Where had they been headed? he wanted to know. Had they been gone long? Well, quite apart from the fact that she was still not speaking to her brother and sister after their meanness to her last night and therefore had no intention of hiking within a ten-mile radius of them, Pippi had to ask herself, Were these the questions of a man anxious to get her into bed?

They were not. On the other hand, she was not one to see her glass as half-empty. A couple of drops of Zach was a whole lot better than anything else on offer. Fine, so maybe he hadn't arrived early specifically to take advantage of the unoccupied house, as she'd hoped, but that didn't mean the house wasn't still unoccupied. And she would take it as a compliment that he was so relaxed in her company that he didn't feel the need to fill every silence with mindless chatter. There'd be none of it from her, either.

'I was reading about your friend Nietzsche,' she said, casually. 'How he pursued Lou Salomé and all that.'

There was no answer.

'Inspired by the romance of the lake . . .'

Again, no answer.

'Down at the Hotel Leon d'Or. You know where that is, right? It's just off the piazza. We should go there for a drink later, maybe? I bet they do good cocktails. Zach? *Zach?*'

At last he looked across at her, frowning. 'Yes?'

Seeing him pluck little plugs of transparent plastic out of his ears, she realised he hadn't heard a word she'd said because he'd had his iPod on. 'I was just saying, I was thinking about Nietzsche and his unrequited love.' While she had his attention she was damned if she wasn't going to plunge right in. 'Do you think places like Orta *make* people fall in love? I mean, people who never would at home? Through sheer force of beauty?'

Actually, if anything, she thought it was through sheer force of boredom—what else was there to do here?—but the phrasing had come out so perfectly she began to believe in her own theory. To her delight, Zach leaned forward with immediate interest. 'Yes,' he said, with an expression of great frankness. 'But I'm not sure if it's the place itself or if it's because you meet people you wouldn't come across in ordinary life. You get the chance to meet the one person who opens you right up, you know?'

The one person who opens you right up . . . She

was astounded by his answer, and overjoyed; she couldn't have scripted it better herself. 'How funny, that's exactly what I think, as well!' She swiftly abandoned the notion of Nietzsche, who, after all, had *not* had his feelings reciprocated and could therefore be no hero of hers, and said, 'Do you ever get that thing, like a *physical* feeling, that everything is completely perfect?'

'Maybe.' He looked a little less excited by this idea than the previous one.

'I don't mean your whole life, like everything's sorted, I mean just this one moment in time, this one place. You wouldn't change it, not a tiny bit of it, and you'll always know it was important as long as you live. There's nothing to blight it.' Blight was a good word, she thought, offering herself secret congratulations. She was on a roll, here.

'Sounds like Wordsworth's "Spots of Time",' Zach said, reclining again. He didn't put the earphones back in, though, which was an excellent sign. 'A different lake, obviously, but same kind of thing.'

Still lying down, Pippi turned eagerly to him, only half-conscious of the deep, polka-enhanced cleavage she was creating in doing so. '"Spots of Time"? Oh, what are they? Tell me about them, go on.'

'Well, they were like key moments or events in his life, so intense and profound that they never faded, and he could draw on them whenever he needed to . . .'

As he went on, Pippi watched his lips; they were pink and kind of dry, quick to pull up at the corners in a smile, which had the effect of making him seem apologetic even as his words sounded

250

so confident, authoritative. After he'd finished explaining, she nodded and said, 'Oh yeah, we did *The Prelude* for A-level.'

He looked puzzled. 'Well, you must know all this already, then.' His fingers began to fidget with the iPod again and, hating the idea that her response might have disappointed him, Pippi began to babble.

'Maybe. I honestly can't remember, it was all such a blur! God, I get palpitations when I think about it too much now. I think my mind has blocked it out, you know, like childbirth or something.' Nonetheless she began to list her A-level papers, the various assignments, the gruelling timetable of examinations, allowing her natural drive to rear up and make her even more animated than she usually was. Zach nodded along, politely rather than with any real interest, and soon she began to wish she hadn't said anything at all. Hadn't Dom warned her that nothing marked out a college fresher better than an obsession with A-level grades? 'No one cares about all that by the time you get to my age,' he'd said, 'it's totally irrelevant, just baby stuff.' She shivered at the memory—her brother could be so cutting—and another of his pronouncements chased the first across her mind, the one from that awful scene last night: *Face it, Pip, you've got no chance there.* What an ugly thing to say!

She was starting to seriously dislike her brother this holiday. It was because he was nobody's favourite, she decided. OK, that sounded cruel, and she didn't *mean* it that way, but they all knew that she was Dad's favourite and Esther was Mum's. Dom had had to find his own special one.

Milla (who inexplicably lived in hope that Pippi's brother might ditch Chloë) said it was this that had made him so unfashionably serious about a girlfriend so young. None of his friends was so committed. And look where it had got him! In some sort of weird gloom.

'Anyway, I hope I don't forget about Wordsworth and the others when I'm studying fashion. It's going to be so easy to forget the more cerebral stuff when I'm at St Martins.' Cerebral was another teacher's word and she enjoyed using it. 'Not that I think clothes are meaningless and trivial, of course. They're a valid form of self-expression, no different from poetry, if you think about it.'

'Except you can't see clothes with your eyes closed,' Zach pointed out.

'No, but you can *touch* them,' she said, but only slightly naughtily, because the intellectual thing was really working for her.

She liked to think he was checking her out then—keeping his eyes *wide* open; certainly his interest had picked up again. 'So, will you live at home when you're at college?' he asked her.

Pippi scoffed. 'God, no, Dad'll get me a flat. That's what he did for Esther at Sussex. She's coming back to London next summer, so I could live with her for a bit, I suppose. I'll see what the budget is.'

Zach didn't reply, just grimaced to himself, and she knew her answer had displeased him. Too late she heard how like a spoiled brat she must have sounded, having quite forgotten what he'd told her about living at home during his own years at university, before sharing a friend's basement for

252

another lengthy stretch. Only recently had he moved into a flat of his own. She added quickly, 'Dom's just got a flat share with some mates from uni, so I might do something like that, actually. Save on bills. And I'll have to work part-time, as well, of course, earn my keep. Hopefully for one of the big designers, maybe Stella McCartney? I'm working for one of Dad's suppliers for six months when we get back home, did I tell you that? He's a serious slave-driver. I won't have a life.' She was protesting too much, she knew, but it hardly mattered because he wasn't listening again, but focusing on something over her shoulder, having his own bloody 'Spot of Time' by the look of it (the moment when he saw the kind of girl he *didn't* want to hook up with, perhaps?). Reluctantly, she turned as well, and saw that he was looking at her mother, who was approaching from the rear of the house.

'Hi, Mum.' Pippi waved. 'I didn't hear you come back.'

'Hi, darling. Yes, I got back about half an hour ago. Dom and Esther are still out, they took a trail into the mountains, but I got tired. It's too hot to go uphill.'

'Way too hot,' Pippi agreed. 'You look amazing.'

'Thank you, sweetie.'

'I haven't seen that dress before. It's not . . . is it Missoni?' She pushed up her sunglasses and narrowed her eyes for a closer look. It was as if someone had woven a rainbow around her mother in silk, that gorgeous heavy kind, except instead of seven colours there were seven *thousand* (definitely Missoni). Her arms had got really tanned and they seemed to emerge from the fabric

253

glowing. In London she swam most days and Pippi was determined to do the same when she was her mother's age, for it had kept her in great shape. Her hair was damp and combed flatter than usual, framing her face differently and giving her a dreamy, hippie sort of look. A younger look.

'What's happened to your hair?'

Her mother put a hand to it, smoothing it in a graceful downward motion, leaving her fingers lingering at the back of her neck, distracted. 'I don't know, the water here, it's so much softer, I suppose. I just had a shower after our walk. I couldn't quite bring myself to jump in the lake again. That was definitely the result of peer pressure.' She laughed, the clear natural sound that Pippi had grown up with and would never stop loving. She knew she was lucky to have a mother with so few irritating characteristics (Milla's was totally neurotic, a *nightmare*), and one who was so good looking, as well. The Missoni dress aside, Pippi had noticed subtle alterations in her mother's style over the last few days. It was less casual, more thought-out; sort of prim and sexy at the same time. She was used to Bea looking more put-together than her friends' mothers—it was a necessity given the family business, she couldn't really get herself known as the local hobo—but this was on holiday, where London standards were usually lowered a little. Normally, by this stage of the trip, she'd be schlepping around in a sarong and flip-flops.

And then, just like that, Pippi understood. Mum must fancy this chef on her course! Even Esther had said he was a bit of a fox. OK, so there was no lesson today, but she was doing what Pippi did all the time, using her day off to try out new looks. Well, good for her. Teach Dad a lesson for buggering off and leaving them to fend for themselves. She'd watch to see if Mum wore the dress to her next lesson, and then she'd know for sure.

'Mum, are you going up to Casa Whatsit today?'

Her mother looked surprised. 'Casa Mista? No, I told you at breakfast, there's no lesson on a Sunday. Sunday lunch is their busiest time of the week: they're swamped. They don't need us hanging around. Why?'

'But you go back tomorrow, right?'

'No, they're closed on Mondays, but we've got a final session on Tuesday.' Bea gave a conspiratorial smile, including both Pippi and Zach in it. 'I hate to be ungrateful to your father, but I think I've had enough now, and I'm pretty sure Esther has, as well. Filippo is a bit of a tyrant.'

'But you like strong men, don't you?' Pippi said.

By her side, Zach sniggered throatily. He had yet to contribute to this conversation.

Her mother raised an eyebrow, disregarding the question. She perched at the end of Pippi's lounger and tucked her feet elegantly beneath her. Pippi could smell the orange flower in her scent. 'To be fair, I don't know how chefs can work all day in those kitchens, especially here, when it's so glorious outside. I'd throw a fit as well, I expect.'

Pippi rushed on, seized with inspiration. 'And this Filippo, the tyrant who's got all the Michelin stars, he's not gay, is he?'

Her mother smiled indulgently. 'I have no idea. Possibly. Esther might know.'

Zach gave another hoarse chuckle. Pippi didn't

like the feeling she was getting that they were teasing her.

'Why are you going back then, if you've finished the course?'

'Because it's Filippo's birthday on Tuesday, so those of us still around have been invited for cake, that's all.'

'He must fancy you,' Pippi declared, '*that*'s why he's invited you back.'

Her mother looked faintly perplexed. 'Oh, Pippi, don't be ridiculous.'

'Don't you think so, Zach?' Pippi persisted, getting carried away. She hooted with delighted laughter. 'Don't you think it sounds like *Signor* Filippo might be lusting after one of his students?'

'I'm sure he is,' Zach agreed. His voice was a growl, like he needed a glass of water. 'You know, he's not the only one . . .' As Pippi looked sharply at him, he cleared his throat and added, '. . . with a birthday. It's mine on Tuesday, as well.'

She squealed. 'Is it? That's fabulous news! Well, we need a cake for you, too, don't we, Mum? Shall I talk to Susanna?'

But her mother looked rather less excited by the idea of a double celebration. 'So, what have you two been up to this morning?' she asked, changing the subject (though by no means removing it from Pippi's imagination). 'Having fun?'

Zach stiffened fractionally at the question, causing Pippi to experience her second epiphany in five minutes. Of course! He didn't want to make a move here at Villa Isola in case someone walked in on them. Hadn't he remarked only yesterday that there was always someone springing out at them here? Someone like Susanna or Emilio or one of the girls who came to clean or a messenger with a delivery. Not to mention Esther and Dom, determined to spoil her fun, and even Mum, popping up like this in her Missoni dress, sitting two inches from his feet. What if they'd been getting intimate and hadn't noticed her come up? He would have been mortified.

OK, so this new modesty theory didn't quite fit with his rock 'n' roll attitude—his occasional reference to his life in Bristol, while never explicit, had nonetheless led her to believe that his experience with women was fairly extensive. (How could it not be? He could have *anyone*.) But if there *was* some strange respect issue at work, well, she'd just have to take this thing off-site. Invite me to your hotel room, she thought, that's what it's there for.

'Just chilling, Mum,' she said, innocently. 'Working on the tan.'

'You've got plenty of sunscreen on?'

'*Mum*, I'm not five!'

Amused, her mother raised her eyebrows again as if prepared to dispute this.

'How are you, Bea?' Zach asked, somewhat belatedly.

She gave him a warm smile. 'Fine, thank you, and you?'

'Good. I slept really well last night. I was completely exhausted.'

'Well, you didn't miss anything here,' Pippi drawled, 'we were all in bed by ten o'clock.' She had already filled Zach in on the horrible row she'd had with Dom and Esther, on her mother having kept from her the sensitive information about the Trustloves (she had kept to herself the

257

part of the argument that concerned *him*, obviously), and she could tell he was as appalled by her family's treachery as she was.

There followed a slightly tense silence. Despite her mother's friendliness, the atmosphere had changed since she'd joined them, Pippi thought. It was suddenly feeling all formal out here. She needed to get rid of her; she was definitely inhibiting Zach's freedom of expression.

'Mum, d'you know if there's any of that *gelato* left? The one Susanna had with the honey and bits of *biscotti*?'

Her mother nodded. 'I expect so, shall I get you both a bowl?'

'No,' Zach said, his voice rather curt. Then he added, more respectfully, 'No, thanks, Bea.'

Pippi turned to him, confused. Was this some sort of comment on her waistline?

'We can get our own ice cream,' he told her. 'We're not paralysed.'

He didn't meet her eye, but looked in the direction of the water, his gaze resting on the small corner of boathouse visible from here. At once, Bea did the same. They were thinking about Ginny, Pippi supposed, the way she always sat in that chair in her garden as if she'd lost the use of her legs. Zach had wandered down there earlier to get some breeze. No one in, he reported when he came back, but he'd seemed caught up in his thoughts as he'd settled back down. Now she came to think of it that was when he'd gone all quiet. He felt sorry for the Trustloves and their horrible loss, a lovely quality in a man (especially compared to Dom—what was it *he* had said about it? 'The baby's dead, moron.' So callous!).

Yes, her hunch about privacy was right; she'd been missing something crucial about Zach. He might *look* as if he didn't give a damn what anyone thought, but in reality he was very well mannered, very caring, especially with the older generation. Not only was there this obvious sympathy for Ginny, but he was also scrupulously attentive to Bea, almost protective, always saying, 'Thank you, Bea,' 'Let me do that for you, Bea.' Bea, Bea, Bea!

She was filled with a sudden and overwhelming longing to hear him say *her* name, say it in that same growl he'd used just now: 'How are *you*, Pippi?', 'Thank you, Pippi,' 'Oh, Pippi, that feels *really* good . . . don't stop . . .' Shifting her position on the lounger, she reached for her cigarettes. She was aware that she needed to calm down. Maybe a dip in the lake was in order—she'd ask him if he wanted to come in with her. If they swam out of sight of anyone up here, along by the rushes, maybe he'd kiss her there, in the water. A delicious shiver passed through her at the thought.

At long last, her mother picked up on the vibe and got up to leave. 'Well, I shall see you for lunch, shall I?' She was looking at Zach; obviously Pippi would be there—especially after having missed most of dinner last night.

He nodded. 'Yes. Thank you.'

'That's good,' Pippi agreed. 'With any luck the others won't be back in time and it will just be the three of us. Oh, Mum? Any word from Dad today?'

'Yes.' Her mother hesitated. 'He just phoned when I was in the shower. He's coming back.'

Pippi sat up. 'Oh goody! *Bene!* I can't wait for him to see the boat, can you?'

259

Again, her mother's glance flickered to Zach, more anxiously this time, and Pippi knew what *that* meant. She almost exploded in disbelief: Mum was expecting her to get rid of him by the time of Dad's return! Well, she didn't see why she should. Dad was the one who had abandoned them and, besides, what was the problem? He was going to *love* Zach. OK, so he was a bit older than her, but he got on really well with Esther and Dom and she'd easily be able to pass him off as a joint friend if she had to.

'You'll finally be able to meet him, Zach,' she said in a defiant voice. 'You've been asking about him, haven't you? He's *so* cool.'

'Hmm.' The set of her friend's face was completely unreadable.

'So when *will* he be here?' she asked Bea.

'Not till tomorrow lunchtime, apparently. He couldn't get a flight today.' Her mother's voice was oddly guarded. Suppressing her fury with Dad, Pippi supposed, but what did she expect him to do? Charter a private plane? Or maybe she just didn't believe a seat on the London–Milan route would be so difficult to find.

'There probably aren't that many flights on a Sunday,' she said, diplomatically, 'Dad said he had a nightmare finding ours last week,' and beside her Zach murmured his support. Once again, his body language had altered perceptibly; he'd shuffled upright, and she could sense the renewed energy in him.

Her mother had only been gone a few seconds when he lit a cigarette, puffing at it restlessly before putting it out almost straight away and getting up. He told her he was going to use the loo.

260

'I might wander down to the lake,' he added. 'I'll get the ice cream on my way back if you like?'

Pippi beamed. 'Oh, would you? And another bottle of mineral water, please. Mum or Susanna'll show you where everything is.'

Was he ever going to do it, she thought, making circles in the air with her painted toes. Was he ever going to touch her? Undress her? She was wearing a *bikini*, for God's sake, how much easier could she make it for him? It had been three days now and she didn't think her body could cope with any more anticipation. Whoever said it was better to travel hopefully than to arrive was totally mistaken— probably that loser Nietzsche or someone else who'd been knocked back by the opposite sex.

As she waited for him to come back with the ice cream, she contented herself by scraping their sun loungers an inch or two closer together and pondering the options for his birthday celebration. The stone girl, squeezed between them, just carried on watering, oblivious to any human machinations.

CHAPTER EIGHTEEN

MONDAY

For Ginny, who had entirely taken for granted the flawless weather in Orta, the storm on Monday morning seemed to come out of nowhere. One minute she was in the garden, settled in her customary spot and idly applying sun lotion to her face, the next she was on her feet and fleeing for shelter. The only explanation was that she must not have looked up at the sky, not once, for black swollen clouds like these didn't just materialise overhead by magic, not even in the mountains; nor must she have heard any of the warnings that Adam had surely given (even without television and Internet, he somehow managed to keep himself up to date with the weather forecast).

Safely inside, it all felt quite cosy at first, even a little exhilarating, as the sound of rain on the glass rose and fell like applause. Then all hell broke loose as rocks of hail began to crash down from the sky and great cymbals of thunder clapped above the roof. She could hear the shriek of birds trapped in the shell down below, the boom of the water like some powerful detonation as it reared up high in the hollowed space. Reacting instinctively, she took a deep step back from the window: for the first time since they'd come here she was properly aware of the structure of the boathouse, what this building was meant for before someone converted it into holiday accommodation for lovers. It seemed to her that it was moving with the storm.

'Wow, look at this!' Adam was at the other window, watching the lake seethe and roll. It was turning quite white, as if in fury. *That*, she was sure, had come out of nowhere. Adam seemed cheered by the sudden savagery, however. 'Them be dragons,' he said, making a face at her as more thunder rolled, 'and not just any dragons. St Julius's dragons.'

She went to huddle against him, something she would not have done so readily two days ago, transfixed by the scratches of lightning now

262

appearing across the sky. They looked pale and feeble, scarcely fizzing through the dense cloud, but when she counted the seconds between lightning and thunder—hardly a delay at all—she knew that the storm was right above them. Adam's arm enclosed her protectively, as if reacting to the same calculation.

That was when she heard it, from outside, out on the water: a child's scream. She whipped her face up towards Adam, bumping her head on his chin. 'There's someone out there, Adam, in the water!'

He frowned, craning for a clearer view through the blurred pane. 'Where? I can't see anything.'

'Nor can I, but I heard a scream. Someone's in trouble.' She began to fumble with the clasp, jerking the windows inwards, and at once the two of them were assaulted by rainwater, shockingly sharp and cold on impact. Adam cursed, but she shushed him as the sound came again, obliterated after a second by the bang of one of the windows as it whipped back on its hinges.

'Ginny!'

She reached to still the wayward window. 'There! Did you hear?'

'Yes, I did, but it's just the wind.' He forced his arms in front of hers to close the windows again. 'Or a bird, maybe.' His voice was exaggeratedly calm, which told her he hadn't needed to listen to know he didn't believe her—in fact, he'd automatically *disbelieved* her. Their physical closeness of a minute ago forgotten, she fought roughly to pull at the windows a second time.

'But if you can't tell which, it could just as easily be a child!'

Now he placed his hands directly over hers, capturing them; the degree of pressure was just a fraction gentler than a jailer's. 'Ginny, in weather like this all children are safely indoors with their parents. I *told* you it was going to rain, remember? Anyone sensible would have come inside hours ago, if they'd even bothered to go out in the first place.'

But the feeling persisted that he was managing her misconceptions rather than considering the possibility that someone could be in trouble, and that made her fear all the more vivid. She began to plead with him, her voice whiny with panic: 'But you saw how suddenly it came on. Anyone could have been caught out. There could have been people swimming or out in a boat. And there's no visibility, how would they even know which way was the shore? These are exactly the conditions where people drown!'

As the scenarios developed in her imagination, complete with pictures of fingers grasping at rushes and mouths sucking for breath, fresh hysteria surged inside her, giving her the speed and strength needed to slip from Adam's grasp and rush to the coat hooks by the door. She found her jacket and began to thrust her left arm through the sleeve. 'I'm going out.'

Adam strode after her, his movements stiff with exasperation. 'Don't be an idiot, you'll get drenched!'

'I have to! I can't ignore someone's cries for help even if you can.'

'There *are* no cries for help,' he groaned, 'except mine! Oh, stay here, Gin, *I'll* go!' And in a second he had flung open the kitchen door and was stomping down the narrow internal staircase. She heard him struggle with the lower door, stiff at the best of times and made heavier now by the pummelling of the rain.

'Not that way,' Ginny yelled, 'the other way! Through the garden . . .' But she issued her instructions to an empty stairwell, to a shut door, the slam of it bringing a more definite shake to the building. Abandoning her jacket, she rushed down after him, shrieking his name through the repeated smack of the water in the cavity beyond. She wrenched the door handle, immediately blinded by water sluicing horizontally into her face, and shielded her eyes with her hands as she strained to see where Adam might have gone. There he was, a little way along the path to the village. 'Adam!' she screamed. 'Not down there, the other way! By the jetty!'

He heard her, thank God, and changed direction. As he flashed past her, doggedly avoiding her eye, she caught the tight grimace of frustration in his face. How would he be able to search properly in a mood like this? She followed him through the passageway to the Sales' lawn and down towards the lake. The tunnel of branches gave brief respite from the elements, but once in the open again the strength of the wind was brutal and they both fought its resistance as if wading waist-deep through setting rubber. Finally reaching the jetty, Ginny clutched at the post nearest to her and hauled herself up. The planks were slick with foaming water, and she could see the Sales' speedboat leaping about on the churn, imagined it being smashed to pieces in front of her eyes.

'Ginny, what are you doing, you'll be blown in!'

Adam grabbed her firmly from behind, holding her steady as his left foot slid on the muddied grass. 'Go back inside, will you? Leave this to me!'

Seeing that he was prepared to waste time escorting her back, she retreated with reluctance to the mouth of the passageway, wiping the water from her face with her sleeves and tracking his pale figure through the thick wet grey. He was off the jetty now and moving towards the northernmost edge of the grounds, the boundary between Villa Isola and its nearest neighbour. It was too far, she thought, anxiously, she was sure the voice she'd heard had been closer to the jetty. She prayed that his bloody-mindedness with her would not obscure his instincts for what was actually out there. Then, with a start, she realised he was already returning to her, and not only that but there were two people, not one, the second just a few steps behind him. She'd been right, he *had* found someone— and that person was alive!

The smudged watercolour figures moved slowly towards her. She could see that they were roughly the same size and she began to feel confused and a little afraid.

'Zach's here,' Adam shouted, the words all but lost to the wall of wind and rain. When he reached her, he gave her a cold, warning nod. He was expecting her to continue with her nonsense about the child, she realised; he was expecting her to embarrass him.

'Ginny . . .' Zach managed a damp, powerless greeting through the wet.

'Zach,' she whispered back, catching sight of him properly and staring. His hair was pasted flat on his head and the bones of his face were sharp

266

under the flushed skin. His eyes, which she had not seen before close up, were of an unusual transparency, almost like dark-grey glass. He looked completely exhilarated, alive with purpose, almost frenzied.

The three of them huddled together under the branches. 'He's been outside since it started,' Adam told her, still fighting for breath, 'and he hasn't seen anyone either.' There was a suppressed fury to those last words; if anything his mood seemed to have worsened with the success of his rescue mission. When he'd left the building five minutes ago he'd been irritated, certainly, but now he seemed downright enraged. But why? Was it because she'd been proved right and he wrong, or was it because he didn't care for who it was he'd found out there? He had no particular liking for the Sales' friend, she'd gathered that much from the occasional comment he'd made, but she had not judged it to be as strong an emotion as dislike. Or perhaps he just resented getting unnecessarily wet? This newly fastidious version of her husband liked to dress correctly for bad weather.

'Come on,' he said, testily, 'I think we should all go back inside before one of us gets struck by lightning.' And the look he shot Ginny left her in no doubt of who would be to blame should the event occur.

'Good plan,' Zach muttered and turned to check the path underfoot before moving quickly on. Ginny alone did not budge, except for a fractional turn of the head away from them, towards the lake.

Adam was on to her at once. 'Ginny, *come on,*' he hissed. 'Just accept that there's *nobody* else out there.'

Ahead, at the sound of Adam's aggravation, Zach eased up, waiting for them. She was keenly aware of how it must look: her husband talking to her like she was a mental patient and she acting like one, poised to dart off and make her escape. She felt she had no choice but to follow them back through the tunnel to the boathouse door, which was swinging open as she'd left it, a negligence that earned her a fresh glare from Adam, and up the stairs.

Inside, sealed from the clamour, the space felt different, more personal, more *hers*. All three of them were soaked through and she fetched towels from the bathroom, reserving for herself the one still damp from Adam's morning shower. Zach had squatted on his haunches by the hearth—not noticing, apparently, that there was no fire lit—and when she reached out silently to hand a towel to him he swivelled round like a wild animal responding to movement in the undergrowth, all its survival senses ignited. It seemed almost comically civilised when he parted his lips to say, 'Thank you, Ginny,' and began dabbing the dry fabric against his wet face and neck.

He's like someone who's just been called to war, Ginny thought, or fallen headlong in love with Helen of Troy, or been told the exact date and time he will die. It was shock or terror or even euphoria that held him in its thrall, she could not tell which, only that he was fully charged by it, electrified. She was not scared by him, however, as she supposed might easily have been the case, but the opposite: she was drawn to him, longing to get close enough to share that unearthly energy.

'I'll make tea,' she said. 'We need something to

warm us up.'

'I'll do it,' Adam said, by her side. 'You dry off.'

But she was tired of his unreasonable mood and sick of him telling her what to do, or rather, what *he* would do for her. 'No. I said I'll do it. You two sit down.'

Over the noise of the boiling kettle, she couldn't hear anything of what the two men were saying to each other. She handled the mugs and tea bags with clumsy unfamiliarity, unable to decide if she was satisfied or not with what had just happened. She tried to work systematically through her original fears: Zach had been found, if not in exactly the place where she'd heard the cry, then close enough to it, and if *he* hadn't seen anyone else, either in the water or on the shore, then it was likely there *was* nobody else (it was something of a shock to realise that she trusted his word on the matter over her husband's). On the other hand, she'd definitely heard that human wail of distress and it could hardly have come from Zach himself. Or perhaps it could . . . wasn't he in an extraordinary mood himself? Heightened and alert? And hadn't she sensed a kind of despair about him the first time they'd met? She'd dismissed it as a fiction of her own making, a desire to attribute pain to all who crossed her path, but maybe it wasn't her imagination, maybe he *was* in trouble. Maybe there'd been some sort of row with Pippi and he'd been out in the storm specifically to release his pent-up anguish, in a spot where he assumed he wouldn't be overheard.

But there was also, she reminded herself, the business of him knocking at their door yesterday, and the more she thought about his curious, faltering manner on that occasion the surer she was that his visit had been something other than an errand for the Sales, something of his own. Today's encounter meant he'd been seen alone in the vicinity of the boathouse twice in two days; odd, surely, since his only reason for being at Villa Isola was to be with Pippi. The memory of yesterday's sighting blended uncomfortably with that of Adam making love to her, reclaiming their lost closeness as if it cured everything, only, twenty-four hours later, for him to be treating her as if he'd reached the end of his tether with her. It didn't make sense, none of it did; if she laid it all out in front of her like physical objects in an evidence room, there wouldn't be nearly enough to make a case—if she even had the first idea of what that case might be.

She brought over the tea. Despite the drama of this meeting, the continued violence of lashing water at the windows, the two men appeared to be struggling to find topics of conversation between them. Zach, at least, seemed more like his usual self. He had moved to the sofa, legs crossed at the ankles, his hair lampblack and roughly dried, sticking out all over the place. Before taking the mug of tea from Ginny he twisted the towel into a roll and slung it around his neck, an act she found so casually intimate she had to look away.

'You really feel like you're on the water here,' he volunteered, at last. His voice had returned to the self-confident drawl she was familiar with from their previous encounters.

'It certainly felt like that a minute ago,' Ginny agreed. 'You could almost feel the place rocking.'

'And you can really hear it, can't you? It's weird how it kind of shrieks.'

270

At this, Adam cast a significant look Ginny's way. He was under the window in the armchair, leaning forward and dripping freely on to the floor. 'That's the birds,' he said. 'They're not usually so loud.'

'I guess they must be freaked out,' Zach said. 'I know I am.'

Ginny lowered herself next to him on the sofa. She sipped her hot tea and the burning sensation of it on her lips was a relief from the atmosphere in the room.

'So what were you doing out there, anyway?' Adam asked Zach, with an unconcealed—and uncalled-for—brusqueness.

Zach shrugged, something close to amusement on his lips. 'Sheltering, as it turned out.'

'Were you up at the house? Won't they be worried you're still out in the storm?'

Ginny had an image of Pippi leading a search party in full waterproof couture; perhaps she'd wear one of those hard hats with a light built into it, but candy-pink or customised with crystals. To her astonishment she had to suppress the beginnings of laughter.

Zach shook his head, scattering droplets over her as he did, smiling his apologies. 'No, no, I haven't been up there yet. I was just down by the lake when it started. It was unbelievable, it just suddenly began crashing down without warning, like the end of the world.'

Ginny couldn't resist a rather petty return look Adam's way: See? Not everyone checks the weather report.

Adam ignored her. Evidently he was puzzling over Zach's last comment. 'You haven't been up

271

there yet, but you were in the grounds . . .'

He was querying Zach's presence on the Sale property for reasons of neighbourly caution, Ginny thought unnecessary, in her view, given not only how welcome he knew the boy to be at the house but also the fact that he counted as a temporary friend of their own. Adam had, however, raised one of her doubts: namely, what was Zach doing *anywhere* on the estate on his own? If he wanted time alone, wouldn't he simply wander about in the village, nearer to his hotel? It was one thing to head down to the water from the house once he'd announced his arrival and said hello—if not reacting to a row, as she'd first speculated, then he might have offered to check on the boat, for instance—but quite another to walk about private grounds before he'd even rung the doorbell. He must have come in through the boathouse passageway, she realised, for the gates of the main villa were operated electronically (but, then again, Pippi might have given him the code; the Sales seemed to care little about security).

'On your way up to see Pippi, were you?' Adam pressed, but Zach neither confirmed nor denied this, just swallowed more of the tea, and Ginny got the impression that he was happy to let Adam go on assuming whatever it was that pleased him.

'You two have got quite close, haven't you?' Though her husband used the same terse tone, an edge of personal disapproval was becoming clearer now, making Ginny uneasy. 'You and Pippi, I mean.'

Finally, the penny dropped—as it must have done for Zach several questions ago. Absurdly, unbelievably, Adam was interrogating him about

272

Pippi almost from the perspective of a father, someone with an interest in protecting her chastity!

'Adam,' she said, finally joining the conversation. Her tone felt miraculously reasonable after her earlier loss of control. 'Zach and Pippi's friendship is none of our business. And I'm sure he's free to come and go at the villa as he pleases.'

'Well, are you?' Adam addressed this to Zach, but somehow managed to direct his rudeness at both of them. '*Are* you free to come and go?'

'Adam,' Ginny repeated, more sharply, 'please stop cross-examining him like this.'

'It's OK,' Zach said to her, shrugging. His eyes had lost their wildness now, but the pupils had grown, making the grey darker. 'I don't mind. They *have* said I can drop by whenever, yeah.'

'They invited him to stay there,' Ginny added, on his behalf, 'instead of his hotel.' But her attempts at defence hardly mattered because Adam continued to ignore most of what she said.

'And you and Pippi?' he asked Zach, even more bullishly. 'You're . . . ?'

'We're friends,' Zach clarified, politely.

'So you're not involved with her then?'

'Adam!' Ginny's indignation on their guest's part was matched only by her mortification; couldn't Adam hear how bizarre he sounded, and how unpleasant?

Again Zach appeared unruffled. He gave a short shake of the head. 'No, I'm not involved with her.'

'She's very young,' Adam said, in the same spirit of condemnation. That was rich, Ginny thought, given that he had married *her* in spite of their substantial age difference.

'It's not that,' Zach said, 'though she is young, yes.'

Adam pounced. 'You mean there's someone else?'

Zach gave the smallest inclination of his head. 'There is someone . . . someone I met recently.'

'And it's serious, is it?'

'It's *private*, Adam!' Ginny cried.

But, yet again, Zach had no need of her protection. His eyes were frank, unblinking, as they regarded Adam, quite equal to this ridiculous inquisition. 'Yes, I think it's going to be,' he said, thoughtful, almost grave.

All of which was more than Adam deserved to know, but *still* he wouldn't let up, now giving a little exclamation of disbelief, like a veteran teacher faced with a particularly obtuse student. 'Well, have you thought about letting Pippi know that? She seems to think you're on the market.'

'Adam, please!' Ginny begged. 'This is nothing to do with you.'

He turned to her, no longer able to ignore her constant interruptions. 'No, Ginny, it's not right. It's not.' His tone was subtly different with her, a reversion to his original irritation as opposed to the naked hostility he was summoning for poor Zach. (Was it possible that the two might be linked, that he was taking out his frustration with her on their guest because he knew she would not be able to handle its force?) 'Don't forget she's planning this big dinner for him tomorrow night. She's invited us, you know,' he added, for Zach's benefit.

'Right,' Zach agreed, mildly.

274

'But isn't that supposed to be a surprise?' Ginny said. She and Adam had had the dubious honour of being present when inspiration regarding the event had struck the youngest Sale. She'd been seeing Zach off by their passageway yesterday afternoon and he had scarcely left the premises before she'd approached Adam and Ginny in excitement, declaring her intention to organise a celebratory dinner in his honour. She would get straight on to briefing Susanna, she said, and seeing the ferocious look of revelation in her eyes, Ginny had been left somewhat dazzled. There'd been a brief moment of camaraderie when the Trustloves discussed how sure they were that *they* had not attended dinner parties at Pippi's age, much less thought to host one. Even now (or, more correctly, even 'before') their efforts at entertaining had rarely lived up to the term 'party'.

'No, she told me all about it,' Zach said. 'Eight o'clock tomorrow.' Ginny sensed he was far from thrilled by the prospect.

'And there's nothing he can do about it, anyway,' Ginny said to Adam, before he could twist Zach's response into further evidence of ingratitude. 'It's up to her what parties she throws. She can have one every night if that's what she wants to do, it doesn't oblige anyone to marry her.' She'd intended sarcasm, but her voice—and imagination—was flaring, making her search for further ways to help spare Zach Adam's unpleasantness. 'And anyway, I haven't said I want to go.'

'You probably should,' Zach told her, affably, 'if you're up to it. We all should. It's only polite.' He sounded twenty times more grown up than either

275

of his elders. This whole conversation was farcical, Ginny thought. 'And you're right,' he added, tipping his head in Adam's direction, 'I should talk to her. I just need to find the right time. It's not easy to get people alone up there. Maybe at this dinner tomorrow . . .'

'Yes, that'd be *really* tactful,' Adam said, scornfully.

For the first time, Zach appeared less than impervious to the other man's insults. He was beginning to look irritated, Ginny saw, and—she was sure she was right about this—disappointed, too, *thwarted*. He had hoped for something different from Adam and her. Given a warmer reception, he would have said more, he would have revealed what was really on his mind about Pippi, perhaps, or about why he had come to see the two of them yesterday—and returned today when he could so easily have sought shelter in the main house instead. It was all connected, she was certain of it, it was right there, about to break the surface, too inflamed to stay hidden for much longer.

But there she went again, imagining that they were all wandering around with only their skins to stop the most intolerable personal agonies from spilling on to the ground in front of them. This was one of the worst parts of feeling as she did, having the deepest, truest instincts about other people and yet not knowing if she could trust those instincts. Hating herself for allowing the thought, she wondered what Martin Sale would make of this conversation. *He* had the right instincts, *he* would be able to draw from Zach what it was that troubled him. He would handle this scene a lot better than Adam had, of that she had no doubt.

276

'Bea's great, isn't she?' she said, reaching for common ground. *Everyone* loved Bea. 'The way she welcomes us all in. She doesn't have to do that.'

Zach brightened. 'Yes. She's an amazing woman.'

'And a wonderful mother. She seems to have no problems giving her children their freedom.' Ginny caught the look Adam sent her way and for once could hardly blame him; of all Bea Sale's demonstrable strengths, this was an oddly specific one to cite.

Zach, however, took it in his stride. 'And herself,' he agreed. 'She has her own life, as well. Her children are only one part of it.'

It seemed to Ginny that there was a kind of sorrow in the way he looked at her then, which puzzled her at first, until . . . until another penny dropped and she was able to see this whole conversation, specifically Zach's sufferance of Adam's rudeness, in a new and clarified light. Of course, someone must have told him about the baby. He felt sorry for them. He was prepared to absorb whatever bullets they chose to fire at him because his pity eclipsed any feelings of offence. He would probably have let Adam hit him if that was what Adam wanted. She hoped that he didn't feel he had to say anything explicit about their loss (was *that* what he was struggling to say? Was *that* why he'd visited yesterday—to pay his respects?), but would continue simply to hold his tongue. She didn't think his belated condolences and Adam's rogue fury would make a pleasant mix.

'Do you have brothers and sisters?' she asked abruptly, earning herself a further incredulous

277

look from Adam. No doubt he thought this basic small talk a little late in the day, but having not spent as much time with the Sale party as he had, Ginny knew very little about their new friend's family background.

Zach nodded. 'I've got two brothers, twins. They're quite a few years younger than me, still at school.'

'Pippi's age,' Adam said, pointedly.

Ginny ignored him. 'And are the three of you close?'

'I'd say so. I *hope* so. I haven't seen so much of them in the last few years, but their school's fairly near my new flat so we get together.'

'This is in Bristol,' Ginny said, remembering that first conversation in the garden, in which she'd taken little part. 'Have you always lived there?'

'Yep, most of my life.'

'And you went to university there, as well?'

'The rain's stopped,' Adam announced, not caring to disguise the obviousness of his interruption. 'Thank the lord!'

Unsurprisingly, Zach took this as a request for him to leave. He sprang to his feet and, before Ginny could stop him, was already at the sink, rinsing his mug under the tap, running his wet hands through his hair in an attempt to smooth it down. She walked him to the door, mouthing a small 'Sorry', which he traded with an apologetic gesture of his own. Then she took his towel from him, said she'd see him the following evening for his party and, with considerably less drama than had accompanied his arrival, he was gone.

She waited a few moments before turning on Adam. As far as she was concerned, the storm still

278

raged. 'Did you have to be *quite* so rude to him? That was humiliating! What *is* it with you and Pippi Sale?'

But Adam looked unrepentant. 'What is it with you and *him*? How has he got you all falling at his feet? What's his secret?'

'You mean he's got *Pippi* falling at his feet. She's the only one. Is that what you don't like, eh? You're jealous of him because he's the one she wants? What on earth did you expect?'

Adam scoffed at her. 'Just because I'm not prepared to behave like he's the *messiah*, it doesn't mean I'm jealous.'

'No one behaves like he's the messiah,' Ginny protested, 'what are you talking about? You're being so *weird* today.'

Adam huffed, somehow managing to bring true contempt to a simple exhalation of breath. 'I suppose it's because he's so good looking, is it? Forty years of feminism out the window for the sake of a half-decent bit of bone structure!'

'What? What *is* your problem?' For all her bravado, Ginny was shaken by this display, and quite mystified. She couldn't remember ever having seen Adam get so worked up about someone he knew so little. A new idea struck. 'Did something happen when you were out on the boat with him the other day?'

'Of course not.' Adam looked stonily at her. 'I just don't trust him, that's all. Can't I be allowed the occasional instinct? Or is that a privilege reserved exclusively for you?'

This was getting dangerously distracting, but out of practice though she was Ginny could recognise a deflection when she heard one, and she was certain Adam was steering—or, more correctly, steamrollering—the subject away from Pippi. She was damned if she was going to let him get away with that. 'She's not your responsibility, Adam. She's got a father of her own to protect her. And from where I'm sitting, she doesn't need any protection from either of you. So what if Zach's got a girlfriend back home? If anyone can handle that, she can. She's eighteen. She's a player. If you ask me we should be more worried for this *other* woman.' She drew breath, beginning to weary of this. Hadn't it begun with closeness, with a cuddle by the window as they watched the storm together? How had it deteriorated so wretchedly? 'And perhaps you'd like to tell me why you were so annoyed with *me*? I was right, wasn't I? There *was* someone out there.'

'Not anyone who needed our help,' Adam said. He couldn't stop himself making this personal. Something about Zach—or Zach and Pippi— really, really bothered him, and Ginny had a feeling he wasn't altogether sure what it was himself.

'Why are you being like this?' she asked, simply. It's me who does it, she added silently, it's me who causes scenes; it's *your* job to reason with *me*. 'Adam?'

And that little shift in tone, a subtle change in her eyes, was enough for his face to fall in capitulation. He stepped towards her. 'You realise what we're doing, don't you?'

'Arguing again,' she said, almost in wonder. In an odd way, she was starting to *need* the conflict between them. It reinvigorated her; it made their time together less . . . less relentless. Along with

280

the unwelcome return to intimacy between them, it gave her something to think about, a tiny bubble of air in the choking spume of her usual thoughts.

On that cheerful note, she sank back into the sofa, the seat still warm from Zach's body, and curled up her feet beneath her. Both of them making a conscious effort not to sulk, she and Adam settled into silence with their books, ready to sit out the rest of the day and wait for the sun to reappear, as it would, he predicted, in the early evening, at which time they'd be able to venture out for an early dinner. They took it in turns to fetch drinks or check the window for an update on drying conditions. Later, they were getting on well enough to be able to laugh a little when Adam made a joking reference to their little search and rescue mission that morning.

Even so, it was a relief to Ginny when the end of the day came and there'd been no news of a drowning.

CHAPTER NINETEEN

MONDAY

After the downpour the sky was an uncertain pale grey, the surface of the lake streaked with pearly currents. Stepping outside, Bea could tell straight away that all the smells of Orta had been blown about, torn from their rightful places and held aloft until the winds allowed them to resettle. The pine from the mountains was distinct, as was the sweetness of the wildflowers, and there was also the scent of brine, as if they were by the ocean. Despite the fragile sky, everything below looked thoroughly renewed, the greens more luminous, the stone sparkling clean; even her own skin responded to the air with a delighted flush. It felt unutterably magical—half an hour later and she was sure she would have missed it.

She wondered where Zach had been during the storm.

She'd thought about him during those hours of confinement, when she and her family had sat downstairs reading and drinking coffee and watching the water lashing on to the terraces, at first streaming in silky curves between the pebbles, later covering them entirely when the drainage system surrendered. She'd thought of little else since she'd woken this morning (was he too new to be in her dreams? she wondered. In sleep, at least, she had some respite).

Having her three children close by had done nothing to censor her thoughts; if anything, their presence provoked new ones, new fears. And, strangely, it was not Pippi who caused her the most anguish, though Bea knew she should be, but Dom. Looking at him stretched out on the sofa opposite, totally unconscious of his own beauty and grace, she'd thought: 'Why would a man in his twenties be interested in me? It makes no sense.' And not merely interested, but fascinated, infatuated—or so Zach claimed to be. There had to be a mistake, a misunderstanding on her part. Or a trick on his: a horrible, heartbreaking joke.

But she couldn't believe it was that. For all his wisecracks, Zach was not the joking kind.

Twenty-four hours ago, in a room across the hall

from this one, he had left Pippi on the sun terrace and hunted her down, intent on being alone with her for just five forbidden minutes. (She'd known he would, wanted him to; why else had she gone out and announced her presence to the two of them?) The sight of his desire had dismantled her as easily as it had the night before and their kisses, dangerous enough the first time, were now, given Pippi's proximity (not to mention Susanna's), reckless, nihilistic. They were, at least, short-lived, for he quickly broke away to demand, 'Just tell me one thing, Bea.'

'What?' She could feel the press of his breath on her face, smell the cigarette he'd been smoking and the sweat on his skin, too, hot from lying in the sun.

'Why are you still married to this man when he can't even be bothered to be here with you?'

This man. It was terrifying, mesmerising, to hear Marty condemned with such scorn.

'Tell me,' he repeated.

'I won't be soon, I won't be married to him,' she whispered, the words tumbling, drawn by his urgency. 'This holiday is the end. I decided long before we came here. I've already seen a solicitor.'

'You're *leaving* him?' Zach withdrew his face an inch or two, his eyes soft and liquid as they refocused. 'Does he know that?'

'No, no one does, except the solicitor.' And it was true. Not her friends at home, even her closest confidante Patricia—especially Patricia, if she was honest—and not Ginny either, for in the peculiar comfort-of-strangers moments the two women had been sharing, Bea had said only that she'd *meant* to leave, once, in the past, not that she still planned

283

to. And yet, within days of knowing Zach, she found she could conceal nothing from him, nothing at all. It was as dangerous as it was inexplicable. 'Otherwise we couldn't really have come out here. It wouldn't have worked.' As if it was working as it was! She had already slept with another man, hadn't she? 'I want to wait till we get home before I tell everyone. There's stuff going on that takes priority.'

'What stuff?' He was moving closer again, locking her hands against the small of her back, pressing his lower body against her. Her groin still ached from the night before.

For once, she managed to refuse him an answer. 'Nothing. Nothing to do with this. And you need to keep this a secret, Zach. You know that, don't you?'

He nodded. 'You know I will.' Then his lips kinked wickedly at the corners. 'So long as you promise to come again tonight.'

There was no point protesting when they both knew she didn't mean it. 'I'll try.'

It was easier than the first time to sneak away. Esther and Pippi—friends again, apparently, though Dom didn't appear to be involved in the rapprochement—were going out to a bar after dinner, hopeful that Zach might join them later, though Bea knew he'd been careful not to promise them. She left after a decent interval, taking the longer route along the upper roads and entering the piazza from the opposite direction. If, by chance, she ran into the girls before she reached the *albergo*, well, the most she risked was their disappointment that their mother preferred her own company to theirs.

In the hotel, fidgeting at the reception desk, she noticed what she'd missed the first time, the general shabbiness of the place—despite its piazza location this was no *palazzo*—and the details of it: the dirty grey marble in that cheap nougat pattern she disliked, the light fittings on the stairwell bought from a supermarket twenty years ago, the crispy nylon curtains at the window. Her nose picked out the lingering smells of old meals and antique drains, of a night porter in need of a shower. It was worlds from the luxurious watchtower suite, from the scented sultan's bed she shared with Marty.

But it had Zach in it, and, as she was discovering, he had a habit of making everything else disappear.

This time her footsteps clattered eagerly on the stairs and he was waiting at the door, closing it quickly behind her, speaking at once. 'You're here . . . you took too long . . .' His voice was in her hair, against her skin, more erotic than any touch. The back of her neck was hot from her walk through streets baked all day in the sun, and the moisture of his breath made her lift her chin and stretch her throat, roll her head to the side. He began peeling her dress from her with his thumbs, as easily as the skin of fruit.

'Happy?' he asked, lowering her on to the mattress. As she began to consider her answer, he said, impatiently, 'Just yes or no.'

'Yes. Of course yes.'

He continued to speak, to ask her questions, the entire time he made love to her: 'I couldn't wait . . .'; 'The afternoon seemed so long . . .'; 'I thought I was losing my mind . . .'; 'Have you thought of

285

me?'; 'What did you imagine us doing?'; 'Tell me how that feels . . .'; 'I love your smell'; and, especially, over and over again, 'I want you, Bea . . . I want you, Bea . . .' It was intoxicating, hypnotic, and all the time she thought her body might combust with the pleasure of it (and it almost did).

Later, she thought she understood that her attraction to him was not only physical, it was of the soul. *Of the soul*: not a phrase she'd used in the last quarter-century and she didn't know if that was because she was only now wise enough to know what it meant or merely indulging in some sort of second adolescence. But this wasn't the cliché of passion making her feel young again, it was simply that the last time she'd felt like this she *had* been young—and so youth was all she had to compare it with. The passion itself belonged to any generation fearless enough to seize it.

Bea said to him, as they lay together, 'You've done this before, haven't you?' Then, at the sight of his amused half-smile, 'I mean . . .'

'I know what you mean.' And he told her he'd been involved with another older woman, not married as Bea was, but someone who had nonetheless beaten her to any protest she might care to make. It had been her reservations, and not any on his part, that had brought the relationship to an end. 'She was fine when we were together,' he said, 'it was when we were apart that she'd do it.'

'Do what?'

'Build the case against me.' He was on his feet, looking about for his cigarettes, lighting himself one (he didn't seem to care for the hotel's no-smoking rule, but that seemed a minor infraction next to his casual appropriation of another man's wife). He returned that frank and beautiful grey gaze of his to her face. 'Don't do that to me, Bea. Whatever you do, please don't do that.'

'What?' she repeated, edging towards him.

He took a long drag on the cigarette, making its end spark orange. She loved the shape of his lips as he exhaled. 'The same doubts, over and over, the same agonising. All totally groundless. Believe me, it's a very tedious way to break someone's heart.'

Bea didn't answer. Already, after just a short time of knowing him, she thought she had sympathy with this other woman's plight. For when she was alone with him, she was fine, too (better than fine: euphoric, happier than she could remember ever having been). Admittedly she got pop-up warnings in her head—neat little speech bubbles telling her she was crazy, that sleeping with him was the most foolish thing she'd done in her whole life—but the fact that he plainly did not was proving a powerful enough reason to ignore her own. And he genuinely didn't seem to think their ages of the slightest relevance. It was not that he had some sort of fetish for breasts past their best or dimpled thighs or permanent frown lines, it was more that they didn't appear to him to *be* that way. It was how she imagined an artist might feel about his model, transfixed by the body in front of him because of that one true fundamental connection. (The soul thing, again.)

It was as he'd said himself: the problem was when she was away from him—

'What, Bea? What is it? What are you thinking?' He was hypersensitive to alterations in her mood, in the degrees of enthusiasm with which she kissed

287

and touched. He rested his burning cigarette on the edge of the ashtray and propelled her gently towards the nearest wall, holding her against it, his fingers threaded through hers, their knuckles scraping against the rough plaster. 'You *must* know by now that I like you. I'd like you whatever.'

'Whatever what?' she asked, smiling.

'Whatever everything. If you grew horns.'

'And I you,' she said, suddenly serious.

'Good, then there's nothing to worry about, is there?'

She liked that he didn't only monitor these switches of emotions of hers, but adjusted himself to absorb them, make their colours his. It was a kind of camouflage that allowed him to appear right for her whatever her state of mind. And he did it quite intuitively; there was no art to it.

'You're so sure about this, aren't you?' she murmured.

'Of course I am. How could anyone *not* be with you?'

'It would be natural not to be sure, it would be sensible.'

Sensible? His face made it quite obvious there was no place for that word in this room.

'Zach, I—'

'Ssh a minute . . .' Keeping one of her hands linked tightly in his, he released the other and moved closer to the front window, stretching their joined arms across the wall between them. 'I thought so.' And with his free hand he delicately closed the nearest shutter.

'What?' Bea said, watching but not moving.

'Pippi and Esther. They're down there, on the square.'

In a single moment of violence she felt turned inside-out. The fear swallowed her whole body, withdrawing its cute little cartoon doubts and instead screaming the worst of all obscenities at her. She snatched her other hand from his, unable to breathe for the terror and also the despair (was it over already, this glorious adventure?) and cried out, 'They're not coming up, are they? Oh God . . .' She peered out of the unshuttered half of the window from behind his shoulder—sure enough, her two daughters were standing there, heartbreakingly familiar for their mismatching dress styles—before moving frantically about the room, not knowing what she was looking for or where she hoped to hide. There *was* nowhere: the wardrobe was narrow and too lightweight, the bathroom, yes, but how would Zach be able to stop one of the girls using the loo if they wanted to? (Quite apart from any other needs, Pippi was constantly reapplying lipstick.)

'Don't let them come in,' she instructed him, 'just go with them, OK? I'll leave afterwards. Quick, put your shirt on, get ready to go.'

But Zach did nothing of the sort. 'It's cool.' He shook his head, calm, in charge. 'They're moving away, look. They didn't even glance up and they don't know this is my window, anyway. They'll be going to that jazz bar place, like they said. Besides, they wouldn't come here because they know I'm not around until much later.'

Bea was not mollified. She hovered in the doorway of the bathroom, grabbing at the nearest thing to cover herself: a damp bath towel. 'What did you tell them you'd be doing exactly?'

From across the room he eyed her mildly, a

smile forming at the sight of the inadequate towel. Oh my God, he's a sociopath, Bea thought; he feels no fear. 'I said I was getting a train into Milan to meet a friend from England and I wouldn't be back till late evening, eleven-ish. Anyway, I told reception not to disturb us. *Non disturbare.*' He smirked at her. 'One of the few phrases in Italian I've managed to learn.'

'But if they think you're in Milan and you've told recep—'

He cut her off. 'If they think I'm in Milan, they'll know not to bother *asking* reception. Seriously, don't panic.' He moved unhurriedly to check the window again, before settling on the ledge. 'They've gone. They were never in earshot, anyway, not even close to it.'

She dropped the towel. Reluctant to rejoin him at the window, she sat on the edge of the bed. It was a mess, the covers kicked to the floor and the sheet pulled away from the mattress. She gathered the sheet in her hands behind her, making a rope of it, as if that might centre her somehow and bring an end to the ghastly pull of dread in her stomach. Zach, meanwhile, recovered his cigarette from the ashtray and smoked the end of it as if nothing had happened. He was still grinning at her, his eyes sliding over her shoulders and breasts. She could see he was contemplating what to do with her next.

'That looks good, like you're all tied up.'

'Don't, Zach, please. This is awful.' But even with her next breath the shock was beginning to abate; for a moment it felt like an ally deserting her, leaving her at the mercy of the enemy. 'I wish you hadn't seen them, I wish I hadn't known.'

'I wish I hadn't told you,' he agreed.

'Oh God, this is wrong.'

He ground out the cigarette and sighed. 'It's not wrong. You act like you're Madame Bovary or something. You're not going to be cast out of society and left to turn feral just because you've slept with me. And want to again in five minutes' time.'

She bit back a smile and, as she did, she felt the last of her terror slipping away, the residual guilt pathetically weak and unconvincing. 'Shouldn't it be *my* job to patronise *you*?' she said.

He shrugged. 'I'm only saying: it's the twenty-first century and you're leaving Marty anyway. You're allowed to be with someone else.'

'Hush.' She put her fingers to her lips.

'What? No one can hear.' His wide eyes narrowed. 'You're not going to pretend you didn't tell me that, are you?'

Bea let her hand drop, looked away. 'No, of course I'm not. I just don't like hearing it like that, as if it's done already. He doesn't know, Zach. *They* don't know. You're the only one who knows.'

'That you're leaving him,' he repeated, with open relish.

'Yes.' She marvelled that a week ago she had not conceived of this man's existence and now he was her closest intimate, her co-conspirator. (Her *lover*.) Again, she felt unable to be anything but truthful with him—she was hell-bent on full disclosure, in fact—even in the face of a faint, niggling instinct that her openness might not be being fully reciprocated. What did she know, after all, about *him*? Who *was* he, standing there looking so beautifully dissolute, so pleased with himself for having seduced her with such ease, surveying her naked body with total composure while she agonised about leaving her husband?

'I'm leaving a lot more than him,' she said, annoyed with herself for being able only to be half-annoyed with him and, in spite of everything she said, hastening through the motions of her defence as if purely for the record. 'I'm leaving my whole adult life, Zach. I'm leaving stuff that happened when you were still just a kid.'

He stopped looking at her breasts, his eyebrows lifting. 'OK. So now we're even on the patronising.'

'Yes, we are. And I should go.' She began scanning the floor for her underwear, but half-heartedly, stirring the fallen bedcover with her foot while otherwise not moving.

At once Zach closed the few feet between them, as she'd known he would. 'Come on, you need to wait half an hour, at least. Let the girls get where they're going. This is by far the safest place to hide.'

She wanted to believe him so badly that when he began touching her again she let the feeling grow, the feeling she couldn't describe, only that it was something between hunger and gluttony and would quickly reach the point where she couldn't have stopped even if she'd wanted to, not as long as he touched her, not even if there *had* come a knock at the door, from the kids, from Marty, from all of them.

An hour later, finally starting to gather her scattered clothes, she said, 'I can't come tomorrow night. He really will be back by then.'

On the bed, Zach's expression clouded, but he nodded.

'What are your plans with Pippi and the others?'

'Oh God . . .' He groaned, half-covering his face with his palms. 'She didn't tell you?'

'Tell me what?'

He took his hands away and grimaced, the closest to embarrassment she'd seen in him. 'She wants to host a dinner party for me at the villa on Tuesday for my birthday.'

Bea gasped, not sure she could process fresh turmoil so soon. 'When did she suggest this?'

'She texted me this afternoon, not long after I left your place. She didn't say anything about it at dinner?'

Bea stared at him, horrified. 'No. She refused to speak with Dom at the table. They've fallen out.'

'Oh yes, she mentioned that this morning.'

All she could think was, *Marty will be back, Marty will be back*, and only when the words stopped repeating themselves did she register their full shame, because she knew she should be worrying about her daughter's feelings before her own, about the news that Pippi had clearly not given up on Zach, as she had hoped, and that sooner or later she *would* be hurt by him. Yes, Pippi showed every sign of being like her father, relishing the chase, the moment of capture, but, still, she had feelings, she had pride. She'd been out on the piazza right near Zach's hotel; she *must* have been hoping to bump into him.

'I'm sure she'll let you in on the plan tomorrow,' Zach sighed. 'Especially as she'll be hoping you'll cook. Or Susanna.'

A reasonable presumption as far as Pippi was concerned, but unthinkable now for Bea. She felt tears of frustration rise in her eyes. 'Well, that's awkward to say the least. Don't you think? I wish you'd said no!'

He propped himself up on his elbow. 'Hey, don't be upset. It will be fine. I did say no, of course I did, but she didn't listen. She was gabbling in my ear about *foie gras* and handmade chocolates and God knows what. Come on, Bea, you know how she takes the ball and bounces it to the moon.'

Startled, Bea stared at him. How did he know this about people? He had just summed Pippi up more perfectly than she, in eighteen years, had ever managed. 'I don't understand,' she whispered. 'You know us so well, not just me, all of us. How do you do it?'

'It's just a question of paying attention.' He crawled across the mattress to kiss her hand, tracing the bones on either side of her wrist. 'Anyway, I'm not sorry. It will probably be my last night here, so I'll want to see *you*, and if that's the only way . . .'

'Your last night?'

'I'll head home on Wednesday, maybe Thursday.' He said this in a terrible, fatalistic way, as though the decision was not his to make.

'But you said you weren't going yet? I don't want you to go,' Bea told him. 'Do you have to? Why?' Now she couldn't imagine the rest of this holiday without him; she couldn't imagine her future without him, but that was something she was going to have to overcome, and quickly, before it took permanent possession of her.

He pulled her down into a sitting position and his hands were in her hair, his lips on her neck and her mouth, and they kissed for a long time. 'You don't want me to go,' he grumbled, 'but you expect me to stay here with no chance of being alone with you. That would be torture.'

'It will be exactly the same for me,' she protested, weakly.

'Will it? Exactly the same?' He looked into her face, the tips of their noses touching. 'I'm not going to be sharing a bed with anyone.'

She lowered her eyes, knowing what he was about to ask.

'Will you sleep with him?' he demanded, sure enough. 'When he comes back tomorrow?'

She looked up again, wondering if she dared brave a joke; he was so frighteningly intense. 'Let's not forget who the other guy is here, Zach. My husband is the one I'm *supposed* to be sleeping with.'

In reply he wound strands of her hair around his fingers, pulling them tight, kissing her again. 'Just tell me, Bea, are you going to fuck him or not?'

She decided to answer him seriously before he tore himself—or her—apart. 'No, of course I'm not.'

'How can you avoid it in that honeymoon suite up there?'

'Because we're an old married couple and there's not the same . . .' She paused, smiling despite herself. 'There's not the same temptation.'

'If this is what we're like here, imagine what we'd be like there . . .' His words were more an utterance of pain than anything else and she had to close her eyes, the rush of desire was so strong. The idea of the two of them in the villa—empty of her family, of course—had occupied her imagination before it had his . . . which only led to more kissing, more hopeless delaying of her exit.

'What about tomorrow?' she said, at last. 'What

are you doing? Are you seeing Pippi or Dom?'

He shook his head. 'I'll probably steer clear—if I can't see you.'

The relief she felt was riddled with disappointment. Once more, concern for her daughter played second fiddle to her own feelings. 'But you'll come on Tuesday, for this party.' In making it a statement and not a question, she prayed that he would not do what she'd just claimed she wished for: back out. Already the idea of a dinner party was becoming less impossible to her, more workable. After all, Pippi had not suspected a thing when the three of them had talked on the terrace that morning, or when they'd had lunch together afterwards, so it wasn't as if she and Zach were altering the laws of physics by being in the same room. No one else knew what had changed.

She decided that, if Pippi had not done so already, she would invite Adam and Ginny to the dinner, dilute the mix a bit. With so many distractions, Marty would be too busy to pick up on any clues. It gave her a cold, uneasy feeling to realise that she had no idea what to expect of her husband when she saw him again: would he be so familiar with the state of unfaithfulness that he could detect it at a glance, or was his trust in her so ingrained that his famous timing would desert him and cause him to be the last to know? In her favour—though that was hardly the right phrase—was the fact that he'd seemed oblivious to the differences in Dom's mood this last week or two, or if not oblivious, then untroubled by them.

Having at last pulled on her underwear and dress and found her wrap (not that she needed an extra layer for the heat was more feverish than ever, reminding her that Susanna had said a storm was expected overnight), she turned to him. 'Maybe we can get a few minutes together on Tuesday during the day . . . Shall I look for an opportunity?'

He was on his feet at once, kissing her a last time. 'Yes. Just say how and when. I'll be here.'

She moved to the door. 'If I can, I'll text. Otherwise . . . otherwise, the dinner for your birthday.' She said the last word in wonder. She couldn't bear to ask.

'I'll be twenty-five,' he said, answering anyway.

That was when she finally left.

*   *   *

Hearing the whine of the main gates opening, she walked around to the rear of the house in time to see the taxi pull up at the door. Marty. And of course it was as if he'd banished the storm and cleared the sky personally, for the sun was suddenly fierce again and the pleasant tingle on her skin had turned in the last few seconds to a warning burn.

She waited for him in the shade of the porch, telling herself that nothing had changed, not where it concerned the two of them. 'You made it, then.'

'Jeez, only just,' he said, kissing her. The kiss landed on the corner of her mouth and she had to stop herself from drawing back from it. 'I thought for a minute we weren't going to be able to land.' It was his one weakness, a fear of turbulence in the air. He had dreams about planes cracking open and watching himself twist to earth like a sycamore

297

seed. It wasn't that he thought he was immortal (or maybe he did—it would be a ridiculous delusion in anyone but him), it was just that he didn't want his life to end before he'd declared his readiness for it. In the beginning she'd been touched by this little vulnerability—the part of him only she shared—and then it started cropping up in press interviews and before she knew it it was one of the handful of things *everyone* knew about Marty Sale, along with his fondness for cheese fondue and the extravagance with which he adored his wife.

'Well, you obviously did,' she said, cheerfully. 'Poor you. Well, come and see everyone, we're all inside. It's only just stopped raining.'

She was reasonably confident she sounded like the woman he had kissed goodbye on Thursday morning and not someone whose body was still sore from the intervening attentions of another man. Before his arrival, she'd worried she might be broken with remorse for those two nights with Zach, for the many times they'd had sex in the hours they'd been together, for the change in ownership (for that, undeniably, was how it felt). Would she be able to stop herself from confessing to Marty the moment she saw him?

Then, passing through the main hall to the sitting room she noticed the console table in whose drawer she had slipped the message from that woman Cally. All at once it was as if the guilt had been washed from her with the rain. What she had done in Marty's absence was nothing compared with his multiple infidelities over the course of two decades (she was fairly certain he'd lost count himself); and finding how seriously she took her own betrayal of him only made her more outraged by the sustained casualness of his. In a funny way he'd walked straight into a catch-22—in cheating on him she might have been inclined to let him off the hook, destroyed the phone message in a spirit of quid pro quo, and yet it was only in being unfaithful herself that she'd finally understood just how unforgivable an act it was.

She allowed him plenty of time to catch up with the kids before she said, discreetly, 'We need to talk.'

He raised an eyebrow. 'Sure, I need a shower anyway. Come up to the bedroom with me.'

He strode up the stairs, overtaking her and then calling pre-emptively over his shoulder, 'I'd forgotten how amazing this place is. Have you found any secret rooms while I've been away?'

When she didn't answer, he said, 'Has something happened? Except for that bloody great storm, obviously.'

Has something happened? She wanted to throw her arms in the air and scream, *Everything!*

Safely in their suite, doors closed, she held out the message to him and said, coldly, 'This came when you were away.'

He frowned at her changed tone. 'What came? What is that?'

'It's a phone message. Who is Cally Hastings, Marty?'

He took it from her, glanced at it, and handed it straight back. 'Cally? I have no idea.'

'Oh, *please*, just tell me the truth.' A strange, liquid relish was spreading through her veins; in all their confrontations, even those involving ambushes like this one when she'd had the element of surprise on her side, she'd not once felt this kind of power. She'd never believed that the bottom line was hers to declare and not his. Well, if this was what guilt gave her then she should have slept with someone else a long time ago. 'You never know,' she added, dryly, 'a bit of honesty now might save you a lot of money later.'

He looked sharply at her, obviously floored by the implication. 'What? What does *that* mean?' Then he recovered and turned away from her, as if to let her know that his question had been rhetorical, after all, and he wanted no more of this discussion. He began pulling at the upper buttons of his shirt, evidently still planning to shower (if he asked her what shirt he should wear when he got out she thought she'd tie the sleeves around his neck and strangle him with it). 'Can I just have a second to get my breath back?' he muttered, with an added note of indignation. 'Clean myself up before you continue with your little "update" . . .'

Bea shook her head, not caring for the inverted commas he'd put around the last word. 'It's not an update, Marty, it's a question. Who is she?'

'I'm telling you I don't know anyone called Cally and that is the truth. Besides, there's no way Angela would have given someone the number here. It's totally off limits.'

She sighed, arching her eyebrows. 'Girlfriends have a way of slipping through the barriers, though, don't they? And who can blame them? I don't suppose I would want to stay off limits either if it were me . . .' And imagining herself as the mistress and not the wife caused an unexpected whoosh of sexual memory, of Zach, of the feeling of him inside her, and she had to steady herself with a hand pressed to her chest. 'Look what they could have!' She gestured to the room, the luxurious furniture, the sheer extravagance of the space. 'All of this, it's the stuff of dreams!'

'I don't know what you're talking about.' Marty stood staring at her, as unnerved as she'd ever seen him, and she knew that it was not so much her choice of words that had caused this (she'd never before articulated a sense of *sympathy* with the other woman—far from it) but the message she was transmitting between the lines, the message that she was no longer fighting for him, that she was at last willing to give 'all of this' up.

He stepped towards her, took the note from her hand a second time, examined it properly. 'Bea, I swear to you I don't know who this is. And look, it just says for "*Signor*"! It's probably just a wrong number. Tell me you weren't serious just then, were you, about . . . what you said?'

She allowed herself to note that he couldn't bring himself to use the word 'divorce', but that was as distracted as she was willing to get. 'Think, Martin: *Cally.*'

He pouted, considering. 'At college, in the year above, there was a girl called Cally, I think, or was it Cathy? Not anyone of any note.'

'I'm sure she'd be delighted to hear it.'

He made an explosive sound. 'She wouldn't know who the hell I was! What's going on, Bea, what's got into you?' His whole upper body heaved with exasperation, his shoulders and arms shifting as he tried to shake the irritation from his frame. Whenever he was angry she was reminded of the sheer solid breadth of him, the physical masculinity that had always been part of his appeal. 'I thought you'd be having a whale of a time out here, not

301

festering over some fucking wrong number.' Then, as it often did in times of danger, a solution presented itself even as he spoke (he would have been a brilliant simultaneous interpreter): 'Has it occurred to you that you could phone this number and put yourself out of your misery?'

It's not misery, she thought, not any more: it's pride. Pride and a need to tie up loose ends, to pave the way for as clean a break as possible and that meant knowing exactly what she was dealing with, exactly who might be waiting in the wings. She needed to know if Cally was going to slot into her place, start building a relationship with her children (newly powerful though she felt, she was not ready to entertain the notion that the other woman might already have met them).

Martin extracted his BlackBerry from his back pocket and passed it to her.

'Why would I use *your* phone?' she scoffed. 'She'll see your number and be able to prepare herself.'

Now it was his turn to arch an eyebrow. 'Hardly. If she's who you seem to think she is then she'll answer as if she's manning a sex line, won't she? Fine, use your phone if you don't want mine.'

'My phone? Do you work out contingencies with them, in case I call? Who do they have to pretend to be? A supplier? An "investor"?' Now it was Bea's turn to put inverted commas around her words.

Marty's eyes narrowed. 'Oh come on, Bea, I thought we were over all this. This is pure paranoia.'

Scared by the thrill she was feeling, the pleasure in the sting her flushed cheeks brought, the pain of her pounding heart, she said, 'No, Marty, it's reality. This is how it feels to be married to you. If you hadn't done it a million times before I wouldn't *need* to wonder about every message.'

'Just phone,' he said, wearily. 'Before one of us says something *really* stupid.'

'Or really necessary,' she said.

'Call her, Bea. Use one of the kids' phones if it makes you feel better.'

In the end, she used her own; it *did* seem unlikely any mistress would have the wife's number pre-programmed, however thorough her sense of self-preservation.

The call was picked up even before the second ring. 'Hello?'

'Hello,' Bea said, coolly. 'Is this Cally?'

'Yes. Who is this?' The woman sounded about Bea's own age, and as unsure of herself as Bea was sure.

By her side, Martin waited, breathing softly.

'I'm calling because you left a message for my husband. At Villa Isola, in Orta, Italy?'

In her ear, there was a reaction of the type you'd expect on breaking the news that a loved one had pulled through after six-hour emergency surgery. 'Oh, thank God, yes! Thank you, thank you so much for phoning. You're married to Adam, are you? Are you . . . Virginia, then?'

Bea was taken aback. 'Virginia? No, I'm not. You mean your message was not for . . . it was for *Adam*?'

Feeling rather than seeing Martin's triumphant expression, she kept her head bowed, concentrating on the rush of words coming through the earpiece.

'Adam Trustlove, yes. I've obviously rung the wrong number, have I? Oh God. But you said Villa Isola and I'm sure that's where the travel agent said he was staying . . .' The woman stopped herself, then, as though she'd broken a confidence and was terrified of the consequences.

Martin shifted position in a bid for Bea's attention and she struggled to ignore his querying expression in front of her. She was finding this phone call more and more perplexing. Having had her assumptions dashed, she didn't think she had the energy to enter into a second personal drama and it was all she could do to keep her voice courteous and kind. 'No, don't worry,' she said, at last, 'you have come through to the right place. Adam is staying nearby, but they haven't got a phone in the boathouse, that's probably why you've had this mix-up. I can get a message to him if you like?'

'Thank you. Please just ask him to phone me, whenever it's convenient.'

That last phrase was sweetly quaint. Convenient, Bea thought; was there anything about this tangle of loves and losses and sheer oversized egos that was *convenient*?

'I will do,' she promised.

'Thank you. You've got the number, obviously, then I guess . . . I guess I'll just wait to hear from him.'

There was a silence, as if the woman had forgotten how to go about ending a call, and so Bea said goodbye and hung up first. Marty had moved out of range again and was by the bathroom door, finishing the job of ripping off his shirt and trousers.

'Don't tell me: I'm not the only man in Italy who has work colleagues of a female persuasion?'

She shook her head. 'I don't think she was from his office.' Neither had the woman sounded remotely like any kind of romantic entanglement. Perhaps she was one of Adam's sisters—Ginny had said he had a large, close family—calling to check on them. But then she'd know Ginny's voice, know she was not 'Viginia'. Remembering the Trustloves' tragedy, Bea felt suddenly much, much smaller, whatever the explanation, all that unassailable power she'd been savouring a few minutes ago quite evaporated.

'I'm having a shower,' Marty said, 'if there's nothing else for now?' He stood in front of her again, naked now, and she could see the flush beneath the tan of his collarbone and chest, a rare sign of fury. He was, she noticed with a shock, *trembling* with outrage, a different outrage from the scenes of old, when she'd learned to recognise his over-protesting, come to know the different grades of it. This time, he actually was innocent. It didn't matter, however; it mattered only if someone was watching from the heavens in the hope of witnessing the perfect demonstration of earthbound irony.

'And when I get out, can someone please tell me what the hell's been going on?'

'Nothing's going on,' Bea muttered. 'It was a simple misunderstanding. Just forget it.'

And it took every last ounce of strength to move her eyes in his direction and meet his accusing glare.

CHAPTER TWENTY

TUESDAY

In the first conversation with the paediatric cardiologist, they thought only about what they might have done differently, what they could have known sooner.

Had these been different circumstances, they would have noticed that he was a charming man with a gently modulated voice you could tell would work well with adults and children alike, those with or without hope. There'd be no question too obscure, no outburst of emotion that couldn't be accommodated by his professional demeanour.

They might even have discussed his hair, dyed a violent black and with a touch of the pompadour about it.

'In most cases—I'd say about eighty per cent—we can do specialist antenatal screening and get an idea of any irregularities early on. Then we can make a diagnosis and discuss whether the parents would like the pregnancy to continue to full term.'

'I would have,' Ginny said, with a leftover ferocity that surprised all of them. 'I would have continued, whether you had found it or not.'

Adam looked less convinced, but in a stunned, uncomprehending sort of way. 'Why weren't we offered that?' he asked. 'The extra screening?'

'Because we had no knowledge of the history of heart problems in Ginny's family. Yours was an undiagnosed emergency.' The reminder—perfectly pitched to soothe even as the words inflamed—was unavoidable, and would be repeated frequently over the next few weeks: don't blame yourselves, but don't blame us, either.

In a second session, with the help of Ginny's aunt's new information, the same consultant eased them into the minefield of her family medical history: the death in infancy of her mother's brother (it wasn't that she'd *forgotten* exactly, only that it had seemed entirely irrelevant when she'd filled in hospital forms sixty years after the event); the four miscarriages she now knew her mother had suffered (and these were just the ones Deanna had been made aware of), including one at eight months, before Ginny herself was conceived; the post-mortem test results that were not known to Deanna but which, if ever unearthed, might cast more light on their situation (or more shadow, depending on how you looked at it). As for the remaining holes in her knowledge, they were like defects in themselves: she didn't know, she wasn't sure, she couldn't remember anyone saying, they'd died before she could ask . . . It was the polar opposite of Adam's long-living clan, the women's easy delivery of baby after baby, their casual references to one another's reproductive health.

Though she and Adam hadn't discussed it explicitly, Ginny had her expectations of how these meetings with the consultant would conclude: they should allow the grieving process its full course before thinking about trying again. Next time, they would be fast-tracked through specialist screening, even if it meant travelling far and wide for the newest techniques and state-of-the-art equipment. But, pressed by Adam, the expert was suddenly offering quite different advice:

'Weighing up what we now know, or at least can deduce, about your family's history of heart disease, as well as the difficulties of this birth and the damage to the uterus, my advice would be to think very carefully about risking another pregnancy.'

She waited for him to add, 'for a year or two', then, realising it was worse than that, breathed 'five years' to herself to see how horrifying that would sound (the answer: *very*). The shock of his full stop knocked the air from her, and it was several seconds before she was able to answer, 'You mean, not have another baby, *ever*?'

'There is a very high risk that the same thing would happen again, and you might suffer even greater damage yourself next time. That's even if you managed to carry to full term a second time. But Mr Roberts can advise more specifically on the obstetrics side of things.'

The views of her obstetrician, or this man's for that matter, on her own physical well-being was suddenly the last thing she cared about.

Adam spoke up. 'But Ginny's OK, isn't she?'

The glossy black head dipped as he consulted his notes. 'I understand he wants to run some more tests, there's a note here about possible PID . . .'

'PID?'

'Pelvic inflammatory disease. It's the—'

'No,' Adam interrupted, fear making him impatient. 'I don't mean the gynaecological stuff, I mean the heart problem. She's lived this long, hasn't she? *She* didn't die at birth.' Ginny closed her eyes tightly, as if darkness could block sound. 'So why couldn't another baby be OK? A girl, like Ginny? Can't you do that thing where you sort out the eggs and see which ones are healthy and which ones have the defect? What's it called again . . . ?'

'You're talking about PGD: pre-implantation genetic diagnosis. There are issues with that, too, Adam, not least to do with funding.' This last provoked in the man a short insider's chuckle. 'But looking at these notes, the main difficulty, as I see it, is the IVF it entails. It can be a long and punishing process, and I'm not sure we would recommend that for Ginny, certainly not for the next few years. We'd have to be confident she was at full strength.' He paused. 'And, as our fertility people will tell you separately, I'm afraid that there's an element of catch-22, because the later you leave this sort of procedure the less likely it is to work. There's every chance it would only bring more heartache.'

'You mean you wouldn't want to throw good money after bad,' Adam said, bitterly.

The cardiologist raised his eyebrows, as if this were a surprising remark rather than an impolite one. 'That's not what I mean at all. I'm only outlining the health risks as I see them.'

Ginny didn't speak. She *couldn't* speak, not least because the consultant appeared to be *smiling* at her. I'm literally unfit for motherhood, she thought. My mother only just managed it, but it ends with me. *It ends here, and I take Adam down with me.*

Later, she wondered what it would have taken for the consultant to have lost his nerve, how much more terrible his pronouncements would need to have been for him to have broken down and sobbed right along with them.

She got the feeling Bea was looking for an excuse to escape the main house—and to escape her family, perhaps—but not before she'd chosen a little treat to bring with her. She always brought an offering when she popped over (this time a bag of bite-sized meringues, glued together in pairs with dark chocolate). Ten days into the holiday, Ginny found she was thinking increasingly in terms of 'always' and 'usually', as though this were not a holiday at all and the boathouse theirs for only a few more days, but a new permanent arrangement and this merely the second week of their settling-in period. Though she hadn't said as much to Adam, not wanting to invite either praise or analysis, she *was* starting to feel settled here; she felt safe, out of the reach of all of London.

Just as Pippi also tended to, Bea hesitated at the gate and politely awaited eye contact before reaching for the latch. Unlike Pippi, however, she did not give the impression of having arrived there expressly to show herself—and her clothes—off. Ginny was starting to appreciate this famous style of Bea Sale's. She was never costumed, as Pippi was, or for that matter visible from outer space by dint of a single accessory; on the contrary, it was often ages before you noticed what she was wearing at all because your attention was drawn always to her face, specifically to those soft-set eyes, the only part of her where feelings might be deciphered. The rest was pure, natural poise. Only later did you see that the colour and cut of her dress framed her to perfection and must surely have been chosen with great care.

Understated, but beautiful: what every woman wanted to be, even the ones with dark, jagged holes inside them, like Ginny.

Bea gestured to the notebook and pen, ever present on her hostess's lap. 'Am I disturbing you?'

'Oh no, I wasn't writing anything,' Ginny said. She didn't explain that she felt stronger when she had her journal on her lap. Not that you could call it a journal, since it contained no words, no dates; it remained simply an unused notepad with a nice cover. Even so, it was her protector, her crutch, her bullet-proof blanket.

'OK, thinking, then.'

'Yes. But it's always good to be stopped from thinking.'

'I'll go along with that,' Bea sighed.

They naturally found mutual ground, Ginny thought. She'd worried she might never be able to relate to other women again, particularly not mothers, but being with Bea proved she could, and slowly, very slowly, the discovery was heartening her. 'You're so kind to bring the meringues. I'll make some coffee.'

'Great.' Bea settled into the second wicker seat as Ginny rose from hers. 'And of course I've forgotten what I *meant* to bring. A message came for Adam, it was a few days ago now but I just assumed it was for Marty, so I've been sitting on it. I got Esther to pop down last night to tell him, but you weren't in.'

'Who was it from?' Ginny asked. Those earlier feelings of safety and separation lurched at the prospect of premature contact with Karen or any of the other Trustloves. She couldn't put it off for ever, she knew, but she certainly hoped to put it off for as long as she and Adam were here. What if they were already trying to fix a date to see them, or planning to meet them at the airport in some grotesque mass-outpouring of family love? Then, before she swerved too far into the unknown, a solution occurred: see them one at a time, not all together. No welcome back wake, no intervention-style lunches. This is *your* life, not theirs.

'Someone called Cally,' Bea said. 'I'm sure Marty will mention it to Adam, but just in case he doesn't, would you let him know?'

'Of course.'

When Ginny returned with the coffee, Bea asked her, in a rare moment of open curiosity, 'So is Cally one of Adam's family?'

Ginny shook her head. 'No, she's not anyone I know. I don't think,' she added, for while it was true that she didn't recognise the name she also knew that the identities of Adam's colleagues, once as familiar to her as they were to him, had slipped altogether from her consciousness. Cally could be his worst enemy or his longest-standing ally for all she remembered. One thing she was sure of was that she wasn't anyone from the hospital, from the retinue of consultants and counsellors and 'special' staff they had become so familiar with. And it was only in thinking this that Ginny understood that she had needed this hideaway as much to escape them as any of Adam's family. Horribly unfair though she knew it was, she felt as if the medical practitioners had been feeding on her corpse these last months, with their warnings and suggestions and tests and probes. Sometimes, they'd made her feel as if *she* was the one who'd died.

312

She hauled herself back to the present. 'It was nice of Martin and Dom to take Adam with them this afternoon. I would have thought they'd want some time on their own, what with Martin just getting back.'

'It was Dom's idea,' Bea said. 'I think he saw how taken Adam was with the boat the other day.'

Of course Ginny immediately made the connection that Bea left unsaid: Dom didn't want to be left alone with his father for reasons to do with the big secret. The others must have opted out too—Pippi and Esther were helping with preparations for the evening, perhaps—and that left Adam to make up the numbers. She very much hoped her husband wouldn't be as rude to the Sale men as he had been to Zach on Sunday. Surely he'd be too overawed by Martin for that?

'He says he wants to book sailing lessons when we get back,' she said. 'Though I don't know how that will be managed in London.'

Bea nodded. 'It is nice to be out on the water. It sounds like such a cliché, but you really do get the chance to leave your troubles on dry land. And when you come ashore again, well, it can feel like you're approaching things from a different angle.'

'Yes, I think Adam finds that. It's good. I'm pleased he's got something new to enjoy.' Ginny could sense Bea eyeing her with an unfamiliar expression and it occurred to her that this was the first time she'd spoken about Adam in this way (as if she really *cared* about him . . .).

'I think it's also good that you've done some things separately on this trip,' Bea said, delicately. 'I know all couples are different, but it makes sense to me that you wouldn't want to be together

313

twenty-four hours a day. There's a limit to how comforting that would be.'

Ginny nodded. We remind each other, that's what she means. We hurt each other just by waking up in the morning with breath in our lungs.

Bea smiled, changing the mood. 'Though I hope you'll be coming together for the famous birthday party tonight?'

'Of course. How's it all going?'

'Very well. I've just been down to the village to choose some wine from the *enoteca* on the square, the one Adam recommended, and we've drafted in a friend of Susanna's to waitress. They're hard at work in the kitchen as we speak.' She chuckled. 'I know it sounds awful, but the lessons at Casa Mista have actually put me off cooking. When we said goodbye to the chef this morning, I felt like I was being set free. Esther feels exactly the same, so I don't feel *too* guilty.'

'Well, you *are* on holiday, why would you want to spend the whole time cooking?' They probably have their own cook at home, Ginny thought, as soon as she'd said it, feeling naive. Or they eat out every night, or attend glamorous awards ceremonies and charity balls. Cooking for her family this holiday has probably been a novelty for Bea. 'I must say, Zach is incredibly lucky to have all this arranged for him. Who stumbles across this sort of VIP treatment when they're backpacking?'

She still wasn't completely comfortable with the gulf between her preconceptions of a high-profile family like the Sales—that they'd want to guard their privacy at all costs, maintain their hard-won sense of superiority—and the evident reality, whereby all comers were welcomed with open

314

arms, taken for jaunts in vintage speedboats, fed homemade meringues and thrown birthday parties. Incredible that Bea should make the trip down to the village in the midday heat to pick up the wine herself and not send a minion to do it.

'Yes, it is a bit over the top, I suppose,' Bea agreed. 'I'm not sure he's desperately keen on it himself, to be honest.' She swirled her coffee in its cup, clockwise, anticlockwise, lost for the moment in her own thoughts, but Ginny found she couldn't help pressing for more. Zach intrigued her: he'd got under her skin yesterday during the storm, and she wanted to know if Bea had the same hunch that he was harbouring something, holding something back.

'Do you ever feel like Zach is, I don't know, being a bit mysterious?'

Bea looked up, lips curving into a smile. 'Mysterious?'

'Yes. The last time I talked to him I got the feeling there was something he wanted to say.'

'Really?' The smile tightened a fraction. She looked uncharacteristically furtive.

'Or maybe it's just because he appeared here so *suddenly*.'

'In Orta? Well, people tend to on holiday,' Bea said, her tone droll. 'We're not supplied with guest lists in advance. Who we meet, who we don't . . . it's all serendipity.'

Ginny couldn't help feeling disappointed that Bea wasn't taking her remarks as seriously as she might have, maybe even deliberately misunderstanding them. 'Well, Adam seems to think he's a bit of a cat among the pigeons. He doesn't like him at all, actually. It's a bit peculiar.'

'Really?' Now, suddenly, Bea *was* serious. She pushed her sunglasses back into her hair, her eyes locking on to Ginny's as she leaned towards her and demanded, 'But do you? Do *you* like him?'

Ginny swallowed the stammer in her voice. She focused on the smudges of mascara under Bea's eyes, a rare occurrence of disarray in the other woman's appearance. 'Yes, I do. I really like him.'

'So do I,' Bea said, and with that she eased back into her chair, rotating her shoulders elegantly before relaxing again. 'I'm not sure why Adam would have that reaction.' She tipped her head to one side, wondering, treating Ginny to the most charming smile. 'And I think this is the first time any of us have been described as *pigeons* . . .'

Relieved to see her obvious amusement, Ginny said, hastily, 'I suppose what he means, what *I* mean, is that I haven't had the chance to find out much about him. I've kept myself hidden away a bit.'

'Well, you'll have the opportunity tonight,' Bea replied, easily. 'There'll only be the eight of us.'

'You're very generous to let Pippi take over the place and play host.'

'Oh, not really, it's lovely to be able to share her energy and spontaneity. She's so like Marty when I first knew him.' Now Bea looked wistful, even regretful. Ginny had never seen so many emotions cross the woman's face in one conversation, and in such rapid succession, too; in a way, it had the feel of a performance about it. 'And between you and me, I feel for her a little bit, as well. A lot, actually.'

'Why?' Ginny hoped she didn't sound too surprised at the idea that Pippi should be in need of other people's compassion.

'Because she really does like Zach and . . . well, you can't force these things. It's either there at the outset, or it's not. You can't *design* attraction.'

That was an interesting phrase, Ginny thought, failing to suppress the connection her mind was making with her own infatuation, for she could no longer deny that this was what Bea's husband had inspired in her. Despite what she'd said to Adam and Zach about not knowing if she wanted to attend the birthday dinner, the truth was she couldn't wait for it, for the chance to be near Martin again, to be able to collect more details of him, to flesh out her growing assortment of fantasies.

She had seen him just once since his return, late that morning, when the men had headed off on their latest jaunt in the Riva. It was another gathering on the jetty, the sun seeming to favour Martin with its spotlight and cast Ginny's own husband into the shadows.

'And how are *you*, Ginny?' he asked in that smooth, lustrous voice of his.

'Fine, thank you.' As she met his eye she felt she could see a difference in him, the half-tone paleness of a few days back in the northern rain, and who knew what mental acclimatisation he'd undergone, too. It felt to her as if the two of them had accelerated in his absence to the kind of close connection whereby the very smallest of alterations could be intuited in the other.

'Keeping to the pavements, I hope?' He said this in an undertone, conspiratorial, flirtatious. Beyond that, he didn't refer specifically to the incident in the road at all and she liked to think this was because he sensed as well as she did there'd been something special, intimate, about the encounter.

'How was London?' she asked.

'Oh, you know, same as it ever was.' But the way he said it made her see—if only for a single jolting second—how utterly preposterous her desires were, how laughable, for Martin Sale was king of the castle and the London he knew was not the London *she* had ever experienced. London was where everything had been made possible for him, whereas for her it would be forever associated with impossibilities.

We need to move away, she thought, abruptly, Adam and I. And not just out of the city, but out of England. Not straight away, not in a hurry, like we've done something wrong, like we're ashamed, but with a proper plan that we've made together, an alternative we know we can live with.

Maybe somewhere like here.

Then, watching Martin at the wheel of the boat, Adam behind him, diminished by the angle of recline the rear seat demanded, all the madness flooded back again, all her longing to be able to rely on someone else, someone bigger and better, to lift her from her dark, halted existence and . . . *elevate* her, place her out of range of all the earth's sorrows.

Yes, she was losing her mind. It was the only explanation for the persistence of these delusions. But at least for the moment she was alone in knowing it.

'And it's not there, then,' she asked Bea, now, 'the attraction between Zach and Pippi? On his side?'

Bea gave a little shrug. 'It seems not. But at least

she's having fun about it. And it's nice for all of us to make an occasion of it. This holiday will be over soon, it'll be as if it never happened . . .' She had begun to speak in a soft, dreamy way, at odds with the careful look she was casting Ginny's way. Ginny couldn't think what was the matter with her—but then *she* was hardly one to judge.

'Adam gave him a hard time about it, the last time we saw him,' she said, unable to leave the subject of Zach alone, if only to oust from her head the continuing presence of Bea's husband.

'Oh, did he? In what way?'

'He just told him he shouldn't be leading her on, I suppose. And . . . oh, I don't know if I should be telling you this, I don't want to worry you, but Zach said there was someone else he was seeing at the moment, which might explain the lack of interest in Pippi. To be honest, it sounded as if he was right in the middle of falling in love.'

'Oh!' Bea looked so flustered by this that Ginny cursed her own lack of tact, rushing to back-pedal. She wasn't reading this conversation at all well. So much for her pride in their common ground!

'Obviously I told Adam to stay out of it. They're both adults. Zach's twenty-five today, isn't he?'

Bea confirmed this with a quick nod, little more than a blink. She continued to look agitated. As if suddenly aware of the make-up smudges, she wiped an index finger under each eye.

'I think Adam forgets things are different now. When he was Pippi's age parents had a lot of influence, but not any more.' Yet again Ginny realised too late how this must have sounded and added, apologetically, 'I don't mean you, of course, I just mean generally. I'm sure you have more

319

influence than most.' When Bea didn't answer, she said, 'Listen to me, you must think I'm obsessed with your daughter's love life!'

'No, no, you're right about the lack of influence,' Bea agreed, beginning to recover herself. It seemed to Ginny that in the period that Martin had been away his wife had acted quite differently; she'd seemed freer, exhilarated even. And yet now he was back she was troubled again. The only conclusion Ginny could draw was that Bea was happier without him, just as she'd confessed on their first meeting.

That was what was wrong with her today: Martin was back. The terrible irony of it!

As if reading her husband's name in her companion's eyes, Bea said, smiling, 'Marty's very revved up for this evening. I warn you, there may be guitar playing.'

'He plays guitar?'

'I wouldn't go that far, but he dabbles. He's one of those men who has a room devoted to his own toys—drum kit, computer games, remote control cars, you name it. Like an adult nursery.' She began to talk in more detail about the Sale house in Kew. At first it seemed as if she were grateful to get off the subject of Pippi and Zach, but soon Ginny grew aware of a quality to her voice that made her think of an old widow reminiscing. 'About fifteen years ago we had the house completely remodelled and the whole of the top floor was given over to the kids—and this playroom of Marty's, of course. There would always be noise coming from above. At first the idea was that we could get some peace from them, all the play dates, Dom and his friends, and Esther

320

was a real tomboy, too. They'd set up battles on the landing or games of cricket. Then, of course, there comes the moment when it's *they* who want the separation from *you*. They start asking to eat their meals up there, they say they want their own front door and an intercom. They want to be able to buzz you in!'

Ginny's eyes widened.

'Of course we said no to all of that. Now Dom and Esther have gone and Pippi's increased her domain. But even she's hardly there now.' Bea paused. 'When I go up there, that's when I feel it most.'

'Feel what?'

Her eyes were full of the softest light. 'That I've lost them.'

'You haven't lost them,' Ginny said, at once, 'they're all here with you now, aren't they? They all look very devoted to you.'

But Bea didn't seem to hear her. She carried on speaking in the same nostalgic voice: 'So anything they want, I try to go along with it, especially on holiday. *This* holiday. In case it's the last.' She seemed to be trying to establish this for herself as much as anything. Ginny could see the conflict in her face, though she couldn't understand the meaning of it. And then, before she could begin to work out how best to respond, Bea seemed to come to, as if released from a state of hypnosis. 'Oh, Ginny, I can't believe how insensitive this is of me, going on about the children all the time!'

Ginny waved her protests aside. 'No, please don't worry, I like it. And I have to get used to the fact that I'm not going to have that.'

Bea looked at her with an expression that was

rare in Ginny's experience these days: the look of someone unafraid to face the full horror of her. She's not scared of me, Ginny realised, she's not scared of my suffering; she wouldn't be scared even if what I had was catching. The thought gave her the strength to add, I have to accept I'm not going to be a mother. The bravado of this statement would have been obvious even to a non-English speaker, but it was not entirely bluff; a tiny portion of it *was* real.

'But why should this be the end?' Bea asked, earnestly. 'You probably don't feel like it now, but don't you think you and Adam will try again, eventually? You're young enough.'

Ginny made herself focus on the green of the rushes, the individual strands, suddenly unable to meet that sincere gaze. 'We can't. We've been told the same thing would happen again.'

Bea stared at her, horrified. All those elusive patterns of her earlier emotions were erased now, her expression open and singular. 'I thought . . .' She faltered, speaking half under her breath. 'I thought there was something else.' Then, 'Isn't there *any* hope?'

'Not really.' As Ginny explained the history, she saw how little she knew for sure herself. It took only a minute or two to share everything she knew. But she accepted that; she accepted that not everything could be known. 'It's all on my side. My parents never told me about it, though I'd been aware they were sad not to be able to have more children. The way it's been explained to me since, I'm a minor miracle myself.'

Bea looked hopeful. 'Maybe there could be another minor miracle?'

'Maybe,' Ginny said. 'That's what Adam says.'

'I don't understand why your family wouldn't tell you something so crucial? If there'd been so many miscarriages before? There must have been some form of diagnosis, even all those years ago?'

'I'm sure my parents would have done, but they died in a car accident when I was nine. I didn't even know the facts of life then, let alone anything about heart disease or fertility. I probably still thought babies were delivered by storks. They would have thought there was plenty of time before they needed to drop the bombshell.'

'But your grandparents, the ones who brought you up, shouldn't they have warned you of what might happen?'

'My aunt Deanna—their daughter—she thinks they probably didn't know the full story. My parents would have spared them a lot of it, especially once I was born and there was a happy ending of sorts. Maybe they all just put the rest down to bad luck. And my grandma was very ill by the time I got pregnant. She hardly knew the basics of her own state of health, let alone anyone else's.'

'But you *could* get pregnant again?' Bea said, gently persistent. 'It's not physically impossible?'

'No, but given all the complications, I can't take the risk. I can't lose another baby, I'd rather die myself.' She couldn't bring herself to look but she knew Bea was gazing at her, that fine maternal heart of hers projected through her eyes. Ginny clutched the notebook closer to her stomach, focused on the texture of its woven cover.

'Oh, Ginny, it must feel like all you've known is loss.' She could hear the tears in Bea's voice.

'Yes, that's exactly how it feels.' Ginny tried a

323

brave smile, but it hardly got a purchase on the corners of her mouth. 'So you see, I'll never be a mother.'

'But that's where you're wrong,' Bea exclaimed, 'because you are already! You're Isaac's mother, aren't you?'

'Not any more.'

'Yes, you are, of course you are. And you always will be.'

At last Ginny found the strength to look her in the eye, and for that one small moment she felt the power of Bea's generosity, the undiluted sincerity of it. For that one small moment it was as if she *hadn't* lost everything, there *was* something left, even if she couldn't hold it in her hands and touch it.

CHAPTER TWENTY-ONE

TUESDAY

Well, it was just *typical* that it should be Dom who got all of the attention that night. Pippi had barely forgiven her brother for one ugly scene and already he was causing another. That was how she saw it, afterwards, when the sting of her own disappointment was so fresh she was still reliving it minute by minute, ghoulishly reproducing the same full-body shudder of humiliation she'd experienced at the time. Even now that she finally understood the reason for Dom's moodiness, she still thought everyone else's reaction to it was just a teeny bit out of proportion. It wasn't like he was terminally ill or anything.

He seemed determined to ruin the party, even before it had begun. First, he kept Dad and Adam out till late in the boat, so late that Ginny had come up to the house to ask if they were lost. 'The mariners', she called them, and it had given Pippi a bit of a surprise to hear her joking like that. Then, once the group had finally returned, Dom made it plain that he wasn't going to make any effort to dress for the dinner party. Even though he'd obviously been swimming in the lake, he just peeled off his used T-shirt and pulled a clean one straight on to his horrible fishy skin (as for his hair, it was a complete freak show!). He then proceeded to sink beer after beer, just sitting out on the terrace on his own while everyone else went upstairs to take a shower, like any normal, civilised person going to a party would. And he really liked Zach, she knew that, so it wasn't disrespect for the guest of honour that was making him be like this. It was disrespect for *her*.

Well, no matter; everything else was just as she'd directed. The food was going to be perfect— Susanna had been baking brioche and stuffing ravioli and doing whatever it was she did with Alpine butter for two days solid now, and Mum had gone down to the *enoteca* near the piazza earlier to choose some special wine. (She'd been ages about it, too, so Pippi knew she must really have pushed the boat out.) By the time the guests were due to arrive, both the terrace and the women were beautifully dressed. Her mother had on the Missoni kaftan again, and a sexy pair of heels Pippi hadn't seen before; Esther wore a soft-pink tea dress (Sale, of course) and the effect of this against her Pears-soap glowing skin made her look like a forties beauty queen saving herself for her soldier sweetheart (the chance would be a fine thing). Pippi herself wore a midnight-blue maxi dress, not a style she normally embraced but this, well, this was a celebration. She pinned her hair up and got Esther to weave flowers into it. 'You look like a bridesmaid,' Esther said, but she meant well. Since their falling out at the weekend she, at least, had been careful to be ultra-nice to her sister, and Pippi was not one to let a penitent off the hook before time.

There were more flowers outside, on the table, on window ledges, great bunches of them in the hand-tied look that Mum always had at home: daisies and peonies and local wildflowers. Not roses—then it really would look as if she thought it was a wedding. And she had got Emilio to string hundreds of extra fairy lights into the trees around the terrace, so many the branches looked as if they'd been encrusted with diamonds. *I want to stay out here for ever*, she thought, dreamily, surveying the effect at dusk. Hollywood couldn't have come up with a more perfect backdrop for her first kiss with Zach; at the end of the evening everyone would melt away except for the two of them. And it was a mild, breezeless evening, too, a fleece of clouds staving off that chill a clear night brought, which was good news because it meant she wouldn't have to put a cardigan over her maxi dress (such a middle-aged look, like a bed-jacket over a nightie!). No, the idea was she'd be taking her clothes *off*.

Adam and Ginny arrived first, which was exactly as she'd planned it, so Zach would get the full hero's welcome. He'd been a little elusive over the last couple of days, off exploring Lake Maggiore yesterday and taking ages to reply to her texts, including the succession of happy-birthday ones she'd sent today. (Pippi could never understand that: if texts weren't answered instantly, then what was the point?) He hadn't come up to the villa at all since Sunday and so had yet to meet her father. He'd love him, though, when he did, of that she was quite confident.

'Oh Pippi, this is all so beautiful,' Ginny cried. 'It's like a magical grotto!'

'Thank you.' For the second time that day, Pippi was surprised, and pleased, to note Ginny's improved mood. She was even wearing a dress in place of her usual jeans and shapeless shirt—albeit a brown rumpled one—and had put quite a lot of make-up on. She's starting to regain herself, Pippi saw, echoing a comment her mother had made after dropping in on their neighbour earlier. Well, thank God; much as she felt awful for the Trustloves, she didn't want Zach's special night to be ruined by long faces. She reserved her brightest smile for Adam, of course, who was slowly rotating on the spot, taking in the galaxy of fairy lights and meadow's worth of fresh flowers with a look of utter amazement. She just *knew* he was wishing he were twenty-five again and that all of this scene setting was because she wanted to sleep with *him*.

Well, maybe it might have been him had Zach not arrived in Orta when he had. Then she remembered the baby again and cast the notion from her mind. She hoped Adam and Ginny would have another one soon; she would send them Sale's bestselling hatbox of new baby clothes when they did.

The group had hardly begun on first drinks when Esther announced, 'Here he comes: the birthday boy himself!' and Pippi bounded over to meet him on the steps. (He always arrived along the lake path, entering the grounds of Villa Isola via the boathouse passageway she'd shown him that first time.)

'Zach, you're here! Happy birthday!' He looked *divine*, there was no other word—except maybe edible. He was clean shaven, his hair adorably mussed up, and he wore a dandyish silver-grey shirt with his usual skinny black jeans and battered deck shoes. Greeting her, his lips curled upwards in embarrassed amusement at the same time as his eyes queried the fuss of it all, like he *still* couldn't work out why everyone wanted to look at him all the time. 'Come on in!' Breathing deeply, she took a chance and reached for his hand, pulling him closer to the gathering. It was not the first time they'd touched—she'd engineered several opportunities before this (the best thing about having the boat was that someone always put out a hand to help you on and off it), but this was the first contact between them to last long enough for her to register fully the length of his fingers, the warmth of his skin, the tight, smooth tendons in his wrist.

'Well, well, well, the famous Zach,' her father said, coming towards them. 'Happy birthday to you!'

Zach removed his hand from Pippi's and used it to shake her father's outstretched one. (Damn, she should have grabbed the *left* one.) 'Thank you,' he said. 'Um, I don't think I've ever seen so many fairy lights in one place.'

'You haven't?' Her father let a professional beat pass before adding, 'I have,' which made Zach laugh too.

Pippi watched with great pride as he next kissed Esther and Ginny hello (he hadn't kissed *her*, she noted, and the omission was surely a manifestation of sexual tension?), shook hands with Adam—who Pippi now saw had a *very* red face after his extended day on the water—and made a point of seeking out Dom, who rudely remained seated. Someone was missing. 'Where's Mum?' she asked.

'Kitchen,' Dom said, with an edge that Pippi knew meant, Shouldn't it be *you* helping Susanna? She ignored him and passed Zach a drink, topping herself up in the process.

'Well, Zach, I'm very grateful to you for entertaining everyone in my absence,' her father said to him.

Zach grinned. 'I'm not sure entertain is the word, but everyone's been really hospitable, yes.'

'And what do you think of Orta?'

'It's beautiful.'

'Have you been over to the island much?'

'Er, just once.'

'Well, I hope you were suitably chastened by the experience?'

'Dad!' Pippi protested, seeing Zach look a little thrown by the question. 'Give him a break, he's just got here.' And Zach slid her a grateful look, which was sweet.

'Tell me what else you've been doing,' her father said. 'I hear you've been out in the boat—pretty cool, isn't it?'

As Zach answered and Pippi watched the two

329

men standing talking together, there was a moment when she had the weirdest feeling, a kind of premonition you could call it, that she was going to—huge breath—*marry* Zach, and this was what it would be like on their wedding day when she arrived at the church: the groom and the father of the bride standing outside, talking slightly nervously as they waited for her (or would her father be in the car with her at that point?—whatever). Maybe it was what Esther had said about the flowers in her hair, but even so Pippi prided herself on her reading of body language and it seemed to her that Zach resembled exactly what you'd imagine a dutiful son-in-law to be. He was kind of like Ferdinand in *The Tempest* (her favourite A-level text), but with much sexier hair, and her father, well, like Prospero he'd be sad to hand over his adored daughter, but he knew it was the natural order of things; it couldn't be stopped, he couldn't be her number one for ever.

They'd come back to Orta and do it, she thought wildly, in that chapel on the top of the cliff on the other side of the lake. She'd heard that was *the* place to get married here.

Encouraged by the earlier hand-pulling, she allowed herself to be a little more tactile with Zach than she'd been on previous meetings. She slipped her arm into his, she stood closer to him, she used her fingertips to brush a petal from his shoulder (just like confetti!). Then, when Ginny came to chat to her father, she began to guide Zach away, only half-listening to the other woman's opening comment, a compliment about her, as it happened, about how incredibly sophisticated Pippi was to have arranged something as lovely as this at such

330

short notice.

Her father's ironic response got her attention again: 'Oh yes, Pippi learned very young the beauty of getting other people to do things for you.'

She smiled and rolled her eyes indulgently. Honestly, wasn't that just what he did himself all day long? Delegate?

'She's forgotten one key ingredient, though,' her father went on.

'What?' Ginny asked. 'It all looks absolutely perfect to me.'

'Music. But she's extremely lucky because *I* can supply that.'

'I'd prefer to stick to the birdsong, Dad,' Pippi quipped to Ginny's delight. 'Seriously.' Leaving the old folk to one another, she beamed at her guest of honour. 'Have you had a good day? Spoken to your family?'

Zach shrugged his shoulders. 'To one of my brothers, briefly, yes.'

'Not your parents?'

He just pulled at bits of his hair, frowning in mild irritation.

She was going to remark that it was a shame he wasn't spending his birthday with them, but it wasn't a shame at all since it would mean he wouldn't be here with her, and, in any case, it might make her sound childish again—thinking you had to be playing pass-the-parcel with your mum and dad for it to be a real birthday.

'I'll see them soon,' he added, with the careless air she'd come to expect when she tried to discover anything about his family. She knew little more about his childhood than the fact that he'd had a pet Westie, who'd died the year he went to university. 'I haven't seen your mother yet, Pippi. Where is she, d'you think?'

'Oh, she'll be out in a minute,' Pippi said, dismissively. 'There's a girl from the village who's helping Susanna, she's probably still organising them.'

'I'll just wander in and say hello to her, and Susanna as well . . .'

He never forgets anyone, she thought, watching him stroll away from her, drinking deeply from his glass, giving a friendly nod to Dom as he passed. He had such naturally noble posture too, straight-backed and graceful, not all heavy and slumped like her brother.

Tearing her eyes away from him, she turned with a euphoric smile to the person standing nearest to her. 'Oh, Adam, that looks *really* sore! Did you not use any sun lotion today?'

*   *   *

It wasn't until they sat down to dinner that Pippi came to appreciate quite how drunk Dom actually was. His eyes were vacant and his mouth slack and he seemed to be having difficulty following the conversation. The whole effect was *very* special needs. And to think this was the same brother her friends were always fancying—if they could see him now! But at least her seating plan meant he was on the other side of the table from her, for she had placed herself between Zach and Adam, with Dom between Ginny and their mother.

'So is this part of a grand tour or are you coming back to Blighty?' her father asked Zach.

'Brighton?' Dom queried, and he gawped

stupidly at Zach. 'Thought you lived in Bristol, mate?'

'Dom,' Esther giggled. 'You sound like Saucepan Man! D'you remember: the deaf one in *The Faraway Tree*?'

'Alcohol will do that to you,' Adam said, drily.

Dom just gave a nasty little chortle, like *he* knew better.

'This wine is wonderful,' Ginny said. 'What is it?' She looked automatically to her host for tasting notes, but Pippi's father motioned at once to her mother. 'Bea chose this one, I think.'

'It's from the village of Gattinara, just south of here,' Bea said, holding the ruby liquid up to her face. With her dark, smoky make-up and loosely curled hair she looked like a (retired) fifties model, Pippi thought, proudly. 'Pretty much unknown outside of Italy, apparently, but we learned a little about it at the restaurant. I thought it would go nicely with Susanna's steak . . .'

(Pippi had specified that there was to be lots of red meat on the menu tonight; Milla swore it was *the* number one aphrodisiac.)

This led to her father exclaiming that he'd forgotten all about the girls' cooking lessons, bidding Bea talk them through the rest of the evening's menu. Pippi took the opportunity to devour the sight of Zach's profile, the heavy dark brows and smooth jaw, those amazing lips. How devotedly he listened to her mother—he was *spellbound*. Honestly, you couldn't genetically engineer a boyfriend more likely to impress and please his mother-in-law-to-be.

Then the question was asked a second time: when was Zach going back to the UK?

'Soon,' he said, forehead furrowing. 'Tomorrow or Thursday, I guess.'

Pippi loved that he didn't know exactly, that he had that free spirit thing about him. Did he really just turn up at the airport when he felt like leaving? She herself tended to memorise flight numbers and check-in times; she *hated* to be late.

'Don't,' Esther moaned, pulling a face at him. 'I don't want to hear that this holiday is almost over and we have to go back to reality.'

'We don't go home till Sunday,' her mother reminded her, but in the same sorrowful voice Esther had used, and Zach gave Bea the most adorable look of sympathy.

'Well, I think you'll be missed,' Pippi's father told him. 'We're very pleased to have met you and Adam and Ginny on this trip, aren't we, Bea?'

As the three guests protested that the pleasure was all theirs, Pippi made a mental note to get Zach's landline number from him before he left. Glorious though it was to have him back at the villa—especially if her hopes for the latter part of the evening were to be realised—she liked the idea of seeing him away from the rest of the family even better. Here, all together like this, they were too much competition for his attention: Esther, Dom, even Mum, and now her father, too, charming him, monopolising him. She began to imagine herself travelling by train from London to Bristol, Zach waiting for her on the platform as the train pulled in, his hair all tousled (maybe he'd be wearing a chunky knit and a big cashmere scarf if it was a cold day), every other woman getting off the train noticing how gorgeous he was and wishing it were she he was kissing hello.

But it would not be any of them; it would be Pippi. *God, just give him to me*, she pleaded, silently, *that's all I ask, all I'll ever ask, I promise!*

Anticipation had not diminished her appetite and she finished every one of the four courses placed in front of her, trying not to think of the effect it was all having on the waistband of her very expensive black lacy knickers. When Susanna signalled that she was about to bring out the cake, she decided she'd pass on a slice of it, at least for the moment. Meanwhile, her father had dipped inside and was returning with his guitar. 'Don't groan,' he told his daughters as he began strumming an introduction to 'Happy Birthday'. (This, of course, had been planned; Pippi had considered the whole Marilyn Monroe breathy solo alternative, but the truth was her voice was not that great and it was better that they all sang in the traditional chorus.)

The double-tiered cake with its yellow blaze of twenty-five candles was duly presented to the birthday boy. 'Er, wow, OK,' Zach said, all cute and overwhelmed.

'Did you make a wish?' she asked him, adding extra smoulder to her eyes to make up for the candlelight he'd just extinguished.

And he smirked at her through the pale curls of smoke—'I did, yes'—and she just knew what *that* meant.

By this time she was bursting to go to the loo and when she returned through the hall afterwards he was waiting for her, smiling like a movie star. *This is it*, she thought. *Finally*. His eyes looked metallic and glittery in the lamplight, and for the first time it occurred to her that he might be *nervous.*

'Thank you for all this, Pippi . . .' His voice was low and boyishly hesitant; it made her want to close her eyes and let the sound trickle over her bare skin. 'I don't deserve it.'

'Why d'you say that?' she exclaimed. '*Everyone* deserves a birthday party!'

'But you've gone to a lot of trouble. I . . . I just want you to know that I appreciate it.'

Show me, she screamed wordlessly. *Don't tell me, show me!* And she was exactly the right amount of exhilarated—and drunk—to close the final distance between them, tilt her head, and kiss. There followed a blissful second when she made sense of how his lips felt against hers—flat and hot and kind of sticky—and another, when she moved in more confidently and pushed her upper body against his, feeling in every living cell of her the animal anticipation of what was to come (she had never, ever wanted anyone like this, it was *mind-blowing*); there was even time for a subliminal glimpse of her own bed upstairs, the two of them on it, naked, moving together very, very slowly . . . before . . . before . . .

'Pippi . . .' With terrible, lethal speed, the abyss opened. He was recoiling from her, touching his lips with his fingers as if he'd been burned. 'I'm sorry, but I just don't think we should . . .'

She stared at him, her mouth frozen in kissing position, half-agape, a fish stuck in a net. Such was the shock, she wanted at first to vomit. Instead, she made a whimpering noise through clamped lips, which caused Zach to flush deeply, obviously mortified by her physical distress, and that made the whole thing far, far worse. There was nothing

336

she hated more than pity. Subconsciously her fingers found one of the flowers in her hair and eased its stem from the grip that held it in place.

'I'm sorry, Pippi,' he repeated, 'but there's someone else. I've been a complete idiot. I should have told you straight away, I realise that now.'

'But it slipped your mind, did it?' The shock had passed (she'd inherited her father's famed powers of recovery), though her voice was not yet hers: thin and desperate, the sound of her drowning twin. More familiar was the alluring little whisper in her ear telling her that this could yet be saved, that she didn't care about this other girl, she'd settle for one night with him. Who said anything about wedding vows? She let her expression soften, her eyes invite him a second time, and she saw the recognition in his face. He knew what she was proposing; he was a man, after all, a seriously good looking one, he must have had a hundred one-night stands . . . But he was shaking his head, rejecting his hundred-and-first. He didn't even want what no one need know about! He had no desire for her whatsoever, no . . . *mercy.*

She didn't feel sick now, she felt angry.

'The thing is,' he said, falling over his own words, 'it's kind of . . . it's getting serious—for me, anyway. I don't want to screw it up.'

Pippi cried out in frustration: 'How can it be "getting serious" if you haven't even seen her this whole time? That's ridiculous!' Whatever happened to 'out of sight, out of mind'? With a black heart, she imagined him locked in intimate phone conversations the moment her back was turned. Was that what he'd been doing today when he hadn't answered her texts? And she loathed herself for allowing this sort of thinking: 'the moment her back was turned'! She was acting so girlish and betrayed, so uncool.

He didn't answer and she decided she didn't want him to. She had no use for names and locations. What he did in his stupid hotel room was his concern. The fact of the rejection was enough. The flower lay shredded in pieces at her feet and her chest felt very tight and hot. Instinctively, she found herself drawing on thoughts of her mother telling her as a child to take her defeats with a better grace, because she'd be glad she had afterwards. Don't be remembered as a sore loser, Pip! (It only gives the winner more satisfaction, her father added, privately.) What would her mother say if she were in this position? Nothing at all, perhaps; she'd simply smile as if nothing had happened and make a dignified retreat.

'It's really hard to explain . . .' Zach began, clearly believing he owed it to her to find a way nonetheless. The glitter had gone from his eyes and she saw now that it had been the effect of dread at having to say something horrible rather than the excitement of doing something wonderful. He had *dreaded* being alone with her.

'No need to,' she said, with tremendous effort. 'Please just forget it. It's your birthday and I just want you to have fun.'

Well, that *was* the sort of thing her mother might have said, though it clearly surprised Zach to hear it. She could see the relief in his face and shoulders and anticipate the consolatory compliment even as it was forming on his perfect lips.

'You're—' he began, but she interrupted him.

'Don't,' she said, turning away. 'I'm not

anything.'

'No, but this is—'

'It's OK, Zach, seriously. Let's go back out.'

Mercifully, he stopped trying to tell her how great she was (though not quite as great as his mystery lover) and did what he was told.

*   *   *

Much as she longed to be like her mother in moments of emotional crisis, Pippi knew she couldn't pull it off for long. In the short time it took to return to the terrace, she had already become aware of her vindictive spirit rising. Zach would not be her victim, however; this she knew in some bleak, subconscious way. She'd handled her defeat as well as it was possible to and she wasn't going to undo that now. Making a fuss after the event would only turn her into an anecdote, the poor little rich girl he told his friends (and beloved girlfriend) about, the one in Italy who he'd had such terrible trouble shaking off.

She wished for the hundredth time that Milla was here with her. Was it just her or were family actually the *worst* kind of refuge in times of humiliation? Already her mother was trying to catch her eye, transmitting sympathy telepathically, as if *she* was the one who'd just been degradingly knocked back and not her daughter.

She took her place at the table, only to find that in her absence her careful seating plan had been disregarded and she was now flanked by Ginny and Dom. Dom, in whom that same vindictive flare was reflected back at her—their only sibling symmetry and not one that was celebrated very often.

She watched him watch Zach return to the table only moments after her, taking Dom's own vacant seat next to her mother. Looking shaken, Zach turned at once to listen to her father, still playing his guitar and now launching into some old Beach Boys number. Embarrassingly, he seemed to be serenading her mother, who soon began trading fondly ironic expressions with Esther across the table. Everyone else was loving it: Adam's right knee was moving in time to the music, Ginny's head rocking, like this was MTV Unplugged or something. With a little shock Pippi remembered that Zach, too, had brought a guitar with him to Orta, though never up to the villa. So why wasn't this *him* serenading *her*? What had she done wrong? She'd lugged the bloody thing to his hotel for him, hadn't she? The least he could have done was play something for her. She should have thrown it off the jetty into the lake.

'Finally got the message, eh?' Dom spoke in an undertone, perhaps not intending her to hear at all (coward!), but she was minutely attuned to signals of offence right then and she heard him quite clearly.

She rearranged her face to something harder, colder, the better to withstand his mockery. 'What message?'

'The love of your life over there. Finally spelled it out, has he?'

'Spelled *what* out, Dom?'

'What, are you a masochist? You want to hear it twice in five minutes? That he couldn't give a shit about you, of course.'

'Oh, fuck off,' she snapped, feeling the heat of tears in her nose and eyes. 'You don't know what

340

you're talking about.'

Dom responded by despatching the contents of his wine glass down his eyes. At once a figure Pippi hadn't even noticed before darted forwards to refill his glass. Susanna's helper, presumably. (Only very faintly did it register that she, as hostess, should perhaps know the girl's name.) After a moment's pause she held out her own glass, in the certain knowledge that however drunk she got tonight she would not be the drunkest here.

'I *do* know what I'm talking about,' Dom said, 'as it happens.'

'How?' She hated herself for needing to hear the answer.

'Because he told Adam.'

'Told Adam what?' Maybe he was right, maybe she *was* a masochist.

'That he's got someone back home. Or somewhere, anyway. And he really likes her. Adam told us earlier today, when we were out in the boat.'

'"Us"? You mean . . . ?'

'Me and Dad.'

And yet her father had still welcomed him and played 'Happy Birthday' for him and told him how lonely they'd all be without him.

'Well, thanks for sharing, guys. Glad you've got my back.'

But she couldn't blame her father; she knew how his mind worked because it was the same way hers did. Knowing about the presence of a rival, well, it just raised the stakes, it didn't end the game. She watched her father as he finished his song about God only knowing how he'd live without her mother, returning to the table all flushed and high. He waved off Esther's cry that he'd been excruciatingly awful and winked across the table at Pippi, his favourite, and she somehow forced the expected smile for him from the muscles of her mouth. Apparently satisfied, her father turned to Ginny, fielding her congratulations about his performance, making her cry out in delight with his reply, which only made Pippi angry all over again. How could it be that even *Ginny* was having a better time than she was?

By now Dom was several mouthfuls into his new glass of wine, returning his sister's scowl with a crude expression of superiority, and she felt spite slide from her pores like melted fat. She wanted to hurt him as much as she'd been hurt, and if she did then maybe it would erase her own pain, just for a moment . . .

'So, now we know my little tragedy,' she hissed, 'when are you going to tell us yours? You've ruined this holiday, d'you know that? Moping around the whole time. I can't believe Mum's let you get away with it. She wouldn't let *me*.'

Nose in his wine glass, her brother muttered something unintelligible.

'What?' Pippi goaded him. 'I didn't hear you. Come on, tell me why you're so bloody miserable?'

The glass was thumped down on to the tablecloth and when Dom answered his voice was sharp enough to make her jump. 'I *said*, *you*'d be moping around if someone told you they were killing *your* baby.'

She stared at him, uncomprehending. 'What baby?'

'*My* fucking baby.' This last expletive was loud, instantly catching the attention of the others, and Pippi was aware of heads turning towards them, of other conversations fading. Dom, also noticing the hush, threw up his hands like some weird cartoon-character emcee. 'That's right: big news, everyone, share! In precisely thirty-six hours' time my wonderful girlfriend Chloë will be killing my child. I should be grateful she bothered to let me know, huh?'

She'd had a fair amount to drink herself and so it took Pippi a little while to digest her brother's announcement, to conclude that Chloë must have discovered she was pregnant and was planning to have an abortion, and was not holding captive and about to murder in his bed some infant lovechild of Dom's that none of them knew anything about. Eyes lowered, she peeped fearfully at the reactions of the others at the table. It was hard to take them in at once, but at the edge of her vision she was aware of her mother putting her face in her hands and Esther gaping in disbelief. Then it became clear that one person's reaction was stronger than the rest: Ginny was making a funny noise, kind of like a farm-animal howl, and she didn't stop the whole time that she was grinding the chair legs on the stone and getting to her feet. She was still making the sound as she moved away, rushing, tripping, the skirt of her dress filling with air as she went. It was almost as if she was being powered by special effects: sucked from the earth by some frenzied, twisting tornado.

Terrible though she knew it was, and a sentiment never to be admitted to in the future, there was nonetheless in some slimy, subterranean

343

part of Pippi a feeling of satisfaction that hers was not the only disaster of the evening.

CHAPTER TWENTY-TWO

TUESDAY

It was eerie the way they all continued to stare after Ginny when she'd fled from view—even Adam—as though her departure constituted the actual moment of impact in this sudden crisis and not merely one person's response to it (though 'merely' was the wrong word; it was obvious from a last moonlit glimpse of her face before she tore off down the steps that she was already sobbing). Later, Bea decided that their collective paralysis was simply a way of delaying the moment when they'd have to turn and face the grotesquely inebriated Dom, acknowledge that they too had heard what he'd said. Wait to see who might be first to try to put out the fire.

It would be her, of course, his mother. How could it not be?

'Dom, darling, please can we talk about this privately . . .' She hardly knew where to start, but he was already forcing the issue by staggering to his feet and making for the open doors of the villa.

'*Don't* come after me,' he snarled at her and, then, to no one in particular, 'I've had it with this shit.' And as he passed by it was heartbreaking to see that his eyes had not changed at all with his public confession, remaining as darkened by grief as they had been all day, all week. It was this, and

344

not his rough words, that stunned her, rooting her feet to the ground and trapping any further pleas in the back of her throat. Her eyes focused on the physical judder of the table itself: in getting up from it, he'd pushed violently and the wine glasses and bottles wobbled in his wake. But none tipped. Red wine on a white tablecloth, that would have been too much, given the context.

'Dom,' she managed again, eventually, but the word was hardly audible and he was gone anyhow, well out of earshot.

Still, no one else spoke.

Bea looked at the face nearest to hers—Zach's! She hadn't seen him slip into the seat next to hers—only to find that his eyes were already on her, frozen in bewilderment, the message in his narrowed expression too complicated to decipher. She had not failed to notice him following Pippi indoors a little while ago, nor missed the hardened set of her daughter's jaw on her return. She had forced herself not to speculate on what might have taken place, on the repercussions it might have on their affair. And now she must do the same with Dom's unwelcome revelation (would there even *be* any repercussions, on Zach's part? His interest in her was so single-minded, so acute; was there anything left in him to care about Dom, *or* about Pippi?).

And so, automatically, she turned for leadership in the tried-and-tested direction: Marty. One desperate look from her and he was on his feet, as fluid and natural as if he were about to propose a toast or address the board. 'I think we need to break up this little party,' he said, his tone measured and professional, making it quite clear

345

that the instruction was non-negotiable. It comforted her a little, that tone, for in their decades together it had inevitably preceded a solution. 'I hope you'll forgive us, Adam and Zach,' he added, pleasantly regretful.

'Of course, of course . . .' Adam, for one, needed no second asking. Under his sunburn he had the look of a man more than ready to put up his hands and surrender. Taking a moment to collect Ginny's handbag and the square of blue silk she'd worn at her throat on arrival but abandoned soon after, he cast a last apologetic look from face to face and hastened off towards the steps after his wife.

Bea said, in a hollow voice that belonged to someone else, 'Oh God, I meant to give him that phone number . . .' That was when she realised she must be in shock herself, because fetching a phone message for Adam should not have been her first concern in this crisis (and it certainly would not be his).

'He's hardly going to start making calls at this hour,' Marty said, but less impatiently than he might have. He placed a hand first on the back of her seat and then between her shoulder blades, physically protective of her. 'I think he has more pressing matters right now, don't you? Look, I'll go inside and find Dom, make sure he hasn't done anything stupid. Give us a few minutes, OK? You say goodbye to everyone.'

To Zach, he meant. As quickly as Marty opened ranks, he closed them again and their guest of honour was utterly superfluous now. Pippi, the rightful initiator of protest, did nothing to intervene. She wasn't even looking at Zach, but gazing towards her father, rigid, mesmerised.

Marty took his palm from Bea's back and stretched across the table to shake Zach's hand in farewell—unwittingly passing his wife's touch to her lover—and then, with a last caress of Bea's nearest shoulder, headed inside.

She gaped at Zach, not knowing what to say, wishing he would go, longing for him to stay right where he was at her side. At last he stood, his eyes not leaving hers for a second. 'I'll take Adam the number on my way out if you like,' he said, in a soft, private voice, as if it were just the two of them. 'I'll put it through their door for tomorrow.' Miraculously, he seemed to recognise that the tying of this inconsequential loose end meant something to her.

'Thank you. I'll go and get it.'

As she rose, he half-turned from her, dutifully including Esther and Pippi in his next comments. 'And thank you, everyone, for my party. Especially you, Pippi. Please say thanks to Susanna, too, and the girl helping. It's been really special.'

Bea nodded, knowing she must defer to Pippi for official farewells, but her younger daughter only smiled correctly at Zach across the table before getting to her feet and following her father's path indoors. Esther, also wordless, at least made the effort to kiss Zach on the cheek before she disappeared, too.

The four Sale exits, one after the other, felt like a magic trick.

She went quickly to fetch the phone number from inside, aware of Marty on the stairs, calling Dom's name, lengthening it to two syllables in an unreal echo of childhood summonses, and returned to the terrace. It was empty. Having

347

expected to find Zach where she'd left him, she felt her whole body engulfed by despair, seizing her breath from her. *Stop this*, she told herself, *stop*. She was behaving as if she thought they'd never see each other again. She was behaving as if that meant more to her than her son's misery (not to mention her daughters' need for support and explanation).

Then she spotted him waiting for her at the top of the steps, felt the flooding sensation of a reprieve.

'Hey,' he said, seeing her approach. 'Beatrice.'

'I thought you'd gone . . .' She stepped very near to him, not thinking—or caring—who might see them. She drank in the sight of him, breathed his smell, as if she hadn't had the pleasure of it that very afternoon. 'Oh, Zach, I'm really sorry about all this.'

'Don't be. He's obviously suffering.'

'He is . . . he is . . .' She couldn't explain, not in the time they had, that Dom's suffering would not last, that it had already become much bigger than it needed to be, and that she, though she'd tried everything she could, had not been able to help him.

She passed Zach the note with the phone number, letting her hand graze his, thinking that was all she would allow herself, but he caught hers in his at once and threaded their fingers securely into place. His touch was more than familiar to her; it was already ingrained. Their arrangement to be together again today had been made within minutes of her coming home from the restaurant and learning of Marty's boat trip with Dom and Adam. Like murder, betrayal seemed only to get

348

easier each time. Buying wine from the shop near the piazza and requesting its delivery had taken no more than a matter of minutes; the rest of her expedition had been spent in Zach's bed. She'd wondered later if she'd dropped in on Ginny on the way back as much to place a third party between her activities with him and her duty to her family as to fulfil any desire to spend time with the other woman. Or, maybe her motive had been something riskier: to see if Ginny noticed anything different about her, anything *special*.

Poor Ginny, who in so many ways had greater need of her comfort at this moment than even Dom—and yet it continued to be someone else who commanded her attention.

'I have to go back in,' she whispered.

'I know you do.' Neither of them moved. This, too, was ingrained, this inability to part. He glanced down at the note. 'Leave this with me.'

'Thank you.' Still she couldn't turn from him, but felt only the pull grow stronger. Still she allowed herself the idea that time had eased, just for now, just for them. *This is bigger than I thought,* she thought, *I don't know if I'm going to be able to let it go.* 'You see . . . you see Dom's going through a bit of a crisis with his girlfriend,' she said, in an effort to prioritise, to correct the pendulum's swing. 'I thought this holiday might cheer him up, but it just seems to have made him feel worse.'

Seeing the appalled look in Zach's eyes, she worried this might have sounded too casual, uncaring even (horrified as she was by the way the evening had ended, Dom's news was not new to *her*). She thought she heard his breath quicken then, felt his musculature tense. He must feel for

349

Dom, after all, she thought. The termination of a pregnancy, it was nothing unique in the world, you could even say it was routine but, here and now in this context, it held symbolic power. It must be bringing home to him what we've been doing together, she realised, heavily. He must be thinking how quickly sex can change from pure pleasure into a lifetime of worry and responsibility. How it can force decisions that, as a man, you will never truly own.

He was withdrawing his hand from hers, turning away his face. (Imagining her as a grandmother, perhaps!) She wouldn't have blamed him if he'd walked down those steps and never came back.

'I hope he's all right,' he managed, at last, and his voice was raw, full of animal effort, more guttural that she'd heard it even in bed, when all their public politeness was stripped from them.

'I'll go and see,' she replied. She felt unsettled, even a little frightened, by the change in him, but she said no more. Watching him walk away she thought she saw, only very fleetingly, a clear likeness in him to her boy indoors: out of nowhere he seemed to be carrying exactly the same torment, a torment so palpable it might be wrung bodily from him.

As she made her way back across the terrace, she saw that Susanna and her friend Rita were beginning to clear the table. There was the air of a crime scene about it, the women's motions those of forensic investigators, as if their job was to preserve the full horror of the picture, not erase it. Bea gestured her gratitude and they smiled back at her. Only then did it strike her that the hard part of this evening was over. Zach was gone and whatever his reaction to Dom's troubles, whatever her own feelings of conflict and guilt, *their* crime had passed undetected. Now, at last, it was family only. It was time to watch Marty repeat to their son the advice she'd already given, to offer the commiserations Dom had already rejected of her.

The four of them were in the sitting room, apparently only just settling themselves; she supposed Dom had had to be retrieved from his room and coaxed to the meeting, while one of the girls had used the time to organise drinks (Bea wondered if they really needed any more of *those*). More powerfully than ever, the just-so arrangement of furniture and meticulous use of complementary colours made the room look like a stage set—it was as if they'd been summoned to hear who the murderer was (though Dom had already told them *that*).

Ignoring the unreal sensations inside her, and the very real residual ache for Zach, she joined Marty on the emerald-green sofa by the fireplace. Dom was hunched on the nearby footstool, his face in his hands, while Esther and Pippi perched on the arms of a ruby velvet armchair set to the side, silent for now but nonetheless essential somehow. They all had stocky glasses of brandy or some other liqueur, to Bea's eyes props of colourless liquid. When Esther handed her hers, she took a gulp and quickly revised her opinion. It burned, but in a good way, like a punishment you knew you deserved.

Marty had begun to gently interrogate their son. 'Come on, how many weeks pregnant is she? The doctor must have told her that?'

Dom shrugged. 'I think nine, maybe ten.'

'And the appointment is when?'

'Thursday morning.'

'Thursday, right. OK, then you need to go back to London and be a part of this, Dommo. You can't be here on holiday while something like that is going on. Go with Chloë to the clinic, show her she's not on her own.' Bea could see her husband thinking how easily this was to be concluded, maybe even feeling faintly regretful that he'd been so quick to send their guests packing.

But Dom was shaking his head, speaking through his fingers. 'I can't, Dad.'

'Yes, you can.'

The hands fell away then and his chin came up; his whole face looked swollen with pain. 'I don't know which hospital it is. Besides, she doesn't want me there. She won't even speak to me on the phone.'

'Why not?'

'She said she didn't want me around, confusing her.'

'Confusing her? Is she in two minds about it, then?' Marty sought Bea's eye with a querying frown and she tried to communicate to him as subtly as possible that he'd misunderstood.

Dom snapped, '*She*'s not, no, but *I* am! I've told her I want her to keep it. She *has* to keep it.'

There was a pause as everyone digested this; clearly the others had taken his original wording at the table—'killing my child'—to be drunken exaggeration and not the moral denunciation Bea had at once known it to be. For the hundredth time she imagined a boyfriend of Pippi's putting pressure on her to keep an unwanted baby, speaking of her to his family in this way, as a killer,

352

a murderess.

Marty recovered quickly. He was well practised in the on-the-spot abandonment of weaker strategies in favour of stronger ones. 'OK, well, that's good too. It's not too late for Chloë to change her mind, is it?' He nodded vigorously, his imagination gathering pace. 'There's no reason why this couldn't work.'

Bea said, 'Except they're both very young and haven't begun their careers yet.'

'That never stopped us,' Marty said, just as she'd known he would. Dom had made the parallel even more explicit when they'd first discussed the situation in London; he'd directly likened the foetus to himself, saying, '*You* were her age when you got pregnant with me. *You* went ahead with it.' He'd expected that to swing it for him, for all of them! He'd not only wanted Bea to go to Chloë and persuade her to keep the baby, but also to offer to take it herself, her first grandchild, and help him raise it. She would never forget the way he'd looked at her when she'd told him it wasn't her baby to take, or her case to plead: it was as if she had failed him unforgivably, withdrawn before his eyes her twenty-two years of absolute love. But she'd stood her ground. He and Chloë were adults, she told him, and all she could do was support the decisions they made.

'You can only support one of us,' he'd said, then. And judging by Marty's present behaviour, he'd made in her the wrong choice of confidante.

'It's not like it's got to be either/or,' Marty said, agreeably, adjusting his sitting position in an attempt to catch his son's evasive eye. 'Chloë can still work. Look how they do it here in Italy. It's the school holidays and all the shopkeepers have their kids just playing in the square outside.'

As if that was going to happen in London! A baby could not be taken to a college of law lecture or a City bank training session. There was no pedestrianized piazza near Dom's new flat in Fulham. Bea didn't say what she was also thinking, that their children, all the kids of their age and background, though a thousand times more streetwise than her own generation at that age, were pitifully under-equipped for the sheer relentless graft of raising a family. Dom and Chloë would never cope: that was her honest opinion. But it didn't matter that she didn't say it, because Marty would have ignored her, anyway; he was too busy pursuing his own fantasy.

'Parents are far too precious in the UK,' he declared, quite forgetting that it was exactly that tendency that had attracted mothers in their tens of thousands to his collection of expensive children's clothing, thus helping to make him a multi-millionaire. 'There's no need for a baby to be such a big deal. Life goes on just the same.'

'Unless someone chooses to kill it before it's begun,' Dom said, viciously. There was a sharp intake of breath from one of the girls.

'I think we're getting off the point,' Bea said, ignoring this last remark. 'Chloë doesn't want to *have* a baby and she's made that clear from the outset.' She made a point of addressing her comments to her husband, for it was obvious he needed to be disabused of his romanticism just as urgently as Dom needed reminding of the basic facts.

'From the outset?' Marty repeated, frowning

deeply. 'You mean you already knew about this?'

Bea felt her shoulders drop in exact synchronicity with her heart. This family conference was going from bad to worse; she'd been crazy to think they could come to Italy and not end up in dissent of some sort. Their holiday together had been a lost cause in so many ways. But at least Pippi wasn't weighing in with some accusation of being left out. Neither she nor Esther had uttered a word so far.

'Who knew when is not relevant,' she told Marty. 'We all know now.' Taking advantage of his temporary silence, she pressed on, 'The point is this has to be Chloë's decision. I know it's hard, Dom, but it just doesn't work any other way.'

Dom straightened, gesturing angrily. 'Well, it should. There should be a legal process when parents disagree.'

'You're not parents yet,' Bea pointed out, gently. 'And even if there was a legal arbitrator, how could that make you agree? You only have one vote each. And there isn't a judge in the land who wouldn't cast in favour of the woman.'

'She's right, Dommo,' Marty said, wide-eyed with sympathy.

Dom looked at his parents in turn, disgusted by their evident slowness. 'I don't mean *that*. I mean she could have it and give it to me to bring up. She could disclaim all responsibility, legally, like a surrogacy.' His face lit up and his next words came out in a feverish rush. 'That's it! We should be the ones!'

'The ones?'

'Yeah. To do it first, to create the landmark case!'

There was a very tense silence. 'We need to be realistic, darling,' Bea said. 'I told you in London, an arrangement like that would only work if Chloë agreed to it, which she does not. You can't *force* someone to have a baby. It would be a form of false imprisonment.'

'Mark and Amanda wouldn't let her, for one thing,' Marty said, naming Chloë's parents, 'and I have to say it sounds a bit complicated. Look, what I suggest is you go back home, talk to her again and tell her you'll back her whatever she decides.' His tone became more significant. 'That's the right thing to do, Dom, seriously. If she wants to go ahead with Thursday, then so be it.'

Dom shook his head. 'I can't be with her any more if she gets rid of it. I couldn't look her in the eye again.'

Love him though she did, Bea couldn't suppress her distaste at this remark. She wondered what his sisters were thinking.

'I think that's a separate issue,' Marty said. 'Resolve the pregnancy, one way or the other, and then decide how you feel about each other. She may not want to be with *you* either, or you may surprise yourselves and decide you've been through so much together you can take on the world.'

He looked at Bea then, and she nodded her support, though she got the feeling he was seeking her affirmation for something larger than this particular suggestion.

Esther spoke for the first time. 'I hate to say it, but she may already have done it, you know, Dom. I don't mean to be cruel, but with you out here, and knowing how much you want to stop her, it's kind of the obvious time.'

'It's what I would do if I were her,' Pippi added, unexpectedly. It was when she added, apologetically, 'I mean, maybe, but it's just *my* opinion,' that Dom began crying.

'Hey, hey! Come here . . .' At once Marty had his son in a tight clasp, cupping the back of his head in his outspread hand as one would that of a much smaller child. Silently, heart squeezed as tight as a fist, Bea got up and shepherded the girls out of the room, though not before hearing her husband outline the plan of action: 'Right. Go and get some sleep. If you can't sleep, lie down and rest. There's a flight at eight in the morning, if I remember rightly. Meet me down here at six and I'll take you to the airport. Whatever you decide to do, you need to go home.'

*   *   *

It was the early hours of the morning before Dom, Esther and Pippi were upstairs and in their bedrooms. Bea hadn't been so grateful to have her three children on a different floor from her since they were in infant school. The villa was in virtual darkness, which was just as well since there were glasses and dishes piled up in the kitchen and the hall, Susanna and Rita having been sent home before they could finish clearing up.

She and Marty were back on the green sofa. At some point the lamps had been turned off, inside and out, the moon had gone in, and the only illumination was from the fairy lights in the trees outside. Bea imagined Pippi, whose bedroom directly overlooked the main terrace, hanging out of her window and wondering what had happened to her perfect evening.

'Sorry I didn't tell you,' she said to Marty.

He nodded. 'Why didn't you? Why didn't *he*?'

It was tempting to answer, 'Because you weren't around', which was partly true—before coming to Italy, Marty had spent two of the previous four weeks in the US—and he would have accepted it readily enough. One thing she'd always valued in him, and had been able to contrast favourably with the experiences of some of her friends, was that he never got competitive about the children; he never overruled her. Unless he passionately disagreed with her approach, he would accept the team strategy with minimal persuasion. 'I asked Dom to keep it to himself. He didn't want me to know, actually, I sort of guessed and then it all came out.' She paused. Years of low-level espionage had made her good at guessing. 'It was just before we were coming here and I thought it would be better for you and the girls if you weren't all worrying about it as well. Of course I didn't think for a minute he'd come out here with us.'

Marty nodded. 'That's why he didn't want to, not at first?'

'Yes. It was Chloë who persuaded him to. And I must admit I thought she had in mind exactly what Esther said earlier . . .'

'What, have the abortion while he was out of the way?'

'Either that or she hoped he'd sort his head out enough to go back and help her through it.'

'Why's he taking it so badly?' Marty exhaled, eyes closed, the embodiment of physical exhaustion. 'It's totally bizarre, the opposite of what you'd expect. Most kids would be relieved the girl was taking the decision out of their hands.'

Bea raised a palm to the heavens. 'I agree, but he has very strong views, it seems. I don't know who's influencing him—not me, that's for sure. I couldn't believe it when he first suggested this idea of using her as some sort of surrogate. It's madness. He hasn't got the first idea what having a baby entails.'

Marty considered. 'It's as if he's experimenting, do you know what I mean? He's taking a stand, like he thinks a proper adult should, but he's taking it too far. And now it's reached the point where he can't back down. Or he thinks he can't.'

'There's definitely an element of that, but it's heartfelt, I think. He really feels like this is breaking him apart.'

'Well, at least he's not copping out. We can say that for him, poor sod.'

Bea smiled. 'Just so long as he doesn't turn into one of those campaigners who stands outside clinics shouting at the poor girls going in.'

Even in the near-darkness, she could see how genuinely rattled Marty was by the idea, no doubt imagining the press he'd get if his son were arrested and brought to court. (He was used to the Sale name being printed after the words 'squeaky clean', an erroneous prefix, as she well knew, but a reliable one.) Was the company famous enough for *that* to be of interest? Perhaps, on a slow news week. And it was easy enough to imagine the 'family values' angle.

'The thing is, Marty, this could be Pippi being railroaded by her boyfriend,' she added. 'At the age of eighteen, not even at university, being told she has to have a baby!'

Marty seized the change of subject. 'So is she sleeping with this character who was here tonight? This Zach?'

Bea felt herself wince at the description, a rush of blood at the sound of Zach's name warming her face, but in the darkened room she felt sure her husband had noticed neither response. 'No, I don't think so. In fact, I think he's told her he's not interested in her in that way.'

'Hmm, that's the impression I got from Adam, who seems to have had some sort of discussion with him. Poor Pipster, she does get carried away. He's a looker, though, isn't he? I can see the appeal.'

Bea said nothing.

'Seems like quite a nice guy, as well. Clever. Still, she's better off with someone younger. He's a bit worldly for her, don't you think? He certainly seems a lot more experienced than Dom.'

'He's older than him, that's why,' Bea managed to say. 'A few years makes a difference at that age.'

'That's what I mean. He's way too old for Pips.'

'Yes.' Bea studied her empty glass, causing Marty to reach for the bottle on the mantelpiece and pour them each another generous measure.

'Doesn't get any easier, does it?'

He meant parenting, she reminded herself, not being married, staying faithful. 'It's the same as when they were little,' she said. 'The only difference is that now they don't act on our advice.'

'I don't think they even listen to it.' He sounded so weary, wearier than she'd ever heard him before. In four or five hours' time he'd be off again, back to the airport. They could have arranged a taxi for Dom but she knew Marty wanted the opportunity to talk to him some more, to make up a little for the weeks of ignorance.

'Did you?' she asked. 'At his age?'

'Of course not. I think I *pretended* to listen to it, though. Ed, too. At least if there was a loan being handed out.'

Bea smiled. Their children didn't know the meaning of the word 'loan'. 'They think they know better now. Maybe they *do* know better.'

'Until, one day, they'll be telling us what *we* should do.' Perking up a little, Marty stretched his arm across the back of the sofa, his forearm resting comfortably against the back of her neck. She could feel the heat of the veins in his wrist. '*That*'s going to be hard to swallow,' he added.

Bea couldn't look at him. She knew he was assuming that they'd be together all their lives. The thought was making him reach out for her properly, draw her towards him into an embrace, kiss the top of her head, then her nose, then her lips. She allowed herself to enjoy the closeness of it, the long-held familiarity, thinking of the song he'd chosen to sing earlier. He'd performed it in a drunken, clownish falsetto, but the selection had been significant, they both knew: God only knows. He'd meant it for her.

God only knew what he'd have played if he'd known she had slept with the guest of honour that same afternoon.

At last, eighteen hours after the day had begun, its bedlam of events overwhelmed her. She considered sobbing into Marty's chest, managed to resist the impulse. Instead, she pulled away from him and stretched her arms above her head. 'I

361

should finish off in the kitchen. I don't want Susanna to be faced with it all when she comes in in the morning. She went way beyond the call of duty today.'

'Remind me to give her a bonus when we leave,' Marty agreed.

And he let her go then, not without a little moan of reluctance.

CHAPTER TWENTY-THREE

TUESDAY

Even before Ginny reached the boathouse she knew she had overreacted badly. Smearing the tears from her eyes, she looked in confusion at the dark marks on her fingers—she'd completely forgotten she was wearing make-up—for in the dark, for a disorientating moment, it looked as if her eyes were *bleeding*.

Waiting for her breathing to correct itself, she stood in the garden, staring at the black lake, and wondered how she hadn't noticed until this moment the sheer hypocrisy of her state of mind. She'd believed her life was no longer worth living—to the extent that in London Adam had virtually kept her on suicide watch—and yet in hijacking other people's crises, as she had just now, in relentlessly seeking to connect their anguishes to her own, wasn't she demonstrating the very opposite of believing it was over? She was forcing her grief on everyone she met, if not by sharing her story explicitly then at least by implication, and in

362

doing so she was insisting they all recognise the profound importance of it. And, what was more, she had put herself in a vicious circle: the apologies she knew she was going to have to make tomorrow would draw yet more attention to her, demand from the others further special treatment.

Oh dear. She teetered slightly as her eyes sought a point of focus on the surface of the water. No doubt Adam would say that this was a good thing, this new clarity, because acknowledgement was a key step, it signified the end of her period of denial. (How she hated to prove his self-help books right!) And he'd be here, she knew, any minute now, her sponsor as well as her spouse. She counted slowly to ten: *One, two, three* . . .

'Ginny! Are you all right?'

Pivoting, still a little unsteady on her feet, she watched him practically vault the gate to get to her. Still he found the energy for her, still he cared enough to worry what she might have done to herself. She felt a sudden cramp of fear: he'd said he would stay with her for ever but, realistically, how much longer could she expect him to? (Even the bereaved must suffer compassion fatigue eventually.) How much longer before that displeasure he'd shown towards her during the storm became everyday or, worse, *all that was left*?

'Don't say it,' she said, surprised by how congenial her voice sounded, how civilised. 'I already know.'

And so, for once, he didn't say it. Instead, he let himself into the house and reappeared a minute later with drinks. They sipped them sitting in their matching chairs, feet touching. It seemed to Ginny that they'd sat like this, drinking together in the dark, for the last hundred nights.

She was the first to break the silence. 'I don't know why I behaved like that. It was just so awful hearing Dom say what he said; I reacted without thinking. I'll go and say sorry to everyone tomorrow.' She began to feel soothed by this mild new voice of hers. It was quite without edges, fresh and soft, like a voice that had emerged from hibernation.

Adam was nodding. 'There was a strange atmosphere from the beginning, didn't you think? Bea was being weird, I thought.'

'Bea?' Only now did Ginny realise how impolitely little attention she had paid to her hostess during the evening, despite Bea's kindness earlier in the day, and despite the evident trouble she had taken to make the evening so special. No, she had been fixated on Martin from the moment of arrival, her response on discovering that they were seated next to each other at dinner the most powerful feeling of delight she had had in the last three months. She had a sudden image of herself just half an hour ago, hanging on to his every word, rocking from side to side to his awful singing like some sort of obsessed fan. She was hardly better than the women who had slept with him during his marriage and brought pure misery to poor Bea.

'Jittery, I thought,' Adam mused. 'A bit on edge. But maybe she was just worried about Dom. Anyway, I had a feeling something might happen right from the start. The dynamic was volatile.'

'Really?' His observation only compounded her sense of guilt: was he implying that *she* had been a part of the volatile dynamic, a second cause for Bea's edginess, because of her admiration of

Martin? Had her behaviour been so obviously that of a woman with a crush? She felt her cheeks begin to burn.

'Yes. And when we were out in the boat, you could tell there was something wrong between Marty and Dom. Marty was saying we had to get back and Dom was just ignoring him, like he was holding us hostage or something.' Adam took a deeper swallow of his drink as he remembered. 'But a student getting his girlfriend pregnant—it's not such a tragedy, is it? Presumably what he was trying to say just now was she was having an abortion? Happens all the time, doesn't it?'

Happens all the time. Such sad words, Ginny thought. You never heard them used to describe something good.

'I suppose in that family, when they're used to everything being perfect, it must seem pretty serious,' she said.

'When they're used to controlling everything, you mean,' Adam said.

'Oh, that's not fair. They've just got a lot more to lose.'

'Maybe. But he'd have been better off not telling them, if you ask me. *I* wouldn't have at his age.'

That, Ginny could well believe. It was all too easy to imagine the Trustlove clan assembling for just the intervention-style family meeting she knew must be taking place up the hill at this very moment. She'd been dazzled by that close kinship of theirs, the unconditional support the siblings gave one another; until she'd met Adam she hadn't known it really existed in modern families. And then, after Isaac, she'd begun to view it differently, more as a form of surveillance, something intrusive

365

to be dodged. Only now was she starting to realise that it could be both.

'I think Bea knew already and they were trying to keep it from the others. I don't think we know the full story.'

'You're right.' There was a short silence, and then Adam said, 'Ginny?' in a new sort of voice, causing an immediate resurgence of apprehension in her.

'Yes?'

'I didn't get the chance to ask you earlier, we were in such a rush when I came back from the boat trip, but why didn't you tell me about running into Marty the other day?'

'How do you mean?' she asked, playing for time. She knew that above all else she must not reveal the extent of her attraction to Martin, because if she did it could only ever be at Adam's expense—and her own. Her infatuation would pass, she was certain of that. They would go back to London and never see the Sales again. She would never be one of Marty's other women.

'The morning we went up to Sacro Monte,' Adam reminded her. 'He said he almost ran you over in his taxi.' There was a pause. 'He seemed very surprised that I didn't know about it.'

'I didn't want to get you all worried,' Ginny said, half-truthfully. 'I thought you might feel like you couldn't leave me alone for more than five minutes without something disastrous happening. I didn't think Martin would think it was worth mentioning, either.'

But her answer failed to placate him, only prompting a second query: 'That's another thing, why do you always call him Martin, when everyone else calls him Marty? It's so formal.'

She sipped her drink, eyes cast low. In a way, this was the more unsettling question of the two because it begged an answer she had never dared voice even to herself. Now, to punish herself, she gave it life: she called Marty Sale by a different version of his name because she was trying to claim a piece of him just for her. What was more, she had convinced herself that he had noticed the little formality and he liked it, he liked there being something private between them. 'I don't know,' she said, carelessly. 'I suppose because that's how he introduced himself to us, didn't he?'

'I don't remember,' Adam admitted.

Ginny did. She would always remember the moment. In retrospect, it had been a turning point for her, a literal one as well as an emotional one, for she had walked to the end of that little wooden pier and spun on her heels expressly for him, for Martin to get his attention, to get him to come to her.

Adam continued to look troubled. 'Ginny, you don't . . . do you, do you see me as some sort of *jailer*?'

They held one another's eyes with deep unease; the low, level-headed rhythm of this question-and-answer exchange was exactly what made it feel so dangerous. *Is this it?* she thought. Is there a part of him that wants me to confess to some sordid betrayal with Marty so he can be let off the hook? 'No, of course not,' she said, quickly, 'that's crazy,' and his evident relief made her grateful enough to blurt, 'In fact, I wanted to say that it's been good that we've given each other a bit of space this holiday. Bea said something similar to me earlier, and I think she's right. We don't need to be together every waking moment to know how the other is feeling.'

Before Adam could answer, they became aware of signs of life in the darkness behind them. A figure was making his way down the long slope of the Sales' lawn. It was inevitable that it should be Zach, the last non-Sale at the party. Ginny, worrying that Adam was going to send him away when he was probably feeling in need of their company, called out pre-emptively, 'Zach, hi, come and join us!' As he approached the gate, she added, 'I want to say how sorry I am for ruining your birthday party. I feel terrible.'

Her eyes adjusting, she saw that he was looking at her with a degree of surprise, not making any of the usual noises of acceptance. It was strange but she almost got the impression that he'd forgotten what had just happened, or why it should be that she needed to apologise. She decided not to remind him of the precise chronology. 'Are you coming in? We're having a nightcap. Can I get you one as well?'

He didn't answer, but Adam slipped inside without complaint to fetch him one anyhow, and in the older man's absence he dutifully pushed open the gate and came to sit on the lake wall near to their chairs. When Adam reappeared and the glass was passed to him, he handled it with the same expression of bewilderment he'd arrived with, placing it heavily on the stone by his side as if unsure what else he was supposed to do with it. Even to Ginny, who'd come to consider herself the frontrunner in erratic behaviour, his manner was curious. Something's happened, she thought, something apart from Dom's outburst and my overreaction. It was to do with Pippi, she guessed. Perhaps he'd done what he'd said he would and spoken to her; and now he was feeling guilty.

At last he spoke—'I've brought that phone number for Adam, from Bea'—and there was a thickness to his voice, recognisable to Ginny as a warning sign of someone about to cry. She noticed the glassy shine in his eyes, their unwillingness to make contact with hers or Adam's.

'He means that Cally woman,' Ginny told Adam. 'You should call her tomorrow.'

Taking the note, Adam made a visible effort to stem his impatience. 'You needn't have bothered, Zach. I told Marty earlier, I don't know any Callys. Never have.'

'No one seems to know who she is,' Ginny agreed. She gave Adam a pointed look—*Be nice*— but wasn't sure if he caught it. In compensation, she smiled warmly at their guest. 'But thank you anyway, that was thoughtful of you.'

Zach said, abruptly, 'I know who she is.' And he began to pluck violently at his hair as if he had a bone to pick with it, causing a tuft to stick out horizontally at the neck.

When he didn't go on, Ginny prompted, gently, 'Who, Zach? Who is she?'

There was a moment of soft, untouched silence and then came the distant sound of an engine across the water. 'She's my mother,' Zach said, into its faint drone. He screwed up his eyes as if in self-protection, watching the two of them through narrowed slashes.

Ginny stared. 'Your mother, did you say?'
'Yes.'

369

'But . . . why would she be phoning Adam?' And she looked in bafflement at her husband.

'Well, she wouldn't,' Adam said, dismissively, but in a voice that had less to do with his strange antagonism towards Zach than with plain weariness. He was dead on his feet, Ginny realised. He wasn't used to the energy with which people like the Sales holidayed. 'It's obviously some sort of mix-up,' he added. 'If she's *your* mother, then she must have been trying to get hold of *you*, Zach.'

'Or . . . or did she want Marty, maybe?' Ginny suggested, her brain awakening. She began to make the natural connections that Adam would not know to: Cally must be one of Martin's women, so that was why Zach had come to Orta in the first place, to confront his mother's lover. She remembered the map she'd seen on his laptop, the directions from the airport to Villa Isola. She'd *known* he was hiding something. But what had he hoped to achieve, coming all this way to challenge a man who was on a private family holiday? Why not wait till the Sales returned to the UK and he could get Martin more easily on his own?

She gazed pityingly at him, unable to fathom his expression in the darkness, or begin to guess his thoughts. Then it occurred to her that he clearly had *not* confronted Martin, that they had only met for the first time this evening, and she knew better than anyone the turn events had taken for *she* had caused it, she and Dom. Her theory didn't make sense for another reason, too: if Martin was having a relationship with Zach's mother, then it surely followed that he would know who Zach was. He might never have met him before, but he'd know

370

the name and age of his lover's son; there'd be enough clues for him to put two and two together.

She didn't think even Martin Sale was confident enough to just ride it out and see if he could get away with it.

'It isn't a mix-up,' Zach said, very softly. 'You probably don't even remember her and, if you do, not as Cally. She must have forgotten that when she left her name.'

'I don't understand,' Ginny said. 'Remember her from where?' It was only when she caught a flicker of acknowledgement in her direction that she realised Zach had been addressing Adam, not her; and that he was continuing to do so.

'She was probably known as Catherine then. I think my dad was the one who started calling her Cally.'

Ginny turned to her husband and saw the faint dawn of recognition in his face. Right, she thought, now he knows. She's an old colleague or something like that. Mystery solved.

Then Zach said, 'She told me you're my father, Adam. My birth father. That's why I'm here.' He spoke very clearly now, three sharp sentences that stapled the silence, that could never be unpicked.

Time ground to a halt. When neither Adam nor Ginny responded, Zach looked away from them, out at the lake, as if wishing to disown his own words.

It was Ginny who forced the clock's hands to move once more. Not trusting her ears, she asked again for confirmation that she'd heard correctly: 'Did you say . . . did you say Adam is your *father*?'

'Yes.'

'But how can that possibly . . . ?' She broke off,

371

frightened by the sudden adrenalin surge that had enveloped her, bringing a rush of white noise. As if expecting to escape its hiss, she leaned forward in her seat towards Adam, who seemed not to have comprehended even the little of this that she had. She plucked at his hand, but it was limp under hers. He was immobilised.

She swung to face Zach. From her new position he appeared hardly more than a silhouette of disarrayed hair and slumped shoulders. Like Adam, he'd become quite, quite still.

Could it be right, what he was saying to them? Could he really be Adam's son?

Under her hand, she felt Adam jerk to life. He was pushing her arm away, straightening in his seat, letting out a short, strained laugh. 'This is completely ridiculous. It can't possibly be true.'

'Adam—' Ginny began, but he interrupted her to speak directly to the Zach silhouette.

'When did she tell you this nonsense?'

For a moment she feared that Zach might have been paralysed, scared stiff, but then his muscles loosened just enough for him to answer the question: 'Just before I came. A few days before. It took me a while to find out where you were.'

'And you did that how, exactly?'

Don't, Ginny pleaded, silently. *Don't do this . . .*

'I managed to get someone in your office to talk to me,' Zach said, 'and they gave me the name of the travel agent you'd used.'

'No one would give that information to a stranger.' The last word resounded. Already it was brutally wrong for who Zach was, who he might be.

'Adam,' she began again, starting to hear an unwelcome echo of that tense conversation the three of them had had during the storm (had that really been just yesterday?), but Adam wasn't suffering fools this time: he was slipping into crisis. She slid from her seat, sinking to her knees by his side. Again she took his hand, never more grateful than when he let her cradle it in hers, didn't shake her from him.

'I said it was a family emergency,' Zach explained. 'I don't know how Mum got the number, though. She was following my trail, somehow.'

'She probably said the same as you did,' Ginny said. 'It hardly matters, does it? You found us, that's what counts.'

There was a long and strange silence. 'This can't be right,' Adam said, at last.

'Are you sure?' Ginny asked him, very gently. 'Are you saying you didn't know someone called Catherine twenty-five, twenty-six years ago? When you were a student?' (Certainly, *she* had not heard him say the name; she and Adam knew almost everything about each other's sexual histories and Adam's was modest enough for him to have recalled the majority of his casual conquests.)

'No, I'm not saying that. I *did* know Catherine. In my second year of university. She was older, a research student. Her surname was . . . ?'

'Agnew,' Zach supplied.

'That's right. Catherine Agnew. We went out a few times, but this . . . this doesn't make any sense. Why didn't she get in touch with me as soon as she knew she was having a baby? If she thought there was a chance it was mine?'

It was a good question, even if the tone made his fundamental disbelief quite clear. Zach sighed

373

heavily. Ginny looked towards him, saw the tremble of his mouth, the gathering of tears in his eyes, and she wished she had enough hands to comfort him, too.

'Look,' Zach said, unsteadily, 'I'm as freaked out by this as you are, but I think it might be true. Your name's not on my birth certificate or anything, because she told everyone I was my dad's. And he still thinks that, as far as I know. Or maybe she's told him by now, while I've been here, I really don't know. I haven't answered her calls either. The whole thing's completely insane.'

For the first time it became apparent to Ginny that Zach shared Adam's rejection of this bombshell—or his lack of desire for it, at least. Oddly, she had no such doubts herself. Tests would prove this Cally or Catherine correct. Women knew who the fathers of their babies were. *What he's saying is true*, she thought, *he is Adam's son.*

Adam has a son.

'Let me understand this,' Adam said. 'She told you this . . . this bizarre tale and you decided to track me down. Is that why *she* tried to get hold of me? Did she plan to tell me the same story over the phone? And if she says she's known all along, then why now? Why here?' It was clear to Ginny that he was unable to stop himself from fixating on the logistical details of the revelation. She had learned this about him; in times of crisis he reached obsessively for untied ends. If he concentrated on tying them then he did not have to look at what it was that they contained. It was this that had helped him hold things together in the period after Isaac's death. Before that, Ginny had been the one to tackle trouble, absorbing all crises

374

before they reached Adam. (Of course she knew now that none had been a real crisis, nothing close to it.)

'There couldn't have been a worse time,' Adam added and, though he spoke in his kindest voice so far, he still made Ginny wince at the harshness of it.

Zach was shifting helplessly on his perch, bringing one knee up to his chest. 'I know, I know,' and Adam said again, 'This is . . . this is unbelievable.' He rubbed his eyes, the knuckles roughly kneading the sockets, and raised his face once more. 'If, in the unlikely event that it is true, then . . . what is it that she wants us to do?'

'She just wants us to know, that's all. She had this idea that we would find you together, in England, obviously. Have a nice civilised talk about it. Nothing more. But I had to meet you, straight away. Maybe I should have waited, I didn't know about everything you've been going through. Nor does she. But I see now that, like you say, it's the worst possible time for you.' Zach gazed beseechingly at Adam, desperate for a word of reassurance. Ginny wondered if she should leave them together, but she didn't trust Adam not to hurt this boy. 'In the unlikely event . . .' He needed to control himself before he said something that might haunt him in the future and, worse, might never be forgiven.

'I'm glad I came, anyway,' Zach said. 'It's been an incredible week in so many ways . . . well, in ways I never expected.'

He means meeting the Sales, Ginny thought. She had a sudden half-glimpse of Bea Sale's face earlier that day here at the boathouse, make-up smudged, eyes ablaze, but it was lost at once.

'I'm glad I came,' he repeated.

Already he was sounding as if he was prepared to accept that this might be his one and only opportunity to be with Adam. Fearing that Adam would interpret this as permission to avoid any further investigation, Ginny left her husband's side and went to sit on the wall next to Zach. She put a hand on his arm, felt its faint tremor. 'I think Adam needs some time to think about this. The shock you've been feeling, still are, I'm sure, well, that's how he feels now. And we've all drunk far too much to take this in properly. I think we should get some sleep and meet again tomorrow. Can we see you in the morning?'

Zach nodded. 'I'll leave you my number.'

She turned back to Adam. His face wore the same concussed look as Zach's. 'D'you think that's best, as well?'

Adam nodded.

Hurrying indoors, Ginny could of course find no pen and paper, nor either of their phones. At last she found a biro in her handbag, tucked into the cover of her notebook, and returned with the two items. It was clear that neither man had spoken in her short absence. 'This isn't bad,' she told them, her voice over-bright in the quiet, 'this is exciting. But we need clear heads to talk about it sensibly, all of us.'

The two of them nodded once more. Zach dictated his phone number to her and then he got up to leave.

'Promise you'll be here,' she said, following him through the walkway to the lane. He looked entranced, his huge eyes unblinking; she feared he might slip off the path and into the lake without noticing.

'Be here?'

'In Orta. Promise you won't go home.'

'I promise.' His voice, at least, seemed present. 'I need to come back and say goodbye to the others, anyway.'

Before he left, Ginny pulled him to her and gave him a quick hug. He tensed perceptibly in her arms, couldn't remove himself fast enough, but she was still glad she'd done it.

She got back to the garden in time to see Adam pick up Zach's untouched glass from the ledge, drink its contents in a single wild gulp that caused him to splutter most of it out again, and then hurl the thing into the lake. The liquid dregs flew up in a thin flame before the glass hit the water with an unspectacular plop and promptly sank.

'Adam? Let's talk about this . . .'

He swung his arm out, keeping her from him. 'Leave it, Ginny.'

'But we can't not discuss it! It's enormous! We need to—'

'I said no, not now! In the morning, OK? *Please.*'

'Adam!' But she couldn't get him to say another word. He just stared and stared down at the water: smooth and reflective again after that sudden, unsatisfying act of violence. His head leaned closer, almost overbalancing him. It was as if he was tormented by the sight of himself, as if he expected to find something deeper than his own image—or, more than that, worse than that, as if he'd never before seen the shape of his own face.

CHAPTER TWENTY-FOUR

WEDNESDAY

He might have stayed like that all night, for all she knew. She'd finally retreated at two o'clock, having failed to persuade him to move even an inch from the water's edge, her reserves of moral support finally depleted by the chill creeping through her skin. Before going to bed she brought him a jacket and a hot drink and left the garden door ajar, hoping the glow of the lamplight might prompt him at some point to give up and join her. In bed her head was an unstoppable spin cycle of thoughts, and only with the sternest discipline did she finally banish them and allow herself a few hours' sleep.

When she woke up, the door had been closed but he was not there, his side of the bed untouched but for the crease marks of her own restlessness. A quick search told her he wasn't in the house or anywhere else on the premises. Still in her pyjamas, she went out to check the jetty, afterwards venturing to the edge of the larch wood that separated the estate from the neighbouring one. She half-expected to find him slumbering under a tree, using the jacket for a blanket, but he was nowhere to be seen.

He must have gone into the village to find Zach, she thought. She didn't know whether to feel glad or uneasy that he had done this without her; either way, how could he possibly think clearly after staying awake all night? The last time they'd done that was during the week of Isaac's life, waiting for him to gain consciousness after one of his surgeries, watching over him as he slept, or talking together through the night, assimilating the last day's information as new supplies of optimism and dread gathered for the next. She remembered very well how it had felt, a hellish battle between fatigue and adrenalin: the highest hopes raised still higher, the darkest doubts dashed still lower, two extremes stretching sanity to snapping point. And, in the end, for nothing.

But this was for something—she was sure of it.

She got dressed, washed her face, set the coffee maker to work. Seated at the tiny breakfast bar, the cup in front of her, she at last allowed her mind to revisit the extraordinary final scene of the previous night. Zach had said he was Adam's son. Zach: the cool, charismatic friend of Pippi's, the friend of a friend whose birthday celebration they had been invited to share purely in order to make up the numbers, no more, no less than that.

Twenty-five years, a quarter of a century, a third of someone's life, and yet Adam had not had a clue he existed!

She remembered now having needed no convincing of the truth of it, but she'd been drunk and—what was the word Adam had used to describe the atmosphere to which she'd indisputably contributed?—*volatile*, that was right. First reactions were not to be trusted and in the sober light of day she might have expected Zach's pronouncement to seem as implausible as it clearly had to Adam. But to her surprise it did not. It felt just as real, just as true. Not only that, but it had already begun to acquire that indefinable sense of

379

saviour she had been yearning for these last months, and that she had found fleetingly, falsely, in Martin.

The question was, would Adam feel the same?

Before the events of last night, he had been in quite a different place from her, recovering from the loss of Isaac faster, readying himself for a return to London and a period of relative harmony. He would not be as quick as she was to welcome a second earthquake.

She reminded herself that it was not she who stood directly above this one.

With her second cup of coffee, her brain began to make the deductions it had been denied last night by alcohol and shock. 'Why now?' Adam had asked, meaning in the context of a whole childhood (and part of an adulthood, too). But the question could be asked for a different reason: Zach had been here for days, almost a whole week, and in all that time he'd said nothing. He'd been up at the house sunbathing, he'd been down on the shore swimming, he'd joined in meals, gone out in the boat, he'd even agreed to a party in his honour ... But then, of course, there had been times when he'd removed himself from the Sales and come to them, when she'd been sure he'd wanted to confide something in them. Only on Monday, during the storm. And he'd come to the door, hadn't he, the time when Adam was kissing her, undressing her? Even during their very first meeting there'd been a sense of something kept unsaid, of something not quite natural.

But they had never made it possible for him. Quite the opposite: they had rejected him.

Why, then, had he done it when he had? It was

to do with the message, she realised. He'd brought it last night on Bea's behalf. He must only have seen it himself then, moments before he came. Recognising his mother's name must have shocked him into his confession. Without that message he might have left after last night and said nothing at all.

They might still not know.

'Oh, you poor, poor thing!' she cried out into the empty room. 'You've had to carry this around with you, this huge thing! We never gave you the chance to tell us, we never wanted to listen!'

Well, if Adam was with him this morning, as she felt certain he was, she sincerely hoped that he was listening now.

*   *   *

Two hours passed before she began to feel worried. She located her mobile phone and turned it on, but there'd been no calls or texts from Adam (as had become habit, she ignored all messages from the outside world). She knew before looking that her notebook would be gone, the one in which she'd scrawled Zach's phone number. Knowing what the notebook was to her—in spite of the continuing blankness of its pages—Adam would have been thoughtful enough to avoid tearing out the one marked page, even in a state of high agitation, and the realisation caused in her a deep twinge of love for him.

Breathless from all the caffeine and too unsettled to eat anything, she put on her shoes and took the path up to the villa. Pippi would be sure to know which hotel Zach was staying in. But the

Sales' terrace was empty; if the family had been breakfasting outdoors as usual then they'd long finished. Seeing the table and its neatly tucked chairs, the closed French doors beneath the high horseshoe arch—normally the chairs were pulled clear, the doors thrown wide—she lost her nerve entirely and returned to the boathouse without checking the drive for their car or trying the front door.

By now, it was past eleven o'clock. She searched the two main rooms for a note from her normally scrupulous husband, and failing to find one she checked the safe: his passport was still there, where he'd placed it on arrival with the other valuables. Was anything else missing besides the notebook? His phone, of course, for the two went hand in hand. She imagined him coming to from his nocturnal hypnosis and dialling the number with the emergency of a 999 summons, already on his way along the path before Zach had managed to pick up the call.

What about the number for Zach's mother, had he taken that, too? And, if not, should Ginny phone it, perhaps? Talk to her about all of this? She began to check the waste paper baskets, the drawers of the bedside cabinets, the pockets of Adam's worn clothes, the pages of his paperbacks and guidebooks, piled high by the bed. It was here, at last, that her search stopped short. In a big hardback novel he had yet to begin, she found, folded in half, a sheet of writing paper. A draft of a letter. She knew immediately who it was to, even before she'd seen the date or read any of the individual words. She'd known a draft existed for she'd been there when Adam made the proper copy from it, writing painstakingly, like a calligrapher, every line and loop of every letter precise and considered. But she'd refused to share in the endeavour or even read the finished article before he sent it on its way. She had vowed she would *never* read it.

But now the world had changed once more and there suddenly seemed every reason to share possession of her husband's past acts:

April 2009, London

Dear Isaac,

Although this is a letter to you, it is also a letter for us. The idea is that we will get some sort of comfort from it in the future—from knowing it will always be with you, a part of us. The problem is it's hard to imagine ever getting comfort from anything, which is probably why it is me writing this on my own.

A special midwife told us that a letter is the best way of telling you how we feel, because there was not the time when you were with us and anyway we were too frantic to think about the right words—I think we'd used them all up. Now, a week later, it is no easier. Maybe it's even harder. Write what's inside you, the midwife says, but what is inside me? I don't know, Isaac, I don't know. Now the last of the hope has gone I feel like there is all this stuff filling up but I have nowhere to pour it and I'm so out of my depth I'm only just managing to breathe. It's not disbelief or anger or confusion or any of those things they keep talking about. It's just love.

383

*Enough love for you for a hundred years. So I'm
sending it with you now, wherever you are going.*
    Your daddy

Zach forgotten for now, Ginny read the letter a
second time, and then a third, crying freely, feeling
the skin of her face heat and soak and swell.
Reading it, memorising it, felt a bit like theft, but
she knew Adam would say it was the right thing to
do.

                    *   *   *

Scanning as she did every passing face, every
distant back-of-head, every fleeting profile, it was
inevitable that she should find a Sale among the
Orta crowds before she did a Trustlove. Bea and
Martin were standing about halfway up the broad
cobbled path that led to the church of Santa Maria
Assunta, a famous landmark in the village that was
spectacularly floodlit at night (Adam had given her
chapter and verse on its date and design, but she
could remember none of that now). It was a shock
to see them together and it took Ginny a moment
to understand why. Was it possible—yes, she
thought it was—that she had not seen them *on
their own* before? Just the two of them, as a
couple? Her immediate instinct was to duck out of
sight—whatever had been discovered since the
party, however apocalyptic it felt, she had still to
face up to the aftermath of her own scene-
making—but this was overridden at once by a
sense of opportunity. After Pippi, Bea was
probably the one who had got to know Zach best;

384

she might know his phone number or the address of where he was staying. Ginny could be minutes from finding Adam.

'Bea! Marty! Hello!'

The Sales turned to her with the now customary expressions of solicitude, and Ginny had a sudden, overpowering sense of incredulity quite detached from her new concerns: had she *really* managed to appear on the radar of a couple like this? Did they *actually* care about her in the way they appeared to? In London, it simply couldn't have happened; their paths would never have crossed.

As she moved closer, the deeper strain on their faces was clear to see. Bea in particular looked drawn, as if she hadn't slept, and Ginny was consumed by fresh shame. She was glad her sunglasses hid the evidence of her recent tears.

'I'm sorry about last night—' she began, but they cut her off, as eager to dismiss her claims of culpability as she was to get them out of the way.

'Dom was the one in the wrong,' Marty said, with definitive firmness, and he placed a hand on her upper arm, tightly, as if to staunch a wound. 'He didn't mean to offend anyone: he wasn't thinking. He asked me to apologise to you specifically.'

'Oh, there's really no need,' Ginny insisted, the unexpected touch making the words spill from her mouth in a breathless rush. 'How . . . how is he this morning?'

'He's gone home. He took the early flight from Milan. You probably gathered that he and his girlfriend have found themselves in a bit of a situation.' He sounded so very English, so coolly capable, she had the overwhelming temptation to

385

blurt out her new discovery and let *him* handle it. Don't, she warned herself; this is strictly Adam's business and the Sales don't need something new to worry about—or to rescue me from.

'Well, I hope they'll both be OK.' The truth was that Dom's dilemma, given the events that had succeeded it, seemed surmountable now, and far less morally injurious to her than she'd had them all believe.

Bea seemed to sense this cosmic shift in perspective in her. 'Is everything all right, Ginny?' she asked. 'Is there anything—'

'No,' Ginny interrupted, 'yes, I mean, something's happened, something completely unconnected, and I need to find Adam. You haven't seen him, have you?'

'No.' Matching clouds of wariness drifted across the Sales' faces.

'What's happened?' Bea asked, with the air of summoning her very last reserves of strength.

'I can't tell you.' But despair had edged into her tone. 'It involves Zach, though, and if I can find out where he's staying then I'll probably find Adam.'

'*Zach?*' Bea exclaimed, but Marty looked as if he might need reminding of who that was. For the first time their expressions differed; his passively attentive, hers alive with interest.

Ginny focused eagerly on Bea. 'Do you know the name of his hotel, or roughly where it is?' For all its compactness, Orta was home to many dozens of hotels and guest houses.

Frustratingly, Bea only murmured something inaudible, the breath catching in her throat, which left Marty to take charge. 'Birthday boy, you

386

mean? No idea,' he shrugged, 'but Pippi will know. She's back at the house, shall I phone her for you?'

'Would you? That would be great. It'll save me from doing the rounds and trying to describe what he looks like in my terrible Italian.'

'*Dove il rock star inglese?*' Marty joked. He fished out his phone and dialled.

'Would you like me to come with you?' Bea asked her, and Ginny noticed that the other woman was breathing very quickly now, picking up perhaps on Ginny's own panic.

But, one ear to the phone and one to their conversation, Martin gave his wife a pointed look.

'No,' Ginny said, quickly. 'I'm fine on my own. I could just use a clue, that's all.'

Marty hung up. 'No reply, I'm afraid. She's probably still in bed.'

'Well, thank you for trying. And thank you for last night. Before . . . everything, it was a really lovely evening. I'll remember it.'

'I think we all will,' Marty agreed, and Ginny couldn't resist a lingering look at his face. The powerful, jutting features, the thick hair, the steady gaze, all were captured by the dazzling noon light, strengthened by it: he was the commander, the summit of maleness.

He was as far from her grasp as the sun itself.

She set off again, moving clumsily on the steep cobbles. She'd barely reached the foot of the hill when she became aware of footsteps behind her. It was Bea, moving so fast she was almost tripping, her face and neck taut with worry.

'Ginny, wait! Tell me, what's happened to Zach?'

Ginny stepped aside to let a large group of

tourists pass by; several of them cast the two women curious glances, thinking, perhaps, that they were arguing. 'Nothing, I think Adam might be with him, that's all.'

'But why? Why would Adam be with him? Please tell me what's going on.'

'I can't, I really can't.'

'Is it . . . is it bad?'

'No, not at all. Nothing for anyone to worry about.'

'Honestly?'

'Honestly.'

'Thank God for that!' With this final exclamation, Bea began to collect herself, smoothing her curls from her forehead, chuckling easily. 'I don't think I could handle any more excitement.'

Ginny itched to move away, but she saw that Bea had something more to say.

'Look, I think he said he was staying just off the piazza, above the café with the green awning. The entrance is in the side street right by it, the first door you come to, just a little way up . . .'

Hope lit Ginny's eyes. 'That's fantastic, thank you.'

'You will let me know if there's anything I can do?'

'Of course.'

Bea was smiling as they parted, but what Ginny remembered as she hastened away was that split-second of unguarded instinct she'd glimpsed before she had been able to assure her friend that everyone was well. What Ginny had seen was terror, categorical terror.

Why would Bea feel terror at the thought of

something happening to *Zach*?

*   *   *

She saw the green awning straight away, but didn't need to follow directions to the entrance because Adam found her first. He came striding towards her from the piazza's landing-stage—overrun with day trippers returning from the island—and greeted her with the gratitude and relief of a small child who thought he'd lost his mother in the crowd. 'Ginny, you're here! I was just coming home.'

They hugged. He smelled bad, of mildew and body odour and too-bitter coffee, but his heartbeat, the bones of two ribcages from hers, was firm and regular.

They eased apart again. 'Coming from where?' she asked.

'I've been over to the island.'

'On your own?'

'Yes.'

'Well . . .' She hesitated, taking in more clearly the feral nature of his appearance. He was still wearing his clothes from last night, the chinos rumpled and stained and the shirt spotted with red, presumably from one of Susanna's sauces, with grey rings under the armpits. His face was smeared and his hair dishevelled—Zach-style. Despite everything, she couldn't help being struck by the comedy of it. 'You look like you've been dragged through a hedge backwards—by the nuns, I presume.'

He smiled, gave her another grateful look. 'That's pretty much how I feel, actually. Let's walk

389

the back route,' he added, 'it'll be crowded on the lake path.'

'OK.' She fell into step with him, unconcerned which route they chose. 'Have you not seen Zach, then?'

'Yes, earlier. We had a long chat.'

She looked sideways at him, trying not to show her anxiety. In profile, you could see the sag in the skin on his jaw and neck, and the way the sun lit the grey in his hair emphasising the stripping of pigment; he'd aged overnight, truly. The sight caused a clutching feeling inside her, as if she were the one who'd just been lost. 'And?' she said.

'And you didn't dream it. He genuinely thinks he's my son.'

Ginny wasn't sure what to make of the way he put this. She sensed that there was a long process of acceptance and understanding ahead of them. 'What about Cally? Did you manage to speak to her about it?'

'Yes. She got quite emotional. But she says it's true, of course.'

'And you believe her?'

'Hmm. I don't *dis*believe her.'

His resistance was palpable. She would need to smooth it away, little by little. She would need to wake up every morning in readiness for his doubts and denials. Ginny felt worried about Zach; who would *he* discuss the meeting with? Who would share *his* disquiet? He was the child in this, however adult he looked to the outside world.

'Adam, you were kind to him, weren't you?'

He swallowed his answer, but she thought he said, 'I tried.'

'I know this must feel surreal, but he wouldn't

have come here if he wasn't absolutely convinced—or if his mother wasn't. No one would want to tear someone else's life apart if they weren't sure, it would be criminal.'

Adam looked as though being convinced wasn't nearly good enough a reason, either.

'I know it's hard for you, but it's no easier for him. Or for her. She must feel absolutely terrible knowing you're both here, trying to get your heads around it without her.'

'She's the one who put the bloody thing in motion,' Adam pointed out.

'Exactly. She'll feel responsible for your reactions.' Worrying she might be pleading too strongly against him, she added, 'And she'll understand them, whatever they are. No one will expect you to come to terms with this quickly. *I* won't.'

He made a movement of the head that might have been a nod. She persevered, keeping the optimism in her voice low-key. 'And if it's true, and we all handle it OK, it could be a great, great thing. There's so much to learn about him, so much to gain. This is a gift.'

The possible nodding had stopped but he didn't protest, which was something.

'So how did you leave it?' she asked.

'He's going home, this afternoon.'

'No!' That was a disappointment. She had imagined Zach would stay, that they'd be together for the rest of the week.

'It's all right, Gin, we're going to meet next week, the three of us: me, him and Catherine. I'll take the day off work and go down to Bristol.'

'What about the father?'

Adam exhaled heavily. 'I don't think he'll be there, not the first time, anyway. He's only just found out himself, apparrently.'

The phrasing, at least, was more encouraging. 'That's probably sensible.'

They strolled a little way in silence.

'Why did she wait so long to tell him, did she say? He's twenty-five; you'd think the natural time would have been sooner.' But Ginny was sure *she* couldn't say what the right age might be; who knew but those in the situation?

'Zach says she kept putting it off—that's what she told him. She'd settled on when he left home.'

'But that must have been years ago?'

'It was, but apparently she started worrying about how it would affect his relationship with his brothers.'

'So she was waiting for *them* to leave home?'

'Maybe.'

'I can see how she could do that,' Ginny said. 'Put it off, find something new to stop her. Especially if he's never had any gut feeling that he's different. You know, out of place in the family in some way?'

Adam began shaking his head, groaning. 'But that's just it: he didn't! He doesn't! He and I don't look or sound anything like each other, do we? Anyone can see that. He probably looks more like his dad than he does me. He wants to get a paternity test done,' he added. 'To be absolutely sure.'

Ginny hoped the suggestion *had* been Zach's, and not Adam's. 'Hey, come on. Children don't always look like their parents. Does he look anything like she did? She must have been his sort of age when you knew her?'

'I just don't remember.' Adam made a helpless gesture. 'She was very attractive, like he is. The eyes, maybe. I think hers were grey. And when I heard her voice this morning, I *suppose* she sounds like him, but I couldn't remember her voice properly from before so it made no difference either way. That's the thing, Catherine and I, we barely knew each other.'

Ginny allowed herself only the briefest of mourning that sometimes it should be that people who 'barely knew each other' could make healthy babies together and people who had pledged devotion to each other for the rest of their lives could not. 'If you think about it, it's the mannerisms and the turns of phrase that make people seem like other members of their family; it kind of tricks you into seeing a likeness. But he hasn't grown up with you and so he doesn't have any of those things from your side.' 'Your side' made her think of the Trustlove clan—it surely had the same effect on Adam—and her hand reached automatically for his, her fingers adjusting to get a truer grip. But they stayed joined only for a matter of seconds before Adam, in his agitation, pulled away again.

'There's always *something*,' he insisted. 'Even if the eye colour and facial features are different, there's build or posture or voice. But with us there's nothing!'

'There will be something, though. You just haven't found it yet. I bet Catherine will be able to see something.'

With the lake gone from view, Ginny had lost track of where they were but Adam seemed to know, taking a narrow alley uphill past a succession of private gardens. The walls were high and the atmosphere very close, the sun scorching the moisture from the air.

'Do you remember his little face?' he asked her.

She was confused for a second or two, thought he was still talking about Zach, but then she realised he meant Isaac. She nodded. *He* looked like you.' In the photographs you could see it, but in the flesh it had been plainer still.

She remembered Karen saying in the weeks leading to the birth, 'Now, don't be shocked, Ginny, but all babies look exactly like their father. Boy *or* girl.' She hadn't been sure if her sister-in-law was jokingly saying that Adam's looks weren't good enough for any mother to want them replicated in her child, or if she thought Ginny herself might be offended to see so little of her own self in its face. 'It only lasts a few weeks,' Karen went on, 'and then they change. And then they change again. They change constantly. Every time you think they've stopped changing, they change.'

Only the rarest remained unchanged, Ginny thought. The forsaken few.

'Adam?'

'Yes?'

'When you go to Bristol and meet Catherine, will you ask her for a photo of Zach as a baby?'

He looked at her with surprise before, understanding, he gently dipped his chin and said, 'I will.'

CHAPTER TWENTY-FIVE

WEDNESDAY

For a horrible moment there, standing at the foot of the Salita della Motta and watching Ginny plunge into the piazza crowds in search of Adam, Bea felt so suffocated with frustration she feared she might not be able to have her conversation with Marty without somehow contriving to see Zach first. To be sure he was safe; to be sure she had not dreamed the very existence of him.

She wasn't certain she could even retrace her steps to where Marty waited for her outside the museum.

Then she reminded herself that she had known Zach for not quite a week. However her feelings for him absorbed her, she couldn't let them eat her alive. She had to put him out of her mind today and concentrate on her marriage, or, more correctly, the dissolution of it. Returning, albeit a little unsteadily, to Marty's side, she suggested they ditch the exhibition in favour of a coffee. They'd already had one since leaving the villa, only half an hour ago, at one of the cafés on via Olina, but that had been taken up entirely with a debrief on Dom's early-morning journey to the airport, his state of mind (less truculent than last night but basically unchanged in his sexual politics) and speculation on how Chloë might react to his unscheduled return (Bea had had to turn off her phone to stop herself from warning the girl).

Now it was time to turn to the subject of them.

She hadn't planned it this way, having intended to get back to London before she breathed a word, but last night had brought a fresh emergency to family life and she had woken up this morning with the certain knowledge that the time had come. When Marty got back from the airport he'd suggested the two of them get out and do something 'normal', but it was already clear to her that normal was the last thing they were going to achieve today. Maybe they never had.

Later, when she reviewed the day's events, she suspected that seeing Ginny—a Ginny who looked so charged, changed, *freed*—had thrown the final switch in her.

In the past, when she'd been about to say something important to Marty, she'd experienced all the manifestations of nerves, the racing pulse and shallow breathing, that feeling of unreality that took you outside of yourself and made you long to know how the world was going to feel in twenty minutes' time, after you'd said what you'd decided to say; only, when the twenty minutes had passed, to wish you could go back again and see how it might have felt if you'd held your tongue, after all, and waited for a different day, a different mood. She'd been willing time backwards and forwards, manipulations no ordinary mortal could achieve, as if that and that alone could make her her husband's true equal.

This time, though, there was none of that. Having chosen a place off the main drag and cheerfully ordered her coffee, she waited for the waiter to move out of earshot before making eye contact with Marty and saying, with simple formality:

'Our marriage really is over. You know that, don't you?'

He didn't say anything at first. He satisfied himself that his ears had not mistaken him by rubbing the side of his face with his fingers, his eyes not once flickering from hers as his brain turned and ground, seeking that one last ingenious appeal that might overturn her judgement. Then, as with thorny creative issues of old, he asked for her advice: 'Is there *anything* I can do to persuade you?'

'No.' *Anything that can be done* has *been done,* she thought. There really was nothing left now. 'We need to see divorce lawyers when we get back.' No need to be cruel and tell him she had already done so; her solicitor had been fully versed over the course of two meetings and now awaited her formal instruction. 'It would be good if we could not get too vicious about it.'

Marty eyed her thoughtfully. 'Did you mean what you said about taking me to the cleaners?'

'When did I say that?'

'The other day. You said if I lied about that phone message, it would cost me. Or words to that effect.'

'Oh, that.' The misunderstanding over the phone message; irrelevant now.

'I didn't lie,' he reminded her. 'That woman is Adam's problem, not mine.'

The schoolboy innocence of his expression, combined with his callous willingness to offload trouble on to an already burdened man, appalled her and she hissed at him, 'Adam doesn't have a "problem", as you put it. Not every man screws around, you know. It's a novel idea, fidelity, but

397

there we are.'

For a moment he looked ready to counter-snipe, but then they seemed to intuit at the same time that this would only lead them down the usual sidetrack and there was no sense in that now its exit had been boarded up.

'I'm sorry,' she said, in a low voice. 'What you said was out of order, though.'

But already he'd dismissed Adam from his mind. 'I don't want this,' he said, unblinkingly. 'For the record, I don't want this. I want to stay married.'

She nodded. It both saddened and relieved her that he had not added 'to you'. It was the marital status that mattered most to him.

'I love you, Bea.' He said the words as a kind of footnote, a clarification, and she decided she never wanted to hear them said like that again as long as she lived.

'I know you do,' she said, 'but we have different definitions of what that means and I don't want to live by yours any longer.'

He drew breath, preparing his protest, but something made him change his mind. 'Am I at least allowed to keep trying? Between now and when it actually happens?'

Goodness knew what sort of last-ditch seduction rituals he had in mind. Nothing could top having delivered her to the gates of Villa Isola—presenting her with the deeds to the place, perhaps, but even that would not work, not in the end. 'There wouldn't be any point, Marty. And I'm not saying you can't fall in love again, with someone else. The opposite: you'll be free.'

She wasn't quite ready to consider who he would choose, for it *would* be a question of choice: he'd have offers from all corners, that was a given. His attributes—personal, physical, financial—ran into pages. Even so, would she have been able to make that gesture if she hadn't had what she'd had with Zach these last days? Would she have been so generous? Feeling the disingenuousness of her position, her composure began to slip. There was no pleasure in this: she still cared about him. Knowing he was with someone else would be scarcely less painful when they were divorced than it had been while they were married. *Where* were their coffees? She searched over his shoulder for the waiter, but there was no one at the counter.

Marty, for his part, nibbled at his fingertips with his teeth, taking stock. She had seen this look, smelled this pain, so many times before. You could bottle it: the scent of a man who had shot himself in the foot.

'What will we tell the kids?' he asked. And she loved him for asking that question first, before the ones that would inevitably follow about the business and timings, the best way to announce the news to the media.

'We'll tell them the truth: that we're separating. I honestly don't think they'll be surprised.'

They'd be upset, though. Esther and Pippi had been horribly shocked by the circumstances of Dom's sudden departure. Breakfast that morning had been subdued to the point of silence, and afterwards Pippi had gone back to bed, a first on this holiday and a rare sign of apathy in one normally so indefatigable. It seemed to Bea that what distressed her daughters most was not Dom's predicament per se, but the sheer caprice of it all, the evidence that adult life was sometimes too

399

complicated, too slippery, to be fully resolved, no matter how much your family loved you.

Their coffees still had not come; the waiter scurried past them to seat a large group, pulling out his pad to take an immediate order.

'How will we do it?' Marty asked her, soberly. 'And when?'

'We'll wait till Dom is on his feet again. But it will need to be before Esther goes off to Guatemala. She'll be away for almost six weeks.'

'I'd forgotten about that. I'm in the States again next week.'

'We'll have to decide whether to tell them all together. It might be better to do it individually.' It went without saying that it was a relief to not have to deal with visitation or residency issues: that was the underlying point of this, after all. She'd done the old-fashioned thing and waited for her children to leave first, and she would never regret that she had.

'You want me to move out?' Marty said.

She nodded. 'It makes sense that way. You're overseas so much anyway.' She hoped that didn't sound as heartless as she feared it did. 'I realise we'll have to sell the house once everything's underway. I'll get some valuations organised once we've talked to the kids.'

'We don't necessarily have to sell, not if you want to stay there . . .'

Bea shook her head. 'Pippi will be gone. It's too big for just me. And, anyway, it was always our house. I couldn't think of it as mine.'

For the first time in the conversation he broke eye contact. She wondered if he was doing the same as she was—imagining a new set of spaces, a new way of ending each day. It occurred to her that he might decide to relocate to the States. He was there so much, and with the children grown there'd be nothing to stop him. A different continent! For a moment the idea tore through her, all set to ravage her, but then it left as quickly as it came, remembering the damage already done, unable to make any greater impact.

'What about the rest of this holiday?' he asked. It felt quite natural, the dynamic of this discussion: he asking the questions, she suggesting the answers. Finally, she was the one leading.

'There've been enough revelations and announcements already. I think we should hold it together for the rest of the week if we can. Just fly back together on Sunday as we originally planned.' She knew that this was something *she* could do because that was what she'd been doing for months now, perhaps years. Her united front was as polished as the medal she deserved for it. But Marty was a different creature; when a decision was made he liked to act at once. 'If that's OK with you,' she added. 'But I understand if you'd rather go back early.'

'No, I can hold it together,' he said.

It was only then that the coffee arrived, lending the act of raising their cups an unscheduled significance, as if they were drinking, not in celebration, of course, but at least in formal agreement.

'What day is it today, anyway?' Marty asked her.

'It's Wednesday.'

It struck them both at the same time: 'I'm not wearing Sale,' he said, horrified. He regarded his Paul Smith shirt as if it had been made by the devil

401

himself.

Bea looked down at her sundress, embellished at the neckline with hand-sewn flowers. 'Don't worry,' she said. 'I am.'

* * *

They parted in the street, agreeing to meet back at the villa at two o'clock and honour their earlier agreement to go out in the boat with the girls, find somewhere on the lake for a late lunch and take the opportunity to talk through the Dom situation as a four.

Bea turned on her phone. Her son would be back in London now and the temptation to contact Chloë had subsided. She saw that Zach had texted her an hour ago:

Please can I see you.

She checked her watch: it was twelve-thirty.

I'm in the village now, she responded. Where are you?

Hotel.

I'll come.

She warned herself not to touch him or let him touch her. Even as she was running up the stairs to his room she was intoning sternly to herself, *Don't, don't, don't*, over and over, aware of course that what she was feeling was a renewed—and admittedly overdue—sense of propriety, brought

402

on by her conversation with Marty. The problem was that her body had read the situation differently; it thought a restraining order had been lifted, not imposed, and as soon as the door opened and she saw him, dishevelled with the heat, groaning at the sight of her, she fell into his arms and returned every one of his kisses.

'I thought,' she gasped, 'I thought . . . after last night, I thought you—'

'No,' he interrupted, 'I would never.'

They looked at each other, neither blinking. 'I'm obsessed,' she said, simply.

'Good,' he said. 'Because so am I.'

He was in the middle of packing his things—that was a shock—and they sat at the foot of the bed amid the arms and legs of his clothing. 'Did Ginny find you?' she asked, still breathless. 'She was looking for Adam earlier and seemed to think he might be with you.'

'I didn't see her, but I was with Adam for most of the morning, yes.' He glanced at his watch. 'They must have caught up with each other by now.'

'You were with Adam?' It was not the likeliest of pairings, but he'd spoken in an unfamiliarly meaningful tone and she felt a return of the chill she'd felt when watching Ginny hurry away from her earlier. What was going on? What was wrong? Then it struck her: he must have confided in Adam about them—before she'd had her meeting with Marty, or, at best, simultaneously. Immediately, she castigated herself for being so arrogant; she thought of him every waking moment (every *allowable* waking moment), but that didn't mean he did her. In any case, why would Zach choose

403

Adam to confide in, the only one of the group he'd failed to connect with, the one, if Ginny's assessment was to be believed, who liked him the least?

Why meet Adam at all?

'Ginny said something had happened,' she persisted, 'not to do with Dom or last night . . . ?'

He raised his head, pressed his lips against her forehead, leaving them there for several seconds before he spoke. 'Something *has* happened. I warn you, though, this is going to freak you out . . .'

Oh God, she was right, he *was* starting to tell people, about them, about her plans to divorce Marty. Did Ginny know, as well? How on earth was she going to handle this? There wasn't only Marty to worry about, but also Pippi and Esther; hadn't she and Marty just agreed they'd all stay for the rest of the week? And yet she knew the Trustloves were not due to leave until Saturday, only a day earlier than them. Dom, at least, was back in London, protected from this particular fallout.

'Tell me,' she said, moving so that their cheeks were touching; his was much cooler than she'd anticipated, hers aflame.

He murmured into her hair, 'I told Adam he's my father.'

'What?' Thrown into confusion, she pulled back, drawing her eyes level with his. 'Say that again, I thought you said—'

'I did. Adam is my father.' He spoke clearly this time, his face, all of him, becoming profoundly still as he watched for her reaction. His grey eyes were the clearest and most readable she'd ever seen them, and what they told her was that he needed her to cope with this.

'But . . . but your parents are in Bristol. You said your father worked at the airport—'

'He does. The man I *thought* was my father does. And that's what he still is as far as I'm concerned.'

Divining danger, terrible danger, her pulse began to jump, painful under her skin. Her voice, at least, remained steady. 'I don't understand, Zach.'

'It's simple. It turns out Adam is my birth father.'

It turns out? The phrase was as inadequate as her response was overwhelming. She felt like a pilot presented with catastrophic engine failure; she needed to find a way to bring the plane down safely.

'I told you you'd be shocked,' Zach said, without satisfaction. He looked, if anything, concerned for *her*, protective of her feelings.

'But how can this possibly be the case?' she whispered.

'Well, he knew my mother back in the eighties, when he was a student. Not for very long, apparently, but long enough.'

She had to bite her lower lip to stop it from trembling. 'And he only told you this *this morning*?'

His hands encased hers, two halves of a shell; glancing down, she couldn't see her own fingers. 'No, no, you don't get it. *I* told him.'

Bea stared. 'But . . . how did you . . . how long have you known?'

'She told me two weeks ago, give or take. That's why I came to Orta. It took me a few days before that to figure out where he was. I had to persuade

405

a work colleague of his to point me in the right direction.'

She absorbed this, hardly realising that she had begun to speak her thoughts aloud: 'That's why you're here . . . That day you came, you met Pippi on the square in the morning . . . she brought you to the house . . .'

He cut in, tightening his hold of her hands. 'Meeting Pippi was pure chance. I couldn't believe it when she started talking about Villa Isola, the actual place I'd come to find. But it's a small town, so I suppose it's not that much of a coincidence. I would have found the boathouse sooner or later. I would have found him.'

Still she couldn't fathom what he was telling her, what it *meant*. He said it was simple but it was anything but; it was huge and dark and bottomless, it made everything she'd thought she'd known fall away from her, out of reach, out of sight. 'Are you saying that Adam didn't know anything about this? You really just told him today?'

'Last night, actually. After I left you.'

Well, that made even less sense to her. Why would Zach imagine that the best time for such a revelation would be after the man's bereaved wife had fled the scene in tears following a cruel remark about killing babies? She struggled to order her questions. 'How did he react? What did he say?'

'He's shocked. And angry, I think. He doesn't know whether he should even believe it.' The faintest of gulps was all that belied Zach's preternatural calm. 'He spoke to my mother on the phone while we were together and that seemed to help a bit.'

Slowly, Bea was making the connections. 'Last

406

night. The message. I gave you the message to take to him. Your mother is Cally?'

'Yes.'

'Oh my God.'

'When you gave me that message and I saw who it was from, I knew I had to tell him before she phoned again. Even so, I wasn't sure until I saw them in the garden that I was going to go through with it. I told myself if Ginny was still upset I'd just walk past, forget the whole thing, at least for now, but if she seemed all right, I'd do it. And she was fine. She invited me in. I think she'd known for a while I had something to tell them.'

I've spoken to his mother, Bea thought. The anxious, tormented woman I thought was pursuing Marty was in fact Zach's mother, searching for her son at the very time I was meeting him for sex.

The timing perturbed her in another way, too. 'Why did you wait almost a week before you said anything?' *You could have told me. I've told you everything.* Terrible, selfish thoughts surged in the wake of these, making her want to cry out, 'Don't you see, this affects what's happened between us! Not only that, it explains *why* it happened!'

And now that she knew that, didn't it also, necessarily, *negate* it?

'I didn't mean to wait,' Zach said. 'I know it must look strange that I did. But when I met them the day after I arrived I saw straight away that there was something really wrong with them. I couldn't just barge in and make my announcement. Ginny—well, you know what she was like, she hardly spoke a word, I worried that she needed to be hospitalised or something—and Adam seemed annoyed that I was there at all, whoever I was. He

407

made it clear he thought I was pestering Pippi, which was pretty insulting.' They both took a moment to consider the irony of *that*. 'Anyway, it was obvious they weren't going to be able to deal with it. I don't know if they can now—I mean, what difference does a week make? But I've done it, I can't retract it.'

With this last realisation his breath caught and Bea became aware for the first time of the hammer of his heart. She was glad: only a monster could be unmoved by this. Fascinated, she pushed their joined hands to his chest; the beat was coming through his ribcage in hot, tight pulses.

'Tell me what you think,' he said, his eyes gripping hers. His pupils were huge and black, the grey circles of iris receding. 'Should I have waited?'

To her horror, her selfish emotions were all but eclipsing her concern for Adam and Ginny—or even Zach himself. She could not answer his question, for she *had* to know the answer to her own. 'So you stayed close to them by making friends with us . . . ?'

There was a sharp intake of breath, a faint flush across his cheekbones. 'I wasn't using you, if that's what you're thinking. You and me, it's something completely separate, Bea, something—'

She could no longer hold back, not even to let him finish his sentence: 'Oh, Zach, please, think about it! What on earth has your state of mind been this last week? You must have had a thousand questions you wanted to ask Adam. You must have been in complete turmoil. I'm amazed you've been able to have a conversation with any of us, let alone anything else.'

He raised his eyebrows. 'If you want to know,

the "anything else" has been easier than the conversations.'

She shook her head, refusing to joke. 'Think about it,' she repeated. 'It's Psychology 101. You've had your whole identity blown apart. First your mother drops this bombshell, maybe you even feel like she's betrayed you, I don't know, I can't imagine how it must feel, but I do know that a week or two is not long enough to come to terms with something as huge as this.' She paused to refill her lungs; each breath was so shallow it was sustaining her for only a couple of seconds. 'You come here searching for your father, only to discover that he's just lost his newborn baby. You feel you can't possibly add to his despair. All those things you must have wanted to know, must have wanted to say, and you couldn't! Then you meet me, a woman your mother's age, or close enough . . .' She was beginning to sound like Hercule Poirot, explaining the sequence of events leading to the murder, but it didn't feel like anything she wanted to laugh about. She wanted to cry, to wail; fluid was filling her nose, swelling her eyelids, turning her voice into a thick whisper: 'I told you about their baby myself, that day on the island . . .' And it had been soon after, *directly after*, that he had turned her existence upside down by kissing her.

You knew, she told herself, *you knew it wasn't real*. She'd thought it was to do with being here—in Italy, at the villa, the heat and the magic of the place, that holiday spirit that made people take risks, behave out of character. But it was something else entirely, something far less elusive, far more definable: one of them was suffering the equivalent of a major head trauma.

'Don't forget I met you before I met them,' Zach reminded her, his voice impressively level. 'Before I knew their story.' Apparently a tear had made itself visible because he was reaching up and blotting at the corner of her left eye with his index finger. Her hands felt shaky without his to cover them and she guided them back into place. He clutched hard.

'Even so, you were in shock. You still are. I've been a displacement activity for you.' She took another swallow of air, straightened her shoulders, lifted her chin, tried all she could think of to pull herself together. 'And maybe you have for me, as well.'

He surprised her then by giving a yelp of genuine amusement. 'I don't even know what that means, Bea! And I don't follow your argument on any level. The timing is insane, I'll give you that, but from my perspective only something miraculous could have competed with what I've had going on in my head. What this boils down to is that two life-changing things have happened to happen at exactly the same time. I have no doubt that this will turn out to have been the most important week of my life.'

She stared at him, confounded. 'You can't equate meeting me with what you've discovered about your parentage.'

'Yes, I can. Of course I can. If anything it's bigger, because it's real, it's mine. It's *ours*. But finding Adam, telling him last night, realising that neither of us wants it to be true, that we maybe don't even like each other, not instinctively—it's a whole out-of-body experience. It's like it's

410

happening to someone else. And I'm pretty sure he feels the same way.'

Slowly, she slipped her hands from his, reversed their positioning so it was hers now that sheltered his. 'I'm sure that will change. It will feel more real with time, for both of you. You *will* like each other.'

He nodded. 'I hope so. I hope so.' His voice gave way then, the final word ending with a faint whimper. It was the first time he'd sounded anywhere close to his age, or even half as vulnerable as she felt; it was a small, necessary split in his skin.

She asked him, very tenderly, 'What are you going to do?'

He took a breath. 'I need to get to know him, share our histories. But first I need to know how my family feels about it. My father, my brothers— half-brothers now, I suppose. Jesus.'

She motioned to the piles of rumpled clothes on the bed beside them, the books and the laptop. 'And you're going home to find out?'

'Yes. I just changed my flight. I'm leaving at four. Can we be together until then?'

She blinked, staving off the return of tears. 'I have to be back at the villa by two. We promised the girls.'

' "We"?'

'Marty and I.'

They stared at each other. 'We have to say goodbye,' she said, simply.

'No.' The shake of his head was resolute. 'I know what you're saying and I don't accept it.'

She frowned. 'You have to accept it. Come on, you need to concentrate on sorting this out,

411

working out a way for you and your family to *be*, in the future.'

'Yes, but that doesn't mean I have to shut myself away from the rest of the world. Not from you, Bea, not from you . . .' His voice was curdled with longing, causing an instant craving of her own. 'If you weren't married, if I wasn't here to find Adam, if there were none of this going on, then you'd want to see me again, wouldn't you?'

'Yes,' she said, truthfully, 'if we were in a vacuum, yes. But the ifs are what life is, Zach. And there are so many. Not just your finding out about Adam, or my sorting out my separation, but all the other stuff as well.'

'What other stuff? Name one other issue?' He was taller suddenly, broader, every inch a man who was equal to this challenge. Bea thought, *If I had a tenth of your self-belief* . . . But she didn't allow herself the second half of the clause. In a single short hour she had become abstracted from the woman who'd faced Marty across a café table, the one who'd coolly laid out the great man's fate for him. The wife and the mother. She felt dispossessed, lost.

'Well, for a start I need to make sure Dom is OK. You saw for yourself what a mess he was in last night . . .'

Zach looked impatient. 'He'll be all right. It's just his first big dilemma without you telling him what to do. He would have got himself into the same state whatever it was.'

His assessment was eerily close to Marty's and her own; she decided not to argue it out. 'And we haven't even begun to think about how Pippi would feel if she knew that we'd been meeting . . .'

412

Again, he was entirely unimpressed. 'Pippi will forget me the moment she meets the next guy, I promise you. There was never enough between us for it to have meant anything more to her than appearances.'

Right again. If he hadn't been so correct, if his own crisis hadn't so manifestly dwarfed everything else in sight, Bea might have resented more his easy dismissal of her children's emotions.

'Even so,' she said, 'the complications can't be ignored as easily as you seem to think.'

'I don't want to ignore them. I want to deal with whatever has to be dealt with. I wouldn't be here otherwise.' Bea knew he was laying himself utterly bare. There was something very pure about him, something very honourable. 'I don't know what else I can say, Bea. I know how I feel, and I want you.' He paused. 'I want you properly. I can repeat it as many times as I have to, but I can't make you feel the same way.'

'Don't say it like you think I don't care,' she cried, distraught. 'You know I do. But I don't know if I can take these life-altering things in my stride as well as you can. As well as you *think* you can. Fine, let's say you *can* handle the news about your father and start a new relationship with me at the same time, I suppose only you can decide that. But I don't know if *I* can start a new relationship while I'm going through a divorce. It will be a long and unpleasant process. I don't know if I'm going to survive it.'

'You will survive it. I'll help you.'

'What about my family? It's not just Pippi, they all know you now—including Marty.'

Again it was as if she raised the most minor of

413

objections. 'They don't need to know we're as close as we are, not at first.'

'But that's just not realistic. I don't want to live my life in secret.'

His lips curled faintly at one corner. 'What, so you were planning on parading your future lovers in front of them then, were you? Getting their seal of approval?'

Bea gave a frustrated groan. 'I wasn't planning on *having* any lovers.'

'Well, *that*'s not realistic. And, anyway, you've already got one.'

She closed her eyes, fighting the smile. 'You have to admit it: there are a lot of variables in this.'

'Fuck the variables,' Zach said. 'It's too late now. We've met. That's all it took, and you know it as well as I do, I know you do.' He began to pressure her, both with his lips and his words. 'Do you have any idea how hard it was not to touch you that first time, down on the square? Or lean closer and smell your skin . . . like this? And when I saw you again, in the evening at the villa, I felt like I'd been stunned. I thought I was having some kind of nervous attack. I couldn't believe none of you noticed . . .'

There was a giving-way in her groin then, a ringing sensation in her chest. 'Maybe when it's all died down,' she murmured, despairing of herself for wanting to close her eyes and let them stay closed, to search for his mouth with hers, 'when I really am free.'

'I can be patient. I can wait.'

'Can you? That's very hard to imagine.'

'So long as I can speak to you, see you sometimes, know you haven't forgotten me.'

Now she really couldn't stop the smile from breaking. 'I'm not likely to do that.'

His fingers began to fork her hair, the touch of his fingertips on her scalp making her shudder. 'Come down to me when you need some time. Tell me what's happening or let me take your mind off it, whichever way you want it to be.'

She suddenly imagined herself sitting on the train to Bristol with Adam and Ginny, going to visit their new son. Explaining how *she* fitted into the brave new set-up. It was absurd.

As had become his habit, he read her thoughts. 'I'll make sure no one's around when you come. It'll be just us. We won't even *speak* to anyone else. You've got to admit there'd be no harm in that?'

And the idea of being with him, away from the rest of the world, compounded by the effects of the touch of his fingers and the kiss he was now driving on the side of her mouth, caused her to whisper, 'Yes,' hardly knowing any longer what it was she was answering. 'Yes.'

His lips were moving all over her face now, across her eyelids, her cheekbones, closing in on her ear and groaning into it his thanks to God. 'You scared me, Bea. I really thought you weren't going to let me see you again. Promise you won't ever do that again, promise me you'll come to me next week, when you're back . . .'

Somehow, moments later, he had the answers he wanted and yet she had not been fully aware of giving them.

But, all things considered, she was not unhappy with the outcome.

CHAPTER TWENTY-SIX

FRIDAY

The day after the day Zach left (she had begun to think of time in this way, a trend she expected to pass), and the first day spent in Orta without coming into contact with any of the Sale family, Ginny put on her swimsuit and lowered herself into the lake.

It was very, very cold. That was the single breath-stealing sensation she experienced on submersion, and it continued to hold her in its brace for a full minute, even before she'd been able to register the wetness of the experience; she might simply have walked naked into a refrigerator. Finding her footing among the rocks she just stood there, utterly numb, as if waiting to lose consciousness. Then, before that *did* happen, she began to swim, creating an icy flow against her skin, most painfully on her breasts and stomach, and in doing so turned her attention to the texture of the water. It was soft and greasy, draping over her in folds, and it swayed strangely, too, wobbling back and forth, she supposed because the lake was not tidal but held in its great giant's bowl with nowhere to drain.

Unlike all those hot baths at home, the water did not soothe her aches; if anything, it accentuated them, brought out their flavours. She thought to herself, This won't be gone by the end of this holiday; it won't be gone by the end of my life. If I accept that, absorb it into my tissue like a new organ, then it will be easier to make the recovery I have to make. Pain is part of every day now, but it doesn't mean the days can't be lived, maybe even to the full.

It was funny, but she associated the idea of living life to the full with Bea Sale. For all her new friend's implications that she had done little more these last two decades with Marty than grin and bear it, they both knew she had led a whole, involving life, right to the present second. Whatever he had done to her, *she* had prevailed. A stranger could see that; a stranger *had*.

The two women had met again yesterday. It was not one of their cosy visits of old ('of old'—by which she meant mere days ago!), but a bumping-into at the counter of one of the *gastronomia* off the piazza. They paid for their respective goodies and left the shop together, standing for a time in the street, chatting. As usual, Ginny felt unglamorous next to Bea, but, as usual, not in any way that provoked envy in her, only admiration.

Bea asked, 'How are you both now?' and though the phrasing was as safe as it could possibly be, there was a nuance, a kind of suppressed hunger to her tone that told Ginny she knew.

Somehow Bea knew that Zach was Adam's son.

And since Adam had not told a soul, she must have learned it from Zach. But why would Zach confess to Bea something he had barely managed to say to Adam? Pippi had been his closest friend in the group and Adam had asked him outright if he'd said anything to her about it. He'd replied no, he had not. Absolutely not. Of course, Adam hadn't thought to ask about any of the other members of the family.

417

Which meant . . . well, it could only mean one thing.

Bea and Zach. Zach and Bea. Bea's face when she'd asked Ginny what she thought of him, livid with attention—not livid, that wasn't right, *radiant*, lit from under the skin—and, later, stricken by the fear that something might have hurt him. Zach: the kind of stand-out male who could take his pick, maverick, *foolhardy* enough to take the queen from under the king's nose. It all fitted together too naturally to not be true. And stupefied though Ginny was, there was also something satisfying in the knowing of it. It explained also the space she and Adam had been given since Zach had left, the visits to the boathouse Bea had stopped making. Agendas had changed; there were new bombshells to guard.

'We're fine,' she said, controlling herself better than she'd ever thought she could, 'given the circumstances.' For her part, it was the phrasing rather than the tone that gave her away. Bea knew the character of her grief well enough to recognise she wouldn't use a phrase like that, not about Isaac. Isaac wasn't 'circumstances', he was life itself, he was all that she was. No, 'circumstances' meant the new, unconnected thing, the true, official secret of the holiday, the one they both knew Bea shared.

'The circumstances are difficult,' Bea agreed.

They looked at each other, lips parted, both seeing what the other concealed, neither willing to name it. Ginny thought, We're different women from the pair who met ten days ago, the ones who divulged things we never planned to divulge. For that brief, strange interlude they'd been quite

418

uncaring of the consequences.

And she thought, If they are together, Bea and Zach, and if it means anything, and if Adam and Zach allow each other into their lives, then we'll find out about it through the proper channels. (Whatever *they* were; was life ever lived through the proper channels?) She wondered if Bea were thinking something similar, calculating the risk she saved by keeping her own counsel. It must be hard for her, Ginny thought, with Zach having gone home and Marty returned, the remainder of the perfect family holiday still to be played out. Or maybe whatever Zach had meant to her had ended with his leaving, and she'd made up with Marty and was thinking something entirely different. Perhaps she was looking at Ginny now and marvelling at how very close to one another fate had blown the good ships *Sale* and *Trustlove*, far closer than they would have come on their own. They'd achieved the finest of degrees of separation, and they might never formally acknowledge it.

They'd almost been family.

'Shall we try and get together again before we all go home?' Bea said, smiling, swinging her shopping bag, a vision of elegance in plum-coloured silk. 'We could all go for lunch up in the mountains?'

'Yes,' Ginny said. 'That would be lovely.'

And then, for the time being, they went their separate ways.

*   *   *

As she was towelling herself dry, Adam came back from his second trip to Sacro Monte.

419

'You've been swimming? In the *lake*?'

His astonishment made her laugh. 'Yes, and I'm not sure I will again, not in there. I can't believe you've all been doing it every day. *Brrr*, it's the kind of cold that never warms up.'

'How long were you in there for?'

'About ten minutes.'

He nodded, as if that explained everything. 'It takes a lot longer than that, Gin.'

'How long?'

'Half an hour, at least.'

'Half an hour! What about hypothermia?'

He grinned. 'We'll go in together next time and I'll distract you.'

As he turned to go indoors, she asked him to stay a moment, reached for his hand. It felt hot and swollen in her stiff, icy one. 'Adam, I was thinking . . .'

'Yes?'

She was still breathing heavily from the swim, her chest rising and falling, aching slightly. 'What will we do about Isaac's room? When we get back?'

Though he had obviously not been expecting the question, he improvised quickly. 'I think we'll have to change it back, not straight away, but eventually. When we're ready.'

'You mean back into a spare room?'

He looked sadly at her. 'It's a small flat as it is; we just don't have enough space to keep the cot and everything else in there indefinitely. I'm sorry.'

Ginny thought about Bea's description of the children's floor at the top of her house. *When I go up there, that's when I feel it the most . . .*

'Can we keep something, though? Something so

420

that we'll always know it was his room?' Not a photograph, but something only she and Adam would understand, so as not to make it morbid for any guests who came to stay. The letter, perhaps, or the journal, tucked in a little box.

He kissed the top of her head. 'Of course we can. Of course we can. Are you coming inside?' he asked. 'You're freezing.'

'In a while. I think I'll dry off in the sun a bit.'

'OK. I'll make us something to eat.'

The garden door and the windows were open and she could hear him pottering in the kitchen, chopping vegetables on the wooden board, rooting about in a carrier bag, banging a cupboard door, splashing at the sink.

Her arms and legs were colourless as stone and almost as cold. She made a cloak of her towel with one hand and perched on the lake wall, the other hand holding her notebook. Adam had returned it to her, of course, and there was Zach's number on the last page. That was my handwriting when we found out, she thought, in wonder. It was wild and eager, scrawled diagonally across the pristine lines like the news of a lottery win or some other life-changing windfall, the four letters of his name underlined thickly below. As if I was going to forget whose it was, she thought.

Turning to the front page, her eyes found the first and only line she'd set down there: *I don't know where to start . . .*

And then she picked up her pen and began to write.